GRANT
PARK

Also by Leonard Pitts, Jr.

Becoming Dad

Forward from This Moment

Before I Forget

Freeman

GRANT
PARK

LEONARD PITTS, JR.

BOLDEN

AN AGATE IMPRINT

CHICAGO

Printed in the United States.

Library of Congress Cataloging-in-Publication Data

Pitts, Leonard.
 Grant Park / Leonard Pitts, Jr.
     pages ; cm
  Summary: ""A novel that weaves together the stories of two veteran journalists from Martin Luther King's final days in Memphis to the 2008 presidential election"--Provided by publisher".
  ISBN 978-1-932841-91-6 (hardcover) -- ISBN 1-932841-91-1 (hardcover) -- ISBN 978-1-57284-762-0 (ebook) -- ISBN 1-57284-762-X (ebook)
  1. Editors--Fiction. 2. Journalists--Fiction. 3. Race discrimination--United States--Fiction. 4. United States--Race relations--Fiction. I. Title.
  PS3616.I92G73 2015
  813'.6--dc23
                        2015021248

9 8 7 6 5 4 3 2 1

Bolden Books is an imprint of Agate Publishing. Agate books are available in bulk at discount prices. Single copies are available prepaid direct from the publisher.

agatepublishing.com

For Onjél, who said, "You've never dedicated a book to me..."

For Lena, who calls me "Pop-pop"

And always, for Marilyn

Well, I don't know what will happen now. We've got some difficult days ahead.
—Reverend Doctor Martin Luther King, Jr., April 3, 1968

But what we know—what we have seen—is that America can change.
—Senator Barack Obama, March 18, 2008

Martin Luther King stood at the railing, facing west. The moon was a pale crescent just rising in early twilight to share the sky with a waning sun. He leaned over, joking with the men in the parking lot below. A couple of them were wrestling playfully with James Orange, a good-natured man with a build like a brick wall.

"Now, you be careful with preachers half your size," King teased him.

"Dr. King," called Orange in a plaintive voice, "it's two of them and one of me. You should be asking them not to hurt me."

"Doc," someone called out from below, "this is Ben Branch. You remember Ben."

"Oh yes," said King. "He's my man. How are ya, Ben?"

Another voice yelled up from below. "Glad to see you, Doc."

As Malcolm Toussaint moved toward King, it struck him that the preacher seemed somehow lighter than he had the last time Malcolm had seen him. It had been late one night a week before, by the Dumpsters out back of the Holiday Inn. The man Malcolm met that night had seemed... *weighted*, so much so that even Malcolm had found himself concerned and moved—Malcolm, who had long scorned the great reverend doctor, who had, in the fashion of other young men hip, impatient, and cruel, mocked him as "De Lawd."

But that was before Malcolm had met the man. That was before they had talked. Now he moved toward King, his mind roiling with the decision that had sprung from that moment, the news he had come to share. King, he knew, would be pleased. There would be a smile, perhaps a heavy hand clamping on Malcolm's shoulder. "Good for you, Brother Malcolm," he would say. "Good for you."

Malcolm was vaguely amused to find himself here on this balcony, anticipating this man's approval. If you had told him just a few days ago that he would be here, ready to go back to school, ready to embrace nonviolent protest, he would have laughed. But that, too, was before.

Malcolm meant to raise his hand just then, to catch King's attention, but a movement caught his eye. Just a reflected ray of the dying sun, really, glinting off something in a window across the street. Something that—he knew this instinctively—should not have been there. He wondered distractedly what it was.

King's voice drew him back. "I want you to sing it like you've never sung it before," he was calling to someone in the parking lot below. "Sing it real pretty."

And Malcolm realized he had missed something, because he had no idea what they were talking about. His attention had been distracted by... what was that?

"It's getting chilly." Yet another voice calling to King from below. "I think you'll need a topcoat."

"Okay, Jonesy," King was saying. "You really know how to take good care of me."

And here, the moment breaks, time fracturing as time sometimes will into its component parts, until an event is no longer composed of things happening in a sequence, but somehow all happens at once. And you can see and touch and *live* all the smaller moments inside the right now. This is how it is for Malcolm Toussaint now.

King is laughing. Malcolm is taking a step toward him. King is straightening. Laughter is echoing from below. King is reaching into a pocket for his cigarettes. He is becoming aware of Malcolm on his left. His head is coming around. There are the bare beginnings of a welcoming smile.

And Malcolm knows. Suddenly knows. And Malcolm is leaping, leaping across space, across time itself, becoming airborne—he was sure of it, that detail felt right, even though by this time King is barely six feet away. Malcolm grabbing two hands full of expensive silk, yanking Martin Luther King off balance, yanking him down *hard* in the same instant they all hear the popping sound like a firecracker, in the same instant he feels the soft-nosed 30.06 bullet whistle past his cheek like a phantom breath, in the same instant he falls awkwardly across King's chest.

And then...

And then time seems to reel for a crazy breathless moment, as if deciding what to do now. The fulcrum of history teetering, the future hanging, suspended in midair.

Until all at once and with a brutal force, time decides itself and slams back into gear.

A woman shrieked.

Someone yelled, "Somebody is shooting!"

Someone yelled, "Doc, are you OK?"

Someone yelled, "Stay down!"

Malcolm's breath was ragged in his own ears. His heart hammered like drums. Then from beneath him, he heard a familiar baritone voice say calmly, very calmly, but yet, with a touch of breathless wonder. "Oh my God. Was that a gunshot?"

Their eyes met. Malcolm didn't speak. Couldn't speak. "Brother Malcolm," said Martin Luther King, his voice still suffused with wonder and yet, also, an almost unnatural calm, "I think you just saved my life."

Malcolm was overwhelmed by the *thereness* of the man. He was not myth and mist and history. He was not a posterboard image on a wall behind a child dutifully reciting in a child's thin, sweet tenor, "I have a dream today." No, he was there, beneath 20-year-old Malcolm Toussaint, who had fallen crosswise on top of him. Malcolm could feel the weight and heft of him, the fall and rise of his chest. He could see his very pores, could smell the tobacco on his breath, the Aramis on his collar. Martin Luther King was *there*, still alive, beneath him. Malcolm opened his mouth to speak.

And then, he awoke.

two

He did not scream. He did not sit bolt upright panting and shivering in the predawn chill.

The dream was an old one, had haunted his sleep off and on for 40 years, and had long since lost the power to shake him. No, by now it was almost an old friend, dropping by every now and again to remind him of the singular failure of his life, that fateful instant when he had seen—he had *seen*—but did not react in time, did not understand in time, froze.

Sometimes, as tonight, the dream gave him a do-over, allowed him to react in time, let him make it right.

More often, the dream unfolded precisely as that awful moment had unfolded, less a true dream than just a memory relived while sleeping. Malcolm failing to act, failing to understand what he saw, failing to realize what was about to happen until the very instant it did. Failing. The shot coming. The bullet driving Martin Luther King down as a hammer drives a nail. The gore spattering.

Malcolm Toussaint standing there, not six feet away, impotent, staring. *Enough.*

He pushed the covers away, sat on the edge of the bed, the hardwood floor cool beneath his bare feet. No more time to dwell on the thing he had failed to do back when Lyndon Johnson was president and the space race was in full swing. It was time to face today. And today, he was going to be fired.

It was even possible he was going to be arrested; he supposed there might be some statute that criminalized what he had done.

He didn't think prosecution was likely—surely, they'd leave him some tattered shred of his previous dignity—though he could not dismiss the possibility out of hand. But at the very least, yes, he would be fired. And he would deserve firing as much as any of the serial plagiarists and fiction writers he had railed against so loudly, the fucking liars who had so spectacularly besmirched a noble profession, *his* noble profession, in the last 20 years.

Now, he was one of them. He was journalism's latest scandal.

A storied career—from a hovel on the south side of Memphis to this palace in Chicago, two Pulitzer Prizes, countless lesser awards lining the walls of his office—would end in ruin today. No more twice-weekly nationally syndicated column. No more *New York Times* bestsellers blurbed by Oprah Winfrey and Bill Clinton. No more daily radio talk show. No more regular appearances on the Sunday morning political programs. No more. Nor would anyone speak in his defense. The National Association of Black Journalists, which had given him a lifetime achievement award just four years ago, would maintain an embarrassed silence, the NAACP would look the other way.

He would be a pariah. And the worst part is, he would deserve it.

Inevitably, someone would ask why he did it. And what could he say? He could tell them the truth, but they would never understand it. He regretted what he had done, yes. But he was not sorry. Even now, having slept fitfully on it, he was not sorry. Did that make sense? Would they get the distinction?

"I just got tired," he would say.

And they would ask him, not understanding, "Tired of what?" But someone in the mob, he imagined, black like him, journalist like him, up in years like him, would not need to ask. Would only close his notebook and shake his head, would understand if not condone and would, maybe...

Enough.

Malcolm got out of bed and padded toward a marble bathroom not much smaller than the house he had grown up in. It was just a little after four in the morning. If he hurried, he could get into the building, pack up his office, the mementoes of a 36-year career, and be gone before anyone got there. The alternative made him shudder. The alternative was to go in there, endure the humiliation of their questions and their anger, and be required to wait outside his office while security—"Loss Prevention," they called it now—threw his things in a box and then escorted him out under the stunned and disappointed gaze of people he had worked with, laughed with, fought with, mentored.

He showered quickly in the walk-in stall, where needles of water hit you from five directions at once. Moments later, he used his towel to wipe clean a circle of mirror and began to shave the face of the old man who stared back at him.

Old man.

It was always something of a shock to apply those words to himself, but the evidence of the mirror could not be denied. His eyes were tired and sad, nested in twin hollows of wrinkles and crinkles. His brown skin seemed papery and thin. The short black Afro he had worn that awful day on the balcony of the Lorraine Motel had shrunk down to a defeated gray frizz, thinning on the top.

Malcolm was 60.

He looked 70.

He felt 80. Arthritis had stiffened his joints. His blood pressure was a problem. His eyesight was going to hell. His feet hurt. Worst of all, there was the fatigue, an abiding exhaustion not so much of body, he felt, as of mind. Of spirit. Living had become an act of penance.

He was tired. Indeed, he had been so tired for so long that he could barely remember being anything else. The happy young man who had approached Martin Luther King in the last instant of the great man's life seemed a stranger. No, a lie. A memory of someone who never was.

Malcolm shaved. He dressed quickly. Long johns, blue jeans, long-sleeved blue shirt with the logo of the *Chicago Post* above the breast pocket, a fur-lined, waist-length jacket, a Bulls cap on his head. No need for one of the natty ties and sport coats that always made his slovenly young colleagues roll their eyes and laugh behind their hands. That was the uniform of a man working in an office, something he no longer was.

He walked slowly, down the hall and down the gently winding staircase, past the African-American folk art, mostly paintings and a few small sculptures, that had been Marie's passion until she died of breast cancer. It had always made him feel a bit like he was living in a museum, all that fancy art covering the walls and tables, but Marie was two years dead and he hadn't yet taken it down. Doing that, he supposed, would be like admitting that she actually was gone, that it wasn't a mistake, an oversight, something for which he could demand a recount. That was something he was not yet prepared to do.

In the living room, he pulled on his gloves, images of his son and daughter and their spouses and children watching him from the mantel. Both were married, raising their families in California. He usually saw them at Thanksgiving, when they inevitably started the argument that was becoming all too familiar since his wife's death, the one about how he should retire, sell the house, and join them on the West Coast. With Mom gone, did he really need the big house? At his age, did he really need the Chicago winters?

At his age. As if, having reached 60, there was nothing left for him to do except wait for death. And the hell of it was, since Marie left him, there were days he found he couldn't think of anything better to do.

Enough.

Enough, enough, enough.

His car was parked at the bottom of the stairs in the driveway that circled the front of the house, looping around a fountain—off for the winter—like a doughnut around a hole. Malcolm drove a red Corvette. It was hard on his knees and a four-wheeled cliché for a man of his age, but he couldn't help himself. He loved that car.

He lowered himself into it now, wincing a bit as Uncle Arthur—his mother's name for arthritis, once upon a time—took a hammer to his bones. As always, he was compensated for his suffering when the car started with a deep, satisfying roar and he eased it around the circle, down the drive, and to the street. At the mailbox, he stopped and lowered his window to pluck out the day's paper.

Malcolm folded the paper open and turned on the interior light. "Day of Reckoning," read the headline, above photos of John McCain and Barack Obama giving speeches. Election Day. With all that he was dealing with, he had almost forgotten. Almost. He wanted to go and vote this morning when the polls opened, but he wondered if his presence—everyone in town knew his face, after all—might cause too much of a distraction, especially today.

What an irony, he thought, if what he'd done forced him to miss the most historic election of his lifetime.

He flipped the paper over and there it was. His sig picture and the column that Bob Carson, his editor, had rejected, the one he'd said was too furious, too incendiary, unworthy of him and destined to be published in the *Chicago Post* only after Sarah Palin wed Jeremiah Wright on a nude beach in Jamaica. "I'm doing you a favor," Bob had said. "Go home. Get some rest. We'll talk about it tomorrow."

He had never had a column rejected before. Granted, he'd never written anything like this before, but still... Malcolm had cursed Bob and threatened to quit, taking with him all the prestige his byline brought to this third-rate paper in a time when even first-rate papers were cutting staff, cutting sections, cutting news hole, and looking to the future as one stares down the barrel of a gun.

But Bob had stood firm. "Go home," he had repeated. "Get some rest."

Malcolm had stormed out. He had taken his case to the managing editor, to the editor, to the publisher. Each had read the column—this column, that now sat below the fold on the front page. Each had paled visibly by the time they reached the end, even Lydia Barnett, the publisher. She had looked up at him, this stylish sister of about 40 years, of whom he had always secretly said in his heart, "Man, if I was just 20 years younger..." and he knew he was doomed from the moment she began to speak in that honeyed voice one uses to instruct children and the feeble-minded.

"Malcolm, you know we can't publish this. Why did you even bring this to me? You think I'm going to interfere with an editorial decision?"

"I think you should. In this case, at least."

"Well, I'm sorry, Malcolm, but I'm not."

"Lydia, I know it's on the line, but—"

"On the line?" Her dark eyes had flashed like the warning lights at a railroad crossing. "Malcolm, this isn't on the line. This is so far over the line you can't even see the line from here. You'd have to board a plane to get back to the line!"

"Come on, Lydia," he said. "I wouldn't expect them to understand." He cocked his head to indicate the white editors, the whole white world, beyond the walls of her office. "But you should get where I'm coming from."

Now thunderclouds rolled into those eyes, and he knew he had gone too far. "Do not," she said, "play blacker than thou with me, Malcolm Toussaint. You know better. There is no form of condescension, paternalism, sexism, or racism that I don't know firsthand. I had to climb over all of that to get to sit in this chair. And the one good thing about it is, after all of that, I don't have to prove who I am, to you, or anybody else."

"Lydia, I didn't mean it like that. I'm just saying—"

"I know what you meant, Malcolm. You should go home, take a few days off. When's the last time you had a vacation?"

"Maybe I could rewrite it? Soften it a little?"

"No. This piece will not run in my paper. Go home."

He had left, but he had not gone home. Instead, he had gone to a bar he knew on the South Side, where he had spent the afternoon staring morosely into one beer after another. And there, he had hatched a plan. When he returned to the *Post* offices in the big building on Michigan Avenue, it was late. *Very* late. Copy editors were pulling on their heavy coats, the police reporter shutting down the scanners, the janitor pushing a big trashcan between the mostly empty desks. The newsroom was quiet. The "daily miracle" had been accomplished once again.

He had slipped past them into Bob's empty office, closed the blinds against the leakage of light, and fired up Bob's computer. Seven months ago, Bob had given him his password, with its administrative access to the *Post*'s systems, to fix some glitch in a column Bob didn't have time to get to. And sure enough, Bob had not changed his password in all those months. Malcolm typed it in—Bob_dylan#1—and Bob's desktop flashed into view.

Malcolm's original plan had been to pluck the banned column from the deleted items basket and put it in its customary spot on the editorial page, back of the CitySide section. But sitting there at Bob's desk, signed on under Bob's name, he had a better idea. Or at least, a bolder one. It was the kind of idea you get when you've had a few and some voice in your mind says, "In for a penny, in for a pound," and you nod to yourself because that seems, under the circumstances, sage advice.

So he had called up the front page, which had already been transmitted to the pressroom. If the pressroom chief was ready to roll the presses and saw that Bob—Malcolm, actually—had the file open and called upstairs to find out what was going on, Malcolm knew he would be well and truly screwed, so he had to work fast, and he did. With a few deft keystrokes and clicks, Malcolm stripped a story off the bottom of the front page—some wire piece about voters who were still undecided on the eve of the election—and dropped his forbidden column in its place.

And then, even though time was critical, even though the pressroom would be looking for this page any second, he paused. There was a moment, a moment of absolute clarity, when he knew what he was about to do and what would happen and what it would cost him and that doing it was absolutely insane. A moment. And then he pressed send.

Now, five hours later, on not quite four hours of restless sleep, he sat in his car and regarded the end result. He had thought he might feel some rough sense of satisfaction, even vindication, at getting the column in the paper. He was disappointed to realize that all he felt was the same fatigue that had walked with him like a shadow for so long now, the sense that he had spent his entire life like a tire spinning in snow, kicking up a great fantail, making a lot of noise, and getting absolutely nowhere. He felt hollow, empty as the wind that moved the skeletal branches of the trees outside.

Malcolm tossed the paper onto the passenger seat and stomped the gas. The car leapt forward into the darkened street.

He had the city to himself for another hour or so. Nobody on the streets, few cars on the road. A police car going the other way, an old white van with rust patches on the hood following behind him, a battered old Toyota parked at a gas pump, a tired-looking woman in a waitress uniform slumped against it.

Was it really so long ago they had thought they would change the world, people—*kids*—like him? Young men and women with big Afros and Jewfros and long blonde locks and strident voices singing songs of peace and love and revolution, a whole generation of them, fresh and raw, untainted by the failures and compromises of their parents' generation, utterly convinced that they were something this old world had never seen, a new people thinking new thoughts that had never been thought before.

Was it really 40 years since they had raised fists and chanted "Power to the people"?

And "Give peace a chance"?

And "Off the establishment"?

And "Revolution"?

Forty years. And look what had become of them. Look what had become of *him*, old and tired and driving a trophy car away from a trophy house and socking away money into a 401k. They had been so smug about their power to change the world.

Malcolm heaved a sigh. He thought of turning on the radio, filling the small space with jazz or Motown or even the ceaseless drone of the news. He left it off. The silence fit his mood. He got on the expressway. Chicago flew by.

Moments later, he pulled up to the entrance of the parking structure beneath the *Post* building. He swiped his ID card and when the gate lifted, he was mildly relieved. It had occurred to him they might already have disabled his access to the building.

The night man on the security desk gave him a curious look but only nodded as Malcolm swiped his ID card again and went through the turnstiles. Riding up on the elevator, he wondered idly what that look had been about. Maybe the guard had seen the paper already and knew that Malcolm was dead meat walking. Maybe the man just wondered what anybody was doing here at this unholy hour of the morning.

The newsroom was quiet as a cemetery and Malcolm felt not unlike a ghost as he wandered through. He was tempted to linger, to look around, to press the memory of this place into his mind like an image in a scrapbook (did anyone use scrapbooks anymore?). After all, the newsroom of the *Chicago Post* had been his home away from home for more than half his life and he knew he would never be here, never be *allowed* here, again. But there was, he knew, no time for that. So he retrieved two empty boxes from the mailroom, let himself into his office, and went briskly, methodically, to work.

He took the photos first. There was Marie's high school picture, showing a stunning teenaged girl with blue eye shadow, a reddish Afro, and a soft smile. There was Jimmy Carter jabbing a finger at Malcolm at some contentious point in their interview. There was a family photo with the kids at his son Miles's college graduation. There was Malcolm shaking hands with Bill Clinton at some awards ceremony. There was the signed photo of Michael Jordan towering over Malcolm, draping an arm upon his shoulder. With each photo, Malcolm had to remind himself not to stop and look, not to lose himself in the memories the images contained.

He looked at his awards, the statues and wall plaques trumpeting this triumph or that. Here was an NAACP Image Award for one of his books. Here were the citations for his Pulitzers. Here were prizes from the National Association of Black Journalists, the Press Club of Atlantic City, the American Society of Newspaper Editors, the Society of Professional Journalists, honorary doctorates from a half dozen universities.

Two boxes would not do it, he realized distractedly. He would have to go back to the mailroom and get more.

In a minute. First, he went through his paper files, then threw his Rolodex and his notebooks into a box. He did not worry about computer files. Though he had learned to use them, Malcolm did not especially trust computers. He understood the technology well enough intellectually, but still, the whole idea of storing information digitally, keeping it in some form that you could not touch and thus assure yourself it was there, struck him as a leap of faith, one he could not bring himself to make. You had to take the machine's word that it had your stuff, that it would not inexplicably take a mood and banish your hard work to nonexistence. That was why he saved a hard copy of everything he did. When they heard this, people always called him "old-fashioned," but he had been vindicated more than once by the agonized, inconsolable moaning of some colleague whose irreplaceable data had been lost to hard drive failures.

But it wasn't just the reliability of computers he distrusted. It was the way they had changed everything.

You couldn't talk to a person on the telephone anymore. You had to talk to a machine. You had to use a machine to pay a bill, buy a concert ticket, write a letter. And everything was wired up these days, interconnected. Suddenly, it was no longer enough to be the best journalist you could be, to do the work and put it out there and let it speak for itself. Suddenly, you were supposed to keep a Facebook page and answer emails and moderate discussions on your message board.

Malcolm had stopped saying these things aloud. He knew how they made him sound. He was conscious of the world moving faster, receding from him, as if he were a sprinter grown winded. The worst part was, he didn't care.

A sigh. Despite reminding himself to hurry, despite knowing he did not have time to linger over photos, he lifted the picture of Marie out of the box, stared into the eyes he had loved for so many years, that lush smile, a teenaged girl facing the rising sun of an unknown future with the kind of confidence that comes only when you're too young to know any better. It was, he had always told her, the best picture she had ever taken. What would she think of what he had done?

And all at once, this idea of slipping in to pack up his office did not seem such a smart thing after all. There was too much. It would take too long. He kept getting lost in reverie and it was making him sad. Besides, he realized suddenly, where would he put multiple boxes? He was driving a Corvette.

Let someone else pack up his office. Let them ship his stuff to his house. Hell, they owed him that much.

So in the end, he didn't take the notebooks or the Rolodex. In the end, he only took the picture of the kids and the one of Marie. He turned off the light in his office without looking back and went out to the elevator. As he was reaching to touch the button, the door opened and there was Amy Landingham, sipping from a tall cup of some designer coffee.

She was a young reporter, a 20-something white girl—*woman*—with a ponytail, big glasses, and a reputation for doggedly chasing down facts other people could not get. Probably, she was coming in early to get the jump on some big project or other. Everyone said she would go places, assuming the newspaper industry survived long enough to take her there.

Malcolm barely knew her, but she had approached him once the week after she was hired and said something that warmed him inside like cocoa after an ice storm. "You're the whole reason I'm here," she had told Malcolm shyly, looking at him up over the rim of her glasses. It turned out he had spoken at her high school career day a few years before and had made such an impression with his passion for journalism that she had decided her future then and there. He hadn't even remembered giving the speech.

Now she stopped short, as surprised to see him as he was to see her. No, he realized on second glance, it wasn't just surprise. She had seen the paper. He could tell. And that look on her face, was it...hurt? Pity?

"Malcolm," she said. Her voice was stiff like new denim and he decided the look was probably anger.

"Amy," he said.

"Awfully early," she said.

"Yeah," he said. "I came in to get some things." He moved past her to grab the elevator door before it could close. "You have a good day." He stepped inside, stabbed at the button.

Amy was looking at him. "Malcolm," she said finally, "I have to ask. Why did you...?"

"I just got tired," he said.

"Tired? Tired of what?"

He was pondering how to answer that when, to his great relief, the elevator door closed.

Malcolm rode down to the lobby with that look on her face before his eyes. It was, he suddenly realized, the one thing he had not considered. He had thought about how his bosses would react, he had thought about what would happen to his career, he had thought about the controversy that was sure to come. All those things, he had thought through, and accepted. But he hadn't thought about people like Amy. Now, walking out past the security gate, pressing the button for the parking elevator and riding it down, she was all he could think about.

"You're the whole reason I'm here," she had said that time, gazing up at him in adoration, like meeting him was meeting Michael Jordan.

Don't blame me, kid. That, he told himself now, was what he should have said. He should have punctured that puppy dog look. He'd have been doing her a favor.

But Malcolm's anger would not hold. How many Amys had he met over the years? How many times had they told him they admired him for the stands he had taken on same-sex marriage, race, Islamophobia, guns, abortion, women's rights, global warming? Hundreds? Thousands? "A prophetic voice," someone had said. "You speak for me," someone else had said. "You make me feel like I am not alone." He had heard it many times. So many times, he realized with a sudden jolt, that at some point over the years he had stopped hearing it altogether.

But he heard it now, as the elevator doors opened and he strode across the empty parking garage. He heard it anew, heard it clearly, and for the first time since he had done what he'd done, he wondered what those people would say, what they would feel, what they would think of him now.

Lowering himself into the car, wincing automatically from the pain, he realized all at once that he had misread Amy's face. That wasn't hurt shining from her eyes. It wasn't pity, or even anger.

It was betrayal. It was the look you give someone when they have let you down.

She had trusted him—no, she had *believed* in him, which was worse—and he had proven her wrong to do so.

Lord, what have I done?

The thought punched through him like a shaft of sunlight through rainclouds. He tried not to think it, as he started the car with the familiar roar that always made him feel better about himself, but did not so much as touch him now.

What did I do?

The thought was relentless. Because suddenly, he knew: It wasn't the acclaim that mattered. It wasn't the prestige.

He accelerated into the 5:30 a.m. streets.

It wasn't even the career. No, it was the *trust*. At a time when, increasingly, nobody believes in anything, people, *some* people at least, had believed in him. At a time when everyone in media is screaming and no one listens, they had *listened* to him. And with a few beers in his gut and a surfeit of anger in his heart, he had destroyed that.

Malcolm stopped at a light. He was barely conscious of the tears on his cheeks.

The light changed. He drove toward home in a stupor. The sun was coming up. There were still barely any cars on the street. An old Cadillac of an indeterminate color limping in the opposite direction. An imperious black SUV passing him on the right. A white van with rust spots on the hood following behind him.

He stopped at another light, wondering—and he couldn't believe this was the first time he had asked himself—what he would do with himself now, having killed his own career. Teach? No. Who would want him? Write a stupid book like Jayson Blair to explain himself? No, he'd explain himself— as best he could, anyway—to whomever he gave his first, probably only, media interview. CNN, he was thinking. Or maybe the *New York Times*. Maybe both. Maybe do two interviews, one for broadcast, one for print.

And then what? Disappear, he supposed. Go out to California where Miles and Andrea were and get to know his grandkids. Assuming, of course, his son and daughter still wanted to have anything to do with him.

Malcolm made a disgusted sound, recognizing the self-pity rising in him. He had to snap out of it.

He glanced automatically into the rearview mirror and all at once, his eyes went wide. He had time to register the white van coming up behind him, time to realize that it did not seem to be stopping, that it actually seemed to be gathering speed. "Oh, God," he said. His brain told him to mash the gas pedal. His foot never made it.

The collision came in a shriek of metal. The airbag deployed with a sound like a gunshot. The Corvette lurched forward from the impact. His body flew. Something punched him hard in the temple. There was a flash of lightning. And then...

Darkness, silence, wetness.

Blood?

His heart thumped heavily.

Darkness. Breathing, pain.

Voices.

"Hurry up! Hurry up!"

"I'm hurryin.'"

"Get him out of there!"

"I got him. No worries."

Darkness.

And then he was briefly aware of the door pulling open with a groan of twisted metal and a strange face leaning over him. Strange, because it was immobile, did not move. A white man with a white beard, his broad face frozen in a cheerful, awful smile.

Hands were on him. He was being pulled from his car. He protested. Thought he protested, at least, but he wasn't sure.

Pain. Oh, God, pain. His leg was on fire. He moaned, heard himself moan. They did not lay him on the street, loosen his collar, call 911. They were...carrying him somewhere?

Darkness was edging back in and Malcolm welcomed it for the relief oblivion promised. In the instant before it claimed him, he realized that he recognized that strange face, indeed, that he had known it all his life. But he had to be wrong. It didn't make any sense.

Why was he being kidnapped by Santa Claus?

three

Bob Carson was an early riser.

He loved the dark silence of the hours before dawn. Being afoot before light and noise overtook the world gave him a delicious sense of being one up on the day, just that much ahead of all the folks still hugging pillows in the warmth of their beds.

So he was already awake, showered, shaved, and padding around his orderly kitchen, humming vaguely to himself as he assembled the ingredients for an egg-white spinach omelet, when his cellphone rang at 5:52. The electronic burring froze him with Ziploc bags of spinach and mushrooms in hand. The sound belonged to later in the day. In the stillness of predawn, it seemed almost an offense.

Bob sighed, put the bags on the counter, turned off the flame upon which a skillet had been warming, and picked up the phone just as it began to chirp again. The caller ID said it was Doug Perry. What could Doug want at this hour?

Bob touched the green button on the screen and spoke without preamble. "Doug. What's wrong?"

"Have you seen the paper?"

There was something brittle in Doug's voice that, for some reason, made Bob shift his weight. "No," he said. And now he glanced with wary foreboding toward the kitchen table where four papers—the *New York Times*, the *Tribune*, the *Sun-Times*, and the *Post*—were neatly arranged, the *Post* on top, the nameplates of the other three peeking out, waiting for him to read them over breakfast and decaf.

"Go take a look," said Doug.

"What's...?"

"Front page. Go take a look."

"Hold on."

Lowering the phone, Bob went to the table and slid the *Post* from the top of the stack. He glanced at the images of Obama and McCain, made certain neither man had been misidentified, looked for typos in the headline. Then he flipped the paper over to look below the fold. And felt a dull thump against his breastbone.

"Oh my God," he said, lifting the phone even as he dropped into a chair. "How did that happen?"

"I was hoping you could tell me."

"I have no idea."

"Are you sure?"

"Of course I'm sure."

"Lydia called me from the gym just now," said Perry. "She is fucking furious, you hear me?"

"I can imagine."

"No, brother, you can't. And she's going to be demanding answers. You sure you have no idea how this happened? Something like this would require administrator level access to the system. It's not something just anybody can do. Maybe you made a mistake somewhere along the way? Maybe you, I don't know, pressed a send button when you meant to press delete?"

"Doug, for the third time: No. Have you spoken to Sam?" Samantha Welles was the night duty officer.

"Yeah, that was my first thought. She swears that when she signed off on the page, it did not have Malcolm's column. It had the AP story on the undecideds."

"Well, I didn't do it," insisted Bob. How many times had he said this now? He was conscious of protesting too much.

Doug grunted. It was a sound that could have meant anything. "Well," he said, "there's a meeting in the publisher's office, 7:00."

"I'll see you there," Bob told his boss. But Doug had already hung up.

Time was short, but Bob didn't go flying to his bedroom to get dressed. Instead, he picked up the paper and, almost as if in a trance, began to read

Malcolm's column, the column he, Bob, had rejected emphatically and then personally spiked to the delete basket, the one that had somehow risen from the dead. It said:

> Good morning, friends and neighbors.
>
> What you read here today are the musings of a tired man.
>
> "Tired from what?" you will ask yourselves. "What can Toussaint have to be tired about? He is a respected journalist, he is paid more than he deserves, he has two of the greatest kids in the world and he was lucky enough to be loved by a woman who was gracious and kind and smart and stunning and who stayed married to Toussaint for 27 years—until her death in 2006—despite the fact that he was none of those things and everyone knew she was far too good for him.
>
> What in the world does Toussaint have to complain about? Well, it's simple, really: I'm sick and tired of white folks' bullshit.
>
> I know the language catches some of you by surprise, but there you go.
>
> Two weeks ago, I wrote a column. You may remember it. It was about Donte Stoddard, the 22-year-old African-American man, father of three, who died in a hail of bullets—52 shots were fired, 27 struck home—when he was confronted by Chicago police late one night outside a McDonald's restaurant. Police say they shot Stoddard because he reached into his pocket and produced a wallet that officers mistook for a gun. Witnesses said that was a lie. Security camera footage backs them up. It clearly shows Stoddard with takeout bags of fast food in each hand. He transfers them both to one hand and begins reaching toward his hip pocket to produce his ID. But before he his hand even reaches the pocket, much less pulls anything out, the shooting begins—and continues for 12 excruciating seconds.
>
> After all that, police said the man they were looking for when they stopped Stoddard on suspicion of armed robbery actually bore no resemblance to him—10 years older, 50 pounds heavier, and with a medium Afro where Stoddard wore dreadlocks. The only thing they had in common is that they were both black men; apparently, that was enough. In the column, I called the cops out for the execution of yet

another black man under dubious circumstances and demanded a Justice Department investigation.

In response, I just received the following email from a man named Joe MacPherson, which I present to you now in its entirety:

"Toussaint, your so stupid. Do you really expect us to shed tears because this guy is dead? Your just another whiny, brainwashed lib who doesn't have the brains to see the truth or the balls to tell it. Fact: niggers committ the majoraty of the crimes in this country, so dont blame the PO-lice for this man being dead, blame yourselfs. If you really want to help your people why dont you tell them to stop committing all the crimes? This guy Stoddart had a record for drug dealing and domestic violence. I notice you didnt write about that. Or you could tell them to stop making babys they cant take care of. Stoddart had three kids with three diffrent women and he was only 22! Thats something else you didnt say. No, you always want to put everything on white people. Your hatred of white America shines through with everything you write. Your such a racist nigger. Always playing the race card. Always stirring the pot. Its race baiters like you who are destroying this country. And its people like me who wont let you. This is America, pal. Love it or leave it."

Now, I don't present this email to you because it is particularly outlandish. It's a rare day when I don't get a half-dozen or more just like it, or worse. No, I present it to you because it represents that final drop of water that makes the bucket overflow.

I repeat: I am tired of white folks' bullshit.

In the first place—and I realize this is petty, but this is my rant, so humor me—does this email not tell you everything you need to know about declining educational standards in this country? Can you appreciate how truly frustrating it is for an educated man such as myself to have his intelligence impugned by someone who failed to master fifth-grade English?

"Your so stupid"? Really? That may be the single most maddening sentence I have ever read in my life—although "Your such a racist nigger" would also have to be in contention. And would someone please buy this man a box of apostrophes?

As to the rest of it, well...I don't propose to go through it point by point. I have already said what I had to say about the execution of Donte Stoddard and, for that matter, about black crime, black babies, and the criminalization of black existence. You may look it up if you care to.

I didn't write this column to say any of that. I wrote it only to say, I give up. I surrender. Uncle.

As many of you know, I once met a great man—his name was Martin Luther King, Jr.—who counseled me to have patience and faith where the people he called "our white brothers" are concerned. I was a young man, with a young man's impatience and rage. My father was a Memphis sanitation worker, one of the men Dr. King had come to town to help, one of the men who paraded through downtown everyday with a sign that said "I AM A MAN," because white folks needed the reminder.

I didn't want to march. I wanted to burn. I wanted to destroy. I wanted to tear down the world until everybody in it felt my impotent fury.

Dr. King told me not to waste my life that way. Patience and faith, he said.

Well, here we are 40 years later, friends and neighbors, and I am out of patience and I am out of faith. I don't want to burn or destroy or tear down. I just want to surrender, to publicly divest myself of the foolish notion that white people can be redeemed, that they can be influenced to once and for all give up the asinine delusion that melanin correlates to intelligence, morality or worth.

I no longer believe they can.

And yes, someone will point out that 40 years after Dr. King spoke to me, here we are with a black man running for president. What about that? they will say. Doesn't that prove patience and faith have paid off?

Well, what about that? Barack Obama has faced not just the ordinary political questions about his policies, his plans and his experience but also a series of extraordinary questions unique to him: Was he really born in the USA? Is he secretly a Muslim? Is he secretly a terrorist? Does he hate whitey? White people ask these questions because they can't bring themselves to ask what they really want to ask: Who is this nigger to think he should be our president?

And when Obama gets his ass kicked and he makes that call tonight to congratulate John McCain on winning the presidency, when the social scientists start talking about the "Bradley Effect" and the hidden racism polling did not detect, ask yourself: could it really have ended otherwise? Could white people have done anything other than what they did?

If you think that, then you don't know white people.

I do. That's why I have given up on them.

So Joe MacPherson, thank you for being that one drop and for thereby helping me to clarify something I have been struggling with for a very long time. Now please, go to hell, and take America with you.

Bob sighed. He sat looking for a moment at the paper, Malcolm smiling a smug little smile and looking younger than he was in a sig photo that was probably ten years out of date. Finally, Bob stood and went about replacing the bags in the refrigerator, putting the skillet in the sink. There would be no breakfast this morning.

As Bob was absorbing that minor disappointment, his telephone chirped again, this time the tone alerting him to the arrival of an email. Bob resented the slightly Pavlovian way the little device had trained him to pick it up at the ringing of a bell to see some ad for erectile dysfunction or plea for help from a distressed Nigerian. For a brief moment, he thought of allowing the chirp to go unanswered—didn't he have more important concerns?—but in the end, he surrendered as he had known he would, picked up the phone, and clicked open his email.

"A name from your past," read the subject line.

Bob opened it. What he saw put him back in the chair.

Old friend, you cannot imagine my delight at running across your name while doing some research on the *Post* website. Well, not just your name...there are a million "Bob Carsons" in the world, after all...but also, your picture. That's what sealed it for me. Even after all these years, I'd have known you anywhere.

I have always regretted the way it was left between us, the things I said to you so long ago in all my youthful self-righteousness and ideological purity. I've thought of you often and wondered what became of you.

These past few months, I have been working in minority outreach for Senator Obama. I am on a plane right now and will land in Chicago at 10:30. I will be homeless for a few hours, unable to check into my room until this afternoon. I know this is criminally short notice and I will understand if you can't do it, but if at all possible, might we have lunch today?

I've missed you, Bob. I'd love to catch up with you. More than that, I'd simply love to see you again.

Let me know.

It was signed, "Janeka Lattimore."

Janeka Lattimore.

He said it in a whisper just to hear it being said, just to have the words on his tongue and the sound in his ear. All at once, Bob realized he had stopped breathing. He breathed.

He was a trim and orderly man in wire frame glasses, pink scalp peeking through the thin canopy of hair at the crown of his head. Once upon a time, back when his hair had fallen to below his shoulder blades, back when he was another man in another life, he had loved Janeka Lattimore.

Helplessly, that was how he had loved her. Completely.

And she had broken his heart.

No, that wasn't quite right. She had not broken his heart. She had broken *him*. She had left him lying in pieces on a dirt road in Mississippi and for the longest time, he had not known if—or even cared if—he could put himself together again. And even when he finally decided to get on with it, even when he did manage to put the pieces back together into something that vaguely resembled Robert Matthew Carson, it had never quite been the same. He felt like a piece of china glued back together by a sixth grader. The pieces didn't quite fit. The break still was visible.

Bob had never loved again—never allowed himself to. There had been relationships, yes. He had even lived for a couple of years with a free-spirited painter in a crummy little apartment in Soho, and she had borne him a son he adored. But he had never married, much less immersed himself in a woman that way again.

Now he was 59 years old and after all this time, here she was, blowing through town, blowing back into his life and wanting to get together...*for lunch*?

Bob felt anger kindling in him at the nerve of her, to show up 40 years later as an email in his inbox, blithely inviting him to catch up on old times. As if what had happened had never happened, as if she had not told him they had no future because he was white and she was not. As if he, with an icepack to his head and blood dripping off his chin, sitting in the back of that ambulance, had not begged her to stay. As if she had not turned away from him—literally turned away from him—to be with "her people." That's how she had put it in that self-consciously melodramatic way of college radicals of the 1960s for whom the revolution was a foregone conclusion. Her people.

"I thought I was your people, too," he had said, his voice wounded and confused, as the ambulance door closed on him. He had always wondered if she heard him and, if she did, if she had answered. He didn't know. The door had closed like finality and he had never seen nor heard from her again.

Then his phone had chirped and there she was, inviting him to lunch. There was an absurdity to it that almost wrung a bitter laugh out of him. Almost.

Bob glanced at his watch. It was a few minutes after six. He needed to hurry if he was going to make the meeting. He pressed a button and the screen on his cellphone went dark. But it was an effort just to get up out of the chair.

"Janeka Lattimore," he said, walking down the hallway toward his bedroom.

His anger had burned itself down to a dull throb by the time Bob entered the glass-enclosed conference room outside Lydia Barnett's office 51 minutes later. He was the first one there and he didn't bother turning on the lights. Bob took a seat near the head of the table, pulling his cellphone from the holster on his hip.

He opened his email and typed quickly before he could talk himself out of it, come to his senses, lose his nerve. "Janeka, so good to hear from you. I'd love to see you again. There's a place on Michigan Avenue called Stymie's, about two blocks from Grant Park. Is noon OK?"

Bob didn't even bother to read the note over for typos. He pressed send. Only then did he allow himself to breathe. And to wonder what he had done.

"You OK?"

Bob looked up. Doug was at the door, rumpled and fat, a bear claw in one hand and a latte in the other.

"Yeah, I'm fine."

"'Cause you look like hell," said Doug. He used his elbow to bring up the lights and took a seat on the opposite side of the table, two chairs down.

"It's not this," said Bob. "Right after we spoke, I got an email from a girl I used to know—a woman, I guess I should say. Haven't seen her in 40 years and she pops up out of the blue, says she wants to have lunch." Even as he spoke, Bob wondered where his sudden chattiness was coming from. Nerves, he decided.

"This girl," said Doug, around a bite of bear claw, "she was something special, I take it?"

"Very," said Bob.

"I guess that would explain why you got that pasty face thing going, like you were just run over by a ghost. I sympathize with you, but you might want to get your head in the game here. Like I told you on the phone: Lydia is not a happy woman."

"And I don't blame her," said Bob. "But why should that bother me? I didn't do anything wrong."

Doug stopped chewing. "You're kidding me, right? You were his editor. If a scapegoat is needed, who do you think gets the nomination?"

Bob stared. Until this second, he had regarded this whole thing as an annoyance—a major annoyance, to be certain, but nothing more than that. But now...

"Are you saying...?"

He didn't finish the question. He couldn't.

Doug met his gaze. "Watch your ass. That's all I'm saying."

He took another bite off the pastry, dabbed at the corner of his mouth with a napkin. "I'm assuming you reread the piece?" he said.

"Yes," said Bob. "Right after you called."

"You were the closest to him. Did you ever have any inkling he felt that way?"

"What way?"

"That he hated white people."

Bob took a moment. "Well," he said finally, "that's not exactly what he said, is it?"

"It isn't?"

"No." A rueful chuckle. "He said he hates white people's BS."

"Yeah, well..." said Doug. He finished the sentence with a little shrug that suggested he found it a distinction without a difference.

"Yeah," agreed Bob. "You're probably right. I mean, he could always be a little bit out there with the race stuff. Seemed like every other column was a rant about some racist conspiracy or other. But no, I never figured he had anything like this in him. Of course, that's not the problem right now. We need to figure out how that column ever made it into the paper."

"We already know how that happened." It was Lydia. She swept into the room, trailed by Denis Lassiter, the executive editor, carrying a copy of the morning's paper. Following them came Mindy Chen, who was in charge of newsroom systems, and Hector Mendoza, director of loss prevention. Two of Hector's men followed him in.

Lydia took her seat at the head of the table, Lassiter sat to her left, directly across from Bob. Bob couldn't help himself. "How did it happen?" he asked.

Lydia's glance grazed him like a bullet. She did not answer.

This was not good.

"OK, everyone," she said, "we've got a lot of ground to cover. Let's get right to it." While everyone else sat, Mendoza and his two men preferred to stand along the back wall, Mendoza with his arms folded across his chest. This was *very* not good.

Lydia swept the room with her gaze, allowing a beat of silence to intervene. Then she said, "Malcolm's column was published through Bob's computer."

Bob felt something hot spike right in the center of his chest. "What are you talking about? Like I told Doug, I didn't do this!"

Lydia didn't even look at him. "I never said you did, Bob," she told him. And then she nodded down the table. "Mindy?"

Mindy Chen cleared her throat. "We traced it back. The digital record is pretty straightforward. The document was saved on Malcolm's computer several times yesterday morning, then filed to the opinion basket at"—she read from a legal pad on the table before her—"12:37. It was accessed from Bob's computer yesterday at 2:15, then Doug's at 2:32, Denis' at 2:56, Lydia's at 4:16."

"That's when Malcolm was taking the column around the newsroom," said Bob, "trying to get one of you to overrule me. That doesn't prove anything."

Still Lydia did not so much as glance over. Mindy cleared her throat. "The column was accessed for the final time last night at 11:16 from Bob's computer. It was pulled from the delete basket and stripped across the bottom of the front page."

"But that's crazy," protested Bob. "At 11:16 last night, I was home, asleep."

Lydia sighed. "Bob, we already know you didn't do this." He turned toward her, surprised. She nodded to Hector Mendoza. He wasn't a tall man, maybe 5'8" or so, but his shaved bullet head and a chest the approximate width of a Buick made him intimidating. Nodding to one of his men to bring the lights down, he produced a silver disc, which he plugged into a console in the back corner of the room. He pressed a button on a control pad and a screen lowered itself across the front of the room from a recessed slot in the ceiling.

"This is security camera footage from last night," he said. On the screen, there appeared an overhead shot of the security desk downstairs, the light muddy, the colors washed out. There was nothing for a moment, and then a figure appeared, a man, and he wore a baseball cap bearing the logo of the Chicago Bulls. He almost could have been Malcolm, but the cap made it hard to say.

Then the man glanced up, right into the camera, and there was no mistaking. Mendoza froze the image for all to see. It was, indeed, Malcolm. The time stamp said 11:02.

Bob brought a hand to his suddenly open mouth. "Malcolm?" he said. He made it a question, though it no longer was.

Lydia's nod was tight. "Yes," she said. "There's another camera at the elevator on this floor. It recorded him getting off 25 seconds later. As you all know, the newsroom is nearly deserted at that hour and nobody who was here recalls seeing him. But the cameras did."

"Also my guy on the security desk remembers him," said Mendoza. "I woke him up to ask him not half an hour ago. He says he remembers thinking it was awful strange to see Malcolm here that time of night."

"Malcolm also came back," said Lydia.

"What?" said Doug.

Mendoza nodded. "Before dawn this morning. Ricky here"—he nodded toward one of his men, a thickset black kid with no discernible neck—"was on the desk at the time and he saw him. That's also confirmed by the security cameras and by Amy Landingham, who was in early to get a jump on some reporting. I've checked his office. It looks like he came in, started packing up, then thought better of it. There's a box on his desk half-filled with pictures."

Lassiter gave a tight nod. "Consciousness of guilt, sounds like to me."

"Has anyone tried to reach him?" asked Doug.

"I called," said Lassiter. "No answer. Can't say I blame him."

"What is there to say to him anyway?" asked Doug. "Beyond 'You're fired,' I mean."

Lydia's chuckle was bitter as charred meat. "Oh, he is the most thoroughly fired human being in the annals of American journalism. You'd better believe that."

Bob was relieved. But he was still confused. "How did he do it?" he asked. "Malcolm's not an administrator. And there's no way he hacked the computer. He doesn't even like computers."

A glance he didn't understand passed between Lydia and Mindy. Then Mindy said. "He didn't hack the system. He signed on, using your password. As far as the system is concerned, you made the change."

"But I didn't!"

Mindy, a petite, pretty woman with the medium-brown skin of an African-American mother and the almond eyes of a Chinese-American father, regarded him patiently. "We know that," she said, softly. "But did you ever give him your password? Or is there some way he could have gotten access to it on his own? Is it written down somewhere?"

"It's not written anywhere," he said. "No need. I know it by heart."

Still patient, she brought him back to the questions he'd ignored. "Did you ever give it to him? Or is there some way he could have gotten access on his own?"

"Gotten access? No. As I said, he's no computer genius and I don't have it written down."

"Did you ever give it to him?" she pressed.

Her manner was quiet and deliberate as she brought him back to the question he had twice ignored. Bob felt cornered and small. "I don't remember," he said finally. "I don't think so."

And now, finally, Lydia looked at him. "You don't think so," she repeated. Not a question, but he answered it. "No," he said.

Mindy spoke. "According to our records, you haven't changed your password since January."

"Maybe." Bob was numb. "Maybe. I don't know."

"You're supposed to change it twice a year," said Mindy. "We send out reminders."

In his personal life, Bob Carson was a disciplined, organized man. He prided himself on this. He paid his credit card balance in full every month. He worked out three mornings a week without fail. He ate a lean, nutritious diet. He spent every New Year's Day cleaning and reorganizing his closet.

But for all the years he had been in the newspaper business, he had never been able to bring the same sense of order to the office. The news, he had learned very early in his career, was a sprawling, unruly, unpredictable mess, careening every single day toward the brick wall of deadlines. To manage it, sometimes you had to simply go with the flow. Things were seldom as neat and orderly as he would have liked.

That was even truer in this new era of cutbacks and shrinkage when he had more to do than ever before and fewer people to do it with. So how, he found himself wondering for a brief instant, was he supposed to have had time to stay on top of Mindy Chen's reminders? How, when he had meetings every half hour on the half hour, a stable of columnists to edit, candidates to interview, editorials to write, a department to run, budget requests to oversee, even as his staff was shrinking like an iceberg in a global warming movie?

No one took Mindy Chen's reminders all that seriously, not even Mindy Chen. And everyone knew it. Sure, they changed their passwords when they remembered, when they got around to it, but it was never anyone's top priority. It wasn't like the passwords restricted access to nuclear secrets or financial records, for crying out loud. This was a *newspaper*.

He looked across at Mindy Chen. "Yes," he said, "I know."

"So you don't think"—Denis was leaning forward, speaking to him in the gentle, saccharine tone you'd use with someone who'd sustained a traumatic brain injury—"you might have given him your password at some point? Maybe to make a quick fix in the column when you were too busy to do it yourself?"

Without meaning to, Bob looked up to the screen where Malcolm was still frozen, his face unreadable.

"I don't know," Bob heard himself say. "I guess I could have. Do you have any idea how many times I've edited Malcolm Toussaint's column over the years? Anything is possible."

"But it would not have been possible if you had just followed protocol," insisted Denis. Bob just stared. He felt wounded and alone.

Doug Perry had finally had enough. "OK," he said, "Bob screwed up. We get that. He gets it. But that doesn't help us now, does it? We can't change the past, but we have to do what we can to manage the future. What're we going to do about this?"

Bob breathed. It felt like the first time in a month.

"We are already doing what we are going to do," said Lydia. "The presses are rolling on a new edition that does not contain Malcolm's offensive column. We've begun recalling the paper from newsstands and racks all over Cook County. As you might imagine, that's a very difficult undertaking. Some vendors, when we explain what's going on, are extremely reluctant to give them up. It's not exactly 'Dewey Defeats Truman,' which our friends down the street have been trying to live down for sixty years, but it's still pretty bad. The vendors think readers will see it as a collectible. They're probably right on that. We're already getting reports of lines forming at some of the newsstands and readers buying by the armloads. I would be surprised if we got more than a fraction of them off the street."

"Then why are we even trying?" asked Doug. "We'll never get this toothpaste back in the tube."

"We're pulling them back," said Lydia, "because doing so sends the message, in the strongest way I know, that we do not approve or condone what Malcolm Toussaint wrote. At this point, the effort is more important than the success."

"Must be costing us a bundle," said Doug with a low whistle.

"I haven't seen the numbers yet," said Lydia, "but yes, I'm sure it's going to cost us plenty—and not just in dollar terms."

"Credibility," Bob heard himself say.

"Exactly," said Lydia.

"We should be braced for a force-five media shit storm," said Denis. "That's surely coming our way."

"It's already here," Lydia replied. "This has already been picked up by Drudge, and I expect Romenesko and Journalisms and any other journalism blog you can name will be all over it just as fast as they can type. Local radio is talking about it and I've already had calls and emails from the overnight editors at Fox, CNN, CBS, ABC, NBC, the AP, you name it. It's going to really crank up once the business day starts in earnest. Thank God there's another, slightly more important story unfolding today, or it would be even worse."

"It's going to be big," said Bob.

She looked at him. "In the elevator on the way up here, I got a call on my cellphone from Telemundo. Fucking *Telemundo!* Yes, Bob, it's going to be 'big.'"

He felt himself shrink again. "We're going to have to report the story," said Doug, coming to the rescue again.

Denis was rueful. "Yeah," he said. "I'm thinking maybe we should give it to Amy?"

"You think?" said Doug. "You know, she's always looked up to Malcolm."

"He was a hero to half the newsroom, especially the kids."

"They're all kids now," said Doug, mouth twisting into a smirk. "Or maybe I'm just getting old."

"You and me both. As to Amy, it's your call, but I don't think she'd be compromised by hero worship." A shrug.

Doug nodded and Denis went on. "I'll be drafting a statement as soon as we break here. It's important that we speak with one voice on this. There will be a newsroom-wide meeting this morning so that people can ask questions about how this happened. I'm sure there will be some venting, too. But I intend to stress that nobody gives any off-the-record interviews to any other media outlets. We've got to control the message."

"You really expect them to abide by that?"

"Hope springs eternal," said Denis.

"This, too, will pass," said Lydia. "That needs to be the tone we take with the staff. We're in for a very difficult next few days, there is no doubt about that. But the way we're going to get through it is by putting our heads down and concentrating on our core mission, which is to provide world-class journalism for the people of Chicago and Cook County. If we just do that, I am convinced the rest of this will take care of itself."

There was a silence, people looking from one to another, their faces taut with the realization of what they were in for. On the screen above, Malcolm still stared up into the camera, mouth open, eyes wide, frozen in the moment of misdeed. Then the screen went mercifully white. Mendoza ejected the disc. Lydia said, "Very well, then, thank you all for coming in so early on such short notice."

Bob stood to join the procession leaving the room. Lydia laid a restraining touch on his wrist. "Bob, you stay. Denis and I need to talk to you a moment."

He sat. *Just like a puppy*, he would later think. Doug shot him a glance as he left the room. It was the sort of look you might give a mortally wounded man.

When the rest had filed out, Lydia turned expectantly to Denis, who cleared his throat. "Bob, there's no easy way to say this and I respect you too much to beat around the bush."

Bob felt his stomach lurch sideways. *Oh, God.* It was happening. Just like that. It was actually happening.

"We have to let you go."

Oh, God.

"Denis, you can't be serious."

"There'll be a generous severance package, of course. And I want you to know, this was not an easy decision for us."

"Not easy for you?" A bark of laughter escaped him. "Trust me, it's a lot harder from this side of the table."

"I know that, Bob, and I'm sorry. But try to look at it from this side of the table. You caused a security breach."

"No, I forgot to change my password."

"Same thing."

"When's the last time you changed your password, Denis?"

Lassiter drew back. His cheeks glowed. "We are not talking about me, Bob," he said.

"Look," said Lydia, palms up in a peace gesture, "let's get back to the business at hand, shall we? Now as Denis said, Bob, we're not exactly throwing you out in the cold here. There will be a very nice severance package. You'll have to talk to HR, of course. And I'm sure the office of the general counsel will draw up some papers for you to sign, a standard nondisclosure agreement and things like that."

"I'm not signing anything," Bob snapped.

Denis and Lydia glanced at each other. Then Denis said, "Bob, don't be a fool. If you don't sign the agreement, you don't get the money."

Bob stared hard at his former boss. "Denis, you can shove your nondisclosure agreement up your butt."

Again the publisher and the editor looked at each other. Bob had the sense they had not expected this from him. He swelled with a momentary sense of triumph. Then, just as suddenly, he felt himself deflating like a leaky balloon. What did it matter if he said something that stung Denis Lassiter and Lydia Barnett? The victory wasn't simply hollow, it was meaningless. All at once, it was as if he could see everything, as if he had a God's eye view of the entire mess. And he knew: The paper needed to be able to say it had taken some action in response to this humiliation, something that went beyond the obvious point of sacking Malcolm Toussaint. In days to come, it would announce new computer-security protocols, new quality-control measures. But for now, it needed to show that it was taking this seriously, needed to put a face on this disaster. And his was that face.

Bob heard himself breathing. He felt his meticulously constructed world falling to pieces, everything he had worked for fluttering apart in a sudden gust. He was a 59-year-old man, suddenly out of work in a dying industry and a bad economy. He had a God's eye view of that situation, too. It wasn't pretty.

"This is all Malcolm's fault," he heard himself say in a soft voice. "I'm going to kill him." He was startled by his own words.

"Bob," said Lydia, "you are not to have any contact with Malcolm Toussaint."

Bob almost smiled. "Beg pardon, Lydia, but I don't work for you anymore, so I don't take orders from you."

There was some small pleasure in watching those words sink in. Lydia was not a woman who was used to taking no for an answer. But for once, he thought with bitter satisfaction, she had no choice.

Bob stood. Denis Lassiter stood in response. "I'm sorry, Bob," he said. "Sorry for all of it. Hector will escort you out. We'll pack up your office and someone will run your things out to your house for you."

"Yeah," said Bob. And here was the point, in any ordinary parting, where they would have shaken hands, wished each other good life. But this wasn't an ordinary parting. This was getting fired. So there was an awkward moment where a handshake would have gone. Then Bob said, "Yeah," again, just to be saying something, just to fill the empty space.

He moved around Denis to the door. Hector and his two men were waiting for him in the lobby of the editorial suite. Like it would take the three of them to wrestle Bob out of the building. He supposed he should have been flattered.

But he wasn't going to make the scene they feared. No tears, no cursing, no punching of walls or of former colleagues. Bob was determined to salvage as much of his dignity from this humiliation as he could. So they fell in behind him as he headed for the elevators, enduring this executive-suite version of a perp walk with his head held high, looking neither right nor left, just straight ahead. The newsroom, thank God, was still relatively empty. Once or twice, a head bobbed up from a cubicle, a jaw dropped open, but that was all.

Still, it was enough. This would be the stuff of newsroom gossip all day, of industry legend by the end of the week.

He saw Doug from the corner of his eye watching from his glass-enclosed office. The expression on his face suggested the mortally wounded man had died. As, thought Bob, in a sense, he had.

Down the hall and into the elevator. Punch the button. The three men behind him, silent and stolid as statues. The elevator opened on the lobby. He went through the turnstiles. The guard at the security desk affected not to see him.

They paused there, the three of them. Hector reached an open palm toward Bob. For an absurd moment, he thought they were going to shake. Then he realized. And he unclipped from his belt his building ID, a press badge with a magnetic strip on the back, and handed it over to Hector. "I'm sorry, man," the security chief said. And then he walked away, his two men trailing him.

Bob moved to the second bank of elevators, the one that served the parking garage. His brain was fighting itself. He didn't know what to do.

And then he did. He whipped out his cellphone, brought up Malcolm's number, punched it. The call went straight to voice mail.

"This is Toussaint," said Malcolm's voice. "Can't take your call right now." And then the beep.

Bob thumbed the phone off. His career was over because of this jerk. He stabbed the down button on the parking elevator.

You are not to have any contact with Malcolm Toussaint?

Heck with that. Bob was going to find Toussaint if it was the last thing he did.

Where are you, Malcolm? Where are you?

four

Floating in a darkness spiked with pain, he heard their voices.

"Those who have ears, let them hear. We are the White Army of Resistance and we—"

"Cut. Stop, stop."

"What's wrong, Dwayne?"

"It's not White Army of Resistance anymore, remember? That spells WAR and there's already a group called WAR: White Aryan Resistance."

"Oh yeah. I remember now."

"Let's do it again."

Still floating, Malcolm took an inventory of his agonies. His ribs throbbed and he thought one or more might be broken. His knee ached. A thunderstorm was grinding through the center of his head. And he was aware of bright lights, hot against his face. The darkness turned blood red. He struggled to open his eyes, swim to the surface.

"Those who have ears, let them hear. We are the White Resistance Army. I am Sergeant Clarence Pym, under the command of Captain Dwayne McLarty. We have captured this coon so that—"

"Hold on. Stop. I thought we weren't going to use 'coon.' Sounds kind of old-timey, don't it? Like something some goobers in the woods might say."

"Well, what should I call him then?"

"Just say nigger."

"Nigger?"

"Yeah, why not? That's what he is, ain't it?"

"Yeah, I guess we can't go wrong with that."

"Fine, then. Nigger it is. You ready?"

"Yeah. Let's do it."

"OK, three, two, one."

"Those who have ears, let them hear. We are the White Resistance Army. I am Sergeant Clarence Pym under the—"

"Wait. Hold on."

"Did I goof up again?"

"No. Look at him. He's awake."

Malcolm had managed to force his eyes open and found himself staring into the harsh glare of unshaded light from a floor lamp. He tried to bring his right hand up to shield his eyes but the hand stopped short with a rattle of metal and something bit his wrist. *Shackles?* He turned to inspect, but a meaty hand clamped on his head from behind and shoved it roughly back.

"Sit still and watch the camera, nigger," said a voice behind him.

"No, no," said the other voice. "That's all right. Give him a moment. Let him look."

The bulb went out. Malcolm tried to blink his eyes clear. He examined his wrists. He was right. Both were shackled. He tried his feet. Same thing. He was chained to a chair in some cavernous room. "What the hell...?"

A man-shaped shadow moved toward him. Malcolm's vision was still a blur of ghosts. "That's right," said the shadow. "Chains. Get used to 'em."

"Where am I? What's this all about?"

Again, a hand from behind him seized him, yanking his head back. "You don't ask the questions. You don't speak until you're spoken to."

"No," said the one in front. "It's all right, Clarence. I don't mind answering its questions." And then, to Malcolm: "What's it about? That's simple. It's about the salvation of the white race. It's about saving America from mongrelization and socialism and putting her back on the path of her true greatness."

Malcolm ignored the hammering behind his eyes and beseeched memory to give him something...anything. After a moment, it did. He had been driving away from the paper. He had stopped at a light. There had been a car behind him. No, a van, with big rust patches, coming too fast.

"You crashed into me on purpose," he said, the memory and the words emerging at the same time. "You hit me. And then...what? You kidnapped me?"

It was outlandish. Even saying it, he couldn't believe it. Why would any-one kidnap *him*?

The stars were fading from his eyes, and for the first time he could really see the man before him. Skinny and twitchy-looking, buzz cut on one side of his scalp, a thick shock of bright yellow hair on the other side falling to a level just above his ear, where it looked as if it had been chopped with garden shears. A stupid hairstyle too young for him by a good ten years, judging from the gray crinkles of his skin—thirty-five if he was a day. Wispy goatee beneath pale gray eyes and wearing a T-shirt with a drawing of an upthrust white fist and the word "Rise."

Tattoos crawled down his arms and up his neck. Guns, snakes, motor-cycles, Viking goddesses.

Swastikas.

And he had a gun, an evil-looking black pistol wedged into his pants at the belt line.

The man smiled. His teeth were brown and crooked, with spaces be-tween them you could drive a small car through. "No, we didn't kidnap you," he said in an agreeable voice. "We took you prisoner. Kidnapping is a crime, and we are not criminals. We are at war, boy. "

"You're crazy," breathed Malcolm,

The man slapped him hard. Malcolm's head jerked viciously. There was a rattle of chains as his hands lurched automatically, futilely, toward his face. Malcolm squeezed his eyes shut against the pain and a sudden nausea roiling in his gut. He tasted blood on his teeth.

When he opened his eyes again, the man's finger was bobbing in his face. "We're not going to put up with any sass from you, nigger. That's the first thing you need to get through your thick monkey skull."

"Monkey skull. That's a good one." The chortling came from the other one, the one behind him. "Hit him again."

"What are you doing?" asked Malcolm. "Why did you"—he almost said "kidnap" again, thought better of it—"capture me?"

"Already told you," said Dwayne. "This is a war. We're fighting to take our country back."

"I have no idea what you're talking about."

"Oh, sure you do. You're just stalling for time. You're a smart one, nigger. I'll give you that." He glanced at the one Malcolm could not see. "Ready, Clarence?"

"Ready, Dwayne."

The one named Dwayne nodded curtly, then retreated to a camcorder on a tripod, aimed at Malcolm. He switched on the floor lamp and Malcolm squinted against the sudden harsh light.

"Okay, Clarence. Go."

From behind him, Malcolm heard the other man clear his throat. Then he began to speak, his voice the careful cadence of a child reciting some memorized thing. It was as if the speech was a minefield and every word had the potential of exploding in his face.

"Those who have ears, let them hear. We are the White Resistance Army. I am Sergeant Clarence Pym, under the command of Captain Dwayne McLarty. We have captured this nigger, the so-called journalist that calls himself Malcolm Toussaint, who for many years has spewed his white-hating, anti-Christian poison in jewspapers all over this once-great nation, including this morning's vicious diatribe against the white men who built this nation. Although the actions we take today were planned long ago, the nigger's diatribe this morning explains better than we ever could why we have felt it necessary to go to this extreme. To put it plainly: at some point, as white men, we have to call a halt, we have to say that we've had enough—or we can no longer regard ourselves as white *men*."

He cleared his throat. His voice rose. "Tonight, there is a good chance this nation will elect a socialist Muslim nigger as its president. The nigger has been clear in his intentions. He has said he wishes to redistribute the wealth. He has said he will pay reparations to his fellow blacks. He has said this country will bow down before the false religion of Islam. The fact that a foreign-born interloper with such radical extreme leftist views might be elected president tells you how sick this country is. This tells us in no uncertain terms that the hour is late and that it is upon our heads to stand and be counted.

"We are not kidnappers. We demand no ransom. We are soldiers and this is an enemy we have captured. We are patriots who are convinced this nation cannot be cleansed except with blood. So let there be blood.

"We leave this document as an inspiration to others so that in case we fall, they will know why we did what we did and they will pick up where we left off. Those who have ears, let them hear. We are the White Resistance Army and this is our declaration of war."

Malcolm's blood was a river of ice. He thought, horribly, inevitably, of Daniel Pearl, the *Wall Street Journal* reporter who'd sat through a madman's rant just like this, delivered to a camcorder just like this and was then beheaded for all the world to see, his lightless eyes and slack mouth held up like some grotesque trophy. All at once, Malcolm knew with a certainty what was coming. He *knew*. And he began to thrash about and buck against the chains, all the while expecting at any instant to feel the steel bite into his jugular vein.

Instead, the light blinked out and the red light on the camera went dark. "What's wrong with him?" asked the voice behind Malcolm.

The one called Dwayne was lighting a cigarette. He exhaled and squinted at Malcolm through the smoke. "He thought you were going to chop his head off."

"What?"

"Sure. Like that Jew reporter those ragheads did in a few years ago. Remember?" He drew his index finger across his throat and made a slicing sound. Then he laughed and bent over, putting his face close to Malcolm's. "Uh-uh, nigger," he said. "We ain't cuttin' off your head. You ain't gettin' off that easy. Won't be easy at all, will it, Clarence?"

And now Clarence came into view. He was...a behemoth, perhaps the biggest man Malcolm had ever seen, a good 6'6" and well over 400 pounds, a mammoth pile of flesh draped by a shapeless T-shirt bearing the legend "Patriots *Act*" above a red, white, and blue swastika with bolts of yellow lightning shooting out from it. His hands were like catcher's mitts. His florid face was topped with a thick mop of brown hair, a cowlick shooting off the back like he was some past-his-prime Dennis the Menace. Malcolm guessed Clarence Pym to be a good ten years younger than Dwayne McLarty, somewhere in his middle twenties.

Clarence caught him looking. "Take a picture, shitbird," he said. "It'll last longer."

Dwayne tugged his friend's sleeve. "Ah, don't worry about him. Come on, we got work to do."

Clarence allowed himself to be led away, muttering, "Just don't like people lookin' at me, that's all."

"I know, buddy," said Dwayne and his voice was oddly soothing. "But when this day is over, they're going to be looking at you in a whole new light."

"Tell again how big the explosion is going to be," said Clarence, sounding not unlike a child asking for his favorite bedtime story.

But Malcolm noted this absently in some small corner of his mind. The rest of his mind was filled with that pregnant word: *explosion*. What had he gotten himself into?

"Later," said Dwayne. "Right now, we've got work to do. Go sit over there while I get the camera."

As Clarence lumbered off to a pair of metal folding chairs set up on the other side of the vast space—a warehouse, Malcolm realized—Dwayne lingered to remove the camcorder from the tripod. Before he joined Clarence, he leaned in and whispered to Malcolm. "You had no call to stare at him like that," he said. "He can't help how he looks."

Before he could think how to respond, Dwayne had crossed the room to a card table where Clarence sat with a laptop open. Dwayne produced a cable and attached the camera to the computer.

Malcolm tried to convince himself this was actually happening. Who kidnapped journalists in America? In the Middle East, yes. In Mexico, yes. It was a job hazard, something you accepted going in. But in *Chicago, USA*? Things like this just did not happen.

It struck him that he could easily be killed in whatever harebrained scheme these two idiots, this Laurel and Hardy of white supremacy, had cooked up. Malcolm felt himself beginning to panic. He ordered himself not to.

He had to focus, had to impose some order on his thoughts. He forced himself to breathe in deeply, to hold it over a seven count, and then to exhale slowly. His heart slowed its gallop to a trot, and his situation shivered into clarity.

He examined the restraints. Handcuffs, one pair on each wrist, with a short length of chain looping through the empty cuff on each side. The chain ran through a metal U-shaped ring bolted to the floor. His feet were held by leg irons around his ankles, similarly restrained. The result was a very limited freedom of movement—not more than a foot or so in any given direction.

"Fuck!" spat Dwayne suddenly, his finger stabbing down on the laptop's keyboard.

"Well, maybe if you try it this way," said Clarence.

Obviously, they were frustrated by some failure of their tech. Malcolm ignored them and continued to survey his situation.

He was in an enormous warehouse space that rose two stories above him. The entire place was largely empty but for a few crates mounted on wooden pallets in one corner, six large metal drums clustered near a man-sized rollup door, and the table in the center of the space where Pym and McLarty were working, a crumpled Santa Claus mask abandoned at their feet. The whole space smelled of dust. Malcolm had the sense it had been abandoned for a long time.

No one knew where he was. No one was looking for him. No one would even know he was missing. He was at the mercy of these two terrorist wannabes. The realization of it made him gulp down a throat full of sand.

Then he saw the face.

Each window was a grid of opaque glass blocks. Except that, in the bottom left corner of this particular window, a block was missing, and through it appeared the face. It was behind McLarty and Pym, unseen by either, a black man with red-ringed eyes that surveyed the scene inside the old warehouse from the other side. There was confusion in those eyes as they fell upon the mammoth man and his small companion, hunched over the laptop, muttering to themselves.

Malcolm dared not make a sound. But he willed the man silently, implored him with all the force he could project.

Look here. Look at me.

And then, to his great relief, the man did. The red eyes widened in confusion. Malcolm screamed at him silently.

Get help. For God's sake, go and get help.

The other man's eyes did not register the plea. Malcolm saw no alarm flare in them, no urgency click into place, nothing but the same dull bewilderment.

Help me!

Malcolm roared this in the silence of his thoughts.

Still, nothing sparked in the other man's eyes. They watched for another few seconds, then slid down out of sight.

Malcolm spat a mute curse.

Outside on a loading dock ringed by weeds taller than a small child, Willie Washington sat amid broken bottles and discarded butts and tried to make sense of the baffling, extraordinary thing he had seen. Who were these men and what were they doing in his home?

Once upon a time, yes, it had been some kind of toy company, headquartered here in a warren of warehouses west of Michigan Avenue beneath the expressway interchange. "Funn Toys!" read the sign hanging from the top of the four-story brick building, just above a placard that read "For Lease."

But for the last few weeks, thanks to a broken lock on the metal rollup door, it had been his home.

Willie knew everybody who lived on these streets, but he had never seen these men before, the fat one and the skinny one and that brother they had in there, trussed up like a slave or something. Whatever they were up to, that was their business, but that didn't give them the right to bring it into his place. His shopping cart was in there, hidden behind those boxes, filled with all his worldly possessions. Had they found it? Had they messed with his shit?

If they have, what are you going to do about it, you stupid motherfucker?

Willie heard voices. He had heard them for 40 years.

"You shut up," he said aloud.

Nhưng mà biết làm sao đây?

It meant, "What can you do?" One of the voices spoke Vietnamese, a language he had picked up during his three tours in that country.

"I don't know," he said. "I'm thinking about it."

He had to do something, he knew. But he had no idea what.

That's 'cause you's a stupid motherfucker.

The English-speaking voice hated him. He had no idea why.

Willie needed a taste. Knock the cobwebs off. Help him think. Most of all, it would silence the voices. He pulled the shortdog from the pocket of his thin, ratty jacket, unscrewed the cap, and took a healthy swallow, draining the bottle.

"Ahhhh," he said to himself, smacking his lips as he screwed the cap back on. As always, the grape-flavored bite settled him down, made the world something he could deal with.

He tossed the shortdog into the weeds and lifted his head to the open place in the window again. The big boy and the skinny fella were still tapping at the computer, the brother was still making faces at him, glaring hard, trying to get his attention. Willie slid back down and sat there, contemplating.

He was not a brave man. Oh, he had been, once upon a time, he supposed, humping that pig, the M60 machine gun and its heavy-ass ammo, through the swamps of Southeast Asia, gook ears hanging shrunken and black on a length of string around his neck, all his senses alive for the slightest hint of the little bastards who always seemed to materialize out of nowhere, rain all hell down on you, then disappear like morning mist before you could get your licks in.

Too much of that changes a man. Even a brave man. That was the thing no one had ever understood. Not his wife, not his folks. And when he began to hear the voices, when they spoke to him and told him things and called him names, his wife, his folks, they kept trying to convince him none of it was real. But he knew better. It was real, all right. All of it was real.

Forty years ago, it was. Forty years.

And the brave man he had been had curled up and withered away inside this old man he had become. Most days, he was just fine with that. Most days, after all, did not require bravery. Most days only required getting over to the mission on time for meals, dodging the few cops who cared to give you a hard time, and hiking over to Michigan Avenue where you stood, trying to look like conscience to some tourist who just spent $90 on a pair of jeans so that maybe he'd drop a quarter or two, maybe even some folding money, into your hand and go home feeling better about who he was. None of that required any bravery.

But this, doing something about these men who had taken over his home? That would require bravery and he was pretty sure he was no longer up to the task.

Willie sat there in the filth, wondering. What to do, what to do?

Inside the warehouse, Malcolm stifled a groan. The man had to have seen him, had to have seen everything that was going on here. But his eyes had not responded, not even with a simple acknowledgment that Malcolm was there, though they had looked right at each other. A drunk. The guy was some pathetic, homeless drunk who was even now working to convince himself that he had not seen what he had. This was the man upon whom Malcolm's very life now depended.

It was, he thought, superfluous proof that God has a perverse sense of humor.

"Goddamn it!" This was McLarty, bolting to his feet, smacking the case of the laptop with the flat of his fist.

"Take it easy, Dwayne," said Pym. "We'll get it figured out."

"I don't know what the problem is. It's just a fucking upload. I don't know why we keep getting this fucking error message."

"We'll figure it out," repeated Pym. "Maybe we should reboot again?"

"We tried that twice! You know that."

"Maybe the USB cable is bad?"

"Maybe."

"Or maybe it's a problem with the website."

"Maybe maybe maybe. I'm tired of fucking maybes." He yanked the gun from his belt. It was, of all things, a vintage Luger. "Ought to just shoot the fucking thing."

Pym gave him a dry look. "Yeah, that'd help," he said.

McLarty's lips kinked themselves into a smirk. "Okay, so I won't shoot it. But how do we pull off the plan if we can't even upload the video? What's the use kidnapping the nigger if nobody knows we have him?"

Pym scratched thoughtfully at a half-hearted goatee sprouting from his chin. "What did they do before they had all this tech shit?" he asked, finally.

"Write a ransom note," said McLarty. "But that's no good. How do we prove we actually have him? They have to know that, or they won't take it seriously."

"We could take a picture."

"We got no printer, Sergeant Pym. Besides, if we just give them a picture, they won't be able to hear your manifesto. Unless we write it out, I guess. But damn it, I had my heart set on seeing the video all over the television."

Pym snapped his fingers. "Why don't we just burn a DVD?" he asked. "Deliver it to the media ourselves?"

McLarty pursed his lips. Then he was nodding slowly, thoughtfully. "That could work. But who gets the DVD? You want to take it to those jackoffs at CNN? You think they have an office in town? Maybe we could give it to that little fairy, Anderson Cooper?"

"We could," said Pym. "But why not take it to the newspaper?"

Malcolm saw disappointment tug McLarty's face. "Aw, Clarence. Nobody reads newspapers anymore. Besides, what are they going to do with a video? Put a picture in the paper tomorrow? Tomorrow's too late. Tomorrow we'll probably be dead. I want to see this before I go."

Tomorrow we'll probably be dead.

The offhand words caused Malcolm's world to swim out of focus for just an instant. They weren't speaking for his benefit, trying to frighten him. Indeed, they had all but forgotten he was there. No, this was their unvarnished expectation, the thing toward which all of this was pointing.

Tomorrow we'll probably be dead.

Jesus.

"But think about it," Pym was saying. "Newspapers have websites. They'll put it online for us. Plus, they'll alert the other media. It'll be like one-stop shopping. Hell, it actually makes more sense than just uploading it to some website and sending out emails to all the media with the link in it. They might not even see the email until it's too late. Besides, police can do all that CSI shit, trace the emails and the uploads, too. We'd look up and have cops at our door by lunch."

"Yeah, I think you're right," said McLarty.

"Plus, it's kind of what they call poetic justice," said Pym, a grin spreading across his fleshy face.

"How do you mean?"

"Well, it was the paper that made this guy famous. They're the ones who published his garbage every week, including that racist piece of shit on the front page this morning. Who better to get the news that we have him?"

Now the grin spread across McLarty's face, too. "That does make sense. Hell, this might turn out better than the original plan. Why don't you burn the DVD, and I'll take it over to the jewspaper while you guard the prisoner?"

"But how will you get it there? You can't take the van out in daylight, not with the armor plate on it."

Armor? Then Malcolm remembered the dark spots he had taken for rust.

McLarty shrugged. "That's no problem. I'll borrow some wheels from somebody."

"Are you sure?"

"Sure I'm sure. If there's one thing I learned from the old man, it's how to boost a car. Easy peasy. I tell you, I'll be out and back before you know it."

A worry Malcolm didn't understand crossed Pym's face, then. "Don't worry," McLarty told him. "I won't use. Don't need to. Hell, this is the biggest high there ever could be."

There was relief in Pym's smile. There was also—Malcolm saw this with some surprise—affection. Who were these people?

McLarty caught him looking. "What are you starin' at?" Malcolm yanked his eyes away. McLarty took a step. "Hell, we already got the video. Don't need you anymore. I ought to put one right between your fuckin' monkey eyes right now." He reached for the gun in his waistband.

Pym touched his shoulder and McLarty stopped. "Don't you think we should hold on to him, Captain? For tonight, I mean?"

A grimace. "Yeah, Sergeant. I suppose you're right."

"Come on. Let's burn that DVD."

Malcolm sighed as they returned to the computer. Tonight? What did that mean? What was happening tonight?

Then his gaze went to the window. The drunk was back, peering through where the glass brick should have been. Malcolm bared his teeth in frustration and anger.

What are you waiting for? Do something! Find a cop! Get help!

Still, the eyes registered nothing. After a long moment, the face slid down the wall and once again was gone.

So here he was, at 60 years of age, trussed up in chains like Kunta Kinte, at the mercy of two white supremacist lunatics and his salvation—if he was to be saved—rested in the hands of some homeless, hollow-eyed drunk. Malcolm heaved a soft, bitter sigh, marveling anew at the bizarre twists a life can take. His life in particular. There had been so many sharp turns and switchbacks on the road that led from then til now.

But the sharpest—and in hindsight, the most consequential—had been one of the very first. Forty years ago, it was. Forty years.

It started...

five

...on a Friday in February of 1968. He was not yet a nationally renowned journalist, much less a hostage of two white supremacist lunatics. No, he was only a failed college student, coming home.

The Greyhound bus pulled into the bay behind the station with an exhausted sigh of airbrakes, and 19-year-old Malcolm Toussaint unfolded his lanky body gratefully from the cracked and faded seat in the back, finally arrived in Memphis after 18 grueling hours of travel from the white college. Home for good, as far as he was concerned.

His father would give him shit, he knew. His father would say, "I told you so. You ain't had no business up there with them white folks." There would be a fight. There was always a fight. But Malcolm was ready. Part of him was even looking forward to it.

Malcolm was the last person off the bus and stood waiting for his bag, watching from behind his shades as older white people grabbed surreptitious eyes full of him—tall, Afroed, goateed, and silent in their midst, his wiry form draped in a brightly colored dashiki over a pair of blue jeans. He was conscious of the vague hostility and, more, the fear in their gaze. Even the brother retrieving the bags from the cargo compartment under the bus—a shuffling, grinning, old-time brother, lifting his cap when the white people dropped their quarters into his palm—watched him warily, the way you might watch a hand grenade.

It was chilly out, and Malcolm could have used a jacket, but that would have meant covering the dashiki, and he liked that wary look in the eyes of white people—and shuffling, grinning, old-time black ones—when they saw it. It gave him a secret, electric thrill to realize that they found him something to fear.

When his bag was pulled out, he reached for it. The old-time brother watched him, that broad, happy-to-see-you-suh smile shrinking away. He didn't even bother extending his palm for Malcolm to drop a quarter in. But Malcolm gave him a tip, all right. He lifted his right fist across his chest and shook it. Black power.

The old brother's eyes turned cold. He scowled. It made Malcolm smile as he lifted his bag and strode through the terminal out to the street.

Melvin was waiting where he'd said he would be, his two-toned white and aquamarine 1954 Buick Skylark parked right out front. Malcolm opened the back door of the car and threw his bag in, opened the front, and threw himself in. Melvin Cotter's wide, dark face opened in a gleaming smile. "Junie," he said, "welcome back, baby."

Malcolm grinned. "Done told you about that. Ain't 'Junie' no more. It's Malcolm. That's legal now, brother. Been to the courthouse, got the papers and everything."

"Yeah, yeah," said Melvin. "OK, 'Malcolm.'" He pronounced the name with exaggerated deference. "But that's gon' take some gettin' used to."

Malcolm had been born Mozell Uriah Wilson, Jr. He'd grown up being called "Junior," then "Junebug," and finally, just "Junie." He'd always hated his corny, country-sounding name in all its permutations. At the white college, he'd learned that changing it was just a matter of filling out some papers and paying a fee. He'd thought about it and finally took the plunge just two months ago. His father still didn't know.

"So," Melvin was saying, "you want to tell me again what your new name is, Junie?"

Malcolm sighed. "OK, " he said, "but remember it this time, 'cause I ain't answerin' to Junie no more."

"Bet you will if your Pop be callin' for you," said Melvin, glancing over his shoulder and wheeling the old Buick out into traffic.

Malcolm ignored the jibe. He ticked his names off on his right hand. "OK," he said, "my first name is Malcolm, after brother Malcolm, or El-Hajj Malik El-Shabazz, if you prefer."

Melvin nodded sagely. Malcolm X, three years in his grave now, had been Malcolm's hero.

"My middle name," said Malcolm, still ticking off his fingers, "is Marcus after Marcus Garvey. Had a big back-to-Africa movement in the twenties til the honkies shut him down."

Melvin shrugged. "Ain't never heard of him."

"You probably ain't heard of Toussaint L'Ouverture, neither," said Malcolm, ticking off a third finger, "brother who fought Napoleon in the Haitian revolution, but that's where the last name comes from."

"Malcolm Marcus Toussaint." Melvin tried the name out.

"Three revolutionaries," said Malcolm.

Melvin cut him a glance. "Yeah," he said, "I kind of got that. Ain't went to no college, but I ain't quite a fool."

"Nobody said you was, brother," said Malcolm. "And you could have gone to college if you wanted."

Melvin made a derisive sound. "Yeah, right," he said. "Wouldn't of got my ass out of high school if you hadn't let me cheat off you. How you think I was going to do in some college? Especially if you wasn't there to help me? I be at some nigger college, you off at that white school. Don't shit a shitter, Junie. I mean, Malcolm."

Malcolm let it ride. After a moment, he reached across and turned on the radio. He caught the tail end of a commercial for Winstons—"Winston tastes good like a cigarette should" trilled the jingle singers—then a station identifier for WDIA, and with the sound of a shotgun blast, Junior Walker's sax was suddenly everywhere at once, walking and squawking, pushed along by a rhythm section with places to go and people to see. "Shotguuuun," he squalled in his unlovely voice, "shoot 'em 'fore he run now."

"So," said Melvin after a moment, "your pop still ain't know you comin' home?"

"No."

"Should of told him, Junie. Malcolm."

Malcolm shook his head, watching as Union Avenue flew by. "Nah," he said. "Why would I do that? What he care? He ain't want me to go in the first place."

"Well, we both know Mr. Mozell got his ways."

Malcolm shot his friend a look. "Hell, he ain't told me he got hurt. If it hadn't been for you, I wouldn't of known nothin' about it."

"He a proud man. You know that."

"Yeah," said Malcolm. "Well, I got my pride, too."

"Let's be honest here," said Melvin. "Your daddy gettin' hurt ain't got shit to do with you comin' home. Reason you comin' home is 'cause you done got your ass kicked out of school for rabble rousin'. And when your old man find out 'bout that..." He shook his head, whistled through his teeth. "Whoo, boy, when Mr. Mozell find that out, I can hear him now: 'Done told you you ain't had no business takin' your black ass up to no white folks' college in the first place, nigger!'"

Melvin laughed at his own impression of Malcolm's father. Malcolm pursed his lips. Even an impression of his father was enough to tighten his jaw. "Well, in the first place," he said. "I didn't get kicked out. It's called administrative leave. I can apply to go back if I decide I want to."

"*If* you decide? What about your deferment? If you ain't in school, you might get drafted, have your ass over there fightin' them Viet Cong. Man, I break out in a sweat every time I see that mailman come past my door."

Malcolm ignored him. "In the second place," he said, "wasn't no rabble rousing. It was organizing and protesting, trying to put structures into place to help combat the inequities of a racist, capitalist system that oppresses the black man from the cradle to the grave."

"Really?" Melvin's eyebrow sprang up. "'Cause I would of swore you told me you was arrested with a spray can in your hand right after you painted 'Fuck The System' on the side of the administration building."

"They dropped those charges," said Malcolm.

Melvin went on as if Malcolm had not spoken. "And I would of also swore you told me you was pullin' a 'D' average and your professors told you it was a damn shame, you done got a chance any other Negro give his left nut for—scholarship, full ride—and here you are, pissin' on it, even though everybody know you could do better if you really want to."

Malcolm snorted. "Just drive, nigger."

Melvin regarded him, something that was not quite a smile playing at the edge of his lips. "I'm just sayin' what you told me in them letters you sent home."

"Just drive," said Malcolm again.

With a shrug, Melvin returned his attention to the road. Malcolm allowed himself a moment to be lost in the sights passing by his window, dark-skinned soul brother in a white straw stingy brim walking with that slide foot bounce to a rhythm only he could hear, rhythm of life, Malcolm supposed. And here came a soul sister, color of caramel, going in the opposite direction, head high, topped by a proud Afro billowing slightly in the breeze, fine, big-legged sister, her thoughts held secret behind mirrored shades.

Damn, it was good to be home.

Yes, he had turned his life upside down, yes there were decisions to make, yes his father was apt to make his life miserable when he heard what had happened. But still...

"Man, I done missed this," he heard himself say.

Melvin snorted. "Shit. You missed *Memphis*? Now I know somethin' wrong with you. I had the chance to get my ass out of here, I be gone so fast my shadow have to run to catch up. Believe that."

"Yeah, man, I know. I might have felt the same way, once upon a time. But I done spent a year up there at that college with them white folks. Don't nobody say nothin' to you up there. Don't nobody smile or laugh or bullshit with you. Food don't got no taste. No, man," he said, waving languidly at the sister, who actually favored him with a smile, "Dorothy was right: ain't no place like home."

Melvin laughed. "Yeah, well, I been off in Oz, maybe I feel the same way. But you need to know, home ain't like you remember. Lot of things done changed, just since you been away."

"You mean 'cause of that strike?"

"Of course. What else is there?"

"I don't get it, man. How a bunch of garbage men going on strike gon' change a city? Make it smell maybe, but..."

Melvin looked at him sharply and Malcolm had a sense—it flashed through him like lightning, gone before it was there—that he had some-how...transgressed. No, *blasphemed*. "Your old man a garbage man," Melvin told him. "You should ask him."

"I'm askin' you," said Malcolm, and was surprised at his own defensive-ness. "Besides, you know, talkin' to him like talkin' to a brick wall half the time."

"Ask him anyway," said Melvin. "Hard for me to explain, but it's just different now. Feel like black people finally 'bout to rise up. Honkies feel it too. You can tell. They laughin', but it's the kind of laughin' like you do when you tryin' to prove you ain't scared, even though you are. Hell, seem like everybody scared."

"All that from a garbage strike," said Malcolm and he did not bother to mask his skepticism.

"Ask your old man," said Melvin. "Ask him, he tell you."

As he spoke, he brought the car to a stop in front of Malcolm's house. It wasn't much, a box of ramshackle on a street of desolation, one more rendition of the ain't-got-shit blues in a neighborhood where that song was constantly on everyone's lips everywhere, all the time. It was a neighborhood of windows boarded, porches sagging, grass gone brown and scrawny, leafless trees. Malcolm's screen door hung open on weary hinges—exactly as it had the last time he saw it.

Home.

It didn't change. Nothing ever did.

Malcolm sat staring at it so long that Melvin finally said, "You gon' sit there all day, or you gon' get out?"

Malcolm shook his head and climbed out of the car, retrieving his bag from the back seat. He was leaning toward the car to wave thank you for the ride when a woman's voice said, "Junie, is that you?"

A grin overspread Malcolm's face automatically as he turned toward the old lady who had called him from the porch of the house next door. Nanny Parker, a spindly little woman with light skin and a head full of thick, gray hair falling haphazardly about her shoulders, had been something of a surrogate mother to him after his own mother died of breast cancer seven years before. "Mornin', Miss Parker," he said.

"Ain't hardly recognized you, all that mess you got on your face."

Behind him, Malcolm heard Melvin cracking up. He ignored it. "Yes, ma'am," he said.

"You need to get a haircut."

"Yes, ma'am."

"What you doin' here anyway? Thought you was away at that white college?"

"Yes, ma'am," said Malcolm. "But I heard my father was hurt, so I thought I'd come back to see about him."

Even though he didn't look back at his friend, Malcolm somehow knew Melvin's eyes were rolling. And he was surprised and even a little embarrassed at how easily the lie now came to him. Not that it fooled the old woman who gazed down on him, arms folded. She stared at him with her skeptical eyes and said, "Oh really, now?"

It was all she said, but it was enough. She had heard the arguments and the slamming doors from inside his house. She knew better. But Miss Parker didn't push it and for that, Malcolm was grateful. "Well, it was nice talking to you," he said, making a move toward the door.

"He ain't there," said Miss Parker.

"Malcolm paused. "He's not? But I heard he twisted his knee."

She nodded. "He did. Twisted it totin' one of them garbage tubs out some white lady's back yard. Tripped over a tree root and fell. Doctor told him stay off it awhile. But you know your daddy. Stubborn. He gone back to the truck two days later. Say he can't afford to miss the work."

"That sounds like him," said Malcolm, and it did.

"Now, with the strike, seem like he gone everyday, down there at the marches on Main Street. That's where he at right now. Some big meetin' at City Hall with all the big mules from the city council. Hope to God they get that mess settled soon and them mens get back to work. My trash pilin' up somethin' awful back there and it's gon' start attractin' rats. I'm scared of rats."

She paused, seeming to consider her own words. Then she said, "Don't tell him I said that. Them mens, they fightin' for something important. Lord know they got enough to worry about without me puttin' more pressure on 'em."

Malcolm was barely listening. His father? In a meeting at City Hall? With all those white men? The thought of it spilled some nameless sense of unease inside him, a premonition he couldn't even understand, much less explain. He knew, rationally, that he should just go inside the house and wait, but…

Malcolm leaned down to the car window. "You mind droppin' me off down there?"

Melvin shrugged. Malcolm left his bag inside the front door of the house, bid Nanny Parker goodbye, and climbed back in to Melvin's car.

That same nameless disquiet chewed at him and he barely noticed the streets slipping past. The idea of his father—too stubborn and too poor to take a few days off even at the cost of his own health—out there hobbling through backyards as best he could, while Malcolm was off at school filling his days with learned, windy dialectics about oppression, socialism, and structural racism, kindled a burn in the bottom of his stomach.

It was filthy work his dad did. They called them tub toters because they walked into people's back yards to carry out metal tubs filled with garbage, with people's chicken fat and Kotex, their dead cats and coffee grounds, their watermelon rinds and pork bones. Sometimes the tubs filled with rainwater. Sometimes, they rusted through on the bottom so that you'd hoist the thing to your shoulder and a rancid sluice of cigarette butts, egg shells, fish grease, and Lord knows what all else would fall down on you.

How many times had Malcolm seen his father undress in the back yard, even in bitter cold, washing up with a garden hose in a little stall they had rigged out there next to a fire kindled in a metal drum for warmth, because he was simply too filthy to come into the house? How many times had Malcolm watched secretly from the kitchen window as his father scrubbed grime from his skin and picked maggots from his hair?

All for $1.27 an hour.

It was barely enough to keep up with the rent and electricity. They had no car. They had no phone. On his father's salary, they couldn't even afford to eat. They had done their shopping when his mother picked up her food stamps on the first of every month. His parents always argued when she did. His father was invariably surly and ill-tempered around the first day of the month.

Indeed, after Hattie Wilson died, for four months her husband had resisted going down to the welfare office to put his name on the roll for food stamps, until the day he conceded that he had no choice. There had been something naked in his face that day, something too terrible to look at, and Malcolm had avoided him, grateful though he was to have food in the house again so that he would no longer need to "happen by" Nanny Parker's place around dinner time if he wanted to eat. Still, what kind of man lives like that? He had too much damned pride to apply for food stamps, but too little to leave a job that made food stamps necessary.

Stubborn, stupid, hard-headed old man.

Even as a boy, Malcolm had thought the tub toters lived a miserable, humiliating excuse for a life, a life that sucked a man's pride right out of him. He did not understand how his father and all those hundreds of other men—almost all of them black—put up with it. There was no way he ever could.

"How did this thing start?" he heard himself ask.

"The strike?" Melvin was making a left turn.

"Yeah."

Melvin snorted. "Man, you *have* been out of touch. Couple of them tub toters climbed into the back of one of them trucks to get out the rain, guess it been three weeks ago by now. The hydraulic thing back there that mash up the trash, it started up on its own. Ain't nobody pushed the button or nothin'. The men say they been complainin' about them raggedy old trucks for years, but the city ain't never done nothin', ain't never cared. So them men, they got crushed to death in the back of their own truck."

It took Malcolm a moment. "Like garbage," he finally said. His voice was soft.

Melvin glanced at him. "Like garbage," he said. "They say one of them almost got out. But the truck snagged his raincoat and pulled him back and that was the end of him. And you know what the city done? It give they families about $800 apiece. That's monthly salary plus $500." Melvin looked straight ahead, then added, "Cost more'n that to bury them."

"So that's why they went out on strike, then? Good for them," Malcolm replied. "'Bout time they quit bowin' and scrapin' to them honkies and start demandin' instead."

They fell into a silence. After a moment, the old Buick pulled up to the corner of Adams and Main—City Hall. A roughly dressed group of black men was milling about on the plaza in front of the building. Everybody seemed to be shouting, arms waving excitedly. Police were everywhere, some with linked arms, forming a human barrier against the black men. One cop was engaged in heated discussion with some black man in suit and tie.

"This don't look good," said Melvin.

"No," said Malcolm, distracted. "It don't."

A moment. Then Melvin said, "I got to get to work. You be all right out here?"

Malcolm lifted a fist across his chest and shook it. "Yeah, brother. Solid."

Melvin grinned. "You and that black power jive," he said. Then a thought struck him. "Hey, you gon' be lookin' for work, since you back? 'Cause I'm in good with the hirin' man at the hotel. I could probably get you on."

"Yeah," said Malcolm, his eyes on the confusion in front of City Hall. "That'd be fine."

"Cool," said Melvin. "I come by and get you on the way to work. We go talk to him tomorrow."

Malcolm nodded. He barely heard. As Melvin pulled off behind him, he started forward across the plaza. More men came boiling out of the building. Snatches of angry words came to him on the breeze.

You seen that cartoon in the paper, ain't you? That let you know what they think of you, don't it?

I ain't no goddamn boy. I was in Korea, goddamn it. I'm a man. Tired of these crackers treatin' me like I ain't.

Well, you seen how they feel in the way they treat you. Question is, what we gon' do about it?

Bring the trash to City Hall. Dump it right here in front. That show 'em! That show 'em for sure!

"What the hell are you supposed to be?"

A policeman had materialized in Malcolm's path, a sweating white man with furious, anxious eyes, his nightstick held out like a crossbar in front of him. Malcolm hadn't seen the man coming, had been too focused on the angry black men coming out of City Hall. Some of them started singing "We Shall Not Be Moved," a chorus of men's voices, reedy and untutored and ugly and somehow, all the more poignant for that.

The cop jabbed Malcolm's solar plexus lightly with his nightstick. "I asked you a question."

"I'm not with them," said Malcolm.

"I can see that," said the cop, his disdainful glance traveling Malcolm's length. Malcolm knew it set him apart, walking about in his dashiki and shades and towering Afro. That was the entire point. But right now, all that was keeping him from getting where he needed to be.

He tried to make himself unthreatening. "My father," he said, seeking a tone that was polite and deferential, "he's over there somewhere with the garbage men and I need to—"

But the cop was done listening. He shoved Malcolm with the night-stick. "Go on, boy, get out of here. I don't have time to fool with you."

Malcolm rocked back. His hands fisted and came up automatically. It was, he knew, a stupid thing to do. But luckily, the cop had already turned away, going to confer with some sergeant who had rolled up in a squad car, bubbletop lights flashing. Malcolm had that sense you sometimes get when the wind rises and you know the storm is soon to break. He had to find his father and get him out of here.

Slipping past the big cop, he hurried onto the plaza. He searched from face to face, seeking one that looked like his. He had been around these men the better part of his life. Most of them were older, in their thirties, forties, even fifties, with the sagging skin and beaten eyes that come from a lifetime of scraping the bottom and smiling like you're happy to be there. Except that they were not smiling now. Their mouths bent around the lyrics of the old song, voices rising—"Just like a tree, that's planted by the waaaaater..."—and bent, too, around angry shouts and defiant cries. And their eyes, something in their eyes, some light, some challenge, some sudden interest in their own fate where before there had been only a dull, almost bovine acceptance.

The crowd was growing, still more men pushing out of the building behind them, but it was held in place, locked fast by police, a phalanx of them. A black man, joined by a rumpled, limping white man in a suit, was in urgent consultation with two of the police officers.

"You've got to let these men march," Malcolm heard someone pleading with the cops. "These are not militants. These are working men who are tired of being mistreated."

The police officer said something Malcolm didn't hear and then another voice said, "There's a lot of anger here. If they don't get some kind of outlet for it, I'm scared for what might happen."

Malcolm recognized a face. Not his father, but a man who knew his father.

"Sonny!" he called. "Hey, Sonny!"

The man, who had been singing lustily, turned at the sound of his name. There was a moment of confusion—Malcolm was rapidly getting used to this—as the man registered the familiar, yet unfamiliar face in front of him, and then he smiled. "Junie?" he said. "Is that you?"

"Yeah. I'm lookin' for my father. Do you know where he is?"

Sonny was one of the younger men—about 30, by Malcolm's estimate—but he and Malcolm's father had become good friends ever since Sonny joined their crew a few years before. They were an odd pair, given that his father was a brick wall of a man given to long, heavy silences and Sonny, as his father had once said, could talk paint right off the wall.

Sonny's favorite topic was himself and his future. He would discourse at length on how this job and this city were just a way station for him, how he had bigger dreams than a Memphis garbage tub could contain, how he was going to go to college, start a business, live in the lap of luxury. Secretly, it always made Malcolm pity him. Sonny thought he could play by the white man's rules and flourish in the white man's system. But even if the white man's idea of success were something to be envied—and it wasn't—how realistic was it for Sonny to think he had a shot at it? You did not start a business and curl in the lap of luxury when you couldn't read beyond the sixth grade—especially if you were a Negro. No, Sonny was going to be a

Memphis tub toter for the rest of his life. Some painful day, he would accept that. Malcom didn't want to be around when that happened.

Even so, Malcolm had always liked Sonny—mainly, he supposed, because Sonny liked him. Actually—and Malcolm always found this strange, because Sonny was ten years older—Sonny looked up to him. He would seek out Malcolm's opinion on current events or quiz him about history, not so much for the answers but just to hear Malcolm hold forth in learned self-confidence and polysyllabic erudition. His father would always scowl at them and often left the room when this happened—he called it "putting on airs" or "getting out your place."

But Sonny saw it differently. He saw Malcolm's precociousness, his raw, unshaped intelligence, as a reflection of promise—Malcolm's promise, even Sonny's promise, maybe even promise for the entire race. "Stop talking that nigger jive and come correct," he would scorn whenever he heard Malcolm slip into slang or throw out a casual curse so that he could fit in, so that he would sound more like everybody else.

"You don't need to do that," Sonny had told him once. "You don't need to fit in with them. Let them try to fit in with you. You the one goin' places, youngblood. Rest'a these fools ain't goin' no further than the corner store."

In his heart, Malcolm knew this to be true. Even Melvin, his best friend since the first day of kindergarten, would probably not go much further than he already had—a job as a busboy at the Holiday Inn that stood sentinel on a bluff above the river. But knowing it was true and accepting it were different things. In effect, Sonny was asking him to be alone—to be, if not exactly friendless, then set aside. A year into his college career, a year spent in the North where the food didn't taste right and the people walked right by you on the street without so much as a nod, and Malcolm still didn't know if he could live with that.

"Mozell?" Sonny scratched his head now in response to Malcolm's question. "Ain't seen him. But he like to be out here someplace. Just about all the mens here, I expect, 'cept for them few scabs ain't had the guts to come out here with us."

He gave Malcolm a look. "What happened to you?"

The question deflated Malcolm's estimation of Sonny a little bit. He'd figured that if anybody would understand the political implications of an Afro and a dashiki, it would be a forward-thinking brother like Sonny Dupree, still young enough that all the spark had not yet been beaten out of him by honky oppression. Malcolm ignored the question. It seemed the kindest thing he could do.

"I'm lookin' for him," said Malcolm. "His knee twisted up, he don't need to be out here."

"Yeah, well you know your father. Once he get his mind set on somethin', you can't change it. "

"What's going on here?" asked Malcolm.

"City council just stabbed us in the back, that's what's goin' on." Just speaking the words seemed to make Sonny's eyes flare. "Made like they was ready to recognize the union and maybe settle this thing, then they voted to support the mayor instead. Henry Loeb, that racist son of a bitch, he the reason we ain't got nothin' settled yet. Think he can treat us any old kind of way. He don't understand, this 1968 now. Ain't no more 1948. Them days gone. Ain't nobody gon' put up with they shit no more. We men and by God, they gon' treat us like men."

"Damn straight," said a man next to Sonny. "Time they learned."

"They say we can march!" Another voice floating high above the charged energy of the crowd. "They say we can march to the Mason Temple!"

If they really were men, Malcolm thought, they wouldn't be out here waiting for permission to walk down the street. The realization filled him with a dull pity.

"Four abreast!" someone else cried. "They say we got to walk four abreast!"

"Hell with that!" This was still another voice. "Take over the street!"

"No. We gon' do this right. Ain't no takin' over nothin'. Y'all line up. Four abreast."

Then the crowd was moving, spilling around Malcolm like water, and bearing Sonny away. "You follow after us!" he told Malcolm. "See your daddy directly. He here somewhere." And then he was swallowed in the crowd.

Malcolm watched, fascinated, as the men organized themselves obediently into ranks of four under the stone gazes of city cops, and then proceeded down Main Street. The sidewalks were narrow and the procession spilled into the street. What, Malcolm wondered, was the point of protesting under rules laid down by the very people you were protesting against? Shaking his head, he crossed to the far side of Main and followed the men. There were hundreds of them, organized as they had been told, into ranks of four, walking past the department stores and TV repair shops, some singing songs of gospel and defiance. Their idea of fighting white oppression was to walk together and sing hymns to the same blue-eyed Jesus who had turned a blind eye to their sufferings for years going on to generations. This was what they had learned from watching "De Lawd"—the great almighty Reverend Doctor Martin Luther King—all these years.

Still watching them from across the street, Malcolm sighed. He was pleased the sense of impending storm had eased, but the spectacle frustrated him. How long would black people content themselves with turning pious eyes to heaven for relief while begging white men to please, finally, treat them like human beings? How long would the evening news be filled with footage of them receiving their answers in the form of swinging nightsticks, exploding bombs, and snarling dogs, or just in the insufferable, insincere smiles of white potentates telling smug lies to TV cameras?

Why couldn't these old Negroes, these "yassuh boss" wage slaves, see that power was the only thing whitey understood or respected, and that only when you spoke to him in his native language—violence—would he finally hear what you were saying? The marches and sit-ins, the prayers and singing, gave the impression of doing something without ever actually doing a damn thing. It was, he supposed, harmless enough to be out there marching and singing songs, but in a sense, that was the whole problem. He'd had enough of harmless gestures. The white man would only move when faced with some threat of harm by an opponent he knew had the will and the ability to back it up. That was why—

Malcolm froze.

A phalanx of squad cars had appeared on the street, riding bumper to bumper in a tight formation. There were five cops to a car, the cars moving slowly up the line of marchers, lights flashing silently. Malcolm saw billy clubs and rifles. He felt his stomach clench like a fist. He watched from the far side of the street, horrified and fascinated, as the cars closed on the marchers.

They were aiming for the men. And then he realized, no. The intent wasn't to hit the men. It was something less deadly, but far more humiliating. The cars were there to herd them, as dogs herd sheep. Sure enough, the formation moved in, pressing close to the marchers, forcing the men to bunch up, step back. It was hard to tell from Malcolm's vantage point, but the cars actually appeared to make glancing contact with some of the men.

"Get that car back and away from us!" This was yelled by a black man with a clerical collar, some kind of preacher who was marching with the men. The police cars continued pressing close. The men retreated, still in ranks.

"Just keep marching," the man with the clerical collar yelled. "They're trying to provoke us!"

Malcolm stepped off the sidewalk, wanting a better vantage point, feeling dazed. The cars were clearly making contact with the garbage men, and with those who were walking with them. Malcolm saw white men. He saw a few women. The marchers were trying to maintain their discipline, trying to hold their ranks. And then:

"Oh! He runned over my foot."

It was a woman's voice. Men had circled around her. A police car had stopped. On her foot.

"Get that car off the lady's foot!" someone yelled.

The car did not move.

"Hell with this!" someone else cried.

The ranks broke. A group of men went to the police car and took hold. They began rocking it, trying to get the woman free. Malcolm took another step, intending to join them. Then he stopped again. The doors on the black-and-white Plymouths had flown open and begun to disgorge police. Nightsticks slapped against palms. A pump-action shotgun was lifted high above the melee. Dark spray bottles appeared in policemen's hands.

"Mace!" the cops cried. "Mace! Mace! Mace!" As if the word itself contained some fearsome power.

And then the nightsticks came crashing down, swinging indiscriminately, the air suddenly filled with the smack of wood on flesh.

And the spray bottles opened up.

The police doused the men as if they were roaches scurrying about a kitchen sink. And, like roaches, the men were stopped in their tracks by the chemical. Some staggered. Some fell. Some wandered blindly, groping for walls, their eyes red, tearing, and sightless.

Malcolm saw the sanitation workers lower their hats and lift their coats around their faces to avoid the chemical. He saw police officers reach under those coats and spray men full in the face.

And still the nightsticks came down.

They bashed the sanitation men, but they did not stop there.

They bashed an old black man who was just standing there.

They bashed a black woman who came out of Kress's department store.

Skin splitting, blood flying. The police officers were out of control. "Mace! Mace! Mace!" they cried.

Pop.

In that instant, Malcolm's eyes finally found Mozell Wilson. He was on all fours on the sidewalk. His face looked as if it had been painted in blood. Some white cop towered over him, rearing back for another blow.

Malcolm ran, crossing the narrow street in a few long strides. "Leave him alone!" he heard himself cry. The cop turned, surprised, and that moment of hesitation gave Malcolm time enough to launch himself. He lowered his shoulder and plowed into the white cop, sending him sprawling. And even as it happened, some part of Malcolm was standing aside from all of it, watching dispassionately and telling him, *You just hit a white Memphis cop. Your life is over now. You know that, don't you?*

He blocked the thought, helped his father to his feet. "Junie?" the old man asked, "is that you?"

No time for that. "Come on, Pop, let's get out of here!" Holding his father's arm, he turned. And got a blast of spray right in the face.

Malcolm screamed. His eyes leaked unadulterated fire that trailed, sizzling, down his face. Every nerve ending was reporting the same thing. Pain. Pure, raw agony. Malcolm fell to his knees, gasping for breath that would not come.

From somewhere far away, he heard the white cop's voice. "It hurts? Go jump in the river, nigger!"

And he would have been happy to do that, would have praised blue-eyed Jesus himself for a blessed baptism of muddy Mississippi water, if he had any idea where the Mississippi was. Or legs capable of carrying him there. He groped about on the sidewalk, blind, miserable, hacking from the poison air.

Then hands seized him under his armpits and he felt himself hauled upright, pulled along the sidewalk, his feet scraping behind him like an afterthought.

"Where are we going?" The words squeezed out of him in a raspy croak.

"We got to get out of here!" Sonny's voice, on his left.

But where was...

"Pop," he managed. "Where is...?"

"Shush up, boy." His father's voice, close by on the right, hard as concrete. Malcolm nearly sagged in relief.

Stumbling, lumbering and awkward, Malcolm barely able to find his feet, they ran.

six

The two men stood talking in front of the door only a few feet away and the moment seemed oddly intimate. Malcolm thought of watching the wife in some 1950s movie as she saw her husband off to war.

"So, you'll be right back?"

"Yes, Clarence. Like I already told you a hundred times. I'll take the DVD to this guy's boss and come right back. I can handle a fucking drop-off, for Chrissake. Which one of us the captain here, Sergeant?"

"You are, Captain. It's just...well, you know."

McLarty grunted. "Yeah, I know. But it won't be that way this time, promise. I'll be quick. Boost a car, zip"—he made a farting sound, sliced the air with the flat of his palm—"drive it over to the jewspaper, give the disc to whoever this shitbird reports to, then right back here so we can get everything ready for tonight."

"I just don't like the way you are when you use. You're mean when you use."

"I won't use. Promise." And McLarty even crossed his heart.

After a moment, Pym nodded. It was, thought Malcolm, as if he had to force himself to be convinced. "All right," he said. "I don't mean to be a pussy about it. It's just...you know, we've spent too much time planning this to fuck it up now."

McLarty reached up and patted his friend's cheek twice. "Hey, don't worry about it," he said. "This is going to work just fine. Trust me."

"Yeah, I trust you, Captain. You know that."

McLarty indicated Malcolm with a nod of his head. "You want me to leave you the gun?"

Pym made a derisive sound. "Why would I need a gun to keep shitbird in line? He's not going anywhere. You're the one going into enemy territory."

McLarty's nod was crisp. "You're probably right," he said. "I'll hold onto the firearm. See you shortly, Sergeant." He lifted the door, which rose with a metallic rattle upon a rectangle of pallid sunlight framing a forest of weeds. Pym called to him then.

"Captain?" he said.

"Yeah?"

"Be careful out there."

"Sure thing," said McLarty. "You know me. Careful's my middle name." He grinned, passed through the door, and then was gone.

Pym brought the door down behind him and then simply stood there, as if lost in the maze of his own contemplations. After a moment, he spoke without turning around. "Ain't nothin' faggy about it, you know."

"What?" Malcolm was confused.

"I seen the way you was looking at us. I know what you was thinking. But we're not fags. We're not like that."

"That's not what I was thinking," said Malcolm, who had, in fact, concluded the two men were gay.

Pym turned toward him and chuckled. "Sometimes, I forget what natural-born liars niggers are," he said.

"There's nothing wrong with it if you are gay," said Malcolm and immediately wondered why he had said it. The words felt cliché and automatic.

Pym's chuckle turned into an incredulous laugh that bobbed his Dennis the Menace cowlick up and down. "There sure as hell is! Look at the plumbing, for Chrissake. You think your body is designed to take a dick up the shit chute? Get real. 'For man shall not lie down with man as he lies down with women.' Don't you read your Bible?"

Malcolm swallowed. "Well," he said. "I did read the part that says 'Thou shalt not kill.'"

Pym's face went still. Then he grinned a sour little grin. "Yeah, I guess I also forgot what a tricky nigger you are. Like to use words to confuse things, don't you? Try to get people all mixed up."

Malcolm didn't speak. He didn't know what to say, didn't know how to play it. His body was throbbing and the metal of the cuffs was cutting against his wrists.

Pym pursed his lips, unwilling to let the thing rest. "Me and Dwayne, we known each a long time, that's all. We're simpatico, you know? We look out for each other and that's all there is to it. Anything else is just something you cooked up in your filthy nigger mind."

"So, what is it you're planning to do? With me, I mean. What's this all about?"

The grin again. "Wouldn't you like to know."

He moved toward the table where the laptop was. Malcolm yelled after him. "I've got money," he said. "I can pay you. I mean, I'd have to go to the bank, but I can get you some money. You don't have to go through with whatever it is you're planning." For some reason—he wasn't sure why—he wanted to keep Pym talking. Somehow, that seemed the wisest course.

It worked. The big man lumbered back. "Money?" he said. "You think this is about money? Shit, maybe I gave you too much credit for smarts. This ain't about money, you dumbass. Didn't you listen to the manifesto? This is about taking our country back from the apes and the Jews and the ragheads... *and* the fags. We're sending a wakeup call to white, Christian America. That's what we're doin', shitbird."

He moved away again. "It's not going to work!" cried Malcolm.

Dutifully, Pym came back. "So you say," he said. "You don't even know the plan."

"Don't have to. It doesn't matter. You and the other idiot can waste all the time you want, pretending to be soldiers, pretending you're on some big mission. But at the end of the day, you're not that. You're not anything. And you know it."

"You don't know what I know."

"Hell I don't," said Malcolm. "You know you're a loser. You'd have to be even stupider than you look not to know that. But go on, don't let me stop you. Keep strutting around here like you're somebody."

"I am somebody," insisted Pym.

Malcolm didn't even deign to look at him. "Yeah, you're somebody, all right. You're a fat fucking nobody, that's who you are."

"You just shut up! You hear me? You just shut up!" Storm clouds had come into Pym's eyes.

Malcolm chuckled. "Whatever you say, you fucking fat-ass nobody."

The change was sudden. Pym snarled like something feral. He wasn't fast, so Malcolm saw the blow coming, not that it did him any good. The meaty fist crashed against his jaw on the backswing and the force of the blow was so powerful he reeled back and would have fallen, except that the hand-cuffs bolted into the floor bit into his ankles and held the chair suspended on its two hind legs, his arms stretched to either side by their manacles.

The pain seemed to come from everywhere. From his jaw, blazing like a four-alarm fire. From his ankles and wrists, the metal shackles sawing into the flesh. From his throbbing and maybe-broken ribs. From the tendons in his arms, creaking and stretching and supporting his weight as he struggled against gravity to bring the front legs of the chair back down.

He had wanted to rattle the big man. He had wanted to see what would happen. Well, he consoled himself bitterly, now he knew.

Pym watched him for a moment, his anger evidently spent. Then he shook his head. He put his right foot on the front crossbar of the chair and slammed it down. The jolt only freshened Malcolm's agony. He sat there with his head hanging and eyes closed, grateful at least that flaccid, 60-year-old muscles were no longer supporting his weight. Beyond the rasp of his own breathing, he heard Pym's steps as the big man walked away.

A few seconds later, he returned. "Here," he said. Malcolm opened his eyes. The disposable plastic cup looked absurdly dainty in Pym's massive fist. Malcolm looked up at his captor.

"Go on, drink," said Pym. "It's just water. Really. I didn't piss in it or nothin'." Malcolm nodded and opened his mouth and Pym held the cup for him. The water was blessedly cool. It tasted like salvation.

Pym waited until he was finished, then pulled the cup away. He produced a paper towel and dabbed roughly at Malcolm's mouth. "I get what you're doing," he told Malcolm. "Try to get inside my head, see if there's a weak spot, find something you can exploit. I'm not stupid. I get that. And I guess I don't even blame you for trying. I'd do the same thing myself, I was in your shoes." He pulled the paper towel away. It was streaked with blood. "But don't make fun of me, you hear? That's the only thing. Don't you call me 'fat ass' or 'hippo' or any shit like that. I won't let you do that. I've had enough of that. You understand?"

Malcolm nodded. "Yeah."

"Good. Then we won't have no more problems." Pym tossed the cup down.

"McLarty never made fun of you," said Malcolm, speaking the realization even as it came to him. "That's why you're friends."

"That's right. He respects me. That's why we're friends."

"But he's so much older than you."

Pym gave a sad shake of his head. "No," he said. "He just looks older. He's had challenges. Now shut up and behave yourself and I'll let you watch the news with me."

Without waiting for an answer, Pym went and dragged the card table with the laptop on it over to where Malcolm sat. He plopped down on a metal folding chair, his great bulk overflowing the sides, and tapped for a few moments at the computer keys. Then he positioned the laptop to the side so that he and Malcolm both could see—as if Malcolm were his guest and not his prisoner. They were watching the live feed of a conservative cable news network. A chipper, Barbie-doll blonde, her lips as glossy and red as a freshly painted fire engine, was holding forth.

"Well, after a hard fought campaign, it's all over but the voting for Senator John McCain of Arizona and Senator Barack Hussein Obama Jr. of Illinois. Both men were out early to cast their ballots this morning. Here we see Sen. and Mrs. McCain voting in Phoenix."

The image on screen switched to the senator and his wife making their way slowly into the polling place as Secret Service agents cleared a path and a woman's voice urged reporters to stand back. The blonde anchorwoman's voice spoke over the image. "McCain, who is trailing in the polls by five or six percentage points in most of the battleground states, is hoping for a last-minute surge of support to help him capture the presidency. And here we have Sen. and Mrs. Obama and their daughters voting at a polling place near their home in Chicago." The image onscreen was now of Barack Obama feeding his ballot into a vote tallying machine. "I hope this works," he joked. "It'll be really embarrassing if it doesn't."

Pym made a sound. "Hail to the fucking chief," he said.

Malcolm looked at him. "You actually think he's going to win?"

"I do," said Pym.

"Why?"

"Because this country is just fuckin' fucked up enough to do it, that's why. There's just enough liberal retards in this country who think it'd be a swell idea to have a socialist nigger as their president."

Malcolm surprised himself by laughing. "You don't have to worry about it," he said. "He's not going to win."

Pym glanced around, mildly interested. "What makes you say that?"

"Because there are too many people like you in this country, that's why."

Pym snorted. "Country needs more people like me."

"He won't win," repeated Malcolm.

"Yeah, that's what you said in the paper this morning, wasn't it?"

"You read the paper?"

"You makin' cracks about me again? I can read."

"No," said Malcolm. "I just meant, people your age, they don't read newspapers."

"Well, technically, I didn't read it in the paper. Saw it online on the website. Had to do somethin' while we waited on you. You almost messed up the plan, you know? We were going to take you out of your house. Then we see you pulling off at four in the morning." He chortled. "Dwayne like to shit a brick when that happened."

"How did you know where I live?"

Pym made a face as if the answer were too obvious for speaking and Malcolm an idiot for asking. "Internet," he said.

"Internet," said Malcolm. "Of course." God, he hated computers.

"So get back to ol' Barry Soetoro," said Pym. "You said in the paper—or on the website, since you want to be technical—that you don't think he can win because of the 'Bradley Effect.' What's that?"

Malcolm sighed. "Tom Bradley," he said. "Black man, mayor of Los Angeles. Ran for California governor in '82. All the polls showed him way out in front. Everybody thought he was going to win. Turns out he loses the election. When it came right down to it, all the good white folks who said they were going to vote for him couldn't bring themselves to pull the lever for a nigger."

Pym's gaze turned thoughtful. "You guys always say that. I never understood it."

"Say what?"

"Nigger. You black guys say that, then you get mad when we say it."

"I wasn't saying it," said Malcolm. "I was saying that's how white voters in California saw it when it came time to cast their ballots. Racist motherfuckers like you. Bradley couldn't win, Obama won't win. Doesn't matter what the polls say."

"Well, from your lips to God's ear," said Pym.

"I didn't say it was a good thing." Malcolm couldn't believe he was letting this fool anger him.

"I expect you wouldn't think it's a good thing. 'Course you're not a white man."

"Thank heaven for small favors," muttered Malcolm.

Pym's chuckle was indulgent. "You know, you're a funny guy. "He was silent a moment, watching the cable news show. When the entertainment report came on, he turned to Malcolm. "Hey," he said in a bright voice, "you want to watch this new Jordan video I got? I saw from your hat you're a Bulls fan."

There it was again, that bizarre courtesy. His kidnapper, his captor, the man who had just rung his skull like a tower-clock bell, was inviting him to watch videos like they were just two buddies hanging out in the den on a lazy Saturday afternoon. Surely, thought Malcolm, he would wake up any moment now, twisted in sweaty sheets, and find that none of it had happened. None of it was real.

Pym took his silence for assent. "You'll like this," he said, producing a DVD from a backpack on the floor. He opened the disc drive on the laptop and popped it in. Moments later, the computer screen showed a familiar figure clad in red, tongue wagging from his mouth as he drove around hapless defenders like a Porsche around traffic cones to slam the ball through the hoop with vicious authority.

"Did you see that?" Pym turned toward Malcolm, beaming. "Fuck Kobe, fuck LeBron. That man there is the best there ever was, best there ever will be. Am I right?"

He did not wait for an answer, turning instead back to the computer, where Jordan was pulling up for a jump shot.

Malcolm lowered his head, closed his eyes. He wondered where that damn homeless man had gone.

Willie Washington had a mission: *find help*.

He could not remember the last time he'd had a mission, something he had to accomplish. He was surprised how good it felt.

For years, he had lived a life free of things to do. He lived off the clock. Hell, he lived off the *calendar*. How many times had he watched the sidewalks teem with the hurried, worried quicksteps of people with places to be and things to do and counted himself lucky he was not among them? His life, he had always told himself in such moments, was the very definition of freedom. He was a man with nowhere to be and all the time in the world to get there.

But now that had changed. He had to find help.

So he set out walking. It was a familiar route, one he shuffled several times a week. East across State, over to Michigan, north on Michigan toward where the high rises and fancy shops stood sentinel. It took him a little over an hour. Along the way, he approached every person who even glanced in his direction. It was just like panhandling, he thought, except he wasn't asking anyone for money. He was asking for help. And that, it turned out, was even harder to get.

"Beg pardon, could you..."

"Sir, I wonder if I could talk to you for a..."

"Lady, this is important. I need..."

But for over an hour they flowed around him, the inconvenient fact of him, like water, not stopping, nor even pausing long enough to let him get a full sentence out. Some automatically extended coins to him, most did not. Finally, Willie just stopped and stood there in the middle of the sidewalk, slumped beneath the full weight of his own inconsequence. He felt invisible. He wondered if he was still there.

What make you think somebody gon' stop for you, stupid motherfucker?

Ông ta cố gắng hết sức rồi! Đừng có sỉ nhục ổng nữa!

"Y'all stop arguing," said Willie, aloud.

This caused a lady to give him a sharp look—and step faster. Willie sighed.

Sure, people sometimes affected not to see you when you reached out a grimy hand from the shadow of a doorway, or when you walked between the cars at the red light holding up a cardboard sign begging for money. He was used to that. But there was something different about this experience of standing right in the middle of them, energetically trying to get their attention, desperately *needing* to get their attention, and having them walk right by before you could get the words out, the sheer rush of them all but spinning you like a weather vane in a high wind.

Yeah, so what you gon' do about it, you dumb ass?

"I'll show you what I'm gon' do," said Willie. And he reached out for the arm of the nearest person. She happened to be a young black woman who was rushing past him, her ear glued to an iPhone.

He spoke quickly. "Excuse me, lady, but this is an emergency. See, it's these two crazy white boys, and they got this brother tied up in—"

That was as far as he got. The next thing Willie knew, he was lying on the curb, looking up at the woman, who was holding some kind of kung fu pose, her weight shifted back on one leg, one palm out flat, thumb tucked in, the other curled into a fist, ready to hit him again if even blinked too hard. The iPhone was on the concrete and she was shrieking in terror.

"Help! He tried to mug me!"

Like he was the one who had knocked her on her ass. If anyone needed help, it was him.

But her cries had the desired effect. The flow of people slowed, congealing around him. So *now* they noticed him.

Oh, shit. You done it now, stupid motherfucker.

"Shut up," said Willie.

"You don't tell me shut up," said the woman.

"Wasn't talking to you," said Willie. "Was talking to—"

"What happened, lady?" This was a big Samoan-looking guy, stuffed into an expensive suit. Looked like he could bench press a Buick.

"This guy tried to mug me, that's what happened! Made me drop my phone, too," she added in an accusing voice as she finally broke the kung fu pose, snatched up the device from the concrete, and began examining it for scratches.

"I wasn't trying to mug nobody!" protested Willie. "I was asking for help. I wanted...I needed..."

And that was when the police showed up.

Willie, ông có chuyện lớn rồi đó!

Translation: "Willie, you are in big trouble now."

"Don't I know it," said Willie.

The squad car glided in to the curb, lights flashing silently. Willie finally felt safe enough to climb to his feet, brushing uselessly at pants so soiled even he could no longer recall their original color. He tried to smile as the two police officers—a young black guy and an older, thickset white one—approached. It wasn't easy. He was deathly afraid of cops.

Then he realized he needn't have bothered. They ignored him, too.

"What's going on here?" the young cop asked the woman.

She pointed. "He tried to mug me!"

"I didn't!" protested Willie. "I just—"

"I saw it," said the Samoan guy. "He grabbed her."

"I wasn't trying to—"

The woman cut him off. "I want him arrested. You hear me? You lock him up right now! It's getting so a woman can't even walk the streets in broad daylight."

The older cop had been watching them and listening. Now he spoke. "We saw it, too," he said. "We were sitting right there across the street. He didn't actually try to mug you, now did he?"

"That's what I've been trying to—"

"Shut up," the cop told Willie. He looked at the woman. "Looked like he tried to ask you something. Reached out for your arm and you put him down with some kind of karate move. Nice punch, by the way."

He seemed to notice the assembled crowd for the first time. "You people go on and get out of here," he said. "Move along now." He looked at the Samoan guy. "That goes for you, too, sir. Thanks for your help. We'll take it from here."

With palpable reluctance, the crowd began drifting apart. Now the older cop turned back to the woman, who drew herself up defensively. "He had no business touching me," she said.

The older cop—Jaworski, his nametag said—conceded the point with a nod. "Yeah, you're right. But you put him on his ass for it, so I'd say we're about even, wouldn't you?"

"Made me drop my phone," said the woman.

"I didn't—"

Jaworski barely glanced at Willie. "I told you to shut up, didn't I?"

You better listen to the man, dumb ass.

"Yeah, I know," said Willie.

The cop gave him a strange look. Then he turned back to the woman. "It still work?"

She examined it for a moment. "Yeah," she admitted. There was something sullen in the admission.

"That's one of those new iPhones, isn't it?"

"Yeah."

"You like it?"

Excitement banished sullenness. "I love it. It's like a little computer."

"And it still works, even though you dropped it?"

She examined it again. "Tougher than it looks, I guess."

"Can I see?"

She handed it over. Officer Jaworski examined the sleek black device, which, to Willie, looked less like a telephone than some prop from *Star Trek*.

At length, Jaworski nodded, then handed the phone back. "I got to get me one of those."

"You'll like it," she said.

"So," he said, hooking a thumb toward Willie without looking at him, "what do we want to do about this?"

She pursed her lips, then shrugged. "I guess there's no harm done," she said. "He just needs to keep his hands off people."

"I quite agree," said Jaworski. "I'll make sure to explain that to him."

"Thank you, officer," the woman said in the voice of the righteously vindicated.

"You're welcome," he said. "You have yourself a good day." He touched his hat.

"Thank you," she said. "Same to you." And she wheeled around, already pecking at her space ship telephone.

When she was out of earshot, Jaworski spoke to his partner. "And that, young Officer Smith, is how you defuse a bullshit situation."

The young officer grinned. "Thank you for the lesson, oh wise Obi-Wan."

"Can I talk now?" demanded Willie, feeling humiliated and forgotten.

Jaworski said, "Buddy, why don't you just count your blessings and—"

"I seen a kidnapping," said Willie, glad to be the one cutting someone else off for a change. "I...I ain't actually seen it happen, but I seen the man they kidnapped. It's this brother. These white boys, they got him tied to a chair in a warehouse. Seen it with my own eyes."

"Oh, really?"

"Yeah, really."

"What's your name?" demanded Smith, not bothering to hide his skepticism. Or, Willie realized, his contempt.

Willie tried to make himself taller than he was and spoke in what he hoped was a voice of grave dignity. "My name is William Washington," he said. "*Corporal* William Washington, US Army, retired."

Jaworski wasn't impressed. "Okay, 'Corporal,'" he said, somehow making the rank sound foolish or dirty. "And you say you saw what, again?"

Need to kick his ass.

Willie ignored this. "I told you: there's this building. Old toy company. It's abandoned, and um...the owner, he...um...doesn't care if I store my belongings in there, you see?"

"I bet," said Smith.

Willie ignored this, too. "And this morning, I go there to check on my things. And I look through this window and I seen what I told you I seen. This brother, chained up to a chair, and these two white guys, big fat guy, little skinny guy, holding him there."

Smith looked to Jaworski . Jaworski shrugged.

Smith turned back to Willie. "You saw this," said Smith.

"Yes."

"With your own eyes."

"Yes."

"You saw it today."

"Yes."

Again, Smith looked to Jaworski. "Probably something came out of a bottle," said Jaworski.

"Yeah," said Smith.

"But we probably ought to check it out."

Stupid motherfucker. I can't believe you got them to listen.

"Shut up," hissed Willie.

"Beg pardon?" said Jaworski.

Willie shook his head, a fast side-to-side motion. "I didn't say nothing," he said.

Jaworski gave him a dubious look. Then he turned to his young protégé. "A lot of the job is judgment, young Officer Smith," he said.

First thing you done right since 'Nam, you stupid motherfucker.

"Shut up," hissed Willie. "You're going to mess up everything."

"What did you say?" demanded Jaworski.

Cẩn thận, Willie. Hãy cẩn thận.

It meant, "Be careful, Willie."

Willie exploded. "Hãy cẩn thận? *Hãy cẩn thận?* How the fuck am I supposed to be careful, when this other motherfucker always telling me what a fuck-up I am? You think I don't get tired of that shit? Forty years of that shit, and you think I don't get tired? Hell with both of y'all. I just—"

He stopped. Jaworski and Smith were staring at him. There was a moment. Then Jaworski turned to Smith. "I believe that answers all our questions right there, don't you?"

Smith just shook his head. "Come on," said Jaworski, moving toward the car. "Let's not waste any more of the taxpayers' money."

Willie felt impaled by humiliation. "Wait," he said. "It ain't what you think."

Smith had his door open. "Go on, get out of here," he told Willie.

"You got to listen to me," said Willie. Smith slammed his door.

"You heard the man," said Jaworski, standing there with the driver's side door open.

"I'm telling the truth." Willie was pleading.

"I'm telling the truth, too," said Jaworski. "And the truth is, the only reason I don't run you in is because I don't feel like doing the paperwork. But that could change real quick if you don't get your ass to moving."

Willie stared. He tried to think of something, anything, he could say to make this angry cop understand: maybe he was crazy, but he wasn't crazy. He knew what he had seen. He knew he needed help.

But there was nothing he could say. And he could see Jaworski waiting, daring him. Willie's head went down. He turned around and began the slow trudge back toward the old toy factory. Behind him, he heard Jaworski's door slam with an emphatic thump and seconds later, the patrol car accelerated past him and was lost in the traffic on Michigan Avenue.

Willie stopped. He almost felt like crying.

At that moment, he felt something being pushed into his right hand. He looked down to see a little button-eyed white girl with dark hair staring up at him earnestly as she pressed a dollar bill into his hand. Beyond her stood her family—mother, father, two brothers, both older, though neither was older than ten. The parents were beaming, proud of their daughter's selfless charity.

Willie knew he should be smiling broadly to vindicate the parents' pride. But he didn't have it in him. "Thank you," he mumbled instead in an ashen voice that did not sound like his own. "Thank you kindly."

"You're welcome," said the little girl in her chirpy little girl voice. And then she skipped off to rejoin her family. The father cast a last quizzical glance at Willie as he shepherded his wife and children away. Willie barely saw.

Cô làm như vậy rất tử tế.

"Yeah," said Willie. "That *was* very nice."

Fuck nice. What you going to do now, you dumb motherfucker?

Willie shrugged. "I have no idea," he said.

seven

He sat in his chair as he had long ago been taught, in darkness, both feet flat on the floor, both palms lying flat on his lap. And he swept his mind clear of clutter, imagined all the apprehensions and fears taking wing, lifting off him, leaving his thoughts a perfect oval of nothingness. And he breathed in on a seven count, held it on a seven count, released it on a seven count. And he said to himself, and listened within himself, for the sound of peace.

Shalom.

Shalom.

Shalom.

It did not work. Before this, it had always worked. *Always* worked. For years, he had meditated. For as long as he could remember, going back to when he was a kid with a ponytail whose every third word was either peace or love, he had meditated. And it had always taken the edge off difficult days, always transported him into a quiet oneness that stilled his worries and settled his heart.

But not this time. This time, when he closed his eyes seeking serenity, he found only the guilty face of Malcolm Toussaint, freeze framed, looking up into a security camera on his way upstairs to destroy Bob's life. And oh, what a job he had done. Twelve hours ago, Bob had gone to sleep reasonably satisfied and fully employed, albeit as a middle manager at a not-very-good newspaper. Twelve hours later, all of it was gone, as surely as if someone had planted a bomb. He had lost everything, he was 59 and out of work, all over some stupid racial garbage.

Bob opened his eyes. Quiet oneness and serenity were a thousand miles away. And he realized with a start that he didn't even want these things anyway. Not really. No, what Bob really wanted was to strangle Malcolm Toussaint.

He switched on a lamp on the table beside him, flipped open his cell-phone, and for the fourth time in the last hour, punched in Malcolm's number. For the fourth time in the last hour, the call went straight to voicemail. "This is Toussaint," began Malcolm's voice. Bob snapped the phone shut.

Obviously, the coward was hiding from him. Fine. Let's see what he would say when Bob showed up at his door. Bob checked his watch. It was 10:17. He was having lunch with Janeka. No way he could make it to Malcolm's house and then back to Michigan Avenue in time. Fine, then. After lunch, he would go and see Mr. Malcolm Toussaint and they would settle accounts.

Malcolm was tired of white people's BS? Fine. Bob was tired of black people's BS. And he was especially tired of Malcolm Toussaint's BS.

Bob Carson was a racist.

Or at least, this was what he secretly feared. He had feared it long before Malcolm published the tirade that ended both their careers. Indeed, Bob had feared it for a long time. Somewhere over the years, he had simply lost patience with black people—beg pardon, *African Americans*—constantly whining about this injustice or that unfairness. He could see it when there were actual laws on the books that kept them from voting or sitting down at a lunch counter to order a hamburger. But those days were long gone. These days, when blacks talked about racism, it was usually about affirmative action—lowering standards so some black person could get a job ahead of some more qualified white one. Or else, it was about trying to defend some lying lowlife. Heck, it was just a few months ago that every "African American" in Detroit had crowded into a church to declare racial solidarity with that city's corrupt mayor, Kwame Kilpatrick.

Yes, Bob forced himself to admit, sometimes they had a point. Those kids in Jena, Louisiana, probably did get a bad deal—charged with attempted murder after a schoolyard fight—and it probably was because they were black. On the other hand, what else could you expect when they were responsible for such a disproportionate amount of violent crime in this country?

Bob was tired of all the complaining. It just seemed like the blacks were never satisfied. Seemed like they just wanted to blame all their problems on "the white man." Translation: on him. Was it too much to ask that they maybe clean up their own communities a little before they started crying about what the white man had or had not done? Hadn't even Bill Cosby said as much? Was it too much to ask that they stop having so many babies out of wedlock? That their kids pull their pants up on their butts, stop robbing people, stop dealing drugs?

Bob was a racist. Or at the very least, he felt, he had lost empathy with a people who seemed to want everything given to them. Who ever gave anything to him? Who ever gave anything to his great-grandfather, fresh off the boat from Ireland?

And Malcolm, always on the race kick. Always writing about the unfairness or the mistreatment or the exclusion or the lack. Whine, whine, whine. It never ended.

Bob stood. He paced through his house without particular aim, walking just to give his feet something to do. He stopped by the window overlooking the street, opened his cellphone to call Malcolm again, then snapped it shut just as quickly. What was the use?

Bob was a racist. Or at least, he thought he was. He hated this in himself. It was something he very much did not want to be.

And he wondered how he could have come to this. It seemed a perverse turn of events for a man who had once marched with—okay, seven rows behind—Martin Luther King, Jr. It seemed an unthinkable fate for a man who had once loved, and been loved by, the incandescent Janeka Lattimore.

Bob sat. He was not the Christian he once had been. Back when he was a young man, back when he had shared the Word with other long-haired young men and women, faith—the certainty that God's hand moved in human affairs—had seemed as real, as tangible, as the person kneeling next to you, eyes closed, mouth moving without sound, breathing out her deepest hopes to the spirit in the sky. That was the sort of Christian he had once been.

Now he was an Easter Christian, a Christmas Christian, when he bothered to be any kind of Christian at all. His faith seemed to have gone the way of his empathy. So it surprised him a little when he lowered his head and closed his eyes and breathed out a fast prayer. He prayed for clarity and courage. He prayed to stop wanting to murder Malcolm Toussaint. He prayed to know what to say when he walked into that restaurant and saw Janeka for the first time in 40 years.

Amen. As he opened his eyes, he wondered what she would look like. Would she be gray as a raincloud? Would she be big as a house? And what would she think of him, still trim enough, thank goodness, but balding and kind of dull looking, his face the unimpressive mask of a million white men, middle aged, middle class, middle managers, just counting off the days til retirement? When had he become...middle?

Certainly, he had not been middle in 1968. No, he had been—the memory bent his lips in a private smile—a revolutionary armed with nothing more than the Word and the audacity to believe it would protect him from angry white men furious at having their prerogatives challenged, apoplectic at knowing some of the challengers were every bit as white as they.

Bob was a dentist's son from Minneapolis who had spurned acceptance letters from USC and Yale to attend a small Christian academy no one ever heard of in northwest Mississippi. But he wanted to go there, he explained to his bewildered parents, because "the South is where it's at." "It," meaning protest and snarling dogs and Freedom Riders and marches and injustice and voter registration and ferment...and change.

His parents had resisted, citing those exact factors. But he wore them down and, in the end, they had relented to their devout and determined son. He arrived on campus in the summer of 1967.

Bob liked to say that he had majored in English and minored in activism. He went to class, he did enough work to pass, but only just. Earning a degree was not his priority. Changing the world was. So unless classwork absolutely demanded it, he was to be found on the quad, passing out leaflets, getting signatures on petitions, or just sitting cross-legged in the grass discussing strategies for ending racism, poverty, and war.

Before long, someone invited him to a meeting of a campus group, Students Organized in Unarmed Love, or SOUL. They met for an hour, about 60 blacks and whites, in the cafeteria in the basement of the student union. The meeting opened with a prayer and then they got down to business, the presiding officer (the group rejected the term "president," sullied as it was by the unjust war being prosecuted by the madman in the White House) asking for status reports on several ongoing projects.

One committee was finalizing plans to have agricultural students do a presentation for local farmers on new scientific methods of soil conservation. Another was trying to raise funds to invite a speaker from the Southern Christian Leadership Conference—maybe even King himself—to appear on campus. Yet another was seeking permission from the dean's office for a program that would provide tutoring to local middle and high school students.

Listening to them all from a seat in the back, Bob had the unmistakable feeling that he had found his way home—that this was a place, and these were people, that he understood. He belonged here.

And then it was her turn to present. She stood.

She was not tall. Even counting the perfect semicircle of her Afro, she was probably no more than about 5-5. But she was commanding. And Lord, but she was beautiful. Her skin was like the color of the sun just as it fell into twilight, her lips were proud as the prow of some sailing ship, her eyes the shade of sea foam on some remote island in the tropics. Her breasts were small and pert and just...*right*. And her butt...

Bob had stopped himself, mortified. What was he thinking?

This was his sister in the body of Christ. She was his colleague in the struggle for human rights. More than that, she was a human being with a mind, and emotions and a soul and inherent, intrinsic worth. Yet, here he was cataloguing her, the pieces of her, as though she were a side of beef. What kind of loathsome male chauvinist pig had he suddenly become?

Worse, she was talking—he could see her lips moving—but he had no idea what she was saying. Bob was scalded by shame. He changed his posture. He concentrated. He forced himself to listen.

Voting rights. She was talking about voting rights and the fact that, although the Voting Rights Act had been passed two years before, there was still fear and intimidation among the blacks in these rural counties that kept them from registering or going to the polls. And what was worse, when they got to the polls, they really had nothing to vote for.

Yes, King's movement had shamed the Democrats into supporting legislation to address the most flagrant human rights violations, but at the end of the day, they were still *Democrats*, as evidenced by their betrayal of the Mississippi Freedom Democrats in Atlantic City. Not to mention the Democrat Johnson's continued prosecution of a useless, immoral war that was chewing up lives at a rate of more than 30 men a day.

"And for what?" she demanded, her voice rising, her fist smacking into her palm. "For what?"

Bob shifted in his chair again. She was not just beautiful. Her passion was energizing.

The problem, she argued, was not just voting rights. It was the fact that black people—poor people of all stripes, really—were being asked to choose between two flavors of the same ice cream: Democrat and Republican. Each was packaged a little differently, each appealed to different prejudices and hopes, but at the end of the day, there was not a whole lot of difference between them. At the bottom line, it didn't matter all that much if you were black or white. If you were poor, you were powerless and you were going to suffer economic exploitation, going to be kept struggling for the same meager crumbs from the same overladen table, going to be so busy fighting against one another on the stupid basis of color that it never occurred to you to get together and fight the real, common enemy.

Meaning the capitalists and fat cats who built and maintained their wealth on the suffering and misuse of others. Economic exploitation, realized Bob with a start. She was talking about economic exploitation and the fact that both blacks and whites—Chicanos and Indians, too, for that matter—were its victims.

Janeka proposed that SOUL confront this situation by forming its own political arm, the American Alliance, to go into rural areas, register impoverished black and white voters, and educate them to go to the polls and vote in their own economic interests—to vote their wallets, not their whiteness; their bank statements, not their blackness. The American Alliance would demand that office seekers all over the state—eventually, she hoped, all over the country—answer a simple question: if elected, what will you do to alleviate poverty? In the long run, she said, she hoped the American Alliance would become a political party itself, fielding its own slate of candidates so that poor people would no longer be restricted to two flavors of the same ice cream.

Janeka's eyes searched the room. "I need volunteers," she said. "I need people to help me register voters."

It was an audacious plan. Moreover, it was stunningly naïve. Bob knew this in 2008. He had known it, at least a little, he thought, back in 1967. But what is youth for if not for being stunningly naïve? What is change made of if not the hard work and sacrifices of the stunningly naïve?

Bob lifted his hand. It rose slowly, but with the irrevocable certainty of an elevator. Searching the room for support, Janeka's eyes came to rest on him and she smiled in relief. "Well, I've got one," she said, and he grinned, knowing that she was righter than she could ever know. She had him, indeed. Bob felt himself being born.

It was August of 1967. Bob Carson was 18 years old.

Dwayne McLarty slid the old Ford four-seater pickup into a parking slot beneath the building. It had been just like he told Clarence, easy peasy. Hell, he hadn't even had to break the window or hot-wire the ignition. The thing had been sitting right there in the parking lot of some designer coffee shop with the window down and sure enough, when he lowered the sun visor, the keys fell. The world was just full of assholes.

He paused a moment to check his reflection in the rearview mirror. A lock of hair on the side where he still had hair had fallen across his forehead. He brushed it back. It was at moments like this, moments when he was just trying to pass for a regular citizen, that he sometimes regretted having such a memorable haircut. But, he reasoned, there was nothing he could do about it now. And besides, it wouldn't matter after tonight.

Still, Dwayne zipped his windbreaker to cover his T-shirt and tattoos—and also the pistol wedged into his waistband. It was a Luger, a good German gun his grandfather had taken off some dead Nazi officer in the Second World War. Mindless Americans under the influence of corporate media elites and biased liberal educators had been taught to hate the Nazis. His own grandfather had hated the Nazis. But more and more, as you looked at the state of the world—the Jews and ragheads fighting over a few godforsaken scraps of land, niggers making it impossible for decent people to walk the streets in safety, fags agitating for the right to marry other fags—you could see that they'd had the right idea, even if they were ahead of their time. It was more and more apparent that the Christian white man needed a homeland of his own.

Over the years, Dwayne had occasionally toyed with the idea of buying a new gun, but he never had. Carrying his grandfather's Luger just felt right. He was sentimental about such things.

Dwayne slammed the truck door behind him, took the elevator up to the lobby level. When its doors slid open, he saw some big nig rent-a-cop sitting at a marble counter next to a turnstile with a swipe card reader that controlled access to the elevators serving the tower. The nig was talking to some old lady who was pissing and moaning about missing coupons in that day's paper. He was telling her he had nothing to do with that, but would pass on her concerns to the appropriate department. Still, the old bitch kept yammering and at one point, the nig looked past her and made eye contact with Dwayne. The look said, "I'll be with you soon as I can." And also, "Can you believe I have to put up with this shit?"

It angered Dwayne that this nig would think he and Dwayne had even that much common ground, but he made himself smile. The smile must have looked as false as it felt, because the nig's expression stiffened. Dwayne stopped smiling. He made himself look around the lobby. Ancient headlines screamed from framed front pages.

WAR! Japs Attack Hawaii—Many Casualties Feared

PEACE! Japs Surrender After Atom Bomb Dropped

Kennedy Killed in Dallas—Johnson Sworn in as President

Man on the Moon—"One Small Step" says Armstrong

Day of Terror—Twin Towers Destroyed, Pentagon Attacked

"Can I help you?"

It was the nig security guard. He had come to his feet and Dwayne could see that he wasn't armed. Only in America would you have a man guarding access to an important building—the elevators were right behind him, for Chrissake!—and not give him a gun. If people came storming the building, what was this guy supposed to use to hold them back? His big, black dick? Unbelievable. Dwayne almost shook his head in disgust, but thought better of it. He brushed at the unruly lock of his hair, suddenly aware of the nig, waiting for him.

"Uh, the guy who wrote that piece in the paper this morning, Toussaint? I want to see his boss."

The nig sighed as if he had heard this request too many times already. Then he began to recite. "The column that appeared on the front page of this morning's paper was unauthorized. The *Chicago Post* does not agree with or support the opinions expressed in Mr. Toussaint's column and had, in fact, rejected it for publication. A computer security breach led to it being published nevertheless. The *Post* would like to apologize to anyone who was offended and you're invited to take a free copy of the corrected paper with our compliments."

"What's that?" asked Dwayne, confused.

"That's what they want me to tell people who have complaints about Mr. Toussaint's column. You want a free paper?" He nodded toward a rack of newspapers stacked against the wall behind Dwayne.

"No," said Dwayne, shaking his head. "I want to see his boss, the guy he reports to." He considered smiling again, but didn't.

"Mr. Toussaint doesn't work here anymore," said the guard.

"Well, then, the guy he *used* to work for. What's his name?" Dwayne fished in his pocket, came out with the DVD. "I've got something for him," he said, hating the eagerness to impress that he heard in his voice. "Something important. Something he needs to see."

"His name's Bob Carson," said the guard, "but he doesn't work here anymore either."

It was as if Dwayne had been reading from a well-rehearsed script and the other actor suddenly decided to improvise. His mouth flopped open, waiting for words that weren't there. He didn't know what to do.

"You've got something for Bob Carson?"

A young woman, big glasses, strawberry blonde hair pulled back into a ponytail, was pushing a cart laden with boxes of books, photos, and miscellaneous paraphernalia out a pass-through gate to the right of the turnstile, heading toward the parking elevators.

Dwayne nodded, dumbly. "Yeah," he said. "Yeah, I do."

She came over. "I can take it to him," she said, reaching out for the jewel case. "I'm headed to his house right now."

A panic of indecision seized Dwayne McLarty then. What to do? If this Carson guy didn't work there anymore, what was the use of giving him the DVD? Yet if Dwayne didn't give it to this woman, wouldn't that make her and the security guard suspicious? He could tell from the way the nig's face had tightened like a screw that he already had his doubts about Dwayne. And the chick, she was watching him expectantly, waiting for him to hand over the jewel case.

What to do? He wished his mind were fast enough to think up an excuse for not giving it to her. He thought of just running out of the building. He thought of pulling his gun and shooting them both.

He gave her the DVD. She smiled, apparently taking his hesitance for concern about her own trustworthiness. "I'll see he gets it," she said, in a voice he supposed was meant to be reassuring.

Dwayne watched the precious DVD disappear into the pocket of her coat. He made himself smile. "Thank you," he said. "I appreciate it," he said.

There was a moment. And then he realized he had no more excuse for being there. He nodded. "Thank you," he said again. He nodded again and, feeling like an idiot, moved to the parking elevator and stabbed at the button.

His thoughts screamed.

What a fucking first-class moron he was!

Now what could he do? Go back to Clarence, *his subordinate officer*, for Chrissake, admit that he had fucked up and burn a new disc? He couldn't do that. He couldn't bear to see that look of...disappointment in Clarence's eyes.

No, he had to get the disc back. He'd give it to the *publisher*. That's what he should have done in the first place. But how to do that?

The elevator door opened. To Dwayne's surprise, the woman with the cart had come up next to him and she boarded ahead of him. He stepped in behind her. Her finger was hovering over the buttons and her glance was expectant. "P1 or P2?" she asked.

It took him a moment to realize she was talking about parking levels. "P1," he managed. She pressed the button. After a moment, the door closed.

His thoughts continued to scream. He had to get the disc back. He had to get the disc back. He had to get the disc back.

But how?

What infuriated him was the certainty that there must be a way, some smooth, slick way, some thing he could say, some excuse he could give, that would allow him to take the disc back, yet raise no suspicion. There was a way. He knew it. But he just couldn't think of it.

She glanced his way, gave him a perfunctory smile. He grinned back, his thoughts grinding furiously through the possibilities. He could tell her he had changed his mind and wanted the disc back, but, again, what reason could he give? Or, he could just punch her in the face and take it. Or maybe pull the gun and shoot her. But then, they'd broadcast his description and he'd have no way of delivering the disc where it needed to be. If he showed up in the building after doing any of that, they'd throw him to the floor, no questions asked.

The door opened. The woman got off ahead of him, pushing the cart. Dwayne watched as she beeped open the liftgate on a forest-green minivan.

He had to get the disc back.

Amy pushed aside kid's toys and dog toys and loaded Bob's things into the back of the minivan. He would not want to see her, of course, especially since she would be showing up uninvited and unannounced. But he would not be able to turn her away, either, since she would be bringing his stuff.

Fine. Once she had a foot in the door, once she had convinced him to give her a few minutes for an interview, what would she say? What questions would she ask?

She still could not believe Malcolm Toussaint, a man she had idolized, a man whose work had helped her decide the very course of her life, had done what he had apparently done. What had gotten into him? What had snapped inside him? And what did he mean, this morning, when she asked him about it and he said, "I just got tired."

Tired of what?

Amy was climbing into the driver's seat of the van when her phone chirped. Doug Perry. She put the phone to her ear, pressed the ignition button, turned down the radio. "Yes, Doug?"

"Amy?" Something in his voice made her sit up straight.

"Yes?"

"I thought you should know. We just got a call from Chicago PD. They're sending a couple detectives over."

Police? Was Lydia trying to have Malcolm arrested? Then she realized she had misheard. "Wait a minute. You said the police called you?"

"They got Lydia, actually. "

"Well, what's wrong? What's happening?"

"They found Malcolm's car this morning at Randolph and LaSalle. It was totaled. Someone hit it from behind."

"Shit," she said. "Is Malcolm okay?"

"That's just it," said Perry. "The car was abandoned. Whatever it was that hit him was gone, too. No one knows where Malcolm is. Cops checked all the hospitals in the area, they even broke into his house, but he wasn't there. There's been no sign of him since he came into the building."

"Oh, my God."

"Yeah. You and that guy Ricky from security were the last ones to see him. Cops are probably going to want to talk to you both."

"Of course," she said. "You want me to come back up?"

"No, no. You go on to Bob's house and do your interview, if he'll let you. We'll wait til they ask."

"Doug, do you think it has anything to do with this morning's column?"

"I don't know," he said. "Whatever happened happened awful early. Who reads their paper at five a.m., gets pissed off, and then takes to the streets to stalk the guy who pissed you off? How could you even find Malcolm in that short a time? How would you know where to look? It doesn't make much sense. I just know that whatever's going on, it's not good."

"I see your point," she said.

"Yeah. Go do your interview and hightail it back. And keep your eyes open."

"OK," she said, and clicked off the phone.

Amy's thoughts were reeling. The day had started out as the most bizarre of her professional life. And it had steadily gotten worse.

She backed out of her parking space, drove toward the exit, and turned onto Michigan Avenue. Amy could not corral her thoughts—or her fears. What was happening? What in the hell was going on here?

Traffic was brisk. She stopped at a light as a herd of people flooded across. Beside Amy, a man in a Mercedes pulled up, speaking angrily into a cellphone. And behind her, an old red Ford pickup truck braked to a stop.

eight

Malcolm Toussaint staggered away from the melee, the sounds of police truncheons smacking into flesh and the anguished, unmanly screams of middle-aged men following hard after. He ran as best he could, gasping for breath, his weight supported by Sonny and Pop. They didn't speak. They only ran. He stumbled along between them until he found himself lying on some woman's lawn in the projects and they were pouring water from a hose into his face and it felt like the very kiss of Jesus, so blessed was the relief. He could not get enough of it into his burning eyes.

And when finally Malcolm wedged those eyes open, there was his father, a rough-hewn man with craggy midnight skin and blunt, heavy features, watching him intently. "You all right?" he asked, in that deep, hard voice he had.

"Yeah," said Malcolm. "Burns, though. Burns like a..." He was going to say "motherfucker." Then he remembered who he was talking to. "Burns," he said.

"I bet," said Sonny, who was standing behind his father.

"Shouldn't of hit no cop, though," said his father.

"He was about to hit you," protested Malcolm.

"I know. Still, you colored and he ain't. You should of known better."

"You think anybody saw?" asked Sonny. "You think they got a good look?"

"Don't know." His father regarded him a moment, then made a gesture that took Malcolm in from head to toe—the dashiki, streaked now with the mud and grass of this woman's lawn, the proud Afro hanging in wet tatters upon his shoulders. "What's all this shit anyway, Junie?"

"It ain't shit," said Malcolm. He had expected the question, had even rehearsed a defense that just now, he could not remember. But then, he had not expected to be lying, gassed and stunned, on some stranger's lawn when he gave it. Beyond his father, beyond Sonny, he saw the woman, three little children gathered to her skirts, all of them watching him like *Green Acres*.

"If they seen him, this what they gon' be lookin' for," said Sonny.

His father nodded. "Yeah," he said. And then to Malcolm: "Take that thing off."

Malcolm started to protest but thought better of it. They were right. So he pulled the dashiki over his head and handed it to his father. Pop accepted it without a word and threw it on the curb. "Can you walk?" he asked.

"Yeah," said Malcolm, shirtless now in the February chill. "Yeah, I think so."

"Come on, then." The father shrugged out of his own threadbare coat and gave it to the son. "Put that on and button it up so nobody see you ain't got a shirt on."

Malcolm did as he was told. He climbed awkwardly to his feet. His balance was unsteady as a toddler's. His eyes teared and stung. He kept squeezing them shut and opening them wide, trying to clear the shadows from his vision. It didn't help. And with every breath, it felt like he was drawing shards of hot glass down into his lungs.

Roaches. They sprayed us like...

His father thanked the woman. They hobbled off.

"They gon' be lookin' for that hair, too," said Sonny.

His father nodded. "I done thought of that," he said.

Malcolm heard this without hearing it. It was as if it was all happening to someone else. They walked in silence down the side streets, the three of them, angling away from downtown, deeper into the Negro section. After 20 minutes, they came to a little barbershop sitting on a corner next to a vacant, overgrown lot. "Smitty's," said the sign above the red, white, and blue striped pole.

Inside, there was one barber and no customers. Malcolm sat in his chair without a word. The man tied the haircloth around Malcolm's neck, fired up his clippers, and leaned over. "How you want it?" he asked, raising his voice a little to be heard over the electric buzz.

Pop answered for him. "He want it all off."

At this, the barber grinned, a gold tooth winking. "Lord," he said, "that's music to my ears. Make me happy every time I get the chance to whack all this shit off one'a these young boys' heads." He gave Pop a look that expected an "Amen" or a "You got that right." Pop gave the man an expression that said nothing. There was a beat of awkward silence. Then the barber sucked his teeth, grabbed Malcolm's head roughly, and started cutting.

Malcolm barely felt it.

Some part of him was still on Main Street, watching men who had done nothing more provocative than carry signs being sprayed *(like roaches)*, being sprayed himself *(like a goddamn roach!)* by men acting under the impunity of white skin and gold badges. And so he could not quite process the barber's smug dig about the length of his hair, could not feel the loss of the hair even as he watched it fall in great dark clumps into his lap.

His father, he suspected, took this silent compliance for sullen surrender. But Pop didn't understand. How could he? Malcolm himself didn't quite understand.

He only knew that something inside him had gone missing. In just that few moments of fighting on Main Street, he had lost something important, something vital. And he didn't even know what it was.

The barber cut his hair and he let him. Afterward, he and Pop said goodbye to Sonny and, neither having money for bus fare, began the long walk home together. There was silence for the first few blocks. Finally, inevitably, Pop asked the obvious. "What you doin' here anyway?"

"They sent me home," said Malcolm.

"You couldn't keep up with them white boys?"

And hard as it was to breathe and as much as his eyes stung, and as removed as he felt from the moment, the question still made something hot flare in Malcolm's chest. "That would make you real happy, I bet."

"No, I'm just askin'," said Pop.

Just askin'. Right. How many of their arguments had begun with this man telling him, "Get your head out them damn books," or "Stop actin' like you think you white"? How many times had his father counseled him, "Don't be gettin' too far ahead of yourself. Stay in a nigger's place"? How many times?

Just askin'? Yeah. Sure he was.

"They put me on administrative leave," Malcolm said. And then he wait-ed for his father to laugh a vindicated laugh.

But instead, Pop frowned, deep ridges furrowing his brow. "That mean you been kicked out?"

"No," said Malcolm, "it's different. It's temporary, like getting suspend-ed. I can apply to go back." *If I decide to.* He thought this, but did not say it.

"You couldn't keep up?" his father asked again. And if Malcolm hadn't known better, he might have thought Pop really wanted to know the answer.

But Malcolm wasn't buying it. "What do you care? You told me I wouldn't make it. You always said I was wastin' my time."

Pop pursed his lips. "Was you?"

Malcolm stared at him. He did not answer.

Something hard came into Pop's voice. "Are you tellin' me you couldn't keep up with them white boys?" he demanded.

Malcolm felt a thin smile bend his lips. "I could have kept up," he admit-ted, finally. "I just didn't."

"Why didn't you?"

"I was doing something else."

"Uh huh. And what was you doin', more important than keepin' up?"

Malcolm stopped walking, met his father's eyes. "I was protesting," he said.

Some ghost walked through his father's gaze then. His mouth worked without sound. Then he nodded and didn't ask any more questions. They walked along.

"Heard you twisted your knee," said Malcolm, after a few moments.

"Yeah."

"But you walkin' pretty good."

"I suppose. Healed up okay."

"You could have told me you were hurt."

His father looked over at him. "You could have told me you was comin' home."

Malcolm hunched his shoulders. "I was mad, them puttin' me out. I didn't feel like hearing you tell me how I wasted my time trying to be white."

His father sighed. "Yeah, I suppose I did say that."

"Pop, I ain't never tried to be white."

It took a moment. Then Pop said, "I know. Tell you the truth, I probably knew it all along."

This surprised him. "Then, why...?"

Malcolm couldn't finish the question. His father didn't try to answer. They walked again through silence. In the next block, father and son passed a group of scrawny black girls jumping rope and chanting "Old Mary Mack." A moment later, they passed two men working beneath the hood of an old piece-of-shit Ford, their beers sitting on the roof. From within the car, the tinny radio speakers lifted the Temptations singing "I Wish It Would Rain." It rose like an offering.

Pop said, "You know, I knew Echol Cole."

Malcolm said, "Who?"

"Him and Robert Walker, they was the two men got crushed up in the back of one of them trucks, reason we's on strike. Never knew Walker, but I knowed Cole, at least a little. We was on the same crew awhile. Nice guy. Good worker. And what happened to him and Walker..."

His voice fluttered. He fell silent.

Malcolm said, "I'm sorry, Pop." He didn't know why he said it. He wasn't even sure what he was sorry for.

"We told 'em about them trucks," said Pop after a moment, his voice leaden now with bitterness. "Told 'em they wasn't safe. But they ain't cared. Now them men's dead, and they still don't care. Ten years from now, 20 years from now, ain't nobody gon' even remember Echol's name. Ain't even gon' remember he was here. That ain't right. But that's the way it is, ain't it?"

Malcolm let it breathe for a moment. Then he said, "Yeah, Pop. That's the way it is." He wondered where this was going.

His father stopped and regarded him closely. Then he said, "You know, sometime it get to where you been takin' it so long, you start thinkin' that's the way it supposed to be. You start thinkin' you *s'pose* to take it. Like that's the whole reason God put you on the Earth. But that ain't right. Ain't no one put here for that. And I guess I just come to realize that now, with Echol dead and Walker dead and people not givin' a damn. I guess I done just got to the point, I'm tired of takin' it, son. You understand that?"

His eyes searched Malcolm. Malcolm nodded. "Yeah," he said. "I guess I do."

"Okay, then," said Pop, "okay. Let's go home."

And they did.

The following afternoon, Melvin came by to pick Malcolm up for the promised job interview. Malcolm threw on a windbreaker and rode with

Melvin over to the hotel on the river. There he stood, mute as a block of wood, next to Melvin as Melvin spoke to a white man he introduced respectfully as "Mr. Rupert Pruitt," promising what a good worker Malcolm would be. And Pruitt, bald and fat as a baby, rolled a cigar stub around in his mouth as he sat there in his booth in the darkened hotel lounge, a shot glass of some brown liquid on the table before him, appraising Malcolm. Abruptly, the man's mouth opened in something that was not quite a smile, revealing small teeth the color of tobacco. "Well, now," he said, cutting Melvin off in mid-sentence, "if Melvin Cotter willin' to stand for you, you must be somethin' special. Melvin's one of our best workers, don't you know? Been here only a year now and been named employee of the month four times."

Malcolm saw Melvin grinning under the praise. Pulling the cigar from his mouth, Pruitt braced himself on the table and worked his bulk up out of the booth. "I swear," he said, clapping Melvin hard on the shoulder, "this boy do so much around here, and do it so well, sometimes I think he's after my job."

Melvin ducked his head, still grinning. It made him look like a ten-year-old. "No, sir," he said. "It ain't like that. But my pappy always told me, any job worth doin' worth doin' right."

"Your pappy a smart man," said the white man, his hand still on Melvin's shoulder. He shot a calculating glance at Malcolm. "So," he said, "you think he'd be a good hire, do you?"

"Yes, sir, I do."

"Well, then, that's all I need to hear. You two go see Della in the office. She'll show you all the paperwork. We gon' put you in maintenance, son. We can always use a good cleanup man. That be all right with you?"

"Yes, sir," said Malcolm. "That would be fine. Do you know—"

He stopped when he realized Pruitt had stopped listening. The white man's attention had gone to a pretty young sister who was coming their way, balancing a tray of empty drink glasses. Malcolm stood aside to let her pass, but Pruitt stepped forward so that she would have to go around him, then stuck out a thumb and forefinger and grabbed himself a chunk of her backside as she did. The sister yelped. He laughed.

"Better get a move on there, gal," he told her. The woman moved away at a quickstep, glancing once over her shoulder. Malcolm felt paralyzed by anger and confusion, by the sudden, urgent sense that he could not just let this pass, that he ought to do something. But had no idea what it was. Pruitt, replacing the cigar in his mouth, noticed none of this. He followed the sister with an appreciative stare. After a moment, his gaze returned to Malcolm and Melvin and he started a little, as if surprised to find them still standing there.

He made a shooing motion. "You boys run on and talk to Della," he said. And he began the work of wedging himself back into the booth to finish his drink.

Malcolm, still stunned by the collision of his own emotions, followed numbly as his best friend obeyed the white man's command. And still, Melvin was grinning. "Told you I could get you on," he said, triumph brimming in his voice like coffee in a cup.

Malcolm stared. It was as if he had never seen Melvin Cotter before.

"What about the sister?" he asked.

"Lynette? What about her?" Then he realized. "Oh, that," he said. He shrugged. "Yeah, Mr. Pruitt a little free with his hands sometime."

"More than a little."

"Yeah, but what you gon' do about it?" he asked. "That's just the way it is, nigger. You know that well as I do."

Malcolm glanced back. The woman, Lynette, was at the bar, putting fresh drink glasses on her tray. Her brow was furrowed with concentration, as if she were focused on this task in front of her and nothing else. Pruitt was reading his newspaper, similarly oblivious. It was as if Malcolm were the only one who felt the pull of a...*wrongness* here. He stared again at Rupert Pruitt and felt a sudden need to rush back in there, haul the fat honky up by his collar, and beat him upside the head with his own shot glass. He could see himself doing this. He could feel the flat smack of his fist against Pruitt's jowls. The need was so strong it made Malcolm tremble.

"You all right?" Melvin was watching him.

"I'm fine," said Malcolm.

But he wasn't. He knew it now, knew it for sure. He had left something behind on Main Street and still, he didn't even know what it was.

"You all right there, boy?"

This was his father, two days later, watching him over the kitchen table.

"I'm fine," said Malcolm.

"Don't look fine."

"Just a headache."

"You done had a headache ever since you got home, then, 'cause you ain't been right since then."

"Pop, can you just drop it?"

His father was dressed to go out. He was wearing his good clothes: a suit coat from Goodwill that he'd had for ten years and a pair of black slacks shiny in the seat from years of use. Behind him, leaning against a wall, was a picket sign. Four bright red words took up the face of it.

I AM A MAN, it said.

This was the new sign the men were walking with. It was their response to what had happened Friday, to being treated like kitchen pests on the main street of their own city. Something about it made Malcolm sad.

I AM A MAN.

He knew they intended it as a dramatic assertion of dignity and self. But there was, he thought, something deeply humiliating in the very fact of those words needing to be said. This was what Pop meant by not taking it anymore? Malcolm pitied him.

"Heard you done changed your name," Pop said now.

It took Malcolm by surprise. "Who told you?"

"Never mind."

"Melvin," said Malcolm. The answer, now that he thought of it, was obvious. "He told you when I went to get my coat for the interview."

"He might of let it slip. That ain't what's important. Why ain't *you* told me?"

"Knew you wouldn't like it."

Pop grunted. "So... 'Malcolm,' now? That's your name?"

Malcolm nodded. "Malcolm Toussaint," he said. "Malcolm Marcus Toussaint."

"Changed the whole thing."

"Yes," said Malcolm.

"You done this legally, did you? Filed court papers and everything?"

"Yes."

"So ain't nothin' I can do about it, I guess, 'cause you of age."

Malcolm swallowed. "No," he said. "Nothing you can do."

"Just like that Cassius Clay done," said Pop. "Guess that's what all you young ones is doing now. Guess I should just be glad you ain't changed your name to Muhammad like he done." He pronounced it *MO-hammed*. "Or X," he added, "like that black Muslim fella you like so much. Ain't never understood that for a name. Just X."

Malcolm nodded. "Well, I did get part of my name from him. Not the X, but the Malcolm."

"Never knew you ain't liked your old name."

"I liked it fine," said Malcolm, a soft lie to spare his father's feelings. "But the new name, it's..." He paused then, groping for words. "It's who I am," he finally said.

"Who you are." The tone revealed nothing.

"Yes."

Pop extended his hand. "Well, I'm Mozell Uriah Wilson, Mr. Toussaint. Pleased to meet you."

"Pop..."

"Thought you was Mozell Uriah Wilson, Jr., Mr. Toussaint, but I guess I's wrong about that. Wrong about a lot of things, I expect. You gon' shake my hand, Mr. Toussaint, or you gon' leave it hangin'?"

With a sigh, Malcolm clasped his father's cool, rough hand and gave it a single, perfunctory pump. "Pop," he said, "this ain't about you and me, man."

"No? Then what it's about, then?"

"I just wanted a name that said something."

"And what your name say, Junie?"

Again, Malcolm sighed. "Revolution, Pop. It says revolution."

"Revolution."

It wasn't a question, but Malcolm answered it anyway. "Yes, sir." And he explained to his father, as he had explained to Melvin, the significance of the three names.

His father regarded him dully as he spoke. When Malcolm was finished, he simply repeated the word. "Revolution."

Something in Pop's voice threw a challenge, made the word sound... foolish. "Yes, sir," said Malcolm. "Revolution." He spoke the word in order to reclaim it from his father's mockery.

"You expectin' to fight a revolution here, son?"

"Black people need to do something more than just march, Pop." Malcolm saw something wounded settle into his father's gaze when he said it. "I'm just trying to say I want things to be different in my life," he explained.

"Different how?"

Malcolm didn't respond.

"Different than they was in my life, is that it?"

Malcolm didn't respond.

Pop smiled. It was the saddest smile Malcolm had ever seen. "I don't right blame you for that," he said.

It was the last thing Malcolm would have expected. He would have expected Pop to yell. He would have expected Pop to curse. But this sad smile and quiet admission? No. He would not have expected that. Not in a million years.

There was a moment when neither of them spoke. Then Pop shrugged and said, "I been callin' you Junie your whole life. Be hard to stop now. I'm still gon' call you Junie, if that's all right."

It was, Malcolm realized with a start, not a declaration. Pop was asking for permission. Malcolm felt something shifting in the air between them. He felt something change.

"Yeah, Pop," he said. "That'd be fine."

His father looked away. "I know things ain't never been...good between us," he said.

"Pop..."

"I expect you blame me for that. I expect you got your reasons. So I probably got that comin', you keepin' that from me. And you right. Once upon a time, and not too long ago, mind, I'd of been mad, all right. Mad as a hive of bees."

He paused, still looking away. Malcolm waited.

"But I wasn't never mad at you, son. Even when I thought I was. Seem like just recently here, first time in my life, I done finally figured out who I really been mad at all along."

Now he looked at Malcolm, held his eyes for a long, precious moment. He said, "Fight your revolution, Junie. I'll fight mine, best I can. Marching." A glance at the clock on the wall. "I got to go."

And he hauled himself out of the chair, the tatty sport coat hanging loose on his wiry frame. He had never had a suit that fit, thought Malcolm distractedly.

Pop picked up the sign. He put on his hat. "I see you, later," he said. And he walked out the door, the placard tucked under his arm, its sad, defiant declaration visible for the world to see.

I AM A MAN.

Malcolm sat there a moment after his father was gone. Then he went out to the porch. Nanny Parker was sitting on her own porch drinking a cup of coffee, watching the world pass. She waved to him. "How you and Mozell gettin' along?" she asked.

"Doin' fine," he called.

He took a seat on the steps, knees drawn up, something unsettled rattling inside him.

Wasn't never mad at you, son. Even when I thought I was.

And the hell of it was, Malcolm believed him. He didn't know why, but somehow, he did.

Never mad at you, son...

No. Mad at himself. Mad at what white folks forced him to be.

Forced him before he even knew. Forced him from the moment he was born, the youngest child on a tobacco farm owned by a white man named Lem Johnston, his mother a sickly, exhausted woman who died on him before he was out of diapers and his father a beat-down remnant of a man who signed Lem Johnston's contracts every year with a mark. Pop had 12 older siblings who regarded him with little interest—another competitor for what little they had of food and living space—and who got the hell out of there as fast as they could. Got married, got pregnant, found work, went off.

Mozell had been the last to go. Malcolm's mother had told him the story. How, in 1943, at 16 years of age, Pop had left his own father, too broken by age and infirmity to work but permitted to live out his last years on land now owned by Lem Johnston's son. How Malcolm's father had not wanted to end up like his father, so he had gone to the city looking for work, looking for a chance to be something different.

But he had ended up working as a tub toter and, excluding a two-year hitch in the Army during the Korean War, there he had stayed. Just as if it had been ordained. Just as if this fate had been stamped on his forehead when he came, screaming and brown-skinned, into the world.

"How that strike comin'?" asked Nanny Parker.

"Slow," said Malcolm.

"Got to give them mens credit," she said. "They done held out. Never thought they had it in 'em."

"Yeah," said Malcolm.

"You seen that sign they carryin' now? Say, 'I <u>AM</u> A MAN.' Seen your father with his'n just a minute ago. Seem like somethin' done got into them men."

"Well," said Malcolm, "you push a man long enough, he's going to push you back. You keep hitting him and what's he supposed to do, stand there and let you keep doing it? Sooner or later, he's got to hit back, or what kind of a man is he? He's no kind of man at all, you know?"

"I guess you got a point there," she said. "I remember—"

He plowed right through her words. "That's what all the good reverends in your so-called civil rights movement don't understand. That's why every time you turn around, there's another riot in another ghetto. And even the tub toters don't get it, not really. You take your signs out there, you march around in circles, and what does it change? When you march in circles, you never get anywhere. And see, the white man knows that, that's why he ignores you. Or he slaps you down. Or maybe he even throws you a few crumbs to shut your mouth. But what does he really care about you marching in circles? If you want to get his attention, you better speak to him in a way he understands. And I tell you, the only thing the honky understands, the only thing he respects, is *power*."

Malcolm fell silent. He felt himself breathing.

"Junie?" The old woman's voice was gentle.

It surprised him. He had almost forgotten she was there. "Yes, ma'am?"

"Are you all right?"

Malcolm smiled. "Sorry," he said. "Just tired is all."

She nodded, but he could tell she didn't really believe him. He stopped wasting the smile.

Malcolm went inside a few minutes later. The hotel had him working an overnight shift, so he slept the rest of the afternoon away. That night at nine, he woke up, bathed himself, and pulled on the gray janitor's shirt that had been issued him. In the front room, his father was slumped in a chair before the television, which was playing loudly. The opening credits of *I Spy* were running, a silhouette figure firing a pistol, then running to escape inside the logo of the show. Mozell Wilson, Sr. saw none of this. He slept. His sign lay on the floor, where it had fallen.

I AM A MAN.

Malcolm lifted it so his father wouldn't step on it when he rose. He leaned it against the chair.

For a silent moment, Malcolm regarded his father. Once upon a time, he had seemed so large he filled the sky. So large, his rages shook the Earth. Now he seemed shrunken—just a tired, beaten garbage man sleeping in a chair with dirty gray cotton showing through the broken seams.

Malcolm touched his father on the shoulder, softly, so as not to wake him, then moved toward the door.

His bicycle—the same bicycle he had used as a boy in high school—was leaning there. He wheeled it outside, closed the door behind him, and carried it down to the sidewalk. Then he climbed on and rode slowly through the shadow-darkened city of his birth. It took him half an hour. He traveled north and west, toward where the hotel sat on a bluff looking down on the big, brown river.

The neighborhoods slept, little houses with small porches and dirt yards, with cracked sidewalks and weathered wood badly in need of paint. But Beale Street, when he detoured up to it on a sudden impulse, seethed with traffic, music from the bars drifting into the street, pawn shops still open for business, their neon "Loan" signs casting garish shadows on passersby. "Things go better with Coke," promised a sign painted on the brick face of one of the buildings. Malcolm passed a group of Negroes huddled on a street corner in front of a bar, men with beers and stingy brim hats laughing too loudly together, women watching them, smoking cigarettes behind patient, waiting smiles. He saw two white men standing across the street watching the Negroes, their faces pinched shut, their arms folded across their chests. He biked faster.

The night felt claustrophobic. He felt entombed by it, the city closing on him like a coffin lid. Was it really just three days since he had arrived back here and proclaimed himself glad to be home?

Melvin had been right, more right than he could have known. This city had changed.

Its streets were piled high with garbage, yes, and though the weather had been cool and that muted the smell, it was not hard, if you took a deep enough breath when the wind turned just right, to taste the moldy bread, fish heads, and old soup cans piling up and overflowing, waiting for this thing to be over.

But it wasn't just the garbage. It was the sense that something had come undone, some sense of white people's prerogatives, some sense of black people's place, some sense of the way things were supposed to work.

Everything was up in the air. It wasn't just a labor arrangement that was being renegotiated here.

You saw the recognition of this in the flinty eyes of those white men looking across at those black ones—and in the way the black ones ignored their hateful stares and laughed together as if, for the first time, they themselves were enough for themselves. And you saw it in the newspaper accounts of the strike, in the frantic way the reporters and editorial writers cheered on the mayor and pleaded with him to stand firm until, if you didn't know any better, you'd have thought Henry Loeb was facing off against the very forces of hell and not a group of rough-hewn men asking for a slightly higher starvation wage and a place to shower the muck off at work. You saw it, too, in those same humble men, marching in circles, singing their gospel songs and carrying their signs that declared the self-evident as if it were the revolutionary.

Malcolm arrived at the Holiday Inn coated in a light sheen of icy sweat. He pushed open the door behind the reservation desk marked Employees Only, wheeled his bicycle down the hall, and opened the janitor's closet. He pushed the bike in and pulled the big floor buffer out. His supervisor, Mr. Whitten, would be looking for him on the fifth floor in about ten minutes. He had said he would teach Malcolm to operate the big machine, after which Malcolm would be left to polish the elevator lobbies throughout the building. It would be numbing, mindless work, but Malcolm thought he wouldn't mind. He thought he would enjoy the solitude.

Then he heard a woman's voice. "No, Mr. Pruitt! Stop that! Please!"

What...?

It came from across the hall, the employee lounge. Malcolm pushed open the door. What he saw stunned him.

On the far side of the room the sister, Lynette, was wrestling with Rupert Pruitt. He had her pinned in a corner and was nuzzling her neck, laughing a little as she tried to ward off his big, flabby arms with her little skinny ones.

At the sound of Malcolm's entrance, Pruitt looked around without interest. "Close the door, boy, and get out of here," he said, turning back to Lynette. The words were mush. He was drunk.

"Get off her!" ordered Malcolm. "Leave her alone!"

His tone got the white man's attention and he came around slowly. "Told you to get out of here!" he cried in his bleary voice.

Malcolm's body moved without his mind. He closed the space between them in two steps, grabbed the white man's collar and pulled him away from Lynette. Pruitt was heavy, but Malcolm was furious. He gave the white man a shove that landed him on the tattered employee couch.

"You leave her alone, hear? You leave her alone, or I will personally whip your ass!"

Pruitt's face was livid. "Who the hell you think you are, boy? Who the hell you think you are?" He worked himself up from the couch, came unsteadily to his feet. "You think you can put your hands one me? Just you wait. I got somethin' for you."

And so saying, he wobbled out of the break room and opened the door of his office across the hall. Lynette grabbed Malcolm's arm. "Come on," she said. "We need to get out of here."

Malcolm yanked his arm away. "No," he said. He was seething. "I ain't goin' nowhere. Be damned if this honky makes me run."

And then Pruitt closed the question altogether. He tottered back into the break room with a double-barreled shotgun held loosely in his grasp, pointing to the floor. "Now," he said, "let's see you put your hands on me again."

Malcolm should have felt fear. He knew this. But somehow, he did not. Instead of flinching away, he walked straight up to Pruitt, and saw Pruitt's eyes grow large as the space between them shrank to little more than a foot. The gun never came up, still threatened only the floor. Pruitt swallowed. Malcolm said, "Big man with a gun, huh?"

The white man gestured the rifle toward the door. "You're fired," he said. His voice broke like an adolescent boy's. "Go on, get out of here."

Malcolm burned the man with his eyes to let him see how much of a damn he gave about being fired. Only when he was sure that his point had been made did he leave the room. Lynette followed as he went to the janitor's closet and retrieved his bicycle and jacket. She stood there waiting as he rolled the floor buffer back in and closed the door. Pruitt watched them the whole time with those large eyes, the rifle hanging down. When finally Malcolm wheeled his bicycle down the hallway to the lobby, Lynette was at his side.

"Thank you," she said. "Good thing you came when you did."

"Are you all right, sister?"

She nodded. He was not convinced.

They crossed the lobby, stepped outside into the cool March evening, and paused beneath the carport. "You don't have to wait with me," she said. "My father will be here any minute to pick me up."

"I'll wait," he told her.

She lit a cigarette with quivering hands, exhaled a jet of smoke. "I'm sorry you lost your job because of me," she said.

"Forget about it."

"Might be all right, though. Pruitt, he forgets half the stuff he says when he's been drinking. Might not even remember he let you go."

Malcolm waved it away impatiently. "Don't worry about that," he said. "What about you? You want to call the police?"

"Police?" She chased the word with a bitter laugh, sucked at the cigarette. "What am I going to tell the police?"

"What do you mean? Tell them what happened."

"Yeah," she said. "Be our word against his. And he's a white man. 'Call the police.'" She made a noise of derision. "You know better than that."

"He pinched you the other day. I saw it with my own eyes."

"Yeah," she said. "It wasn't the first time. He's not the only one. So?"

"So he has no right."

"White men do a lot of things they have no right to do. Men period, you want to know the truth."

"But you can't just do nothing."

"It'll be all right," she insisted. "He gets like that when he's been drinking. He always apologizes when he sobers up."

"So this is a regular thing?"

She shook her head. "No," she said. "I mean, he's put his hands on me before, yeah. But he's never pinned me in a corner like that. But he'll apologize. He always does." Another laugh, bitter as her cigarette smoke.

She took a seat near a big stone planter. Malcolm sat next to her. "You don't mean to say you're coming back here?"

She snorted. "What else am I going to do? Jobs are hard to come by. I got tuition to pay."

The anger rose in Malcolm so hard he actually trembled. "To hell with that," he said. "There's got to be something else you can do."

"It's my problem," she told him.

"You're a black sister," he told her. "That makes it my problem, too."

"Sister," she said. A fatigue older than rivers rode the curve of a closed smile. "That sounds nice. That sounds...noble. But what you gon' do for me, 'brother'? You gon' protect me? You got some way to make that white man in there leave me alone? If I raise too big a stink and he fires me like he just fired you, are you going to pay my tuition? Are you going to help me put food on my parents' table?"

Malcolm had no response.

She touched his hand. "I thank you for the thought," she said. "I do. But that's all it is, isn't it, a thought? All it ever can be. Whole reason I'm going to school is so I can learn something and better myself, so I don't have to live here and I don't have to put up with this kind of shit anymore."

Still, Malcolm struggled for words. There had to be something he could do. There had to be something. But for the life of him, Malcolm Toussaint could not name it. The inability made him feel...impotent. So that was the way it was? A white cop could gas you, a white man could try to rape a sister right in front of your eyes, and there was nothing you could do about it, nothing you could even say?

For some reason, he thought of Pop and that pitiful sign. I <u>AM</u> A MAN. Malcolm almost laughed. How could you be a man if you couldn't even protect a woman? What was left if they took even that much away from you?

She seemed to read his mind. "It's *my* problem," she repeated.

A pair of headlights raked over them before Malcolm could respond and an old Chevy rumbled up the driveway. A tired-looking man was behind the wheel. Lynette stood. She dropped the cigarette and mashed it out with the toe of her shoe, began smoothing her blouse and skirt.

"That's my father," she said. "Do I look okay? I mean, do I look like anything happened?"

"You look fine," said Malcolm.

"Don't say anything to him, okay? Don't tell him what happened."

"Why not?"

"Because if he finds out, he'll act just like you. Worse, since I'm his daughter. He'll feel like he has to do something, because he's a man and that's how men think. But there's nothing he can do. Same as you."

She was gazing hard at him, waiting for his answer.

"Yeah," he told her after a moment. "Same as me."

She squeezed his hand. "Thank you," she said.

For what? he wanted to say. What the hell had he done? But then, all at once, Lynette became someone else. This new Lynette wheeled around and trotted toward her father's car, waving excitedly, her face lit with a smile light as cream, a smile that knew nothing of care, much less of almost rape. The tired man's face lost its fatigue in a smile as she slammed the door behind her, leaning over to kiss his cheek. They spoke for a moment, then the car rumbled off. Lynette's father gave Malcolm a quick once-over and a noncommittal nod as he passed.

"Been lookin' for you," said a harsh voice from behind. "Might have figured you out here chasin' some tail. All you bucks the same."

Malcolm turned. Ronald Whitten was a stocky man who stood not much more than five and a half feet beneath a brush cut the color of rain clouds. "You were supposed to get the buffer and meet me up on five," he said. "Or did you forget?"

"I don't work here anymore," said Malcolm.

"What are you talking about?"

"Pruitt fired me."

"Fired you for what?"

"It doesn't matter."

"Hell it doesn't. I've been asking for help on the nightshift for a month and he finally hires somebody and now you tell me he fired you? Fired you for what?"

Malcolm sighed. "He was drunk. He was trying to rape that girl, Lynette. I pulled him off her. I may have told him I was going to kick his ass if he laid a hand on her again. He went and got a shotgun and told me to get out."

Whitten shook his head. "Son of a bitch," he breathed.

"Yeah," said Malcolm, lifting a leg to straddle his bike. "So anyway, I don't work here."

Whitten said, "Wait." Malcolm looked at him. "Look, I'll go get the buffer—probably not a good idea for you to go past his office right now. I'll meet you up on the fifth floor."

"But I'm fired," said Malcolm.

"No, you're not," said Whitten. "I'll talk to him. It'll be fine. He gets in his cups sometimes and says stupid things, does stupid things. Half the time, he doesn't even remember afterward."

Malcolm was not at all convinced he even wanted the job. Whitten seemed to sense this. "Look," he said, "you're not fired. Just trust me on this. I promise I can make it okay. Now, I need somebody to work this shift and unless I'm mistaken, you need work. So what's it going to be?"

Malcolm considered for a long moment. "Trust me," the man had said. And Malcolm had almost laughed. Because he had lost something three days ago on Main Street and finally, in that moment, he knew what it was.

He had lost trust. No, he had lost *faith*.

Faith in the idea that white people would ever really see black people, ever really accept that Negroes were human, too. This would never happen. They would never change. They *could* never change. He knew that now.

It was as he had told Nanny Parker. There was no reaching those people, no persuading them. They understood only power. Negroes needed power. *Malcolm* needed power. And suddenly, he knew what he had to do.

So he burned a half dozen responses away in the incandescence of a smile whose falseness he knew this man would never see. "Okay," he said.

Whitten gave a tight nod. "Good," he said. "Put your bike behind the desk. I'll get that buffer and meet you on five. It'll be fine. You'll see."

Malcolm worked that night. He worked the next night, too, and saw Lynette, who told him her prediction had been right: Rupert Pruitt had left her flowers. He saw Pruitt, too, in the hallway outside the break room. Pruitt stopped him. "Look," he said, "last night, we both said some things, did some things, we probably shouldn't have done..."

Malcolm waited out this speech, nodded when Pruitt got to the part about leaving it all in the past, said okay, and then wheeled his mop and pail away to go clean the women's restroom in the lobby. He was aware of the questions in Pruitt's eyes as they followed him down the hall. He ignored them.

Malcolm worked, and the days passed. He worked the night after Pop— *Pop!*—was arrested at a City Hall sit-in. He worked the night somebody set garbage fires and angry black boys hooted at firemen who tried to knock the blazes down. He worked the night Pruitt patted Lynette on the ass as she walked by him, balancing a tray of hamburgers and french fries. He pretended not to see this. He worked. He buffed floors. He emptied ashtrays. He cleaned toilets. All this he did scrupulously and without complaint. He smiled when Whitten told him to do something. He nodded when he passed Pruitt in the hallway. He kept his head down. He did his job. He worked the three weeks until his first payday. When he got his pay envelope, he took the check and cashed it at a liquor store, then rode the bus to a freestanding stucco building he knew with a neon pistol hanging over the door.

He walked in. He did not bother looking at the display cases. He went straight to the man behind the counter, a longhaired white guy in an old Army coat, who stood there regarding him as if he had been waiting for Malcolm all along, as if he had been expecting him all these years. Malcolm tented his fingers on the glass of the counter and met the white man's eyes.

"I want to buy a gun," he said.

nine

Once upon a time, he had been a soldier.

Corporal Willie Washington was someone trusted to handle important information, make life and death decisions, get things done. In fact, his heroism in the battle for Quang Tri City had won him the Purple Heart and the Bronze Star. Not exactly a Medal of Honor, but not nothing, either, and when he had received his honorable discharge, he had gone home to a life pregnant with expectation.

This was the plan: finish college, get a job, start a career, live a good life. Or so he had thought. But somehow, it never happened. Somehow, he managed to return to the world and yet, not return to the world, hunkering instead in a fearful, shadowy place out on the margins, where every string of firecrackers popping off on the Fourth of July might be a firefight, every helicopter chopping the air over a gridlocked freeway might be a Huey hitting a hot LZ, every child with Asian features running in your direction might be some kid the gooks had rigged to explode. He would look around him in amazement that other people did not react to these things. He wondered what was wrong with them that they didn't understand what he understood, didn't see what he saw.

Then, on a sunny afternoon at a barbecue in his mother's backyard, the voices started talking to him. And they would not stop.

It got worse after that. He cried a lot. He stopped shaving. He stopped eating. His wife tried to get him to see a doctor. A head doctor. He told her no.

She insisted, following him down the hallway outside their room. "Willie, we can't go on like this. You have to see somebody to help you with your problem."

Problem?

He slapped her.

"I am *not* fuckin' crazy!" he screamed, spittle spraying off his lips.

That's telling the bitch, one of the voices said.

"Damn right," he replied.

Her hand to her bloodied mouth, Pam had stared at him, a dozen emotions competing for primacy on her face. Awe incredulity anger shock sorrow...pity.

When he saw that last one, it was like a hammer hit him in the heart. *She pitied him?* His shoulders rounded and he went back into the bedroom. He didn't leave it for two weeks.

Once, he had been a soldier. But that was a long time ago.

Now, he was a homeless drunk, and he wasn't even quite sure how that had happened. All he knew was that one day, Pam said she'd had enough; one day, she'd told him she couldn't put up with him anymore. And then he'd gone from their home to his old room in his parents' house, and then, after a couple of more years, to a friend's couch, and then to his own car, and then to the streets, slipping, frictionless as a child on a playground slide, down the path to uselessness.

For a long time, he had hated himself. For a long time, he had drunk simply to feel nothing, simply to make the voices shut up and leave him in peace. In a sea of cheap wine, he had tried to drown his capacity for humiliation. Where others walked past him and shook their heads or went *tsk-tsk* at the miserable straits into which his life had fallen, Willie had learned to accept those straits, to embrace them, and to want nothing more. There was, he had found, an invigorating freedom in not wanting more. He took life as it came, let tomorrow worry about itself. So he could not remember the last time he had felt humiliation.

He felt it now, though, trudging back toward the old warehouse.

You fucked it up, you miserable fuck! Can't you do anything right?

Mặc kệ ông. Đừng xỉ vả ông nữa!

Willie jammed his hands over his ears. "Stop it," he whispered aloud. "Stop it, please."

Find those cops, dumbass. Make them listen to you. Kill them if you have to!

"Not going to do that," Willie said. "Not going to do that."

Still, he could not deny the dismay he'd felt watching the officers go. It was as if God or whoever had allowed him some reminder of what it was like to be a man people saw, a man they listened to. Then that glimmer of respectability had been snatched even as he was admiring it.

And now, Willie just felt...low. Lower than he had felt in more years than he could recall.

Useless. Stupid motherfucker. Need to just kill yourself.

"Corporal William Washington," he had told them. And what had possessed him to draw himself up like that, to give them his full government name and the rank he had not used in a half a lifetime? Pride, maybe? Some stubborn determination to make them see him?

Bây giờ ông muốn gì, thằng cha lính kia?

This was asked in a voice of quiet solicitude.

"Ain't but one thing I *can* do," he answered.

Willie had seen what he had seen. He knew that. And now, the only way to vindicate himself—not to mention the only way to get his stuff back from inside that building—was to handle this alone.

Fine. That's what he would do. Wasn't he a trained infantryman? Wasn't he a soldier in the United States Army? It had been a long time ago, yes, and he had lost a lot of himself since then to wine and hard living and the cruelties of age. But surely whatever remained was more than enough to take care of some 400-pound white boy who looked like he couldn't move quickly even if you stuck a cattle prod up his ass.

Willie giggled at the image.

In the next block, he passed a favorite liquor store and paused there, looking with longing toward its neon signs and advertising posters of happy people smoking cigarettes and drinking drinks. It was like coming upon an oasis in the desert. And he had a little change in his pocket, too, thanks to those people who had given him coins when what he had really wanted was attention. He could afford to buy himself a little taste. It would make the voices go away.

You might as well, you stupid motherfucker. What can it hurt?

But no. He had to be strong. He had to be clear-headed for this. Later, after he had rescued the brother being held hostage, after he had been interviewed on the local TV news and they had gushed over him and asked him how he did it, after the two cops Smith and Jaworski had apologized for treating his Army rank like a joke, then he would have a drink to celebrate. But only then.

He continued past the liquor store, crossed a bridge over the river, came again to that warren of warehouses beneath where the expressways met. Willie climbed onto the loading dock of Funn Toys and peered tentatively through the broken window.

Nothing had changed. The brother was still chained—handcuffed, actually—to a chair. The white boy was doing something on a laptop computer and the two of them seemed to be talking, calmly.

"Told you I saw it," he said.

He found himself wishing he had one of those spaceship phones like that crazy bitch who'd knocked him down. Then he could call this in and just sit here and wait for the cops to arrive. But he didn't have such a phone and Lord only knew where there was a payphone. They didn't have those so much anymore.

He would have to handle this himself.

You're just going to fuck it up, you stupid fuck!

"No, I can do this," he said. He said it again, whispering. "I can do this."

Willie lowered his head from the window before the brother could see him and start making demanding faces. He could not rush this. He had to think. He had to plan.

He wished he had a drink.

A preppy white man in a red, white, and blue bowtie had replaced the blonde with the fire-engine-red lips.

"President Bush is keeping a low profile this Election Day," he said. "The president spent the weekend at Camp David before returning to the White House where, according to aides, he will celebrate the First Lady's sixty-second birthday and, later, watch election night coverage. This is in keeping with the campaign itself, during which the president, whose approval rating is mired in the mid-20s, has been conspicuous by his absence."

Pym was eating cold chicken from a red-striped bucket. An image of the president walking across the White House lawn flashed on the screen and he flipped his chicken wing at the laptop. "There goes ol' fuck nuts," he said, chuckling. "Boy, Dwayne hates that guy." The chicken wing bounced onto the keyboard and he swiped it to the floor, then plucked another from the bucket.

"Most observers," continued the man in the bowtie, "think Republican Senator John McCain faces an uphill struggle to surmount Democrat

Senator Barack Hussein Obama's lead in the polls. But in the face of that daunting reality, the former Navy flyer was upbeat and combative at an Election Day rally in Colorado."

McCain appeared on the screen. "I feel the momentum. I feel it, you feel it, and we're going to win the election," he told a cheering crowd. The bowtie-wearing man's voice came on over the image of the Arizona senator. "McCain's defiance was in sharp contrast to the gloomy tone struck by his own campaign manager, Steve Schmidt, while talking with reporters on the flight back to Arizona."

Schmidt now appeared, a bald, burly white man. "We did our absolute best in this campaign in really difficult circumstances," he said. "We had some tough cards to play all the way through, and we hung in there all the way."

"Sounds as if he thinks the election is already over," the anchor said, turning to his partner.

Pym muted the volume and made a sound of disgust. "It's over, all right," he said. He turned toward Malcolm and added, "Like that time Jordan was with the Wizards, scored just 6 points, lost by 27. You remember?"

He grinned, waiting for Malcolm's response. Malcolm stared at him, silent and cold.

Pym tried again. "You remember that game, right? December 27, 2001. Dude should never have come back a second time, am I right?"

Still, Malcolm gave him nothing but a stony stare. He was dizzy with the sheer absurdity of the question.

Pym's grin shrank and it was as if he had read Malcolm's mind. "You don't have to be that way," he said in an accusing voice.

"So what are we supposed to be now?" demanded Malcolm. "Friends?"

To his surprise, the big man looked stung. "Well, no," he said, "but I just figured, since we both got to be here, we might as well pass the time friendly-like."

It was too much. "We don't 'have' to be here!" cried Malcolm, rattling the chains that held him to the chair. "We're here because you and your numb-nuts friend chose to kidnap me and bring me here."

"I wouldn't expect you to understand," said Pym, and Malcolm gaped. The big idiot was *pouting* now. "It's getting so a white man doesn't have a chance in his own country," he said. "I wouldn't expect you to know how that feels."

Malcolm shook his head. "What in the hell are you talking about?"

"Dwayne talks about it all the time, how you niggers are taking over. Fucking affirmative action and shit. I mean, look at you: gettin' paid to write your racist bullshit, write your books and whatnot, living in that big mansion, driving that fancy sports car. And here I am, driving a piece-of-shit van, living with my mom. It's not right. You can't tell me, deep down in your heart, you think that's right."

"So your life didn't work out the way you want and it's my fault?" Malcolm was finding it difficult to breathe past his fury.

"It's niggers' fault," said Pym. "Dwayne says that all the time."

"'Dwayne says this, Dwayne says that.' You got a brain in that fat head of yours? What do *you* say?"

Pym stared at him for a long moment. His smile came slowly. "Oh no you don't," he said. "You don't get between me and Dwayne. Might as well stop wastin' your time."

Malcolm met his eyes. "Oh? Maybe I was wrong before. Maybe you two are fags."

He was hoping for a reaction, something he could work with. But Pym's eyes just frosted over. "Told you about that," he said. "We're friends."

"Yeah," said Malcolm. "*Special* friends."

Still Pym refused the bait. He rolled his eyes and turned back to the computer, unmuting the sound. A famous African-American civil rights leader was framed in a box next to another box containing the white man in the patriotic bowtie. The civil rights leader was heavy lidded, with graying temples and a distinguished mien, and he spoke with ponderous solemnity. "The election of Senator Obama to the presidency would be a watershed moment in the tortured racial history of this country," he was saying, apparently in response to some question, "but we would be foolish and premature to believe that, in and of itself, it represented the full redemption of Martin Luther King's dream."

The bowtie man arched an eyebrow in a practiced imitation of shock. "But Reverend, how can you say that? During King's lifetime, what might happen tonight would have been unthinkable. Surely you are not denying the country has changed dramatically for the better in matters of race."

"As I said," the civil rights leader responded, "the election would be a watershed. But we must avoid the trap of treating the extraordinary as if it were the representative. On the day after Brother Barack's election as on the day before, an African-American family would still face a disproportionate chance of

living in poverty, an African-American man would still face a disproportionate chance of being jailed for drug crimes, an African-American woman—"

Pym muted the screen again with a snort of disgust. "Oh, please don't
start that shit," he told the civil rights leader.

"What are you talking about?" asked Malcolm.

Pym glanced at Malcolm. "I'm talking about that 'poor, pitiful me' shit
you niggers always shovel." He made his voice a nasal whine. "'Oh, we is
treated so bad,'" he mocked, eyes rolling piteously to the ceiling. "'Us can't
do no better. De white man be keepin' us down.'"

"Well, isn't he?"

Pym reached for another chicken wing. "I look like I been keepin' anybody down, dumbass?"

Malcolm glared at him. "You're sure as hell keeping *me* down."

Pym almost chuckled. "You know what I mean," he said. "You people
don't want to do anything, want to lie on your asses shitting out babies and
collecting welfare. That's what Dwayne always says."

"Really? And what does *Dwayne* do for a living?"

Color rushed into Pym's cheeks. He stopped chewing. "Dwayne's not
working right now. He's had issues with drugs, okay? I already told you that.
But he's cleaned up."

"Yeah, right."

"Okay, well at least we're not out there slinging drugs and knocking
people in the head."

"No," said Malcolm, his voice even as a blade. "You're just kidnappers."

"We're not kidnappers!" Pym was indignant "We're not some damn
criminals."

"Last I heard," said Malcolm, his voice still even, "kidnapping was a
crime."

"But we're revolutionaries!"

Malcolm laughed. "Okay, Che Guevara. You could have fooled me."

"Stop laughing!" Pym came up off his seat, the forgotten chicken wing
clenched in his fist. "Stop laughing at us!"

Malcolm met his eyes. "Dwayne got any kids?" he asked. Some glimmer
in Pym's gaze told Malcolm he had struck pay dirt. "He does, huh? Is he
married? Probably not. He take care of his kids at least?"

There was a telling silence. Malcolm laughed. "So let me get this straight.
Your buddy is an unemployed junkie, he's a criminal, and he's got kids he

doesn't take care of. Hell, I don't know why you and him hate niggers. You *are* niggers."

"*We're not niggers!*" Indignation thundered through Pym's voice. A silence followed. When he spoke again, he did so softly. "We're white men," he said. "That's the difference."

Malcolm regarded him for a moment. Pym's chest was heaving. His face was florid. And were those *tears* in his eyes?

"You've got to be kidding me," said Malcolm.

"Why are you doing this?" asked Pym.

Malcolm lifted his manacled right hand. He spoke almost gently. "I could ask you the same question," he said.

"Already told you why," said Pym.

"Yeah," said Malcolm. "But it doesn't make any sense. And you know that."

"Don't know nothin' of the sort."

"Yes, you do," said Malcolm.

Pym sank back onto the chair. "Just shut up," he said. He was almost pleading. Belatedly, he realized he still had the chicken wing in his hand. He threw it across the room. "Just shut up," he repeated. He sounded tired.

Malcolm shook his head. "I look at you, all the crazy bullshit you spout, and I wonder what the hell has happened to this country."

Funn Toys had been a regional maker of children's playthings: sporting equipment, model cars, dollhouses, and action figures of obscure superheroes. Never a Mattel or a Hasbro, it had nevertheless endured for many years, its profits respectable but never spectacular. But the company, which never bothered to develop an electronic games division ("It's a fad," Benito Funicelli always said, "it'll pass."), had declined through the '90s, its already small market share shrinking even further as children put down plastic bats and obscure action figures and began to spend all their playtime in front of the television with "Tekken," "Call of Duty" and "Grand Theft Auto."

Ben Funicelli ("It's Ben Funn!" read his business cards) had eventually bowed to reality, liquidated a business he had inherited from his immigrant father, padlocked his building, and retired to Boca, where he died two years later, heartbroken, still wondering how children could have changed so much. His own children had been trying to sell or lease the property since he died, without success. It sat on that corner of the warehouse district, as forgotten as dollhouses and model cars, except by the occasional junkie or squatter or homeless, alcoholic Vietnam veteran who drank to keep from hearing voices.

Now Willie Washington scrambled up the fire escape to the second floor.

Using his elbow, Willie broke a pane out of the yellowed old window of what had once been, although he did not know this, Ben Funicelli's office. He poked his head through, waiting to see if the sound brought any reaction from below. All he heard was the dull murmur of voices from the warehouse floor. Satisfied that no one had heard, Willie pulled his head back, reached in, unlatched the window, and pushed it open. With a glance around to make sure no one was watching, he hoisted himself through.

It took a moment. His lumbago was acting up. He wasn't as young as he used to be.

Finally Willie landed, with less than catlike grace, in the gloom of the old office.

Too loud, you stupid fuck.

"Shhh," he admonished the voice in a hissing whisper, hunkering low to a floor littered with scraps of paper and bits of glass. He waited again, listening for any indication he had been heard from below. There was none.

After a moment, Willie straightened. He felt a peculiar tickle at the nape of his neck as he began to look around. He had never been up here before. The room was wood-paneled like something out of the 1970s, draped here and there with cobwebs. There was a door leading to a small private bathroom. Willie poked his head in. The plumbing fixtures were gone—scavenged, most likely, though the ceramic top to the toilet tank lay in two jagged pieces, one large, the other small, on the floor.

Thieves must have dropped it and broke it, so they couldn't sell it.

"Yeah," said Willie, "that's probably what happened."

Shut up, you stupid fuck. They might hear us.

"Yeah, you're right," said Willie.

He went back to looking through the office, but there wasn't much to see. The floor was littered with some junkie's things—an old spoon burned black, a short length of yellowed hose, cigarette butts and beer cans and a blanket that reeked of piss. Of the original occupants there was little evidence, except for a warped old desk they had apparently thought too little of to move and a banged-up gray metal file cabinet, its four drawers standing open and empty.

There was also a white banner hanging from the wall, primary color images of birthday cake, scooters, baseballs, dollhouses, and clown faces spelling out the words, "It's Ben Funn!" The banner had gone grimy and dull with age and neglect. It struck Willie as one of the saddest things he had ever seen.

Slowly, he edged his way into the outer office. It was also empty. In the rust spots and scratches on the old tile floor, he could read the placement of cubicle walls long gone. The ceiling was torn open, a tangle of wires hanging down. Thieves looking for copper and other valuable metals, he supposed. Willie made his way forward, toward the door marked Exit. He opened it upon an enclosed stairwell. The rectangle of light at the bottom was the warehouse floor.

Willie swallowed and took a breath to steady himself. He wished he had a weapon. He wished he had a drink. Then he wouldn't care that he didn't have a weapon. He took a step. After a moment, he took another, moving as cautiously as if one of the stairs might be rigged. He felt sweat drooling down his temple.

Then the voice exploded.

"We're not niggers!" it cried.

In the dark stairwell, three steps above the floor, Willie froze like January. Movement stopped. Breathing stopped. Blinking stopped.

He waited, but he couldn't hear anything else. After a moment, the muted burr of voices resumed. Had he actually heard that? "We're not niggers?" It didn't sound like either one of his voices. Why would they say something like that?

Willie stood there frozen, contemplating his options. He decided he couldn't go down there without some kind of weapon. That white boy was a monster. What could Willie do against him, frail and old as he was? He had to find something he could hurt that big man with. But Willie had no idea what he could use.

And then, he did. He turned around and headed back up the stairs.

"'What's happened to this country?'" Pym asked, repeating Malcolm's question. "Hell, people like you are what happened to this country. You niggers are ruining—"

"Oh, shut the fuck up."

Malcolm was surprised by his own words. Apparently, Pym was, too. He fell silent. Malcolm regarded him for a moment, then shook his head. "You're too young," he said. "What are you, in your 20s? Twenty-five, maybe?"

"Twenty-six," said Pym.

"Twenty-six, then. So you've never really known a world without Fox News and Pat Buchanan and Sean Hannity and all these other right-wing lunatics telling you all day what a victim you are because you're a white man."

"The white man *is* a victim. You hear that Jeremiah Wright, that so-called preacher who said goddamn the white man? Hell, you niggers are the biggest racists in this country."

Malcolm surprised himself by laughing. It broke out of him like water breaching a dam and he couldn't make it stop. After a moment, he had to lean his head down to his manacled hands to wipe away tears.

Perplexity squinted Pym's eyes. "What's so fuckin' funny?" he demanded.

Malcolm regarded the big man for a moment. "You are," he said, finally. "You. Have you any idea of the sheer cognitive dissonance of accusing me of racism while calling me a nigger?"

"I told you about making fun of me," said Pym, stepping toward Malcolm, fisting his massive hands. But somehow, thought Malcolm, he suddenly seemed like a man playing a role. Malcolm had the distinct sense he was making the threat only because he had to.

"Yeah, yeah," said Malcolm as the last of the chuckles rattled in his throat. "I remember. I make fun of you, you'll treat me like one of those chicken bones."

He fell into a stillness then, remembering. Clenched fists. And sit-ins. And pot smoke wafting on the breeze. And power to the people. And the hope—the abiding *expectation*—that things could be made better: that you could, if you wanted it bad enough, if you worked for it hard enough, force this old world to change. Where did it all go, he wondered? When did it all change? "When did we get so small?" Malcolm heard himself ask. "That's what I think of when I look at you. When did everything get so goddamned small?"

"I still don't get what you're talking about."

Malcolm glanced up. Pym seemed honestly confused. "It wasn't so long ago," explained Malcolm, "that you and I would not have been here arguing over who was the bigger victim. It wasn't so long ago that white guys just like you were putting themselves on the line and even dying because they knew that unless everybody was free, nobody was. I just wonder sometimes, how we got from people like that to people like you."

Pym's eyes narrowed even further. "What do you mean, 'people like me?'"

Malcolm met his eyes, but did not answer.

"What do you mean, 'people like me?'" This time, he shouted it.

The edge of Malcolm's mouth hooked into a tiny smile. "Small-minded people," he said. "Hateful, closed-minded, self-righteous, damned ignorant and proud of it. We were not like that—and white people were not like that—when I was your age."

Pym's faced twisted as if he had just smelled an odor. "You mean, back in the '60s when all you liberals were taking drugs and spitting on soldiers and refusing to bathe? Back with all that free love and no respect for authority and burning down the cities? That what you're talking about?"

Malcolm's smile opened. "Yeah," he said, "there was drugs and there was sex. But there was also vision. We had ambition. Not for making money, but for making a difference."

Pym swallowed. "You aren't the only ones with dreams," he said. "We dream, too. We dream of taking our country back from the faggots and niggers and Islamofascists and freeloaders."

"Do you really believe half the crap that comes out of your mouth?" asked Malcolm. "I really don't think—"

His voice caught. Through an open door 25 feet behind Clarence Pym, he saw feet descending a stairwell.

Damn.

The brother couldn't have been more obvious. He had stopped talking at the sight of Willie. Now Willie stood, still as a lamppost, tense as a guitar string, waiting for the inevitable discovery. He mapped escape routes in his head.

The brother turned back toward the big man, trying to cover his lapse. "I really don't think you do," he resumed.

Still Willie waited for the white boy to turn around, waited for him to see Willie there, and come lumbering after him with murder on his mind. It was so obvious. The white boy could hardly fail to see what was going on, could he? There was a moment. Then the big man leaned close to his captive. "I believe every damn thing I say, hoss. I guarantee you that."

"Then you're an idiot," said the brother. He was provoking the big man, trying to hold his attention. Willie breathed. He put his weight on the last stair. It didn't creak. In the movies, they always creaked. He gave thanks for small favors and stepped off onto the floor.

"If I'm such an idiot," said the big man, "why are you the one chained up to the chair?"

That is one big motherfucker.

Got that straight, thought Willie.

Anh có chắc không đó?

No, he told the voice silently, he wasn't sure about any of this. Not in the least. He almost said this out loud. He bit his bottom lip instead to keep the words inside. He crept forward.

It struck him that he was living through an absurd parody of his own life. Forty years before, he had crept just like this, crouched low and moving on mouse feet, through a South Vietnamese jungle, lugging that damn M60. Forty years later here he was, creeping through an abandoned Chicago warehouse, lugging a damn broken toilet tank lid.

Life played strange tricks sometimes.

I'm telling you, that's one big motherfucker.

Willie wanted to scream at the voice. *Shut up! Shut up! Shut up!* He needed to concentrate. He needed a drink. He crept forward.

The drunk came slowly, his eyes round and white with terror. In his hands, he clutched a toilet tank lid, broken off at the end.

Malcolm reminded himself not to look. Above him, Pym smirked in satisfaction. "Can't answer that one, can you?"

"Huh?" Malcolm couldn't even remember the question. Then he could.

"You being an idiot has nothing to do with who's in the chair," he said. "It has to do with you believing a bunch of bullshit. It has to do with thinking you can be better than somebody else just because you were born a different color. Do you have any idea how stupid that is? Why do you let that other fool make you believe something so stupid?"

His words sounded thin and uncompelling even to his own ear. He couldn't concentrate on this stupid argument with this stupid man. Not while he was busy watching out of the corner of his eye, willing the homeless man forward.

"You know why you think it's stupid?" Pym was bent so low over him Malcolm could smell the chicken on his breath. "Because you never had a country stolen from you. But that's okay, because we're going to take our country back."

Malcolm tried to think of something to say. He could not improve on what he had already said. "You're an idiot," he said.

"You'll change your tune," said Pym, straightening up.

"I doubt it," said Malcolm, shooting another surreptitious glance at the homeless man. He was maybe nine feet behind.

"You will," said Pym and an easy confidence had entered his voice, "when me and Dwayne kill Obama tonight."

"What?" Malcolm wasn't sure he had heard correctly. Even the drunk was stunned. To Malcolm's consternation, he stopped creeping forward and simply stared.

"Oh yeah," said Pym, and his grin was cool as water. "We're going to get him at Grant Park when he comes on to make his speech. That van we got parked outside? It's a bomb with armor plating. We're going to drive it right into the park tonight and blow his black ass straight to hell."

Even the voice that hated Willie was stunned.

That motherfucker is crazier than you are.

"You got that right," Willie said.

It was only when the big man turned that he realized he had said it aloud.

Oh shit!

The broad face registered more surprise than alarm. "Who the fuck are you?" he demanded. "How'd you get in here?"

Run!

And this wasn't one of the voices of his undiagnosed mental illness speaking. No, this was the sweet, reasonable voice of self-preservation and basic common sense telling him to get the hell out of there before that big man smashed him to pieces.

Willie ran.

He ran straight toward Clarence Pym, who simply stood there in utter befuddlement. He ran like the soldier he once had been, some long-forgotten war whoop ripping from his mouth, the toilet tank lid raised high in both hands like a club. He ran.

Pym's forearm came up. Too slowly.

Willie brought the toilet tank lid down. Pym flinched backwards at the last instant, so he didn't catch the full brunt, but he caught enough. The jagged porcelain raked his face, laying open his left cheek. Blood squirted out.

The giant screamed. He grabbed for his wounded face.

Corporal William Lincoln Washington never stopped moving. It was as if he was 22 again, fighting his way through some godforsaken jungle hell. He pivoted, shifted his weight, brought the toilet tank lid down again, and this time the blow was solid, landing on the crown of the giant's head with a thunk so emphatic Willie was sure it had broken his skull. It certainly broke the porcelain, a slab of which fell to the floor, leaving Willie with just a stub in his hands.

He didn't need it. The big man staggered, his feet crossing one another. His eyes rolled. Then he fell backwards, crashing heavily to the floor. His head bounced off the concrete and he was still.

Willie could hardly believe it. He stared. He gaped. The big man did not move. He lay there flat on his back, blood flowing, eyes closed, dead to the world. Maybe dead, period.

I don't believe it. You did it.

"Me neither," said Willie. He dropped the stub of porcelain. He still didn't move.

"The keys," hissed the brother, still chained to his chair. "Find the keys."

The keys? Willie couldn't stop staring

"Come on!" the brother told him, his voice low but urgent.

The keys! Of course. The keys. "Okay," Willie said. "Okay, okay."

Hãy bình tĩnh đi.

"I *am* calm," Willie said. But of course, he was anything but. For years, he had failed at everything he did, failed so badly so often that failure had come to feel like home. Now, in this singular moment, he had succeeded, he had done the impossible thing he set out to do. It was like cold air in a sauna bath. The rush of it was intoxicating.

But you ain't finished yet, you stupid motherfucker.

"Got to find the keys," said Willie.

That's right. You got to find the keys.

Finally, he moved. He went to the table where the computer and the chicken bucket sat with some papers, the backpack, a Styrofoam chest, and two boxes of computer discs. Willie searched it all thoroughly. No keys.

"They're probably in his pocket," said the brother.

They probably in his pocket.

"Yeah," said Willie, agreeing with them both. "Probably in his pocket."

The big man was wearing jeans. Willie went to him on tiptoe. He reached out gingerly, as if toward a live explosive, and patted the left front pocket. Nothing. An ink pen, some change. Nothing. He patted the right front. Nothing.

"Got to be in the back pocket," said the brother.

Check the back, you stupid motherfucker.

"I don't want to."

"You have to," said the brother.

You got no choice.

Willie sighed. Failure was so much easier.

He went to one side of the giant, knelt down, wedged his hands under one massive buttock and lifted. There was a wallet. Willie pulled it out, tossed it aside without looking at it. Nothing else in the pocket.

Try the other side, you stupid motherfucker.

"Shut up," said Willie. "I know." The brother's eyes tightened in confusion when he heard that. Willie hunched his shoulders and grinned an apologetic grin.

Made bold by adrenaline, Willie crossed to the other side of the big man. He crouched down and lifted his right butt cheek, ran his hand beneath and patted. And there it was.

Willie reached into the big man's hip pocket and pulled out the key. He held it up.

"What you got to say about that?" he asked the voice that had been calling him a stupid motherfucker for almost 40 years.

That voice did not reply. The other did.

Ông làm tốt lắm, Willie.

Good work.

"Thank you," said Willie.

He climbed to his feet and went to the brother, holding the key out before him. "I am so glad to see you," said the brother, whispering. "I thought you were going to leave me here."

"Went for help," said Willie, "but nobody would believe me. So what's this all about? Why they got you in here?" He stuck the key into the lock and turned. With a click, the cuff sprang open.

"They're crazy, that's why. You heard 'em. They want to kill Obama!"

Willie shook his head. "Crazier than me," he said, reaching for the left manacle. "And that's saying something."

He put the key in the lock. Then the brother said, "Oh, shit."

Willie glanced at him. "What's wrong?" he asked.

The brother didn't answer. His face had gone slack, his eyes wider than the Interstate. Willie turned, slowly. Behind him, the white boy was rising like a harvest moon. His face was a fright mask crimsoned with fury and blood.

He got you now, you stupid motherfucker.

Willie cast about for something he could use as a weapon. There was nothing.

Run!

This was the voice of self-preservation and common sense again. But it was no use. Willie felt as if an electric current ran through him. He was rooted to the spot. He was pinned.

The white boy wasn't fast. Willie had time to follow the massive fist on the upswing, to see it sweeping toward him on the backswing. It hit him like a wrecking ball hits a derelict building. The blow smashed him to the floor. The key flew. He heard the brother cry out something, but he didn't know what it was.

Oh, shit. You stupid motherfucker, you done it now.

"I know," said Willie. His arms and legs spasmed uselessly as he tried to climb to his feet. It was no use. They would not work in coordination. "I know," said Willie again.

"Stupid, son of a bitching, motherfucker!" The white boy's voice roared from above, hoarse, garbled and furious. "You hurt me! You actually hurt me!"

Willie moved. That is, his foot finally found some traction and he felt himself inching across the floor.

"Get back here!" the giant cried. And his hands closed on Willie's throat.

"Leave him alone!" the brother cried.

The white boy didn't even hear him. Malcolm could see it in his eyes: he was someplace else. He tightened his grip on Willie's windpipe and bore down with all his mammoth, terrible weight. Willie's body went into a panic. He tried to pry the grip loose, but it was like trying to pry a rusted lugnut by hand. The massive fist forbade him air. Willie felt the bones give. He felt darkness. It edged in like twilight.

"Stop it," the brother cried, "you're killing him!"

Willie swung at the big man and actually managed to hit him, but the blow seemed to land harmlessly as summer rain. The big man snarled. Willie's feet scrabbled uselessly against the floor. The darkness came on more swiftly. No air! No air!

Ah, you poor, stupid motherfucker.

It was the last thing William Lincoln Washington ever heard.

ten

Bob opened his door and almost walked into Amy Landingham, who stood on his porch with her fist lifted, about to knock.

"Oh," he said, startled.

"Oh," she said.

There was a moment, neither of them sure what came next. Amy recovered first, hooking a thumb toward a green minivan, parked at the curb behind Bob's Camry. "Hey, Bob," she said. "Listen, I've uh...I've got your stuff. From the office, I mean."

Bob glanced at the van without interest. "I know you didn't come by to bring me my stuff," he said.

She smiled. "Well yeah," she said, "there was another reason, too."

"They've got you working on the story?"

"Yeah," she said again.

"Congratulations," he told her. "That's going to be front page for sure. Good exposure for you."

"Thank you," she said. "But listen, I was hoping maybe you wouldn't mind—"

Bob cut her off. "I'm headed out," he said. His tone was curt, just this side of rude, and he immediately felt guilty about it. Amy didn't deserve his attitude; she was only doing her job. "Lunch date with an old friend," he added, appending the explanation in a belated attempt to soften the discourtesy.

Amy took this in, appeared to think about it. "Maybe after?" she asked. Her voice lifted girlishly and Bob knew he was being worked. She really was a good young reporter.

Still, he shook his head. "I don't think so," he said.

"Bob, I understand how you feel."

"No you don't."

"Okay," she conceded, "I don't. But I can imagine. And one thing I imagine is, if I was you, I'd want my side of this told. How will it look in the paper tomorrow if they blame all of it on you and the only thing we have from you is a no comment?"

Bob pondered this. Part of him—the greater part, truth be told—simply didn't care if they blamed it on him. But he was self-aware enough to realize he was still in shock over everything that had happened. He might change his mind, might care a great deal, once the numbness passed.

What finally decided him, though, was the fact that, at the end of the day, Bob Carson was a newsman. He believed stories should be told as fully as possible so that people could understand how a given thing had happened and why. Was he really going to impede the telling of this one story out of pique?

Bob's surrender came in a sigh. "I can't talk now," he said. "Like I told you: I've got a lunch date."

"Later, then?" Her voice lifted again. She knew she had him.

He looked at his watch. "2:00," he said. "I'll meet you back here."

"2:00," she said. "Great."

He stepped out the door and pulled it shut. "What about your stuff?" asked Amy. "I wasn't kidding. I do have it."

"It'll keep," he told her. "Bring it back with you."

"Okay," she said. "I'll see you then." She turned to go.

He stepped off his porch behind her, glanced again at his watch, had a thought. "You know what?" he said. "Make it three. I almost forgot: Toussaint hasn't been taking my calls. I intend to go to his place and have it out with him. I'll bet I feel a whole lot better once I've wrapped my fingers around his throat." A bitter laugh gurgled up out of him like brown water from a rusted tap. "Who knows? Maybe the interview will be a murder confession."

He winced as he heard himself, wondering how Amy would react to an attempt at humor that was in such flagrantly bad taste. But then he realized, somewhat to his own surprise, that he wasn't sure he didn't mean it. That scared him. Bob had never been as angry as he was now.

Amy turned back toward him, but he saw immediately that he need not have worried; she had barely registered what he said. She was frowning. "Oh," she said, "I guess that's right. There's no way you could've known yet. Malcolm is missing."

"Yeah, I do know," said Bob, stopping short. "He's been ducking my calls all morning. Not that I blame the jerk. I'd my turn my cellphone off, too, if I'd done what he did."

She shook her head. "No," she said, "he's not ducking phone calls. He's *missing*, as in nobody knows where he is. Police found his car abandoned this morning at Randolph and LaSalle. It had been in an accident. Totaled."

"So? He probably went to the hospital."

"They checked the hospitals," she said. "They even went to his house. It was empty."

"So what, then? Somebody took him?"

Amy shrugged.

"That doesn't make any sense. Was it because of the thing in the paper this morning? Somebody got angry at him?"

"Maybe," said Amy, "but it doesn't seem very likely, does it? The accident happened maybe an hour after the paper hit the streets. The timeline doesn't work."

"Maybe somebody saw it online."

"Could be," said Amy, not bothering to hide her skepticism. "Still far-fetched."

"Yeah," said Bob, "it is."

There was a moment. Then Amy looked at her watch. "So, 2:00, then?"

"Yeah," said Bob. "I guess I'll see you at two."

With a nod, she went to her car. Bob went to his, but he didn't start it. Instead, he sat behind the wheel for a long moment, index finger pressed to his lip. After a moment Amy pulled past him, giving a good-natured tap on the horn. He automatically beeped in return, but he barely saw or heard her. There was so much to think about, Bob didn't even know where to start.

Suddenly, the thing that had consumed him for the last few hours seemed of secondary importance. His fury, his sense of having been done wrong, his need for an accounting felt...dulled.

What had happened to Malcolm? He could think of no explanation that seemed logical, no story that satisfied every question. It simply made no sense. How could you just total your car and then disappear? Was this some crazy attempt by Malcolm to fake his own death? No. That was stupid.

But then...what?

Bob started the Camry. He waited until a red Ford pick-up truck had lumbered past him, then pulled out.

And Lord, what about Janeka? There was that to think about, too. What with Amy showing up at his door like that, he had almost forgotten. What would he say to her in—Bob glanced at his watch—45 minutes, when he saw her for the first time since 1968?

I thought I was your people, too.

Once again, the last thing he said to her—somewhat pathetically, he had always thought—came back to him. So how do you pick up the conversation after that, plus four decades? For perhaps the tenth time since he had impulsively responded to her email this morning, Bob found himself wishing he had just ignored it instead.

He had Googled her once, a few years ago, found that she was running a small public relations firm in San Francisco. There had been no picture and he had only read a little bit of her company profile. Looking her up that way had felt creepy and stalkerish. It had felt—and here was that word again—pathetic.

Bob had closed the web browser and admonished himself sternly never to go looking for her again. And because he was a man of great personal discipline, he never had, though he was periodically tempted to. But even with all that discipline, he had been unable to prevent her from drifting to the top of his mind more often than he would have liked—more often, he thought, than was probably healthy for him. And now, steering toward Michigan Avenue for the second time in five hours, his thoughts were simply dominated by her.

Her, and that moment in time they had once shared.

As Bob saw it, there had been two 1960s. The first was the early '60s, the hopeful '60s. That optimism had been tested, to be sure. Bombs had exploded in churches, police dogs had been loosed on children, and there had been growing unease about what US troops were doing in Southeast Asia. And then had come that bleak and rainy Friday in November, when Bob was sitting in fifth-period English and Principal Buddiger came over the P.A. sounding like he'd been crying and made the announcement that the

president had been killed in Dallas. In the awful silence that followed, Bob
Carson had looked to Tommy Zelnecker, who had looked to Freddie Logan,
who had looked to Cynthia Sheridan, who had looked back to Bob, because
who knew a president could be killed like some gas station pump jockey in
a holdup? And once you had this terrible and irrevocable new knowledge,
what were you supposed to do with it? His friends' eyes had been as empty
of answers, he supposed, as his own.

But hope had marked that era. At least, that was how that part of the
1960s had always felt to Bob. He was conscious that maybe, as it receded
into time and became history, as he himself became a man with more life
behind him than before him, he was guilty of idealizing those years.

Maybe.

But he couldn't help what he felt. And what he felt was that the early
1960s, that hopeful 1960s, had always managed to overcome grief, maybe
because it had little time for grief. That 1960s—that "New Frontier," as the
murdered young president had called it—had been about progress, about
marching through status quo, hateful stares, and unequal laws, marching
forward and keep on pushin' and people get ready and answers, my friend,
blowing in the wind, yeah yeah yeah.

Then the '60s had gotten angry. Those other '60s, the later '60s, were
not about marching forward, but fighting back. Segregation, determination,
demonstration, integration, aggravation, humiliation, obligation to the nation, they had exploded in a ball of confusion, riot, and rage that burned
halfway through the next decade. And the band played on.

The entirety of Bob's relationship with Janeka Lattimore had unfolded in the crease between those two '60s, in that pregnant moment as the
one was yielding to the other. They had known each other from the late
summer of 1967 to the first week of spring in 1968, a time before hope was
fully lost and fury truly won the day, yet you could still see fury coming,
like lightning in black clouds massed on a far horizon. "There's something
happening here," the singer sang, one eye on that horizon, "what it is ain't
exactly clear."

Of course, this was all visible to Bob only in hindsight. View-
ing it through that prism, he thought, recalling it through the lyrics of
once-troubling songs that had since become something called "classic"
rock, imposed upon those sprawling times a clarity and order that had not
been there back when he was living them. It framed it all as neatly as a

picture on a wall, and thus robbed it of fear, bafflement, immediacy, the smell of smoke. He surely hadn't been considering the niceties of musical and historical context back then. Indeed, in the moment, when then was now, the only thing visible to him, the only thing knowable or even worth knowing, was her, Janeka.

The memory gave him a private smile, sitting at a traffic light in Chicago on Election Day 2008, waiting to make a left turn. Does anyone ever love as completely, as ferociously, as they do when it's the first time, and they are young?

No, he told himself, they do not.

With three other volunteers—two black guys and a white girl—he had followed her out of that first meeting and into an intense burst of planning and strategizing, making up pamphlets, researching voting laws, testing and retesting their arguments. They spent hours role-playing how they would remain nonviolent in the face of white intimidation and provocation. Janeka always played the part of the white Southern sheriff, and despite having been born and raised in San Diego, she acted the role with gusto, leaning in close, invading your space, yelling and cursing at you.

Janeka

(smacking Bob upside the head)

What's a nice white boy like you doing hanging around with trash like this? What are you, some kind of goddamn nigger lover?

Bob

I try to love all people, sir, as Christ commanded. Even you.

Janeka

(smacking Bob again, harder this time)

Are you getting smart with me, goddamn nigger lover?

Bob loved every second of it. He probably loved it too much. His grades suffered. Alarmed professors pulled him aside to warn him of the catastrophe he faced if he didn't pull himself together. Bob hardly heard them. Bob hardly cared. He was immersed in this. In her. As far as he was concerned, there was no difference between the two.

It had occurred to him more than once in later years that, had he and Janeka stayed together, he might never have graduated college.

But of course, they had not stayed together.

He'd had no idea that moment was coming, that it would broadside him like an 18-wheeler. To this day, he couldn't say if knowing would have changed anything he did.

"I was thinking, we've been working really hard and maybe, I don't know, you'd like to go into town, maybe catch a movie Sunday after chapel? Maybe get something to eat?"

This was Bob, the same day she slapped his head and called him "nigger lover," trying to keep an odd, fluty sound out of his voice as he asked her the question he had rehearsed til three that morning in his dorm room mirror. He had lingered in the student union basement while the others filed out of the meeting, hoping to catch her alone.

"A movie?" she said, and the tone of her voice was as if something so frivolous were beneath the dignity of the serious work they were doing. But Bob had been ready for this.

"Yeah," he said. "*In the Heat of the Night* is playing over in Buford."

She looked up at him with interest. The new drama starred Sidney Poitier as a Northern cop who ends up tangled in a murder investigation in some backwater Mississippi town. It was said to be a dangerously provocative film and that Mississippi didn't come off well in it. There was even rumored to be a scene in the film where Poitier's cop knocked the heck out of some white man.

"I'm surprised they're letting that show anywhere in the state," she said. "Especially in some little town out in the boonies."

"So am I," said Bob. "Probably won't be there for long."

"Are you sure you can get tickets?"

Bob nodded. "I'm friends with the assistant manager," he said. "He owes me a favor. I helped him pass his English exam."

"But what about…" She left the question unvoiced, her index finger flicking from her chest to his.

It took him a moment to get it and he was embarrassed when he did. "The race thing?" he said. "Don't worry about that."

"Bob, that's easy for you to say. You're white."

His embarrassment deepened and he felt the flush rising in his cheeks. She was right He was naïve. He hadn't thought about it. This was the state where they had killed those voting rights workers just a couple years ago. This was where they had lynched Emmett Till. Bob was white, and wary as he was of Mississippi, he hadn't learned to think about that kind of stuff all the time, to take it into account in deciding what he could or could not do. So now, Bob improvised.

"You're right," he said. "I'm sorry. But hey, the theater is in a Negro neighborhood. We'll probably be okay."

"Probably," she said. It wasn't quite agreement, wasn't quite a question.

Bob pushed on, committed now. "I don't think they'll care," he said. "I don't think they'll bother us. Black people aren't like that."

She arched an eyebrow at that and he saw, to his horror, the ghost of a smile on her face. "They're not?" she said.

"No," he assured her, with far less confidence than he'd felt just seconds before. "And if we see any white people—"

She cut him off. "If we see any white people, they'll think you're just some rich white boy sowing his wild oats with a colored gal the way rich white boys always have."

He had intended to say they wouldn't try to start something in a Negro neighborhood. But Janeka, he realized, was probably right. "Yeah," he said, his voice edged with resignation and chagrin. "Yeah, they probably will."

A silence intervened. Bob sighed. "Look, Janeka," he began.

She looked at him. That look almost dared him to go on. But he did.

"I like you, okay? I'd like to get to know you better. As for the black-white thing, well…you're right. I didn't think it through. But I have to tell you: what is it we're fighting for here, why are we doing all the planning and strategizing, why am I letting you hit me upside the head and call me a you-know-what lover if it's not to create a world where a white guy can invite a black girl to the movies and it's no big deal? And besides that, the

Supreme Court just said it's okay, so who are any of these...these...*honkies* to say it isn't?"

She gave him an amused look, but didn't speak. Bob plowed a hand through his hair in frustration. "Look, I know it's frightening. I get that. Maybe it's even a risk. But maybe we've got to step out on faith, you know? Maybe we've got to live in it before it's real in order to make it real. Anyway, that's what I think."

He fell silent then, acutely aware of having blabbered too long and said too much. What had come over him? Where, he wondered, had this sudden and uncharacteristic boldness come from?

I like you? I'd like to get to know you better? Jesus, give me strength.

Then he realized she was smiling at him and he felt the awesome and exquisite pain of ice cracking in his chest.

"I like you too, Bob," she said. "And you're right. Let's go to the movies."

They went to the movies. They drove the '65 Corvair his father had given him. The movie was as riveting and provocative as advertised, down to the scene where Sidney Poitier's Virgil Tibbs slapped Endicott, the powerful white businessman, after Endicott had slapped him first. Though he knew the scene was coming, it still made Bob gasp in shock, though all the Negroes in the audience, including Janeka, sitting next to him, chuckled at it.

The theater was in a Negro neighborhood, as he had been told, but there were still whites in the audience—more than Bob would have imagined. They had to see it, he supposed, for the same reason an Army general seeks intelligence on enemy troop movements. Or maybe he was being unfair. Maybe they were simply curious. Maybe they had simply gone to this movie for the same reason anyone ever does—to be entertained.

That thought died when the film ended, the lights came up, and he and Janeka walked out together. White people stared after them. Negroes did, too. They didn't bother to hide it. A matronly woman with dark skin and a purse held protectively at her bosom watched them with eyes that held their judgments secret. A white man, his hair piled in satiny white drifts, ran his eyes up and down Janeka, a knowing smirk playing at the corners of his mouth. Some young white guy with a brush cut, holding hands with a stringy-looking blonde, turned his head after them, his whole face stony with some unspoken rebuke. A young black woman smiled a friendly smile.

Bob felt the touch of all those eyes on him as they passed. Janeka must have felt it, too. "Got to live in it to make it real," she reminded him in a whisper.

"Yeah," said Bob. "Wonder what fool said that?"

She smiled and did not reply.

They chose not to eat at the diner in town. This decision was made without either of them speaking it or even needing to speak it. They both simply knew. So they got into Bob's car and drove. As they reached the edge of town, passing a little church with a Negro cemetery in the back, headlights appeared in the rearview mirror. Without meaning to, Bob caught his breath and held it tight, old headlines of brazen racial murder looming up in his thoughts.

He did not breathe again until the headlights were right behind him and he realized the vehicle was a delivery truck. The rush of air when he inhaled again almost made him dizzy as the truck, with its Hamm's beer logo on the side, swept into the oncoming traffic lane and roared past, the little Corvair rocking a little in its wake.

"You okay there?" asked Janeka.

Bob's grin felt unsteady, as if it seesawed on his face. "Yeah," he said. "For a minute there, I just thought—"

"Yeah," she said, "I know. Me too."

He looked over at her. They both laughed.

"Well, other than that," he said, "how did you like the movie?"

"I loved the movie," she said. "Thank you for inviting me."

They laughed again and the silence that fell then felt companionable as the car raced along the darkened road through the fields and trees of the Delta. Half an hour later, they passed through the front gates of their campus, and a few moments after that, they pulled up in front of the girl's dorm. Bob had been rehearsing this moment in his mind all day. He would go around and open her door for her, of course, but then there was the big question: to kiss, not to kiss, what to say, how to say it.

He turned toward her now, still not knowing what he would do. And Janeka shocked him. She placed her hand over his and kissed him on the lips—or at least, very near the lips—a quick peck that was over before he even knew it was happening, then bounced out of the passenger's side door while he was still fumbling to register that the kiss had actually happened.

"Thanks again for the movie," she said now, leaning through the passenger side window. "I had a great time." Pause. "You want to have lunch together tomorrow? Say at noon in the cafeteria?"

"Sure, that sounds great. I'll see you then."

Or at least, this was what Bob wanted to say, in an easy, carefree voice. But he realized to his horror that he no longer had a voice, easy, carefree, or otherwise, because his throat had constricted to a tunnel the approximate circumference of a pinhead from which no intelligible sound had a prayer of escape. So he nodded instead—vigorously. He nodded as if nodding were a power source, as if his head were a pump handle in the desert, as if he got paid by the nod.

And she gave him a dubious look, then a dubious smile, then said, dubiously, "Well, okay, I'll see you tomorrow."

He waited until she had opened the door of her dorm building. She waved. He waved. He started the car. It floated him home.

Forty years later, the memory was still good for a smile as Bob drove past Stymie's Steakhouse on Michigan Avenue and began looking for a place to park.

Fifteen blocks north on the same street, Amy Landingham pulled into a parking slot in the garage beneath the *Chicago Post* building. She climbed out of the van—her "mommy bus," girlfriends called it when they made fun of her for being 27 years old and already having two kids. Amy beeped the lock, feeling rather pleased with herself.

Mission accomplished. She had gotten the interview. Or at least, the promise of an interview. She would go upstairs now and get the cops out of the way, spend half an hour repeating the particulars of a 30-second encounter until they finally realized she knew nothing of value, then hop in the van and zip back out to Bob's. Maybe, if the cops didn't detain her too long, she'd have time to interview Lydia and Doug before she left. The more reporting she got out of the way now, the more time she'd have to massage the piece tonight before the desk started screaming for copy.

This was an important story—and Bob was right, it was a great opportunity for her, too. She wanted to get it right.

Amy was 27. She knew that logically, she should be strategizing a transition into television news—or better yet, the Internet. That's where the future was, and everybody knew it. When people her age found out what she did, they tended to look at her the way you would a two-headed calf. The old heads in the newsroom called people like her "true believers," meaning Gen Y kids who somehow missed the memo that a thing was not worth doing unless it was done digitally. The term was not uttered without fondness.

Sometimes, she wondered if she were not really a 58-year-old reincarnated inside a 20-something body, but Amy couldn't help herself. She loved print. She also loved black and white movies with Henry Fonda and Bette Davis and vinyl record albums by Marvin Gaye and the Beatles.

Humming a little, at peace with the world and her place and prospects in it, Amy moved away from the van—and got hit by a speeding bus. At least, that was how it felt. Something hard and heavy came from the left and smashed into her jaw. Her glasses flew off her face. She went down hard, too stunned even to brace her fall. Her head banged off the concrete.

The pain was unimaginable, ferocious. Amy held her jaw with one hand. That whole left side of her face felt crooked, felt...misaligned. She would have sworn her bottom teeth were where her uppers should have been. And her mouth was filled with the coppery warmth of her own blood. Amy writhed on the concrete, eyes squeezed tight, trying to scream, but unable to get her mouth to work. The best she could manage was an outraged growl that rumbled deep down in her throat.

Then, she felt a hand reaching into her jacket pocket.

Amy's eyes came open. It was the guy, the weird-looking guy with the dopey haircut who had been in the lobby. She grabbed his arm, buried up to the wrist in her pocket. He swatted her hand.

"If you'd done what I told you to do, bitch, none of this would have happened. I was watching you. You didn't give it to him."

She tried to tell him she was going back to see Bob this afternoon, but she still could not get her mouth to work. Somehow, her teeth were in the way of her tongue and the sounds she produced were unintelligible.

The man pulled his arm from her pocket, the computer disc in his hand. He regarded her with a sneer. "Could have saved yourself some trouble," he said. And he turned to walk out of the garage.

Something happened to Amy Landingham then. Something got into her. It simply infuriated her that this skinny, scabrous *nobody* with his doofus haircut and glassy eyes had sucker punched her, had put her down and then had the unmitigated gall to lecture her while he violated her person searching for some stupid DVD. Something got into her. She didn't know its name, but in that instant, it drove out pain, drove out weakness, drove out fear.

Amy Landingham, all of 5'3" tall and 125 pounds, rolled to her feet, came up with fists clenched, and went after the man who had hit her.

He heard her coming. He whirled around, his eyes bulging. "You get back now! You get away! Don't make me hurt you!"

He was sidestepping back from her, one palm up, retreating as if from a snapping dog. His other hand lifted his windbreaker and Amy saw the butt of a pistol in his waistband. He reached for it, but mishandled it in his panic. The gun slipped into his pants and he chased after it, plunging his arm into his crotch up to the elbow. But the gun would not be had. He lifted a pant leg and shook it. A moment later, the pistol clattered onto the concrete.

Amy had stopped. She had been too amazed to move. Now, as the man reached down for his weapon, she closed the distance between them. She hit him with a solid punch to the jaw that tore skin from her knuckles and radiated agony all the way up to her shoulder and caused her to realize, distractedly, that hitting people was a whole lot more painful than it looked in the movies. But the blow had the desired effect. It put the man on his back pocket. He cradled his jaw in his right hand and gave her those bulging eyes again.

"Fuck this," he said. "You are one crazy fuckin' bitch!"

He scrambled backwards then, found his feet, and took off running. Amy chased after him. Through the garage they went, past Chevys and Toyotas, up the driveway, out into the pale sunlight of a midday in November, the small woman chasing the panicked man.

And that's when whatever had gotten into Amy suddenly went out of her. That's when reality finally caught up with her. As they reached the sidewalk, her steps slowed, then stopped. She wobbled, then had to lean against a lamppost for support. The world seesawed about her. Nausea bubbled in her esophagus and she was afraid she might retch. A dull, heavy pain throbbed her skull.

"Miss, are you all right?"

"Lady, do you need some help?"

"Look at her, she's been hurt!"

The voices came from all around. She tried to answer them, but she couldn't. She saw that the skinny nobody was running away from her, getting away through the crowd, and she wanted to scream for somebody to stop him, but she couldn't do that either.

The world went gray, then black. Her legs turned to air. The last thing she felt was some stranger's hands, lowering her gently to the concrete.

eleven

Pym stood slowly. The body lay crumpled at his feet like dirty laundry.

"You killed him." Malcolm could not suck in enough breath. "You crazy bastard, you killed him."

Pym's chest heaved like a bellows. His eyes jittered and glittered in their sockets. He looked around and seemed not to know where he was. Finally, when they had gone everywhere else they could go, his eyes fell upon the disheveled heap at his feet and he stared hard as if waiting for it to move, as if willing it to do so. There was a long moment.

Then he said, "Didn't mean to do that. Sorry. Didn't mean to do that." The words were spoken in a mumble so soft, Malcolm could barely hear. He couldn't tell whether the big man was apologizing to him or the corpse.

There was a long moment. Finally, with dull resignation, Pym reached down, clutched the collar of the dead man's ratty green jacket and, head bowed, dragged him off. The only sounds in the world were the thin scratch of voices from the laptop computer streaming cable news and the lonely rasp of the dead body sliding across the floor, pulled into a dark corner to repose out of sight.

After a moment, Pym wobbled back on unsteady legs. He landed heavily in the metal folding chair, which bowed with his weight, reached into the Styrofoam ice chest, and came out with a beer can. He held it against the side of his face.

"You killed him," said Malcolm, again. His throat was full of hot glue. His eyes burned.

Pym didn't look at him. "Stop saying that," he said. His voice seemed to issue from a deep cave.

"You killed him," said Malcolm, defiant.

The giant shook his head slowly, wincing at the pain. "You should have told me he was behind me," he said.

And that was amazing enough that Malcolm fell silent.

"God, this hurts," said Pym. Voices still chirped from the laptop. He slammed it closed. "God, it hurts," he moaned again.

He pulled the beer can away from his face. The scar was livid and dripping blood. It ran in a ragged line from temple to jawline on the left side of his face. The toilet tank lid had gotten him good. "How bad is it?" Pym asked. "Probably need stitches, huh?"

Malcolm stared at him. He did not respond. He felt a tear trickling on his cheek. The little homeless man had proven so valiant at the end. He wished he knew the man's name.

"Dwayne's going to be so mad at me," continued Pym. "He's going to be so mad. And my head hurts like a son of a bitch, too. Little bastard cracked me good."

Malcolm gave him more silence.

"First time I ever killed anybody," said Pym. "Always knew I'd kill somebody someday, though. Was always scared of that."

And this, finally, was too much. "Scared of it?" Malcom cried. "Scared of it? You just said you plan on killing Obama and probably thousands of other people in Grant Park tonight. How in the hell are you 'scared' of killing someone?"

The giant shook his shaggy head and paid for it with a bolt of pain that screwed his eyes shut. "Not talking about that kind of killing," he said through a wince of agony. "I mean killing with these." He lifted his great hands, one of them still holding the beer he was using as an icepack. "Always knew I'd kill somebody with these," he said. "They used to always tell me to watch myself, watch my temper, 'cause on account of my size, I could hurt someone if I lost my temper. And I always did real good with that, until now."

He rested the beer against his temple again and repeated himself. "You should have told me he was coming."

"Are you crazy? Why would I do that? Why would I help you?"

Pym looked up. His expression was that of a lost child. "I didn't mean to kill him. I swear I didn't. I just lost my temper."

Malcolm met his eyes. "Yeah? Well, you did kill him," he said. His voice was cold and bleak. "You're going to kill a lot more people if you keep this madness up. You have to end this. You have to let me go."

Pym appeared to consider this for a moment and Malcolm was foolish enough to hope. Then Pym said, "No, can't do that. Dwayne wouldn't like that. Him and me, we made a promise to each other, to take our country back. You know, from the niggers and the fags and all. We swore an oath to see this thing through."

"Let me go!" demanded Malcolm.

"Can't," said Pym. "But it'll be okay. I won't lose my temper anymore."

"Fuck your temper!" roared Malcolm.

"Wish I could," Pym said after a pause, "all the times my temper has fucked me. Kids giving me shit, calling me fat retard and stuff, and I'd pound 'em good. But every time I done that, it just made matters worse. Get suspended and go home and have to tell the folks what I done. My old man'd get so mad he'd get that stick of his and go upside me every kind of way. Man, was I glad when he walked out on us."

Pym laughed. It was a rueful sound.

"Let me go," said Malcolm. His tears were falling freely now. The realization shamed him.

Pym regarded him thoughtfully for a moment. "Can't," he finally said. "We're in too deep now. There's no way to turn back."

"There's always a way to do what needs to be done. Didn't Jordan show us that? Remember the flu game? Nineteen ninety..." Malcolm racked his brain frantically. "*Six*," he said. "Nineteen ninety-six. They're down by 16 and they're on the road and Jordan is half dead with the flu, but he brings them back. He scores 38 points, shoots 48 percent. Remember that?"

Malcolm fell silent when he saw the pity in the big man's smile. "Nineteen ninety-*seven*," he corrected. "June 11, 1997, Game 5, in the Finals against the Jazz." Pym paused again, then turned away. "But this ain't a basketball game, is it?"

"Let me go," said Malcolm again.

Pym ignored him. "You want to know how we're going to do it? Dwayne said not to tell you til the end, but what the hell—I've told you this much. You might as well know the rest. Just don't tell him I told you."

He reached over for the backpack, rummaged in it for a moment and brought out a first-aid kit, a white plastic box with a red cross on the top. "So anyway, you want to know how?"

To his surprise, Malcolm felt himself nodding dumbly.

"We're going to do it like McVeigh," said Pym, "on account of Dwayne really loves that guy." He pulled out a pad of cotton gauze, used it to shield his eyes, and then with his free hand, groped for a can of over-the-counter antiseptic. He sprayed the wound on the side of his head. "Ouch. Shit! Fuck!" he hissed.

"McVeigh?" prompted Malcolm.

"Yeah. Only we're going to do it with style," said Pym. "Dwayne's real big on that, doing things with style. So we've got the van armored, you see? Like Clint Eastwood did in that old movie from the '70s. Spent all day yesterday welding the armor plate on.

"Then, of course, there's the bomb." A nod toward the metal drums near the door. Malcolm's gaze followed him, disbelieving. Pym grinned. "We built a good one," he said, "but I don't mind telling you, that thing was a bitch to put together, what with mixing all those chemicals: nitromethane and ammonium nitrate fertilizer and what have you. I kept messing up—I never was good with science—but Dwayne, he was real patient with me."

He used scissors—ridiculously dainty in his hands—to cut the gauze into two rectangular strips. "We're going to ram through the barricades, and they're not going to be able to stop us. Get as close to the stage as we can. Then we fall out of the van shooting and yelling, 'White Power' and like that. And the fuse goes off and this fertilizer bomb like the one McVeigh used in Oklahoma City blows up behind us. Like I say, we'll probably get killed, but what a way to go, huh? And if we're lucky, it'll take ol' Hussein Obama with us."

"You're crazy," said Malcolm.

This brought a wry look. "Yeah, we expect a lot of people to say that, especially the left-wing media elites. But the right people, they'll understand what we're trying to say. And they'll pick up after us. You'll see. And you know the cool part?"

Malcolm just stared at him. Pym laughed. "I'll show you," he said, putting the gauze aside. With a grunt, he lifted himself to his feet and lumbered off, the side of his face shiny with a smear of antiseptic and blood. A minute later, Pym returned, grinning and lifting high a garment sheathed in a clear plastic bag. It was so big and so blindingly white it could have been a bed sheet.

Then Malcolm registered what he was looking at. Pym's grin broadened. "That's right," he said. "White tie and tails. That's how we're going to be dressed. Both of us. Had to have mine tailored special on account of my size. Cost a shitload, but like Dwayne said, you only die once. And check this out."

Pym had been holding something hidden behind him. Now he whipped the hand from behind his back to reveal a snowy white top hat, which he plopped atop his Dennis the Menace cowlick. He patted the top of the hat, which sat at a jaunty angle above his broad face. It struck Malcolm that if he lived another 50 years, he would never see a more ridiculous sight.

But Pym was pleased. "Going out in style," he told Malcolm. "That Dwayne believes in doing things with style." He looked down at his watch then and sudden concern creased his smile. "You know, he should have been back by now. Hope he hasn't run into trouble."

"What about me?" Malcolm heard himself ask. His throat felt dry. The words croaked out of him.

The great head came up. "Say what?"

Malcolm swallowed. "I said, what about me? What's my part in this crazy scheme of yours?"

"You?" Pym grinned. "You'll be with us in the park."

"I'll be in the van?"

Pym shook his head. "You'll be *on* the van," he corrected.

Malcolm was not sure he had heard. "On it?"

Pym bobbed his head. His grin was boyish. "Oh yeah," he said. "Chained right on the front, like a hood ornament."

Something swept over Malcolm at that, a sense that he was not here and this was not real. Could not be real. The room seemed to tumble about him. He felt a nausea so strong he thought he might vomit.

Pym didn't notice. He checked his watch again, muttering to himself. "I wonder where the hell Dwayne is."

Dwayne was running pell-mell, south on Michigan Avenue, trying to put as much distance between himself and that woman as he could. He finally stopped four blocks later, on the bridge crossing the river. Only then did he realize people were staring.

"Take a picture," he told some old lady. "It'll last longer."

She put her nose in the air and turned away from him like something dirty. He hardly noticed, too busy looking over his shoulder to make sure that woman wasn't coming. He hoped he had gotten away from the crazy bitch—he was pretty sure he had—but even if he hadn't, he could not go another step. A thick, ropy ache had settled itself into his legs and made them useless. He doubled over now, hands gripping his knees, a line of spittle dripping from his mouth, cursing her over and over again in his mind.

Stupid, crazy-ass *bitch!*

Dwayne's jaw still ached from where she had socked him with that bony little fist. How in the hell was she able to get up and slug him like that after he had knocked her down? Man, was he out of shape. Look at him, chest heaving, legs quivering like a Jell-O factory in an earthquake, and all he had done was run four blocks. Four fucking blocks! And the worst part was, he was running from some stupid cunt who by rights should still be lying on a parking garage floor wondering what hit her. Instead, she had gotten to her feet and chased him. *Him.* And he had panicked and run like some little girl and even left his grandfather's Luger behind.

Damn. He loved that gun.

Dwayne thought briefly of going back to get it; it would have his fingerprints on it, after all, and probably some DNA, too, and the cops could use it to do some CSI shit and identify him. Besides that, it was worth a whole lot of money, an heirloom like that. But going back would be crazy. That garage would soon be lousy with cops. And even if they figured out who he was, there was probably no way they could find him in time. Besides, he could hardly walk. In fact, he thought he might be sick. He lowered his head until it almost touched his knees, nausea bubbling like some witch's cauldron in his gut.

Forgetting for a moment that he did not expect to be alive after tonight, Dwayne Ray McLarty made himself a solemn promise. He was going to get his ass to a gym. He was going to get back in shape.

"You okay there, bud?"

Dwayne glanced up. Some citizen was standing over him, some clean cut, clear-eyed guy had laid a consoling hand on Dwayne's back and was gazing down with concern. Dwayne snarled at him. "Fuck..." it took a moment to gather sufficient breath "...off."

The guy's eyes sharpened. "Well," he said, "you just looked sick is all."

He waited—for an apology, Dwayne supposed. When he saw that none was forthcoming, his nose went up and his back went stiff. And he went storming away.

Fucking priss, thought Dwayne. Too bad he had lost his grandfather's Luger. He'd love to shoot that guy right in his tight ass.

After a moment, the nausea passed and Dwayne was able to unbend. He clung to the railing. A tour boat was passing below—one of the last of the season before the cold would clamp down on this city and nobody with any sense would want to be outside, much less near the water. The deck was crowded with asshole tourists who had paid almost $30 apiece to look at buildings they could see for free and listen to some asshole tour guide's corny spiel. The tourists were bristling with cameras—cellphones, point and clicks, Canons and Nikons with foot-long lenses.

In fact, he realized, some orange-haired woman was pointing one of those long lenses right at him. Dwayne gave her the finger, bobbing his hand for emphasis. She lowered the camera, looking shocked. Then she gave him the finger in return. But that wasn't enough. She tapped the man next to her and pointed. The man—black hair, thick black moustache and built solid as a load-bearing column—scowled up at him. So Dwayne gave *him* the finger—and grinned.

Fuck him. Fuck *everybody*. Dwayne was in a mood.

He tried to think what he should do, now that he had the disc. He didn't want to just return to the warehouse without accomplishing his mission. Obviously, there was no way he could walk it back down to the jewspaper. But what about that editor guy? Even if he no longer worked there, he could probably still get into the building, couldn't he? And he probably knew who to take the disc to. All he needed was the right incentive.

That was the smart move, then. Dwayne would go back to the editor guy's house. Sitting across the street in the stolen pickup, eyes and ears straining, Dwayne had heard him yell to the crazy bitch that he would be back by two. So Dwayne would meet him there and somehow get him to take the disc to the jewspaper.

But that meant Dwayne would need a new gun, in order to convince the editor guy to do what Dwayne wanted him to. Luckily, he knew exactly where to find one.

His course settled, Dwayne's mood improved. He stood straight. His legs felt almost like legs again, his lungs no longer flamed. This clusterfuck could be fixed. He was convinced of that. Secure in that conviction, he headed north, back in the direction he had come.

Ten minutes later he reached the stolen truck, which was illegally parked on a side street right across from the newspaper. Dwayne snatched the parking ticket from beneath the wiper blade, crumpled it in his fist and threw it on the floor between the two front seats. He climbed in, started the engine, and took off. He was headed home.

He hated going home.

Dwayne's mother, the former Edith Hinkley, still lived in the house where he'd grown up, a brick bungalow where the front yard was largely dirt and there was an oil stain on the street from a car she had once owned. He went there as little as possible. In fact, he hadn't been there, hadn't seen her, in almost three months, having spent most of that time crashing with Clarence, living off Clarence's disability check, as they laid their plans for today.

It wasn't like he didn't love her. He did. She just made him crazy, is all. Still, she was his mother.

So it was with a sigh of resignation that Dwayne pulled up to the house, parking over the oil spot. He checked his hair in the mirror and was dismayed to see a little purple bruise blooming near his mouth where the crazy bitch had clocked him. It made him shake his head. How could such a small woman hit so hard? Maybe she took some kind of karate class or something. Maybe she was even a black belt.

Dwayne liked that thought. He decided to believe it. It made him feel less like a wuss.

He fished his keys from his pocket as he climbed out of the truck, unlocked the accordion security gate that guarded his mother's door, then unlocked the door itself. Some little kid pedaling a Big Wheel paused on the sidewalk to watch. "What are you lookin' at?" demanded Dwayne over his shoulder. Then he saw the girl's mother, walking about six feet behind her, staring at him angrily. Dwayne darted inside. He'd had enough of crazy bitches for one day.

Daryl was sitting on the couch watching ESPN and spooning Fudgy O's—a cheaper, store-brand knockoff of Cocoa Puffs—into his face. He'd been sitting in the same spot doing the same thing the last time Dwayne had seen him. Now Daryl glanced up. "Well, well," he said. "Nice of you to drop by."

"Fuck you," said Dwayne.

Daryl and Dwayne were fraternal twins. As far as Dwayne was concerned, this meant they were twins who hated each other.

You always saw this stuff on TV about how real twins shared everything, how they looked alike and talked alike and confided in each other and finished each other's sentences. But Daryl could not have been less like Dwayne. Fat and already balding at 27, dumb as a bag of hammers, he worked some loser job at a gas station at $11 an hour, 35 hours a week. They had an older brother, Earl. He was doing time in Stateville for armed robbery. They also had a younger sister, Karen. She had gone off to college in Rhode Island and never returned, though they got cards from her every year at Christmas and on Ma's birthday. A large portrait of Karen, blonde, pretty, and resplendent in her blue cap and gown, dominated the room from the wall above the mantel. Dwayne walked beneath it on his way to the kitchen.

"Denise has been by here a couple times," called Daryl. "Says you promised to have some money for her."

Denise was the mother of Dwayne's two kids and a first-class cunt. "Fuck her," said Dwayne, pulling a beer out of the refrigerator.

Daryl's chuckle was full of scorn. "You already did, you dumb bastard. That's why she's after you."

The amusement left Daryl's face when Dwayne came back into the room, holding a bottle of beer. "Hey," he said, "you don't put nothin' in the fridge, you don't take nothin' out of it."

Dwayne took a long, deliberate pull off the beer. "Fuck you," he said again.

His brother shook his head. "You already said that. You have a very limited vocabulary, you know that?"

Dwayne nodded toward the back of the house. "She in there?"

"Where else she going to be?"

"How she doing?"

This brought a shrug. "Same, I guess. Doctor says it won't be long now."

"What the hell do they know?"

"They know," said Daryl. "You would, too, if you were ever around. You should stay in closer touch. She asks about you."

Dwayne shifted his weight, tried to think of what to say, and came up with nothing. He took another pull off the beer instead.

Apparently done with the conversation, Dwayne's brother used the remote to raise the volume on the sports network, then spooned another helping of chocolate cereal into his mouth.

Thus dismissed, Dwayne nevertheless lingered a moment more, making a pretense of watching an interview with some hockey star. But he knew he couldn't put this off forever. Finally he drained the beer, set the bottle down hard on the counter that separated kitchen from living room, and went to see his mother.

The hallway was dark, but Dwayne still paused before a grouping of school pictures of him and his brothers hanging on the wall across from the bathroom. The symbolism, Dwayne had always felt, was explicit. The mantel was for Karen and her college picture. He and his brothers resided here in the shadows across from the toilet. Ma had never been particularly subtle.

For a moment, Dwayne stood face to face with his second-grade self, smiling a crooked, goofy smile that was missing three teeth. Like Daryl and Earl, he had failed to finish high school, so there were no graduation pictures. There never would be.

There were four doors in the hallway. Dwayne passed his own room without looking inside. Karen's was locked, but he knew without opening it that it was still maintained exactly as she had left it. No one was permitted to open that door except Ma, who went in sometimes to clean it or just to sit. His mother wanted the room to be there for her just as Karen remembered it in the event, increasingly unlikely though it was, that she ever decided to return home. Facing Karen's room was Daryl's room. Dwayne poked his head in. The walls were bare; the only furniture was a particleboard dresser, the pieces of which were slowly surrendering to gravity. Daryl slept on a mattress on the floor in a corner of the room. A copy of *Hustler* lay on the floor next to this makeshift bed, open to a picture of some dull-eyed babe fingering herself.

Dwayne withdrew his head, vaguely amused. Daryl always acted so superior, but look at this.

There was one door left at the very end of the hall. Dwayne took a moment to steel himself. He knocked on his mother's door, then pushed it slowly open and poked his head through. "Ma, it's me. It's Dwayne."

Edith Hinkley McLarty was sitting up in a tangle of sheets and blankets, with plastic tubing running from her nostrils to an ever-present tank of oxygen that rested on a little rolling handcart by the side of the bed. She'd been watching television, but she lifted her remote and brought the volume down at the sight of her son.

"Well," she said, "isn't this a pleasant surprise. The prodigal returns." She didn't smile.

"Hey, Ma." Dwayne crossed the room and gave her a hug. His mother had once been a robust woman. Now he feared to hold her too tightly. You could feel her bones moving beneath her thin nightshirt.

"Where have you been?" she asked as he drew back. "We were worried about you."

"Had stuff to do, Ma. That's all. You know I would have been here if I could." He knew she knew he was lying. But the way he figured, caring enough to lie about wanting to be there was almost as good as actually wanting to be there.

She said, "You got a cigarette, honey?"

"Ma, you know the doctors say you can't be smoking."

She made a derisive sound, turned her head. "Doctors," she said.

"If you want to get better, you need to listen to them," he told her.

She cut him with a grin. "Get better? Is that what you're expecting? Oh, you poor child."

"I'm just saying, Ma. You should never give up hope."

The grin took another slice. "You always were a little slow on the uptake, honey."

"Ma, come on. Don't be like that."

"Don't be like what? I'm dying, Dwayne. You'd have to be pretty damn dumb not to have figured that out."

"I'm not dumb. But miracles happen everyday, Ma."

His mother looked at him. "Miracles," she said. She pronounced the word the same dull way she'd said "doctors."

Dwayne shifted his weight. He wanted so badly to be out of there.

"Dwayne, you need to face reality. And reality is, shape I'm in, one cigarette is not going to make a whole lot of difference."

"Well, you still shouldn't be smoking. It's dangerous around the oxygen tank."

This time she laughed. "You're worse than that other one," she said, meaning Daryl. "He always says the same thing."

"Well we're just trying to look out for you, Ma."

"Yeah. You and your brothers, you been real good at that."

Dwayne was desperate to change the subject. "So, how you been, Ma?" He hated the words even as they came out of his mouth. What a stupid fucking question. *How you been?* Emphysema. That was how she had been.

Dwayne braced for her comeback. But she did him the favor of ignoring his question. "I got a call from Karen this morning," she said. "She's doing real good at work, just got a big raise. Says she thinks she's going to go ahead and get her master's degree. Of course, that'll keep her away from home a while longer, but it's probably worth it, don't you think?"

He wanted to scream at her.

She's not coming home, you stupid cow! Don't you get it? First chance she got, she ran as far away from you as she could without swimming. Didn't that give you a clue? She hates her whole fucking loser family and I can't say I blame her!

"Yeah," said Dwayne, and the words tasted like ashes on his tongue, "I think that's good for her. Get all the education she can."

"And then she'll come home, don't you think?"

Dwayne hated the hope he saw in her eyes, the way her voice lifted on the last words, reaching for assurance. He knew she had never in her life had that tone in her voice while asking about him. He swallowed. "What you watchin'?" he asked.

She sucked her teeth. "News," she said. "They keep interrupting my stories to talk about that damned election."

On the screen, Barack Obama, in shirtsleeves, was walking in a phalanx of Secret Service men, waving to a crowd that lavished him with cheers. His mother regarded the image for a moment, then said, "Looks like they're going to elect this guy."

"Yeah," said Dwayne, "looks like." He was relieved to see the conversation move to safer territory.

"Almost makes me glad I won't be here to see," said Ma. "He's going to mess this country up real bad."

"Ah, don't give up hope, Ma. For all you know, he won't ever become president."

"They say all the polls have him way ahead."

"Yeah," said Dwayne, and he felt something secret, delicious, and electric tingle through him, "but you never know what could happen."

She was still watching the screen. "Well, we better hope something does happen. Otherwise, this whole country is screwed."

After a moment, she turned back toward her son. "So where's the Incredible Hulk?" she asked.

This was her name for Clarence. How many times had he asked her to stop calling him that? "Ma, come on. He's got a name. He's got feelings, too."

"That elephant hide of his, I'd be surprised he could feel anything this side of a tranquilizer dart."

"Ma, stop it. You're being mean. I've told you before: he's got a condition."

"I just asked you where he was," she protested. "You two been thick as thieves lately. See one, you always see the other."

"Clarence is...busy. We're working on this project."

"I'll bet," she said.

"We are," he insisted.

"What kind of project could you two losers be working on?"

"I can't tell you, Ma. But you'll see."

"Oh, I will?" Her eyes sparkled with a merry malice that infuriated him.

"Why do you always do that?" he demanded.

"What?" she protested, the very soul of innocence. "What do I always do?"

"You always act like anything I do is shit."

"Well," she replied, "it isn't like there's a whole lot of reason to believe otherwise. Look at you. Your hair looks like somebody took garden shears to it, your mouth is all messed up from that crap you smoke. What else should I think, Dwayne? You tell me."

She glanced to a picture sitting on her nightstand in a cheap frame. A dark-haired, flinty-eyed man stared back, unsmiling. "I'm just glad your father didn't live to see," she said. Earl McLarty, Sr. had been killed holding up a gas station 11 years before.

"Ma." Dwayne was reduced to pleading. God, he hated coming here.

She was sniffling now, dabbing at her eyes with a crumpled piece of Kleenex. "We just had such high hopes for all our children," she said. "We thought you all would do such great things."

"You just wait, Ma. When you see what happens tonight, that's me. It's me and Clarence. You remember I said that, hear? When you see what happens, you remember, okay?"

He waited for her response. Needed it. Finally, she looked around from the picture of his sainted father, the dead stickup man. "I have to pee," she said, still sniffling. "Help me out of this bed, would you?"

Dwayne felt himself deflate, the air going out of him like a blow-up toy with a slow leak. "Sure, Ma," he said.

He took the hand she proffered. It was weightless. With his free hand, he braced her arm and she climbed gingerly down from the bed. She seemed unsteady on her feet and he moved to walk her to her bathroom, but she swatted his hand. "I've got it," she snapped as he pulled his hand away.

Ma grabbed the handcart with the oxygen tank on it. "Me and my shadow," she muttered as she trundled across the room. Then the bathroom door closed behind her with finality.

It was, Dwayne suddenly realized, a blessing in disguise. He had meant to ask her for the use of her pistol. But how could he have done that now, after going on and on about his big project with Clarence? She would have been suspicious. She would have asked questions he could not answer.

No, he realized, it was better this way. Now all he had to do was steal the gun.

The decision made, Dwayne crossed to the other side of the room. He opened the top drawer of the nightstand and there it was, right where she always kept it, the pistol his father had given his mother one Christmas many years ago.

It was, Dwayne had always thought, a ridiculous gun. For one thing, it was a .22, which meant that if you shot somebody with it, you were as likely to piss him off as to do any damage. Even worse, it was pink. Every visible surface—the grip, the slide, the trigger guard, the trigger, and the barrel—were the color of a Barbie Corvette. Also the color of Pepto-Bismol, which Dwayne felt was probably fitting, since the idea of carrying this damn thing around made him sick to his stomach. Instead of scaring somebody, this gun might make them fall over laughing.

But any port in a storm, he reassured himself. Whatever it looked like, it was a gun. It would shoot and it would kill. And that's all it needed to do.

Dwayne plucked the weapon out of the drawer and checked the magazine. As he had expected, it was fully loaded.

"An unloaded gun," his father had always preached to his family, "is like tits on a bull. It's interesting to look at, but it don't do you a damn bit of good."

Dwayne shoved the gun into his pocket. Now that he had what he had come for, he couldn't wait to be out of there. One more minute with Ma, he was sure, and he would be ready for the funny farm.

He came back around the bed, leaned close to the bathroom door. "Ma," he called, "listen, I'm going to take off. I've um...got an appointment I've got to get to. So um...I'll see you later, okay?"

She didn't answer. Ordinarily, Dwayne would have been happy to take that silence as a victory and get the hell out of there as fast as he could. But as he moved toward the hallway, it struck him: this was probably the last time he would ever see her, these were the last words she would ever hear from him. That deserved to be marked somehow, didn't it?

So he went back to the bathroom door. "Okay, so um...you take care of yourself and do what the doctor says, okay? Don't give up, Ma. You never know what could happen."

Still there was silence. Dwayne tried one more time. He rapped the back of his knuckles lightly on the door. "Ma, I...I love you, okay?"

Silence. Then he heard the toilet flush. Dwayne left the room, closing the door behind him.

In the hallway, he breathed. It felt as if he hadn't done so for an hour.

In the living room, he went straight for the door without a word. "You have a nice visit?" trilled Daryl.

Dwayne stopped, one hand on the knob, the other in the pocket of his windbreaker, curled around the grip of his mother's gun. He tried to think of reasons he shouldn't whip out that stupid pink pistol and shoot his brother right in his mocking mouth. In that moment, he couldn't think of any, but he knew there must be at least one. So he turned the doorknob instead and contented himself with flashing a malicious grin. "Fuck you very much," he said.

He went to the truck at just less than a trot, started it up, and pulled out so abruptly that a guy driving by in a Chevy had to slam on the brakes. The guy leaned on his horn. Dwayne leaned on his own horn. He jammed the gas pedal to the floor.

By his watch, it was 12:30. He still had time to kill before he had to be at the editor's house. And he knew just where he wanted to go.

The realization of where he was headed made him think, guiltily, of Clarence towering over him this morning as they parted, not wanting to use the actual words, but reminding him—*begging* him, really—not to use while he was out.

But goddamn, what a day it had been. And it was the last day, after all, the very last either of them would ever know. What could it hurt if he got a little something to steady himself, ready himself for what they had to do tonight? He needed this. Hell, he *deserved* it. The more he thought about it, the more sense it seemed to make.

Yes, Clarence would be disappointed. Yes, Clarence would stand there with that hurt puppy dog expression on his face. Yes, Clarence...

Shit.

Clarence.

Dwayne checked his watch again. 12:30? God, he'd been gone for more than two hours. Clarence must be worried sick wondering what had happened to him. The mission had gone operational, which meant, according to their plan, they were to observe strict radio silence. The Secret Service, the NSA, the CIA, the FBI, the NAACP, they all had means of spying on electronic communications, and he didn't want them swooping down on him and Clarence.

But surely it couldn't hurt if he just made one little call to Clarence's cell, just to say that he was okay. He could use code. "Papa bear is still searching for the honey tree," or something like that.

Dwayne reached into his hip pocket for the prepaid cell he had bought the last time he bought cigarettes. What he pulled out shocked him. Cracks spider-webbed the screen, the buttons were askew, the plastic casing was in two pieces. Thunderstruck, Dwayne stared at the mangle in his hands with such intensity, he almost ran through a red light. He slammed the brakes.

What had happened to his fucking phone? Dwayne had no idea. Then he knew. When he was knocked down by that crazy bitch with the black belt in kung fu, he had landed on his backside, right on the pocket where he carried the phone.

Damn, he thought. He turned his hand sideways and let the pieces of the ruined phone fall into the passenger seat.

Damn, damn.

But what could he do? Clarence would just have to understand.

Dwayne shook his head in disbelief. What a day he was having. Thankfully, it was about to get a whole lot better real soon. The light changed. Dwayne hung a quick left, cutting off drivers in the oncoming lane. A chorus of bleating horns followed him as he took the ramp down onto the expressway.

Twenty minutes later, he was walking into a bar on Lake Street, the El train clattering by overhead. The air inside was damp with stale beer, bitter with the smoke of too many cigarettes. From the jukebox, some morose country singer serenaded a sprinkling of drinkers who sat quietly handling their business at the bar and in the booths. It occurred to Dwayne, as it did every time he came through the door, that this place really lived up to its name, even though the owner had probably intended it as a joke. Misery, the bar was called.

Dwayne waved off the bartender and walked to the last table in the back, just the other side of the men's room. Sal looked up at his approach. He had been nursing a ginger ale—Sal didn't drink—and squinting over a copy of the *Post*.

"You see the shit this nigger wrote in the paper this morning?" he asked without preamble. "He's tired of white people's bullshit? Un-fucking-believable. Somebody needs to haul his black ass out from behind that desk and teach him some manners."

"Maybe somebody will," said Dwayne. He was bursting to say, but he tried to be enigmatic. He'd already said way too much to Ma.

"Yeah, from your lips to God's ear," said Sal. He folded the paper, creased it, and laid it aside. "So, D, long time. What brings you to my place of business? Can't be what it usually is. You ain't doing that shit no more. Isn't that what you said?"

"Let's just say I changed my mind."

"Changed your mind? No, son, that ain't what I heard. I heard you went and got religion."

"Come on, Sal. Don't break my balls."

After a moment, Sal leaned back and grinned. He had a movie star grin. "Okay, kid, no more breaking balls."

Sal was maybe 30, three years older than Dwayne. He called everybody kid.

Dwayne lowered his voice. "You got any of that Go Fast?"

"You know me," said Sal. "Always got what you need. Big party? Small party?"

"Small party," said Dwayne.

A knowing look. "Chippin' a little, are you? Easin' your way back in?"

"No," said Dwayne, "this is my last time."

"They all say that," said Sal.

"No, I really mean it," said Dwayne.

"They all say that, too."

Dwayne gave up. There was no way to make Sal understand without telling him. And he couldn't do that. "I'll just put it like this," he said. "When you see the news tonight, that's us, me and Clarence. Remember I told you so."

Sal's expression creased. "What am I going to see tonight, kid?"

"You'll see. Just watch." Dwayne went into his pocket and fished out a crumpled $20 bill. It was his last money. He pushed it across the table to Sal. "Got to go," he said. "Let me get my shit."

For a moment, Sal simply regarded him with the same dubious expression. Then he plucked up the $20. His smile was slow. "Okay, kid, be that way. I'll keep an eye on the news."

"My shit?"

"Keep your shirt on." With a furtive glance around the bar, Sal stood. When he was satisfied with what he saw, he lifted the seat cushion upon which he had sat and turned it over on top of the table. In the hollow beneath, secured by tape, were a dozen Baggies of various sizes. Some held pot, some held rocks of cocaine, and the small one Sal removed and handed to Dwayne contained Dwayne's drug of choice, shards of what looked like cloudy broken glass. He thought of it as instant well-being.

God, he loved meth.

It was hard to explain to someone who had never been there, who had never known the hard clarity, the endless energy, the simple ability to get shit done, that could be found in a few pulls on a meth pipe. "You need to quit using that shit," Clarence had told him so many times. "That shit's going to kill you."

And finally, Dwayne had agreed, finally said yes, if only to shut Clarence up. That was two weeks ago. But Clarence, he had come to realize, simply didn't understand. Nobody did until they had been there for themselves.

Yes, Jesus, he loved meth.

Dwayne tucked the little baggie into his pocket. Now that he had it, he was itching to be away, find some place to park so that he could sit with his pipe and let the sun shine in. "All right," he said.

Sal replaced the seat cushion and sat back down. "Nice doing business with you," he said. "See you next time."

Dwayne barely heard him. He floated out of the bar on wings of sheer anticipation back into the lattice of sunshine and shadow beneath the El.

"Hey."

Dwayne turned. A big man, squinting in recognition, was coming toward him at a quickstep, some frowsy orange-haired woman sprinting along behind. The fact that the man seemed to know him confused Dwayne, froze him to the sidewalk.

Who was this guy? Dwayne didn't know this guy.

Then he did. In fact, Dwayne recognized him in the same instant the man's right fist came out of nowhere and smashed into his jaw. Same fucking spot the crazy bitch had hit him, but harder. *Way* harder.

Dwayne dropped like a bag of gravel. Lights flashed purple and white. A low, throbbing sound filled his mind. Cars passed, driving upside down.

The woman grabbed the man's bicep. They, too, were upside down. "Come on, Carl, leave him alone. He's just some asshole."

Carl leaned up from the sky and poked a finger thick as a kielbasa at Dwayne through flashes of the white and purple light. "Who the fuck do you think you are, giving the finger to my wife?" Dwayne got the sense the man was screaming, but he could barely hear him over that deep, almost electrical thrumming. "Next time you'll get worse, do you hear me? Next time I'll really kick your ass."

He kicked Dwayne in the ass one time for emphasis, then allowed the woman to lead him away. Dwayne could do nothing but writhe on the sidewalk, waiting for the world to come back. He heard shoes clicking and scuffling around him. The El rumbled overhead, metal singing against metal.

After a long moment, Dwayne pressed his hands against the sidewalk and pushed against it. He was on his knees. Then he was on his feet. He stumbled back. The side of the building caught him.

Dwayne held his jaw, eyes screwed shut against the light. Blood filled his mouth. He spat some of it on the sidewalk. This only freshened the pain. God, he was having the worse fucking day of his life.

twelve

Martin Luther King was coming to Memphis.

The word leapt from pulpit to pew to pool hall. The great man had heard about the plight of the sanitation men, how you could be crushed to death like the garbage you hauled and the city didn't even care. But the great man cared.

"I'm glad he comin' to see about us," said Malcolm's father when a television reporter stuck a microphone under his nose and asked for his thoughts. Pop and Sonny watched this at the house that night. Malcolm, shrugging on his work shirt, stood behind them. His father was a dual image on the beat-up old black-and-white TV, a grainy shadow of himself standing next to himself in front of a group of strikers, holding their I <u>AM</u> A MAN signs down in front of them.

But his voice, thought Malcolm, buttoning his shirt, was certainly clear enough. *Comin' to see about us.* As if his father thought the barrel-chested Baptist preacher was Jesus himself. As if King were not so much flying in to Memphis as descending upon it.

The white television reporter seemed to feel the same way. He did not bother to hide an indulgent chuckle. "And what," he asked through that snigger, "do you expect him to be able to do for you?"

At this question, the two Mozell Wilsons on the television brought their eyes up and in them was a sudden, disconcerting directness that had not been there before. "He ain't gon' do nothin' 'for' us," he said, and was that actually scorn Malcolm heard at the edge of his voice? "We men, so we got to do for ourselves. But Dr. King can help us get the mayor and the city to *see* that we are men and we ain't gon' go for nobody treatin' us like we ain't. Not no more. Them days is done."

And he looked at the white man as if to dare him to ask another question.

Sitting there in his ratty chair, Malcolm's father allowed himself a barely there nod of satisfaction as he watched surprise register on the reporter's face. The white man looked like he had swallowed a hot pepper as he said, "And there you have it. This is Ken Simpson, reporting live from City Hall," and threw back to the studio anchor.

Sonny erupted in a high-pitched laugh, slapping Pop on the back. "You got him good," he trumpeted. "Oh, you got him good!"

The expression on his father's face loosened into something that was pleased, if not quite a smile. "That's what he get for askin' that damn fool question."

"So when Dr. King coming to town?" asked Sonny.

"Next week, way I hear," said his father.

"You goin' to see him speak, right?"

Malcolm's father looked at Sonny as if he were a fool. "'Course I'm goin'," he said.

"What about you, youngblood?"

Malcolm had been leaning into a wall mirror, brushing his close-cropped hair into place. He looked back at Sonny. "I don't know," he said. "Maybe."

Sonny was incredulous. "Maybe?"

"Junie don't have no use for Martin Luther King," explained Pop.

Malcolm returned to the mirror. "I don't have anything against King," he said. "I think he wants what we all want. But if you ask me do I see the point in marching around carrying signs and letting some whiteys beat you upside the head...no. I'm sorry, but that don't make sense to me."

"So what do make sense to you, youngblood?" asked Sonny. He sounded as if he really wanted to know.

Malcolm didn't want to be drawn into this conversation but apparently there was no avoiding it. He turned from the mirror. "We need power," he said.

Pop said, "You talkin' that black power shit, ain't you?"

Malcolm shook his head. Sometimes his father could be so obtuse. "We black, ain't we? So any power we get is going to be black power by definition."

"You talk like all the rest of them young fools," said Pop.

Malcolm sighed. "Look, Pop," he said, "ain't no point fightin' about this. We ain't never gon' see eye to eye. Your whole generation is based on asking white folks to give you what you're already supposed to have. My generation sees it differently, that's all."

Pop just shook his head. "Foolishness," he said.

"It ain't all foolishness, Mo."

Sonny's words surprised them both. Malcolm and his father looked at him and he shrugged. "It ain't," he insisted. "I done listened to them young ones talk and some of what they say make sense to me. They say we need to control our communities, control our own money and like that. We need to take more of our destiny in our own hands. And if you call that black power, fine. I want me some black power, then, 'cause it's a stone drag, livin' without power."

"Well, to get power," said Malcolm, "you got to learn to fight back. You got to show 'em you ready to defend yourself."

"What you think we been doin'?" said Sonny. "Why you think we out there everyday, marchin' around and totin' them signs?"

"You really think that's fightin' back, Sonny? You really think the white man cares about you all singing freedom songs and carrying some signs? That ain't nothin' to him."

Pop came to his feet. "You think it's *nothin'*? Take a lot for us to carry them signs. You might not think so, but it do. 'I AM A MAN?' That's a lot to say, right there."

Malcolm faced his father. He had that sense again, like he so often did when they spoke, of the sheer futility of trying to explain concepts and ideas Pop was simply not equipped to understand. His ignorance was not his fault, Malcolm supposed, but that didn't make it any easier. "I said it ain't nothin' *to the white man*," he told the older man in a slow, careful voice. "If it was, the strike would be over by now, wouldn't it?" Pop didn't answer. Malcolm sighed, giving up. "Look, Pop, you remember what you said to me that time? You fight your revolution and let me fight mine? How about we just do that, huh?"

He looked from his father to Sonny. Neither man spoke and that was fine with Malcolm. "I got to finish getting ready," he said. "I'm going to be late for work."

Malcolm did not wait for a response. He went back to the tiny chamber where he slept, the room on the back of the house in which he had grown up, the room where he used to furtively watch through the window as his father showered off the grime of another long day in the makeshift stall rigged in the yard. Malcolm lifted his thin mattress and pulled out the pistol hidden beneath.

He carried the gun everywhere now. He didn't feel safe without it. Malcolm didn't quite know what he planned to do with it or even quite why he had bought it. He only knew he would never be caught helpless before a white man again.

Twice it had happened in just the last month. And that was two times too many.

He slipped the pistol into the front pocket of his pants. The bulge it made was barely discernible.

De Lawd came to town the following week.

Malcolm, reluctant but resigned, rode the bus with his father and Sonny—Sonny's gas tank was on empty—over to the Mason Temple, a stone fortress of a church on Mason Street. It was not yet 6:00 when they got there, but traffic on the street had already congealed, acres of Detroit steel sitting bumper-to-bumper going nowhere. The meeting was not scheduled to begin for an hour.

"Good thing I didn't drive," said Sonny, surveying the mess.

But the human traffic jam was hardly less than the steel one. The front of the church was clotted with people making their way inside. Someone was yelling to let the sanitation workers go first so they could sit together down front.

Pop and Sonny joined a wedge of brittle-eyed men in ill-fitting thrift store suits and work clothes edging toward the entrance. It occurred to Malcolm that once they were inside, he could head back home if he wanted, maybe grab a nap before work, and his father would never know. He was debating this when he heard his name.

"Malcolm! Hey, what you doin' here? This ain't your scene." Melvin Cotter was coming up behind him.

"Came with Pop," said Malcolm. "Him and Sonny just went inside. I was actually thinking about heading back home. I got to work tonight."

"How that goin' anyway? Ain't hardly seen you since the day I took you to get the job."

This was Melvin's idea of subtlety. *Where you been? Why you been avoiding me? You owe me.*

Malcolm felt a pinch of guilt, because the unspoken accusation was true. He *had* been avoiding his friend.

Melvin had come by the house just the previous Saturday. Pop was at some union meeting and the insistent knocking at the door brought Malcolm shambling out to the front room in his underwear. He had moved aside the bed sheet that served as a curtain over the front window and seen Melvin standing out there chatting with Nanny Parker.

Malcolm had regarded his friend's profile for a moment, made a decision, and lowered the sheet. He moved away from the window so his shadow could not be seen from outside. After a few seconds Melvin knocked again, emphatically. A minute after that, Malcolm heard the sound of his feet walking away, and then Melvin's car started. Malcolm lifted the bed sheet again and watched the old Buick pull away from the curb. At the time, he'd told himself he didn't answer the door because he was tired and didn't feel like being bothered. Until this very instant, he supposed, he had even believed that.

Now he shrugged. "Just been busy," he said. "Workin'. You know, that night shift is a real drag. I'm still gettin' used to it. I sleep most of the day."

"Yeah, I hear you," said Melvin, but Malcolm could see he was not convinced.

"So, you come here to pray to De Lawd?"

But Malcolm's attempt to change the subject only made Melvin frown. "Man, don't be like that. I know Shabazz was your man. But this man, he got some good things to say, too."

"Yeah, I guess," said Malcolm, without conviction.

They fell into an awkward silence then. And that was odd in itself. Junie Wilson and Melvin Cotter had been friends forever. Rapping had been like breathing with them, an easy, unaffected thing that just...happened. Now, all of a sudden, it was work.

Finally Melvin said, "So, you decided about school?"

"Yeah," said Malcolm. "I'm not going back. I've had enough."

"How Mr. Mozell feel about that?"

"Ain't told him yet."

Melvin said, "Uh-huh." Another silence. Then he said, "So I heard what happened with Lynette. She say you saved her."

"I just pulled that asshole off her, that's all."

"Good thing you was there. Pruitt, that bastard, need to be ashamed of himself."

Malcolm laughed. "Oh, he's a bastard now?"

"Always been a bastard," Melvin said.

"When you were standing there talking to him, the day you got me my job, the day he pinched Lynette on the ass, did you know then he was a bastard?"

Malcolm had his own ideas on subtlety.

Melvin's eyes flared like a struck match. "You got somethin' you want to say to me, Junie? I mean, 'Malcolm?'"

Malcolm shook his head. "No," he said. "Just asking a question, is all."

But Melvin would not let it go. "It ain't easy as you think, Junie. You used to know that. Maybe you went away to that white college and forgot. But a man—especially a black man—do what he got to do to survive, even if it ain't somethin' he like doin'."

"Oh, is that what you call it? You survivin'?"

Melvin's hot eyes went cold. "Fuck you, nigger. You think I don't know you look down on me? Maybe I ain't been to college, but I ain't no fool, neither. You done always looked down on me. Especially after I got you your job by talking to that bastard, as you say. But it ain't just me, is it? Hell, you even look down on this man." A nod toward the building, indicating Martin Luther King. "That take some balls, you know? I mean, I get why King ain't your thing. But give the man this much: he put his ass on the line for what he believe. What you ever done, 'cept talk shit and paint 'Fuck the System' on some wall?"

Malcolm was stunned. Who the hell did Melvin Cotter think he was to talk to him like that? Melvin, who had stood there grinning like a bashful child at that racist bastard Rupert Pruitt?

He was about to say this when a third man approached. He wore a denim jacket, a moderate Afro, and dark shades that made his face a stop sign. He had been a few years ahead in school. His name was Eddie.

"Brothers," he said.

"Hey," said Malcolm.

"Hey," said Melvin.

"You here to see the man?"

Melvin shot Malcolm a pointed look. "I am," he said. "Don't know what he here for."

"That's cool," said Eddie. There was something indulgent in the way he said it, as though they ought to be pleased to have his approval. "King is all right in his way, but you do know that he fails to comprehend the magnitude, the complexity, and the true nature of the problem he seeks to address."

"Is that right?" asked Melvin.

"Yes it is. The man wants to help our brothers who work the sanitation trucks to achieve recognition for their union, better working conditions, and better wages. But all that does is seek better treatment within the same old system. Even if they get everything they're asking for, the system remains broken and tilted against the needs of the working man, the *black* working man in particular. It's like what they say about rearranging the deck chairs on the Titanic. You can make the chairs look nice and neat, but the ship is still taking on water."

"Yeah?" said Melvin. "So what's your program?" A challenge edged his voice.

Eddie smiled. "We believe in black power."

Melvin jabbed Malcolm with a look. "Same thing you always goin' on about, ain't it?"

"Same thing every righteous brother is goin' on about," retorted Malcolm.

From his vest pocket, Eddie extracted a folded flier printed on red paper with blocky black letters. "We are having a gathering to discuss what we in the younger generation can do to aid the sanitation workers in their moment of need," he said, passing it to Melvin. **BLACK POWER IS THE KEY,** it said at the top.

"You see," said Eddie, "we don't believe you can fix the system. We believe you must tear down the system and build something new in its place. The evils of capitalism cannot be reformed, because whatever reform you create, the fat cats at the top of the power structure will always find some way around it. So you have to remove the fat cats first. Only when power reposes in the people can there be any hope of meaningful change."

"Okay," said Melvin. "Thank you for the speech."

Eddie's eyes might have sparked. The sunglasses made it hard to tell. "I wasn't trying to give a speech," he said in a voice stiff as a freshly starched collar. "I leave the speechmaking to the man in there. Me, I was just trying to hip you cats to what's really going on."

He tapped the flier, still in Melvin's hand. "Hope to see you there," he said. And with a nod, he walked away.

"Sound more like your thing than mine," said Melvin.

He handed the flier to Malcolm, who studied it for a moment. "Yeah, maybe I'll go check it out," he said.

"You do that. I'm going to go listen to Dr. King."

Melvin didn't wait for Malcolm's response. He lifted his hand in an indifferent wave and went to join the line of people waiting to enter the building.

Malcolm stood there alone under the darkening sky. Melvin's words still stung.

What you ever done?

Who the hell was Melvin Cotter to ask him that?

What you ever done?

He had protested, that's what. He had raised his fist. He had shouted defiance.

What you ever done?

He had painted "Fuck the System" on a wall.

And the great Reverend Doctor Lord Almighty Martin Luther King, Jr.? The dreamer of dreams and high apostle of let-whitey-kick-the-shit-out-of-you-but-love-him-anyway?

He put his ass on the line for what he believe.

Yeah, right.

Yet still the people came to see him, wedging into the church. Hundreds of them, thousands of them. Every Negro in Memphis, it seemed. Malcolm watched.

What you ever done?

Malcolm folded the red flier and slipped it into the same pocket where his gun slept. He stood there another moment, watching. Then his feet carried him forward without conscious command and he got in line to enter the Mason Temple.

He was here. Might as well hear what the man had to say.

It was a long wait before Malcolm finally squeezed through the door into the church sanctuary, a vast room with a low ceiling. Despite its size, there was a closeness to the room—especially now, packed as it was. People sat nearly on top of each other. It was hot and the air carried the indistinct buzz of a thousand conversations all going at once. And still people kept coming, crowding through the door behind Malcolm like ants boiling out of an anthill.

Malcolm fought his way back out to the lobby and took the stairs up to the balcony, where he claimed some of the rapidly diminishing space against the back wall just as the singing began below.

The audience sang "We Shall Not Be Moved," the same song the men had sung on the plaza in front of City Hall, except that this time, the untutored reediness of their voices was swallowed by thousands more, a woman's roughhewn contralto leading the way and calling out verses, thousands of hands trip-hammering in time.

Then there was more singing.

They sang "We Shall Overcome."

They sang "God Bless America."

They passed a metal garbage can for donations to the strike fund. They passed a petition for the recall of Mayor Loeb.

A white man with horn-rimmed glasses, some national union leader whose name Malcolm didn't catch, stood at the lectern beneath banners proclaiming church programs and slogans and recounted how Echol Cole and Robert Walker had been crushed in that faulty garbage truck.

"These men tell us that all their lives they've been wanting to be men," he shouted. "As men, they've been struggling to be dignified. And they tell us that this may be their only chance. And we're not giving up!"

"Tell it like it is!" someone shouted.

"Say that!" cried another voice.

A black preacher spoke. He had white hair and a dignified bearing.

"I see God's hand moving in this business," he said, and his voice was filled with warning. "Mayor Loeb, you need to get on the right side of this thing, for the Lord will not be mocked. Right there in the book of First Timothy, it says, 'The laborer is worthy of his reward.'

"These men have labored for you, Mayor Loeb." He slapped the podium and repeated it. "These men have *labored* for you, sir. They have toted your tubs and driven your trucks and handled that garbage and they are not asking you for anything but what they have coming. They have labored and they are worthy of their wages."

He paused and something puckish came into his eyes. "Where's that brother who was on the TV the other night?" he asked, abandoning for a moment the studied formality of his preacher's cadence. "Did any of you see him? TV reporter asked him what he thought Martin Luther King could do for the sanitation men. And he said, King can't do nothin' for the men, 'cause if you are a man, you got to do for yourself. But he said Dr. King can *help* this city and this mayor to *understand* that you are men and you will no longer stand for being treated as if you are not."

The preacher shaded his eyes. "Is that brother here? Let that brother stand."

Far below, a tiny figure came hesitantly to his feet. The crowd erupted. "There he is!" the preacher roared. "That brother spoke the truth! That brother told it like it is!" Malcolm felt odd watching them cheer his father.

Another preacher spoke. There was more singing. There was still more speaking. Anticipation hummed through the crowd. Any moment now. Martin Luther King was coming to see about Memphis.

The man was coming.

And all at once, the man was there.

He entered Mason Temple by a side door, came into a room where there was no more room, people sitting on stairs and standing in doorways and crowding the aisles. It was shortly after nine when he came, walking in the center of a wedge of men linked arm by arm to get him to the podium. The crowd was on its feet, their cheers booming like thunder, people shouting at him, some of the women lifting steepled hands beneath glittering eyes, some of the men holding clenched fists aloft.

He seemed small in the belly of the tumult.

Slowly, the man made his way up the stairs, pausing to shake hands with other dignitaries on the rostrum. He was introduced and then he stood before them, silent for a moment, waiting, in no hurry, and the pandemonium, which had never quite crested, refreshed itself and rose anew. Malcolm thought he had understood the power the great man held over his people, the reverence and awe with which they beheld him. But he'd had no idea.

King began slowly. His voice heavy and solemn, he congratulated Memphis for what he called its "great movement." He praised the black community for its unity. He assured the sanitation workers, those men people called tub toters, that they had value and meaning.

"So often," he said, "we overlook the worth and the significance of those who are not in professional jobs or those who are not in the so-called big jobs. But let me say to you tonight that whenever you are engaged in work that serves humanity and is for the building of humanity, it has dignity and it has worth. One day our society must come to see this."

King went on. As Malcolm watched, King seemed to change. Some new light came into his eyes, some new urgency rose in his voice. He invoked a Biblical parable about a rich man named Dives who went to hell for ignoring the pain of the poor man who lingered every day outside his gate.

"And I come by here to say," said King, "that America, too, is going to hell if she doesn't use her wealth. If America does not use her vast resources of wealth to end poverty and make it possible for all of God's children to have the basic necessities of life, she, too, will go to hell."

His voice rose on a righteous wind. The crowd was fully with him, talking back to him.

"*Yes*, sir! *Yes*, sir! *Yes*, sir!"

"We can all get more together than we can apart," said King. "This is the way we gain power." The word made Malcolm stand up straight. "Power," continued King, "is the ability to achieve purpose, power is the ability to effect change. And we need power!"

Power, he explained, was defined by the labor leader Walter Reuther as the ability to make General Motors say yes when it wanted to say no. "That's power," said King. "And I want you to stick it out so that you will be able to make Mayor Loeb and others say yes, even when they want to say no."

Malcolm was surprised. There was confrontation in those words.

Then King surprised him yet again. Indeed, he even seemed to surprise himself. "Now you know what?" he said. His voice had gone quiet, and his face took on that speculative, thoughtful expression that comes over a man when he finds himself speaking an idea even as it is still coming to him.

"You may have to escalate the struggle a bit," said King. "If they keep refusing and they will not recognize the union...I tell you what you ought to do, and you are together here enough to do it. In a few days, you ought to get together and just have a *general work stoppage* in the city of Memphis."

And all the cheering and all the thunder and all the shouts that had come before were as nothing to what came now. King's words detonated the crowd like a bomb. People stomped. Their hands jackhammered. They screamed exultation, adoration and yes, Lord, yes.

A work stoppage? Yes.

Show 'em we mean business. Yes.

Demand our rights. Yes.

I AM A MAN. Oh, yes. Hell yes.

Malcolm watched from a distance as the crowd went wild. He felt like a stranger. He felt as if he were marooned on a raft in an ocean of other people's ecstasy.

Shocked. That's what it was. The realization came to him as if through a dull haze. He was shocked.

But De Lawd had delivered. Say that for him. Martin Luther King had said exactly what needed to be said. Now, Malcolm watched as the men behind King hurriedly deliberated with him about this sudden inspiration of his. He saw hands chopping the air. He saw heads huddling together. He saw consensus reached.

King returned to the podium. March 22, he said. Friday. That would be the day. No Negro would work. No Negro would go to school. They would demonstrate instead. He would return and lead them himself.

At that, the pandemonium renewed. In all the tumult, Malcolm checked his watch. He was surprised. It was after ten. And he still had to catch the bus home before he could grab his bike and cycle over to the river. He was going to be so late. He had not expected the meeting to go this long.

His mind already working on an appropriate excuse for his tardiness, Malcolm shouldered his way through the crowd, through the cacophony. Voices from the podium below were still banging off the low ceiling. People next to him were yelling in his ear.

Down stairs that were choked with people. Through a lobby that was clogged with people. Out a door that was thick with people. Finally emerging into a courtyard that was thronged by people.

The air, warming up as spring came on, was sweet to Malcolm after so long in the stifling room. It tasted of possible rain. He gulped it greedily, glad to be out.

Eddie came out of the building just a moment later, still wearing his shades even in full darkness. He was scowling as if greatly displeased. Then he saw a brother standing between two parked cars and approached him, a hand with one of the red fliers in it leading the way. The brother took the flier and studied it grimly.

Black power is the key, it had said. And so it was. Malcolm believed this, knew this, with every molecule of his being. At some level, Martin Luther King must finally know it, too. What was it he had said? "We need power."

And who could disagree with that, who could disagree that black power was necessary, when even King had come to see it? Not just to see it, but to embrace it by calling for action that went beyond speeches, marches, and platitudes. A work stoppage, that was something real, something tangible, something whitey could not ignore. But why stop with that? Maybe there was even more they could do.

Malcolm took off at a trot, driven by the clock, but also by the stunning thing he had just experienced. Martin Luther King himself had spoken of power, admitted that Negroes needed power. And in four days, he was coming back to Memphis. Anything could happen now.

thirteen

Stymie's was only two blocks from Grant Park, which was where the Obama people would hold tonight's rally. Bob had chosen it for convenience—Janeka probably already knew the area.

But he realized as he came through the door that at some level, he had also chosen it to send this woman a message. Stymie's was an old-fashioned steakhouse done up in wood the color of dark chocolate, with high-backed booths and brass fixtures. Its menu depicted a drawing of a cow seen in cross-section, with the various cuts of meat delineated. Its owner had contributed heavily to the doomed effort to defeat the state smoking ban that had gone into effect on January 1. If a building could vote, this one would vote—it would *scream*—Republican.

Not that Bob was a Republican—or, for that matter, a Democrat. A registered Independent, he didn't identify with either party. But if Janeka was still spouting the hippie rhetoric of their youth, if she now embraced some Left Coast, free-range, organic food ethos, or if, God forbid, she had gone vegan on him, then walking into this temple of red meat and cholesterol would tell her emphatically that times had changed. That *he* had changed.

At his request, the maître d' seated him in a booth in the back where he took a seat facing the front door. As the server was pouring his water, Bob opened his menu and asked, "What is your fish of the day?"

It was salmon, seared over wine-soaked cedar planks, served with grilled asparagus and pine nut couscous.

"Sounds good," said Bob.

"Will you be eating alone?" the server asked. He was a lanky kid with long hair.

"No," said Bob. "I'm meeting someone. I'm a little early."

"Very good, sir."

Bob was, in fact, early by design. He had not wanted to walk in and find her already sitting there, scrutinizing him while he stood in the doorway waiting for his eyes to adjust to the darkness, searching the lunchtime crowd for her. To allow that would be to surrender a tactical advantage, like a general who allowed an enemy to seize the high ground. No. He wanted to see her first.

Hearing himself think these things, Bob was mildly appalled. Was Janeka really his enemy? Was that how he thought of her now?

He had certainly not regarded her as such in that sweet fall and winter of '67 and '68. No, she had been his deepest friend. She had been his future. Or at least, this was what he had very soon come to believe.

They made love for the first time three weeks after they saw *In the Heat of the Night* together. He was her first and she was his and they had agonized over the decision, both of them being good Christian kids from good Christian homes whose parents would be hurt and mortified at the thought that their son and daughter were down here breaking commandments and sinning their fool heads off. Plus, there was pregnancy to worry about.

In the end, however, reluctance and good intentions had been overmatched by simple lust. And dawning love.

Once the decision was made, they had to figure out where they would do it. The dorms were out. They were strictly segregated by gender and the monitors were known to be humorless and incorruptible. No visitor of the opposite sex was allowed past the front desk, period, ever, end of discussion.

So they settled on a hotel near campus—the only hotel near campus, this being Mississippi, where a ten-minute drive in any direction put you in the middle of cotton fields.

Bob had gone to the registration desk that afternoon, carrying an empty suitcase to make it look real. He registered, then went to the room and called Janeka's dorm. When she came on the line, he said simply, "254," feeling not unlike a spy in some Cold War novel. She said, for the benefit of the dorm monitor, "Jim! How good to hear from you, little brother. How's mom and dad?" He could picture her standing in the hallway leaning against the cinderblock wall, smiling so the monitor could see there was nothing out of the ordinary here. He wondered if she were as nervous as he was.

Two hours later, there was a knocking at the door of Room 254, two hours having been the amount of separation they felt was needed between his arrival and hers so that it would not look suspicious. Bob had been sitting on the bed with the television on, half watching a rerun of *I Love Lucy*. Now, feeling almost as if he were in a dream, he opened the door and there she was and he could hardly believe she was real. She came in and he closed the door and there was an endless moment. Then Bob swept her into his arms, and by God, she was real. Indeed, he was overcome by the realness of her, the *thereness* of her, and they kissed with a passion and an abandon, all the while going at buttons and hooks and clasps in delicious haste. And they fell into bed...

...and what happened next was, of course, an unmitigated disaster, as how could it be otherwise with two kids who had never done anything like this before and had only the vaguest idea of how it went and had to read the helpful instructions on the box even to get the condom on? All that was bad enough. Then it got worse. She lay down, she opened herself to him, and Bob pushed eagerly inside her. He shuddered, his eyes rolled, and it was over.

Just like that.

Over.

Mortification made him very still. His cheeks flamed. And a second later when she asked, "Did you...did you...finish already?" his humiliation was complete. Bob groaned with unutterable self-loathing, buried his face in the pillow and prayed very fervently that God allow him to tunnel through the floor, through the crust, mantle, and core of the Earth and out the other side in China where he could flee to some hinterland village and live under an assumed name for the rest of his life.

"It's okay," she said, realizing now what had happened, trying to be helpful.

"No, it's not," he said, his voice muffled by the pillow.

"It's okay," she insisted.

He rolled off her and lay there staring at the ceiling. This was the worst moment of his entire existence.

Janeka placed her head on his chest. After a moment, he put an arm around her.

They lay together for a few minutes and then, somewhat to his surprise, Bob felt...a stirring. Janeka saw. "Do you want to try again?" she asked. After a moment, Bob nodded.

So they tried again. And later, they tried yet again.

And by the end, it was glorious.

And Bob and Janeka became inseparable. They also became increasingly bold about showing their feelings, race be darned, walking around campus hand in hand, even going across the street together to the launderette to wash their things, or to the burger joint next to it with the clean rectangular spot above the door where the *Whites Only* sign had hung until just two years before.

Some older white woman with cat's-eye glasses stared at them one day as they sat across from one another in the cracked vinyl booth, Janeka idly poaching French fries from Bob's basket. Finally, she came up to them. Ignoring Janeka, she addressed herself to Bob and spoke without preamble. "You're such a fine-lookin' boy," she said in a voice of tender, grandmotherly concern. "I'm sure you could have any white girl you wanted. Why would you want to date outside your race?"

Bob had always been proud of how he responded to that. He smiled sweetly and spoke in a placid voice. "Ma'am," he said, "my race is human. What's yours?"

The woman colored. She clutched her purse tightly and walked away, her steps pinched and quick. He looked at Janeka. Janeka looked at him. They managed to wait until the door closed behind the old woman before they broke out laughing.

"There's this girl," Bob told his mother.

This was a few days later and Mom was calling long distance, wanting to know why he wasn't coming home for Christmas.

"Girl?" She pronounced it like a word in some exotic foreign language. He could all but hear her eyebrows arching.

"I'll write you about her," he said. "This is probably costing a fortune."

"Never mind that," she said, and her voice mingled curiosity and concern. "Tell me about this 'girl.'"

Bob sighed. He had been standing at the wall phone in the hallway next to the dorm monitor's desk. Now, resignation pushed him down to the floor, where he sat cross-legged. This earned him a sympathetic smile from the monitor.

"Her name is Janeka," he said. "Janeka Lattimore."

"Janeka? What an odd name. Tell me more."

So he did. He told her how Janeka was from California and her family couldn't afford for her to come home for the holiday and he didn't want her to have to spend Christmas here by herself.

"That's very sweet," said his mother, her voice measured like baking powder. "This girl is obviously special to you, Bobby. What's she like?"

Bob heaved another sigh and told her still more. He told her Janeka was majoring in political science. He told her Janeka was about the smartest person he knew. He told her Janeka and he were working together on a voter registration project. And he told her, when she pressed him on it, that, yes, Janeka could indeed be The One.

He didn't tell her Janeka was black.

Even when his mother asked him what she looked like, he said only that she was petite with brown hair and dark eyes and was just about the most beautiful woman he had ever seen.

"She sounds lovely," said Bob's mother.

"She is," said Bob.

On Christmas Eve, five days later, Bob walked out of his dorm into a biting winter afternoon to meet Janeka. She was standing out front waiting for him. They kissed, he took her gloved hand in his, and they were about to set out for chapel, where there was to be a holiday service. Then a woman's voice called his name, but made it a question.

"Bobby?"

He looked up and there they were at the curb, his mother and father, Mom holding a tin of her famous Christmas cookies, both standing stock still with mouths agape. And there, behind them, were his three younger brothers grinning behind their hands and punching each other in the shoulder.

"Dad? Mom? What are you doing here?"

"We came to surprise you," said his mother. There was a helpless note in her voice. The surprise was on her.

The next three seconds took an hour to pass, the longest, most excruciating hour of Bob's life. Finally, his father recovered his power of speech, reaching for Janeka's hand. "I'm Robert Carson," he said, his big fist swallowing her tiny one and pumping it. "I'm Bobby's father. These are my other boys, Sidney, Reed, and Stevie. And this is my wife, Estelle."

It was right then that Estelle Carson finally recovered her own power of speech, to Bob's everlasting regret. "You're black," she said. She said this in a tone that suggested Janeka would find it as much a surprise as she herself did.

"Yes," said Janeka. She looked at Bob. "All day long and seven days a week."

They all laughed at this, relieved at how artfully she had defused the moment. Janeka smiled, but there was ice at the edge of it that only Bob saw.

"I'm sorry," his mother said, embarrassed, "but we didn't know. Bobby didn't tell us."

'I see," said Janeka.

His mother shook Janeka's hand. "Do you watch *I Spy*?" she asked. "We're all crazy about that Bill Cosby."

"Yes," said Janeka, "we like him, too."

If a truck had come barreling down the street just then, Bob would have stepped calmly in front of it and thanked God for sending it.

His mother clapped her hands together. "Well," she said, and her voice was brighter than a klieg light, "who wants dinner?"

She had made reservations at a swanky restaurant in Memphis. Memphis was an hour away. They drove toward it in a rented station wagon, Estelle Carson filling half the drive with questions until Bob was sure Janeka must have felt like a suspect in an FBI interrogation. She wanted to know where Janeka was from (San Diego), what her parents did for a living (her father published a black newspaper, her mother was a housewife), if she had any siblings (a brother who was older and two sisters, both younger).

Panic coursed through Bob's veins. He wished his mother would shut up. His mother had ruined everything.

Halfway to Memphis, thankfully, the interrogation ended and his mother started telling stories about her oldest son as a child, beginning with the 26 hours of labor it took to bring him into the world, and going on through such family favorites as the time Bob opened a lemonade stand and charged $50 a glass on the theory that he might not get many customers but at that price, wouldn't need many. Ordinarily, Bob would have preferred death by firing squad than to have his mother telling a girl these hoary, embarrassing tales.

But given the alternative, he was happy to have her dredge up the misadventures of his childhood. Even if she whipped out the second-grade picture of him when his teeth looked like the New York City skyline, he was willing to take it, so long as she didn't mention Bill Cosby again.

Pretty soon, his mother had them all laughing, and by the time the lights of Memphis appeared on the horizon, Bob was beginning to feel a little better. Yes, conversation stuttered to a stop when they entered the restaurant with Janeka in tow, but they were able to ignore that. And yes, at one point, some man two tables away did stare at Janeka as if she was some odd species of dog and he was trying to figure out how she had gotten in to such a swank restaurant. But by this time, Bob's father was feeling so protective of her that the mild-mannered dentist from Minneapolis threw down his napkin and went over there, ignoring his wife's, his son's, and Janeka's protests. They heard him promise to knock the man's teeth out if he didn't find something else to stare at.

The other man said, "Well, shit fire." But he stopped staring.

Robert Carson, Sr. came back to the table and calmly finished his coffee. Bob's mother stared at him as if wondering who he was and what he had done with her husband. But the expression on her face was not displeased.

A little over an hour later, the rented station wagon pulled up in front of Bob's dorm and disgorged him and Janeka. He leaned into the passenger window to accept his mother's kiss and to promise that he would join them for Christmas at the hotel in the morning. It struck him dimly that his parents or his brothers might wind up sleeping tonight on the same bed where he and Janeka had made love. The thought made his stomach hurt and he resolved to never think it again.

As the station wagon pulled away, he turned to face Janeka and saw what he expected. Her face had gone to stone.

"I'm sorry," said Bob, cold smoke leaking from the side of his mouth. "I apologize for them. They're not usually that bad."

Janeka was incredulous. "You apologize for *them*? You need to apologize for yourself."

"Me? What did I do?"

"Never mind," she said. "Just forget it, all right?"

Janeka spun around to walk away. It was the first inkling Bob had of just how angry she was. He put a hand lightly on her shoulder. He had misread something—that much was obvious. But what it was, he had no idea.

"Janeka, what is it?"

She came back around, her eyes large and filled with anger. No. It wasn't anger, was it? Disappointment. That's what was in those eyes. Somehow, he had let her down. But...*how*?

He felt himself teetering as at the edge of a cliff. "Janeka?" There was a soft insistence in his voice. "What did I do? If it was the surprise, I'm sorry. I didn't know anything about it."

She shook her head and there was pity in the gesture. "Bob," she said, "why didn't you tell them I was black?"

It surprised him. "That's what you're upset about? Why should I tell them that?"

"Are you ashamed of it, Bob? Is that it?"

Panic stabbed his heart that she could even think such a thing. "No!" he said. "Never. Of course not."

"Then why didn't you tell them?"

"Because," he said after a moment, "if I tell them, it's like I'm warning them. It's like I'm saying, 'Oh, here's something you better prepare yourself for. You might want to sit down for this. She's...*black*." He waggled his fingers on the last word, pronounced it with horror movie exaggeration, like the name of some monster from a black lagoon. He waited for her to laugh. Instead, she regarded him with sober, unblinking eyes.

"That's exactly what you should have done, Bob. You should have warned them. The way you did it was extremely unfair."

Bob sighed. But she had a point, didn't she? "I guess you're right," he said. "That was unfair to you. But in my own defense, I didn't expect them to just show up out of the blue."

She shook her head. "You still don't get it," she told him. "It wasn't just unfair to me. It was also unfair to your family. Your poor mother, I felt sorry for her. Did you see her, for heaven's sake, stammering about how much she loves Bill Cosby?" Janeka chased the memory with a sad laugh.

"I didn't tell them," said Bob, "because telling them is like saying it means something."

"It *does* mean something," she said.

"It *doesn't*," he insisted. "It can't. That's the whole point of what we're doing, isn't it? With the voting rights and the whole freedom movement? We're saying it doesn't matter. I'm Bob, you're Janeka, and we love each other and that's all that's important."

She didn't answer. She folded her arms across her chest and looked away. A thought struck him then. "So wait a minute," he said. "Are you're saying you've told your parents that I'm white?"

Janeka looked at him as though he were an idiot. "Of course I have," she said.

Bob was shocked. "And?"

"My mother's okay with it," said Janeka. "Daddy's trying to be okay with it, but it's going to take him a minute. But my older brother, David..." The words dissolved in a rueful, private smile.

"He doesn't like it?"

"He said he's ashamed to see a sister of his consorting with the white devil. He said if I ever bring you home, he's going to knock your block off."

"Nice guy," said Bob.

"David's been hanging around with the Black Muslims. I think he ate too many bean pies or something. Mom and Daddy are really worried about him."

She regarded Bob for a moment. Her arms were still folded. "You should have told your family," she said. Her voice was quiet but definitive. "The fact that you didn't makes me wonder if you really understand the struggle the way I thought you did."

"Wait a minute," said Bob. This was going too fast, veering off into crazy new directions that made no sense. What did this have to do with the struggle? "Of course I understand," he said. "I told you: I just didn't want it to mean anything."

He hated the pity he saw in her smile just then. "But it does, Bob. You have to see that and deal with it. It has always meant something and it always will, even when people are well intentioned, even when they don't want it to mean anything, even when they say it doesn't mean anything. It always does."

Her words set off a dull ache inside of him. "So, is that what you think of me?" he asked. "Just some clueless white boy who doesn't get it?"

She looked up at him. "What I think of you," she said, "is that you are the sweetest, gentlest, most thoughtful and caring man I have ever known, and I am truly crazy about you. But I also think you're naïve and you really haven't thought about what it means for us to be together, what it means for you to be with me."

"Because it doesn't mean anything," insisted Bob. He was conscious of repeating himself, but he could not understand why she didn't see this.

"My God," she said, incredulous. "You don't even see it, do you? The ability to say that, and to believe it, to think it's true, that's a luxury you have only if you are white. Only then. "

"Janeka…"

"I don't have that luxury, Bob."

"Janeka, come on…"

But she was already moving away from him.

"Janeka, please…"

But she was already gone.

Christmas Day dawned bleak and cold. Bob rose early. He got dressed and hiked over to the girls' dorm on the far side of campus, hoping that a night's sleep had soothed her. He rang the bell, got the dorm monitor out of bed (she was not happy about this), and asked her to ring Janeka's room and tell her Bob was there. The dorm monitor did this. Then she listened. Then, instead of handing the receiver to Bob through the sliding glass window of her booth, she hung it back on the wall.

"She doesn't want to talk to you," she said.

"But…"

The middle-aged face that stared back at him from beneath a crown of pink curlers was unyielding. "She doesn't want to talk to you."

"Can you try her again? I'm sure there's some mistake."

This, the woman didn't even deign to answer. She simply stared at Bob until he got the message. His shoulders rounded. He left the dorm and dutifully hiked into town to meet his parents and brothers at their hotel. The Carson family sat in the lobby beneath a fir tree, one of three or four clusters of people unlucky enough to spend the holiday in this place. They exchanged gifts and talked about maybe driving down to Jackson for dinner.

Bob barely heard any of it. All he heard was the woman at the dorm pronouncing his doom over and over again.

She doesn't want to talk to you.

She doesn't want to talk to you.

She doesn't want to talk. To you.

"Honey?" His mother approached him delicately now, the way you might an unfamiliar dog. He caught his father and his brothers exchanging worried glances. "Where's Janeka? We had thought she was going to be with you today."

"She couldn't come," said Bob.

His mother's face creased. "I'm sorry," she said. "I must have made a terrible impression, didn't I? I don't know what got into me, rattling on like that about Bill Cosby. And the funny thing is, we *don't* even like him that much. It was just the only thing I could think of to say."

Bob looked up at his mother. "It's not you she's mad at," he said. He felt tears pooling in his eyes and turned away so that she would not see.

"She's angry with you? What did you do?"

Bob only shook his head. He could not have answered the question even if he'd wanted to.

His parents and brothers flew home the following day. They stopped at Bob's dorm on the way to the airport to say goodbye, the back of the station wagon crammed with suitcases. Standing there on the sidewalk in front of the dorm, Bob's mom kissed his cheek and promised him everything would be all right. His father clapped his shoulder and told Bob the same thing he had always told him for 19 years whenever things got rough.

"This too shall pass," he said and went to get behind the wheel of the rented car. Then he seemed to think better of it. He came back to Bob and leaned his mouth toward his son's ear. "Do you love this woman?" he asked in a private voice.

"Yes, sir," said Bob. He was afraid to say more.

"You really think she's the one?"

Bob nodded.

"Then go get her," his father said. Like it was the simplest, most obvious thing in the world.

Bob's head came up. Father's eyes met son's. Father nodded once, as if in confirmation. Bob nodded once, as if in receipt. Then his father got behind the wheel and, with a chorus of goodbyes and arms waving from every window, the car pulled away from the curb.

Bob watched them until they were out of sight.

Go get her.

Three words, but it was like a pep talk from Vince Lombardi.

Go get her.

Bob marched over to the women's dorm under a full head of steam and asked the dorm monitor to please call Janeka Lattimore and tell her Bob Carson would like to see her. The dorm monitor did this. Janeka would not see him. Bob nodded and marched away.

He marched back the next day, Wednesday. Janeka would not see him.

He marched back on Thursday. Janeka would not see him.

He marched back on Friday. Janeka would not see him.

He marched back on Saturday. Janeka would not see him.

He marched back on Sunday. The dorm monitor listened at the phone for a long moment before returning the receiver to its cradle. She gave Bob a searching look.

"Well?" he said.

"She said she'll meet you tonight on The Hill at 11:30."

Bob pumped his fist at the news. He thought the dorm monitor almost smiled.

The Hill was the closest thing the campus had to a make-out spot. It was, as the name suggested, the highest point on campus—in fact, the only high point on campus—a grassy slope at the top of which a 15-foot-tall white granite Christ stood with palms spread in a "come unto me" gesture. During the day, people went up there to read or have lunch or nap in the grass. At night, they went up there to kiss and, well...not much more. It was difficult to think of rounding the bases with a girl when Jesus himself was watching you.

Bob climbed the slope at precisely 11:30. Janeka was already there, sitting in the grass leaning against Jesus. Lights from the walkway below painted the scene in a faint orange glow.

"Hey," said Bob.

"Hey," said Janeka.

Bob sat down next to her, careful not to be too close. He didn't know if closeness was allowed. "Listen," he said, "I just want to thank you for meeting me."

She gave a little smile. "You're persistent. I'll give you that. You impressed the heck out of Mrs. Hooper."

"The old lady with the glasses?"

"Gladys Hooper, yeah. I think she was secretly rooting for you."

"Nice to know I had somebody on my side," he said.

They were silent together for a long moment. They had The Hill to themselves tonight, which was not surprising. It was New Year's Eve, after all. Most people had gone home for the holiday or they had found parties to go to, or they were in their dorm lobbies watching Guy Lombardo on television. Faintly, Bob could just make out the sound of a party from somewhere in town. "I'm a Believer" by the Monkees was playing on the stereo.

Janeka's right hand was on the grass between them. Bob covered it with his own. "I'm so sorry," he began. "I'd rather die than hurt you. You have to understand that. I guess there's just things I didn't know. And the worst part is, I didn't know I didn't know them."

She looked at him, and his heart thumped when he saw she was smiling. "It's my fault, too," she said. "I shouldn't have assumed you would somehow magically understand. I should have taken more time, explained it to you."

He shot a frustrated breath through his nostrils. "It shouldn't be this hard," he said.

"Should be and shouldn't be have nothing to do with it," she told him. "You're white and I'm black and as long as that's true, it's going to be hard. We may love each other, we may want the same things and believe the same things, but we've come from different worlds and we bring different perspectives and expectations to the table."

Bob tried to swallow past the golf ball that had lodged in his windpipe. "Does that mean it's hopeless?" he asked her.

She scooted over, closing the distance between them until their shoulders were touching. "No," she said, "of course not. But it does mean we're going to have work at it."

He thought about this for a moment. "I think we're worth it," he told her.

"I think so, too," she said.

He put an arm around her and they sat quietly for a long time, not speaking and not needing to. The tinny sounds of music still drifted up from the house party in town. Lulu was singing "To Sir With Love."

Bob looked at his girlfriend. Relief flooded him. He felt a fullness, a *rightness*, unlike anything he had ever known in his life. "I love you, Janeka," he said, because it seemed to need saying.

Her eyes were large and tender in the soft light. "I love you too, Bob."

All at once, from below, there came the sound of whoops and cheers. Car horns blared and there was scattered gunfire.

Bob and Janeka were kissing as 1968 began.

"Would you like an appetizer while you wait for your friend?"

Bob shook off the memory. The lanky server with the long hair was standing above him, placing a basket of warm black bread on the table.

"No," said Bob. "That's fine." He glanced at his watch. It was a little after noon. "She's late, though."

"Your wife?"

"A friend," said Bob.

"Tell me what she looks like and I'll keep an eye out for her."

"I have no idea," said Bob. When the young man gave him a quizzical look, he explained, "I haven't seen her in 40 years."

"Wow," said the server, impressed.

"Yeah," said Bob. "'Wow' is right. All I can tell you is that she's about my age. She's African American." Pause. "And she's beautiful."

Something in his face as he said this made the server grin. "Yes, sir," he said. "I'll steer her your way if I see her."

Bob was embarrassed. He was grateful when the young man—boy, really—walked away. He picked a piece of bread from the basket, thought about butter, thought about cholesterol, decided to eat it dry. Idly, he watched the server bantering with the couple at the next table. So young he was. Probably not yet 25. Probably not even 23. Barely bruised yet. Probably thought that because things were a certain way, they would be that way all his life—because he felt a certain thing now, he would feel that thing always. Too young to understand how life can turn itself inside out and upside down so that all the things you thought you knew, the bedrock upon which you built, could come tumbling out and flying about like the contents of a woman's upended purse.

And you could learn that you didn't know nearly what you thought you did.

Kissing Janeka in those first seconds of 1968, he had been absolutely certain they stood at the beginning of something transformative and new. He'd had no way of knowing that they actually stood very near the end.

They threw themselves into their voter registration program, trundling in his car down the back roads of the Delta, walking the black earth of January-dead cotton fields to the tar-paper shacks where shoeless children watched from corners as he and Janeka made the case to wary-eyed parents and grandparents that they should support the formation of a new political party that had their interests at heart.

They listened patiently, the women sometimes bringing their hands up self-consciously to cover gapped teeth when they smiled, the men often flinty and suspicious but not willing to simply turn polite, well-mannered young people away from their door. Especially when one of the young people was white.

Still, it was frustrating work. For every person who agreed to sign a petition of support—an "Agreement for Change," Janeka titled it—there were
five who nodded when the presentation was done and then said they would
have to think about it. Which, in practice, meant no. And the two of them
would have to trudge on down to the next tar-paper shack and try again.

Sometimes, Bob forgot they were in Mississippi. Sometimes, looking
at the bloated bellies of children too listless even to bat away the flies that
crawled brazenly upon their faces, he felt like he was doing missionary work
in Ethiopia. It took an effort of will to remember that this was America, too.

Janeka's little committee numbered five in all. Besides herself and Bob,
there was a white girl, Rebecca Spivey, and two black guys, Hank Cates and
Parker Ross. Janeka tried sending her teams out in different configurations,
hoping to tap some personal or racial chemistry that might induce these reluctant tenant farmers to do more than listen.

She went into the field herself with Hank and Parker and Rebecca. She
sent Bob out with Rebecca. She sent Hank and Parker out together. She never, of course, sent either of the two black guys out with the white girl. Not
that there was any reason to believe doing so would have made a difference.
Nothing else had. No matter the racial or gender configuration of the teams
that showed up at their doors, the tenant farmers were apt to do the same
thing: listen politely and then say, "Well, you let me study on that for awhile."

Janeka fumed. "It's as if these people have been exploited for so long it's
become habit to them," she told Bob once as they were sitting on The Hill
watching clouds roll by. "It's as if it's become second nature."

"Maybe there aren't enough of us," said Bob. "Maybe it's going to take a
larger operation or a more concrete program like with Freedom Summer in
'64. They had—what? Dozens of people? Hundreds of people, maybe? We
have five."

This brought a rueful smile from Janeka. "We be small, but we be
mighty," she said.

Bob laughed. "Aye, Captain. That we be."

It was a good moment, a moment that bonded them in shared frustration
and laughter. Those moments came less frequently now than they once had.

The truth—and Bob didn't dare acknowledge this, even in the privacy
of his own thoughts—was that there was something fragile in their relationship in that early part of 1968. It was like a broken plate that has been glued
back together and looks more or less the same as it always did, but will always
be just a little weaker at the point of the break.

Yes, they still laughed together. Yes, they still held hands as they walked across campus. Yes, they still loved.

And yet...what had been easy and unforced once upon a time now sometimes felt—*sometimes* felt—mannered, formal, and on guard, particularly when they were talking about race. Bob had never before felt that he was "white" in those discussions. He had felt only that he was who he had always been: himself.

Now he sometimes caught himself being careful, caught himself weighing his words for blind spots and hidden traps. He caught himself being on guard. He did not like the feeling.

And as Bob had never felt he was "white," he had also never felt Janeka was "black."

He knew better than to say any of this out loud. He knew enough to realize it would insult her, though for the life of him, he could not say why. But at any rate, the point was moot; these days, it sometimes seemed to him that she went out of her way to force him to think of her as black, as if she would not allow him to think of her in any other terms. He had the sense sometimes that she was testing him.

At the end of January came the stunning news out of Vietnam. The Cong had broken a holiday ceasefire—it was the lunar New Year, what the Vietnamese called Tet—to launch a major offensive strike against more than 100 cities across the war-torn nation, battles raging in Hue, in Khe-Sahn and even in Saigon, on the grounds of the US embassy.

There was a protest on their campus, as there were on campuses around the country, demonstrators carrying signs denouncing the war, denouncing the president, and demanding the withdrawal of US troops. Janeka was one of the speakers, and instead of just condemning the unjust and unnecessary war, she spent most of her allotted ten minutes complaining that black soldiers were fighting and dying in disproportionate numbers.

Bob understood that this disparity was happening and that it was wrong. But as far as he was concerned, it was secondary to the overall issue— the wrongness of the war itself. He wondered why Janeka could not see this. But he kept that question to himself.

In February, during one of the twice-a-month meetings of SOUL, Janeka floated a resolution. She wanted to invite Stokely Carmichael to speak on campus. The meeting erupted.

Someone wanted to know if the fiery black power advocate was even a Christian.

Someone else asked if they shouldn't invite Martin Luther King if they were going to invite a black leader.

Even members of her own committee sharply challenged the resolution.

"When he was chairman of SNCC, didn't they vote out all the white people?" demanded Rebecca Spivey. "What's the difference between that kind of discrimination and the discrimination we're all fighting against?"

"And this whole black power thing," said Parker Ross, "just seems to me like a cover for a philosophy of Negro supremacy. I don't believe in Negro supremacy any more than I believe in white supremacy."

This brought a snort of derision from Hank Cates. "Stop Tomming, Park. It's not about Negro supremacy and you know it. It's about black *self-sufficiency*, about us getting our own instead of always having to crawl to them."

"I don't think there's any need for name calling," said Parker, stiffly.

Rebecca said, "Am I a 'them' now, Hank? Is that what I am to you?"

Bob caught Janeka staring at him then across the room. It was a look that implored him. But to do what? Did she really think he would stand up and say, "Yes, by all means, let's invite Stokely Carmichael, who preaches black supremacy and violence, to the campus of our Christian university?" Did she really think that might happen?

He loved her. God, he loved her. And he believed she loved him, too.

But it was in moments like this that he felt the distance between them, and he had no idea if the love they felt would be enough to bridge it. So he did the only thing he could. He turned toward the imploring look and hunched his shoulders in a helpless shrug. And he wondered if she knew that the impotence and inability it expressed were not just about this moment in this meeting, but about many things far beyond.

"Bob Carson? Is that you? Lord have mercy."

The voice came to him over the muted rumble of restaurant chatter. Memory broke. Bob blinked, startled. And just like that, 40 years had passed and he was looking up into the face of Janeka Lattimore.

fourteen

Doug Perry was out of breath and promising himself he would never again eat bear claws for breakfast as he trotted across the parking garage and up to the street.

The ambulance was still there. Amy was sitting upright on a gurney in back, one paramedic taking her blood pressure, another writing something on a clipboard. She looked ghastly. One side of her face was crooked and stained by a garish bruise the color of sunset. Her glasses were askew. She was holding a cold pack to her head.

Doug was in shirtsleeves and his armpits were dark with sweat from the unaccustomed exertion. At the sight of Amy, he shouldered his way through the crowd of tourists, shoppers, and office workers who had stopped to see the spectacle. Amy's eyes were foggy. They sharpened all at once when she saw him.

"Yag," she said, and Doug guessed that this was supposed to be his name.

"Amy?" he said. "What the hell?"

"Yag, e ah le ma fuh efo..." It was no use. Her jaw would not properly close and gibberish was the only language she could speak. Consternation pinched her features. But Amy was not to be defeated. She snatched the pen from the paramedic with the clipboard and mimed writing until, with a grimace of exasperation, he handed her a piece of paper.

Amy wrote on it with great concentration, wincing occasionally from pain. When she was done, she handed the paper to Doug, returned the paramedic's pen, and sagged a little as if fatigued. Doug studied the paper. In the margins of a memo on the cleaning and maintaining of emergency rigs, she had written in a spidery hand: *This wasn't random! The guy who was here before, he hit me. He took the disk back. Ask Jalil. He saw.*

Jalil. She had to mean the big, black kid who worked day security. That was his name, wasn't it? Something Arabic, at least. But what was this about a disk? And a guy from before? Doug looked the questions at her. She nodded emphatically, brushed at the air as if shooing him off.

He turned to go, thought better of it and turned back. "I'll meet you at the hospital," he said. "I'll call your husband. Where's he work?"

"E ou a houn," she said.

It took him a moment. "Out of town?" he finally guessed.

She nodded. Then the pain winched her eyes shut.

Again, Doug turned to go. Again, he thought better of it. She had kids, didn't she? He wasn't sure, but he seemed to remember two little ones capering after her last year at the holiday gathering that had once, in a less politically correct era, been called a Christmas party.

"What about your kids? You want us to see to them?"

"Wih a si-ah."

Doug whispered the strange sounds in his mind until he understood them. "With your sister. Okay, got it. I'm sure we have her number. We'll call and let her know."

The paramedic with the clipboard interrupted. "Okay, mister, we got to roll."

"Where are you taking her?"

"Mercy," said the paramedic as they pushed the gurney into the wagon. Doug heard it lock into place.

One paramedic went around to the driver's side door. The second climbed in back with Amy. He closed one side of the rig and was reaching for the other when Amy called out.

"Ock ou Ya-il!" Doug heard her command.

Talk to Jalil.

"I will," he called. But the door had already slammed shut.

Siren howling, the ambulance pulled away from the curb and out into Michigan Avenue traffic. Doug wheeled around to head back into the building and ran into a phalanx of *Post* employees pouring out through the glass doors of the elevator lobby. Like him, they had heard something was going on right at the entrance to their garage. Denis was leading the way.

"What's this I hear about a mugging?" he said. "Is it true?"

Doug didn't answer immediately. He lifted both hands, index fingers wagging toward the elevators. "Everybody back to work," he ordered. "There's nothing to see out there. Amy Landingham was jumped here in the garage, but she's going to be fine. The paramedics have already taken her away."

A few of them—the younger ones, mostly—stopped and went back, their questions answered. The rest paused, listened, then walked past him to see for themselves. Doug shook his head. The same thing that made some people good reporters made them absolutely lousy at following directions.

"Amy was mugged?" Lassiter was at his elbow.

Doug shook his head. "No," he said. "She was attacked, not mugged. She—"

And then he stopped, stunned by what he saw. Lassiter stared at him, first quizzical, then impatient. "Yeah?" he said. "Go on."

"Gun," said Doug.

"What?"

Doug pointed to where a black Luger lay on the concrete next to the right, rear tire of somebody's car. "Gun," he said again.

Lassiter looked where Denis was pointing. He started when he saw it. "Holy shit," he said. "You figure the guy who attacked Amy dropped it?"

Doug found himself wondering—and not for the first time—how it was that this guy was his boss instead of the other way around. "That'd be my guess," he said. "Yeah."

A low whistle. "Holy hell. What should we do?"

"Call Mendoza. Have him seal the garage and put a couple of his guys down here to make sure nobody touches the gun. Get a photographer down to get pictures. Call the cops."

It struck Doug how bizarre it was that he was giving orders to Lassiter this way. But Lassiter didn't seem to notice. His nod was thoughtful. "Yeah," he said, "those sound like good ideas. I'll call Mendoza."

"Good," said Doug, moving away. "You'll want to keep an eye on things til his men get here to make sure nobody messes with that thing. This is a crime scene now." Several of the reporters were now staring at the gun and taking pictures with their smartphones.

"Where are you going?" asked Lassiter.

"Going to talk to the kid in the lobby."

"What for?"

Doug stopped. "Amy said it wasn't just a random mugging. She knew the guy—or at least she'd seen him before. He came through here earlier today. She told me the kid in the lobby saw him, too."

Lassiter stared at him for a beat, taking all this in. Then he said, "First Malcolm disappears, now this. What the hell is going on here?"

"That's what I want to know." Doug strode off through a second, late-arriving group of reporters, reached the elevator, and punched the button for the main lobby. Behind him, he heard Lassiter telling people to step back.

Doug couldn't make sense of it. Someone coming after Malcolm at least made some kind of sense. He wrote an opinion column, after all. Opinions piss people off. But Amy? She was a good-natured young reporter who, as far as he knew, didn't have an enemy in the world—unless you counted that married alderman who used campaign funds to take his boyfriend on a ski trip to Aspen. When he wouldn't give her an interview, Amy had ambushed him in a public meeting and questioned him so relentlessly he broke down crying at the podium.

Other than that, who would wish ill on Amy Landingham? Heck, who, beyond the most assiduous newspaper junkies, even knew her name?

Could it be a coincidence, her getting attacked the same day Malcolm went missing?

It could be, he supposed, but the idea just didn't feel right. No, somehow, all of this was connected. He just didn't know how. Doug felt as if he were trying to solve some bizarre puzzle to which he held a few random pieces, but had no idea what the finished product was supposed to be.

The elevator opened on the lobby. The security guy was just sending off an angry subscriber with a replacement copy of that day's paper. He saw Doug coming. "What's going on?" he asked. "I heard them say somebody got mugged down in the garage?"

Instead of answering, Doug nodded toward the retreating customer. "Been like that all day?" he asked.

"Yeah," he said. "All day. So what's happening in the garage?"

"You're Jalil, right?"

"Yeah."

Doug had folded and creased the memo from the paramedics. Now he unfolded it and placed it beneath the big man's eyes. "A few minutes ago, some guy coldcocked Amy Landingham down in the garage."

Jalil looked up from the paper, eyes rounded by distress. "Amy? But she ain't big as a minute. Was she hurt?"

"They're taking her to the hospital," said Doug, "but I think she'll be all right. She looked all right, at least, more or less."

"So what's this I'm lookin' at? Some kind of paramedics memo?"

"No. Amy wrote that note out for me, the one right there in the margins. She said you would know what it means."

Jalil read. Then the line of his jaw stiffened and something pulsed in his temple. "I'll be damned," he said.

"Yeah?"

Jalil looked up. "Yeah," he said. " I know who she's talking about. Came here asking to see Malcolm Toussaint's editor. Said he had something important for him. Some computer disk. I knew there was something hinky about that guy. I knew it."

"He was angry about Toussaint's column?"

Jalil shook his head. "Actually, he didn't even mention it. I mean, we've had a lot of folks through these doors today so pissed off they could spit. But that didn't seem to be where he was comin' from. He just kept demanding to see Toussaint's boss, and when I explained to him that Mr. Toussaint didn't work here anymore and his boss didn't, either, that seemed to throw him."

"When was this?"

"Couple hours ago, I guess."

"Can you show me?"

He nodded and beckoned Doug to join him behind the security desk. There he had a console with five screens, one showing the parking elevator downstairs, one showing the front of the building, one showing the newsroom upstairs, two watching the lobby from different angles. None, Doug noted, with a view of the garage where Amy was assaulted. "We need more cameras," he told Jalil.

Jalil nodded. "Yeah," he said, tapping the keyboard. "I told Mendoza the same thing. He said no way that happens. Budget cutbacks."

There was weariness in Doug's sigh. "Yeah," he said. "Lot of that in this business lately. You want my advice, kid?"

When Jalil glanced up, Doug told him, "Keep your eyes open for another job opportunity. Grab it if it comes."

The younger man grinned. "All due respect, sir, I ain't dependin' on this place to take care of me forever. I'm in school. Got one more semester til I get my degree in video game design."

"Video game design? That's a thing now? You can get a degree in that?"

"Oh, hell yeah," said Jalil, still grinning. "That's what I'm doing. I'm looking to start the next Rockstar Games."

Doug did not know what that was. He felt old.

As he spoke, Jalil was fast-forwarding through images from a little more than two hours ago, a procession of people who darted up to the desk, spoke rapidly, gestured broadly, darted away. All at once, Jalil slowed the playback. "There he is," he said.

Doug fumbled for the glasses he kept in his shirt pocket and leaned forward. He saw a thin man in his forties with nervous eyes and a bizarre hairstyle, buzz-cut on one side, thick on the other, chopped off just above the ear "He ought to stab his barber with his own scissors," muttered Doug.

On the screen, he saw Jalil in the foreground, talking with some older lady, while the man waited his turn, reading headlines of old newspapers. There was something odd about it, almost as if he were making a show of being calm. But all you had to do was look at those jittery eyes and you knew it was only a show.

"He give a name?" asked Doug.

"No," said Jalil.

On screen the old lady moved away from the desk and the man approached Jalil. "Okay," said Jalil, poking one stubby finger toward the screen, "this is where he's asking me about Mr. Toussaint's editor and I'm telling him he doesn't work here anymore, yadda yadda, he comes out of pocket with this DVD, says he has to get it to Mr. Carson, yadda yadda yadda, and then, boom." Again, he pointed to the screen. Amy had entered the frame, pushing a cart full of Bob Carson's belongings. "She tells him she's going over that way and she'd be happy to give Bob the DVD. And he says yeah, but you can kind of tell he doesn't really want to do it."

Doug peered at the screen. You really could tell. The jittery eyes were dancing a buck and wing, the lips pursed in resignation, as the man handed the DVD to Amy.

"Can you burn copies of that?" Doug asked.

Jalil nodded. "Sure."

"Make three. Cops are going to want one. Give one to Lassiter. And make one for me."

"Machine's slow," Jalil warned him. "And it can only make one at a time."

"Fine," said Doug, pulling a cellphone out of his front pocket. "Make mine first."

"I'll tell you one thing about this guy," said Jalil. He was placing a DVD in the open bay of a dubbing machine.

"What's that?" Doug was scrolling through the contacts list on his phone, looing for his own office number.

"He didn't like me very much."

Doug looked up. "How do you mean?"

"I mean he didn't like me."

"Did the two of you have words?"

"No," said Jalil, "it wasn't a personal thing. It was a race thing. He didn't like having to deal with a black man."

Doug looked down into the young man's eyes. They were straightforward and clear. "How did you know this? Was there something he said? Something he did?"

Jalil gave him a little smile and to Doug's surprise, he read pity in it. "No, sir," said the security man. "But you can just tell."

Doug did not bother to mask his skepticism. "You can tell."

Still those straightforward eyes. "Yes, sir. Usually, you can."

"Okay," said Doug, returning to his cellphone directory. "Thanks."

He was dubious. In his experience, black people—Malcolm included—often cited race to explain stuff race had nothing to do with. It was a default position for some of them. Even an excuse.

He called his office, got his secretary, and gave her terse instructions. Get his suit coat and his laptop computer and bring them both to the lobby. Call Amy Landingham's sister and tell her what had happened and where she was.

As he spoke, Hector Mendoza and two of his men—one was a woman, actually—came through the turnstiles without a word and strode to the parking garage elevators. Jalil was directing a customer to the classified advertising desk. Doug glanced at the progress bar on the CD burner. Only 65 percent. Jalil was right. The thing really was slow.

On a whim, Doug opened his phone again. He touched Bob's name on the screen. Granted, Bob no longer worked here—Doug still couldn't believe it, even though he had known it would happen—but he still ought to know what was going on. Especially since the guy who slugged Amy had been looking for him. What if he was still after him? Besides, thought Doug, he wouldn't mind hearing the guy's voice, just to make sure he was okay.

"Hello?" said Bob.

"Bob, hey, it's Doug Perry. Listen, I thought you ought—"

"I can't talk right now."

"No, listen, I just need to tell you…Hello? Hello?"

Doug stared at the phone as if it had done him wrong. Surely the call had just been dropped. Surely, the sonofabitch didn't just hang up on him.

Doug touched Bob's name on the screen again. The call went straight to voicemail. Doug swore softly in disbelief. The sonofabitch had, indeed, hung up on him.

As he pocketed his phone, his secretary came through the turnstiles with the items he had requested. Peggy Toyama was a thin woman of Japanese heritage with half-moon reading glasses and a matronly dignity. Doug thought she must have been a knockout in her day.

She held his coat for him as he shrugged into it. "You tell Amy to feel better soon," she said. Amy and Peggy were great friends.

"I will," Doug said. She handed him his briefcase.

"I can't believe somebody hurt that sweet little girl," she said.

"It's been a crazy day," he said, "and it's not even 1:00 yet. Don't forget to call her family."

The elevator from the garage opened. Lassiter came through. "Police just arrived. Mendoza's got it covered," he said. Then he noticed the suit coat and briefcase.

"You're leaving?"

"Going to the hospital."

"I understand you want to check in on her and that's fine. But we've still got a paper to put out. Heck, we've got to get an opinion page together—without an opinion page editor."

Doug spoke more sharply than he'd intended. "Yeah, well maybe you and Lydia should have thought of that before you sacked the opinion page editor we had."

Lassiter's eyes widened and Doug knew he'd gone too far, snapping at the executive editor in front of two of his subordinates. He had a moment to calculate the job prospects for a 61-year-old manager in a dying industry. They were not good. After a moment, he said, "I'm sorry, Denis. I didn't mean to snap at you. It's just been a hard day. I'm worried about Amy and Malcolm. Don't worry. I'll be back soon." Doug added this last, even though he wasn't at all sure it was true.

Still, it had the desired effect. Lassiter gave a short, sharp nod, mollified for the moment. But Doug knew this wasn't over. He was conscious of all their eyes on him—Doug's, Peggy's, even Jalil's—as he moved to the elevator and stabbed the button, reminding himself again of his uncertain employability. And yes, this did concern him.

But damn it, something was going on here and he needed to know what it was. For all any of them knew, some lunatic was out there targeting *Post* employees. At the very least, it might well be news. And, budget cuts aside, that was still the name of this business, wasn't it?

The elevator door opened. Doug got on and rode it down to the parking garage. A police detective was using a pencil to lift the Luger by its trigger guard. Doug walked to his car, a little canary-yellow coupe. He threw the briefcase on the front seat, cranked the engine, and drove out into the weak late autumn sunshine.

About a mile south on Michigan, he saw police barricades going up. It reminded him of what he had almost managed to forget. It was Election Day. They were sealing off streets, rerouting traffic. Tonight, Barack Obama was coming to Grant Park.

fifteen

She wore her hair in short, salt-and-pepper dreadlocks now. Her skin was still the color of the sun just as it fell into twilight, her lips still proud as the prow of some sailing ship. Time had piled up in her eyes and left a residue of wisdom there, but those eyes were still the shade of sea foam on some remote island in the tropics. Her breasts were still small and pert and just... *right*. And her...

Easy, boy. Easy. Get a grip.

He was alarmed at how readily it all came back, as if 40 years had somehow instantly been scrubbed away. Without meaning to, he planted a hand on the back of his head, uncomfortably aware that he was a little balder every day.

And wasn't that funny? Bob had never been self-conscious about that, never cared much about his hair loss one way or another. Until just this instant.

"Bob?" Confusion wrinkled her brow. "That is you, isn't it?"

He realized he had not yet answered her. "Uh...yeah," he said. "Yeah. I'm sorry, Janeka, where are my manners?"

He stood, awkwardly, embraced her, awkwardly, all thoughts of tactics, all thoughts of maintaining the high ground, all thoughts, period, suddenly gone.

"Please, sit down," he managed to say.

She sat, still smiling, and he took her in. She was stylish in a way she never had been when they were young, wearing a waist-length, reddish brown leather jacket, a high-necked, sand-colored blouse, and a gold necklace with matching earrings. Bob did not remember her ever caring enough about what she wore to coordinate it so deftly. Color coordinating clothes, after all, did nothing to challenge the structures of institutionalized oppression.

"I'm so sorry I'm late," she said. "As I'm sure you can imagine, it's been quite the busy day."

"Janeka Lattimore," he said. He was conscious of almost praying her name.

"Bob Carson," she said. "How have you been, old friend?"

"Mostly good," he said. "Today hasn't been the best day, but mostly, good."

"Oh? What's wrong with today?"

He waved it off, sorry he had brought it up. "Don't even want to talk about it," he said. "So tell me, how are you? I hope life has been good to you."

"Better than I deserve," she said.

"Married? Single? Children?" He heard a hopeful note in his voice that made him wince.

"Married," she said. "And then divorced. I guess it's been…11 years now. We had a good run—19 years. Had three wonderful kids. My daughter, Angela, is a doctor in San Diego. My son Eldridge scores movies. He lives in Los Angeles. And my youngest, Bryan, is an Americorps volunteer at a school in some small town in West Virginia. I'm still waiting on grandkids. Getting a little impatient about it, to tell you the truth. How about you?"

"Never married," said Bob. "One son, Adam. He's an actor in New York City. Well, mostly he's a bartender in New York City, but every once in awhile, he's an actor."

She smiled. "They have to follow their own paths, don't they?"

"Yeah," he said, "that they do."

"Makes you appreciate what our parents went through with us. I can't tell you how many times my father gave me the lecture about how you can't make a living carrying protest signs."

"So, what did you end up doing?" he asked, though he already knew some of it.

She was buttering a piece of the black bread. "Oh, I did a bunch of things, but for the last 20 years, I've owned a little public relations firm in San Francisco. Of course, that's been on hiatus since I started working with the campaign. I'm doing West Coast minority outreach for the senator. Which reminds me: have you voted yet? I'm supposed to ask everybody I meet today."

Somewhat to his surprise, Bob realized that he, in fact, had not voted yet. "No," he said. "I'll do it this afternoon."

"Good," she said. "Make sure you do. I hope we can count on your support?"

Bob hesitated. He didn't know why he did, but she saw it. "Oh, come on, Bob. Please don't tell me you're voting for the cranky old man and the naughty librarian."

Bob intended, in fact, to vote for Obama. Eight disastrous years under George W. Bush along with nightmares about the two most terrifying words in the English language—"President Palin"—had left him little choice but to gamble on Obama, despite reservations about his lack of experience and the vagueness of his agenda. But even so, something combative rose up in him at Janeka's airy dismissal of the Republican candidates.

And then, a second later, he realized: it wasn't her dismissal of McCain and Palin that raised his ire. It was her dismissal of the idea that *he* might vote for them, her assumption that she still knew anything at all about him, all these years later.

Bob drew himself up. "And what if I was?" he said.

The bread paused, halfway to her mouth. "You're not," she told him. Assured him, actually.

Bob repeated it. "What if I was?"

"Bob?" She made his name a scandalized shout. It was as if he had suggested they strip to their underwear and dance on top of the table.

"What if I was?" he insisted. "What would you say?"

She considered the question for a long moment. Finally she said, "I would say you have changed a great deal. I would say you're not the boy I used to know."

And this, he realized, was the admission he'd wanted from her all along. Except, now that he had it, he wondered why having it had seemed so important.

He smiled. "It's been 40 years, Janeka. Lots of things change over that much time."

"I see," she said, and the new note of caution he heard in her voice pleased him. "So are you saying you'll be voting for the Republicans?"

"Heck no," he said. "I mean, I might have if McCain had picked a better veep. Let's face it: she's an idiot. But your guy has problems of his own. He's not exactly the most experienced candidate who ever ran for president."

"He has the exact same experience Lincoln had."

Bob rolled his eyes. "I wish you Obama folks would stop saying that," he said. "Your guy is not Lincoln and in any event, Lincoln was 147 years ago. It's a different world now."

"You know what?" She raised her palms. "Uncle. I surrender. You win. I don't care why we have your support, so long as we have it."

He grinned. "If you knew the whole truth, you might not be so happy to have me," he said.

"What do you mean?"

"I mean, I've got a losing streak going back 20 years. Bush the elder is the last guy I voted for who actually won."

"You're kidding me."

"Nope." He squeezed his eyes shut, the better to pluck the names from memory. "Bush in 1992, then Dole, then Gore, then Kerry: my litany of losers. I never seem to find myself in step with what the rest of the country is thinking."

"So your voting for Senator Obama is—"

"—the worst possible omen for your side, yes."

Janeka took this in, her expression thoughtful and reflective as she chewed bread. Then she swallowed. "You know," she said, "sometimes I think Sarah Palin has gotten a raw deal from news media with their snobbish emphasis on reading books and understanding geography."

Surprised laughter broke out of him, a sound warm and welcome after all that had happened so far on this bizarre day. She laughed with him and for that moment, the world was a good place.

"I've missed you," he heard himself say. He spoke softly and he wasn't sure she heard him over the sound of her own laughter.

The skinny waiter appeared at their table. "Have we had a chance to study the menu?" he asked.

"Actually, we haven't," said Janeka, still chuckling as she flipped it open. "But I'll be quick. Go on and order, Bob, if you already know what you want."

Bob did. He ordered the seared salmon with the pine nut couscous.

When it was her turn, Janeka tapped one elegantly manicured fingernail on the page. "This is what I'll have," she said. "New York strip steak with mashed potatoes and gravy and fresh, steamed broccoli. That sounds just right."

"Yes, ma'am. And how would you like that prepared?"

"Medium rare," she said. The waiter nodded, collected their menus and left. She looked at Bob and said, "What?"

Bob realized he must have been staring. "I don't know," he said. "I guess I just figured…maybe you'd have gone vegan or something by now."

"Really? Why?"

"I guess…well, you know, we were both pretty far left of center back in the day."

With a glance, she took in the room, which was overseen from above the front door by a steer's head. The steer did not look particularly happy about it. "If I were a vegan," she said, "I'd be out of luck in this place, wouldn't I?"

Bob felt petty and obvious then. "Janeka," he began, "I didn't mean to—"

His cellphone chirped and he was grateful for the interruption, because he'd had no idea how that sentence might end. He lifted the phone from the holster on his hip. Then he saw the caller ID and his mood soured like milk.

"This will just take a second," he told Janeka as he pressed the button to accept the call.

She gave an amiable shrug. "Take your time," she said.

"Yeah?" said Bob into the phone.

"Bob, hey, it's Doug Perry. Listen, I thought you ought—"

"I can't talk right now." He clicked the phone off without waiting for an answer. Bob knew he had no reason to be angry with Doug Perry, but that didn't help much. He was angry with all of them.

Janeka was watching him. "Wow," she said. "You weren't kidding."

"What?"

"You said it would take about a second."

"My ex-boss," he said.

"Ex?"

A sigh. "You remember I told you it hadn't been the best day?"

She nodded.

"I got axed this morning."

"What? Why?"

The cell chirped again. Bob glanced at it. Doug wasn't taking the hint. He pressed a button to dismiss the call. "I assume you saw today's paper," he said.

"Picked up a copy at O'Hare, yes."

"So you saw that column by Malcolm Toussaint on the front page."

"I sure did. I was surprised you guys would run it at all, much less on page one."

"We didn't intend it to run it," said Bob. "Malcolm was one of my writers. He submitted the column and I rejected it, precisely because of how angry it was. He tried to go over my head, but my bosses all agreed with me. He snuck into the building late last night, just as the early edition was being put to bed. Apparently, he had my computer password—maybe I shared it with him at some point, I don't know—and he used it to remake the front page and strip his column in there."

"They blame you for that?"

"My writer, my password, my fault."

"Oh, Bob," she said. "I'm so sorry."

He shrugged. "Yeah," he said. "Not a good day."

"What does Toussaint have to say for himself?"

"Haven't been able to reach him. He's not taking my calls. As a matter of fact, I'm headed to his house when I leave here."

"You sure that's a good idea?"

This surprised him. "How do you mean?"

"You're obviously upset."

"Don't I have a right to be?"

"Sure, you do. But what's the point of going to his house? The only thing that can happen is an argument—or a fight. I don't see how either of those outcomes helps you any."

"The man ruined my life, Janeka. I'm entitled to my pound of flesh."

She regarded him for a moment. "You know," she said finally, "they used to call you Bobby Peaceful back at school. You were so committed to all that stuff we used to sit up and talk about: nonviolent revolution, the weapon of love, passive resistance, peacefully challenging the social order."

"Yeah, I remember all that," he said. "So?"

"So you really have changed."

"Haven't you? Haven't we all?"

"Yes," she said. "I suppose that's true. But I'm curious about something. When Toussaint brought that column to you, did you try to reason with him? Did you suggest ways he could make the same point without the inflammatory language?"

Bob was incredulous. "His point was that white people are full of crap," he said. "I don't know any kinder and gentler way to say that."

"Actually," she said, "I think his point was that he's tired. Wasn't that what he said in the first or second line?"

For a moment, Bob did not speak. Was she actually going to sit there and defend him? This woman of all women was going to defend the man who cost him his job?

"Malcolm Toussaint," he said, speaking slowly and with great care, "drives a Corvette and lives in an exclusive neighborhood. He hangs out with presidents, he appears on television, he writes best-selling books and he makes, I would guess, probably three times my salary. So tell me, Janeka, please: what in the hell does he have to be tired about?"

She looked at him. She held up the surrender hands again. "I apologize," she said. "This is obviously still a very raw subject for you and it's not my business to be telling you what I think you should have done. Let's talk about something else."

"No," he said. "Let's talk about this. Explain to me what he has to be tired about."

"Bob..."

"Explain it to me. Please."

She sighed. "He explained it to you himself, didn't he? Right there in the column? He said something about giving up on the notion that white people can be influenced to give up the idea that color dictates intelligence, morality, or worth."

"Is that how you feel? White people are all lost?"

Her eyes sparked like struck flint. "If that was how I felt, Bob, I wouldn't be sitting here," she said.

"Then what's your point?"

"My point is that I understand why he might feel that way. The Bob Carson I used to know would have understood it, too. Or at least been willing to try."

"Bobby Peaceful has left the building."

"So I see," she said. "Maybe I should join him." She picked up her purse.

"No," said Bob, reaching to touch her arm, "please stay." She hesitated. "It's been 40 years," he reminded her.

"Maybe it should be 40 more," she replied.

"Okay," said Bob, "I deserve that. But I'm serious: I do not understand how Malcolm Toussaint can feel the way he does. Or why you can sympathize with him, even if you say you don't quite agree."

She removed her hand from her purse and sat back, her eyes warning that this was only a conditional surrender. "It's not about whether I agree or disagree," she said. "I just know where he's coming from."

"So help me to understand it," said Bob. And when he saw the skeptical look on her face he said, "I'm serious. Please."

Janeka released a soft breath of exasperation. "You know, white people always do what you just did."

"What did I just do? Say please?"

This actually made her laugh. "No, Bob. I mean before. You talked about Toussaint's money and the good life he has as if because of that, he has no right to complain about the effects of racism, no right to be frustrated."

"I'm just saying it hasn't kept him back."

"We don't know that," she said. "For all that he's made and all that he's achieved, we don't know that he could not have made even more and achieved even more except that somebody who could have made a difference looked at him in some pivotal moment and didn't see a talented writer, but only a black man."

He opened his mouth to reply. She held up a hand. "But assume you're right," she said. "Assume he has achieved exactly what he would have achieved even if were white. You think that makes it any less frustrating? In a way, it's more. You go to school, you build a career, you check off all the boxes of achievement, you're feeling pretty good about yourself and yet, invariably, somebody will come along and remind you that for all that, you're still just a nigger."

"Why should he care what some random idiot thinks?"

"It's more than a few random idiots, Bob. That's something else white people don't get. And anyway, it doesn't take but a few idiots to make your life miserable. You said he drives a Corvette?"

"Yeah."

"Did he ever tell you about the time—or maybe the times, plural; I don't know—he got pulled over by some snide cop who thought he was a carjacker?"

"That's such a cliché, Janeka."

"Things become cliché because they are repeated. And because there is truth in them."

"You're so sure that's happened?"

"I would bet money on it," she said.

"Okay," said Bob, "but even so, it's just a bad cop. Stuff happens. It happens to everybody, no matter what color you are. So why can't he accept it as just one of those things and keep on moving? That's what I would do."

She smiled without humor. "That's easy to say when it never happens to you. Or when it happens rarely. What if that and a dozen other indignities like it happen every day, not just with cops, but also with doctors, waiters, cashiers, bosses, friends? It's like walking around your whole life with a pebble in your shoe that you can never remove. How long before that makes you crazy?"

"A pebble in a shoe? That's your explanation for Toussaint?"

"I don't know Toussaint," she said. "You do. I'm just trying to explain what you asked me to explain. All I'm saying is that white people always think having a fine car or nice clothes or money or social standing puts you beyond racism—and it doesn't. That's the whole point. That's why it's racism."

For a moment, Bob didn't know what to say. "Janeka," he finally managed, "I'm sorry. I have to apologize."

"For what?"

"For dropping my bad day in your lap. For asking you to explain how somebody else feels."

"The man I used to know would have had more empathy, even if he didn't understand."

"The man you used to know." He chased the words with a bitter snort.

"What's so funny?"

He looked away from her. He would not be able to admit what he needed to admit if he was looking at her while he said it. "Janeka, I've got to tell you the truth. Sometimes, I think the man you used to know grew up and became a stone racist. Because you're right: I *don't* have the empathy I used to have. I don't have the patience. Toussaint writes about that stuff all the time—*all the time*—and I read it and I'm thinking, 'Stop whining. Get over it. I'm tired of hearing it. Just sick and tired of hearing it.'"

Bob lowered his eyes to the table. "I don't know what's happened to me," he said. "Sometimes, I'm not very pleased with the man I seem to have become."

"Bob?" He lifted his head until his eyes met hers. "If you're sick and tired of hearing it, how do think Toussaint feels, living it?"

Bob nodded. He didn't trust himself to do more.

She smiled to lighten the mood. "Listen to me," she said, "lecturing you about race. I would think that's the last thing you'd want to hear from me."

"No, it's okay," he said. "I asked for it, remember?"

"You know why I wanted to see you?" she said, and there was a bright note in her voice that he did not trust.

"Why?" asked Bob.

"Well, because it's been 40 years, of course. But I also wanted to see you because I felt I owed you an apology."

"An apology for what?" asked Bob.

She took a deep breath, seemed to gather herself. "For the last time I saw you," she said. "It has always—" she paused, and he could see her searching for the right word "—haunted me, the way I left things between us. The last time we spoke, I was lecturing you on this same subject. And I said a terrible thing I never should have said. I was such a young fool, so full of myself, so full of revolution. All you wanted to do was love me. And that should have been enough for me. I know what I said hurt you; I could see it in your eyes. And I've carried that knowledge with me all these years because I never had the guts to find you and ask you to forgive me."

It was the last thing he had expected. Bob Carson felt something shift inside him. It scared him. "Janeka," he said. And then his phone buzzed.

It was sitting on the table where he'd placed it after Doug's call. The screen lit up with a text message and he only glanced down, not even intending to pick it up, not wanting to lose this moment. Then he saw what was written there. The words were in urgent capital letters and he snatched up the phone in alarm to read them closer. Janeka called his name uncertainly. He held his hand up.

The message was from Doug Perry. It said:

PICK UP THE PHONE—WE THINK YOU MAY BE IN DANGER!!

Then the phone rang.

"Yeah?" said Bob.

"Finally," said Doug Perry.

"What's this about me being in danger?" asked Bob. He saw Janeka's eyebrows dart at the question.

"I'm at Mercy Hospital," said Doug. His voice was breathy like he was walking fast. "I'm on my way to see Amy."

"Amy? I just saw her an hour ago."

"I know," said Doug. "She was assaulted. I mean, not sexually, but, you know…"

"What? Is she okay?"

"I think she's going to be."

"What happened?"

"She got back to the building and some guy jumped her in the garage. Beat her up pretty good and took some computer disk she had."

"Computer disk?"

"Yeah. Near as I could piece together from talking to the kid at the security desk, this skinny guy with this bizarre haircut shows up at the building this morning with a disk he says he has to give to you. Well, actually, he said it had to go to Toussaint's boss, but, well…you know…"

"Yeah, I got it," said Bob, eager to get Doug past the awkward moment and on to the point.

"Well anyway," said Doug, "Amy's passing by headed down to the garage and she says she's going out to your house and she can give the disk to you. So he lets her take it. But he must have followed her or something because he knows she didn't give you the disk. He's waiting for her when she gets back to the garage. And he coldcocks her and snatches the disk from her."

"Who is this guy? What's on the disk?"

"Your guess is as good as mine," said Doug. "I have no idea. But if he followed her, then he knows where you live and probably what you look like. So I just wanted to make sure you were aware. You need to be careful. If I were you, I don't think I'd go home right now."

The waiter was putting their plates in front of them. He asked Bob if he wanted ground pepper. Bob waved him away impatiently. He caught a look at Janeka's eyes. She was watching him with concern.

"You think the guy might be looking for me?"

"He was as of a couple hours ago. Oh, and there's one other thing: Malcolm is missing."

"Yeah," said Bob. "Amy told me. You think the one has something to do with the other?"

"I don't know," said Doug. "Be a hell of a coincidence though, wouldn't it? Two of our people in the same day?"

It took Bob a moment. "Wow," he finally said. "Doug, what's going on here?"

"I don't know, buddy. But you need to watch your ass."

Bob felt dazed. "Yeah," he said. "Will do. I'm having lunch now. Maybe I'll go by the hospital after and look in on Amy."

"Good deal," said Doug. "Stay in touch."

Janeka was staring at him as Bob set down the phone. "My goodness," she said. "What's going on? Is everything all right?"

Bob shared with her the details of the call from Doug. "My goodness," she said again.

"Yeah," said Bob. Their meals were still untouched. "Eat," he told her.

She ignored him. "So he thinks this individual might be after you?"

"That's what he said. Seems like a reasonable assumption, I guess. Eat."

"You have to call the police."

"I have no idea what I would tell them. Or even what I'd want them to do. Now come on, your steak's getting cold."

She looked at him a moment. Then she picked up knife and fork and began to eat. For a few minutes, neither of them spoke much.

"How's your steak?" Bob finally asked, because the silence was becoming uncomfortable.

"Delicious," she said. "And your fish?"

"A little undercooked."

Silence intervened again. Finally, Janeka said, "Bob, before the phone call, we were talking about the way we left things between us all those years ago."

Bob kept his eyes on his plate and did not speak. He had been hoping she would let that go. She wanted to apologize and that was all well and good, but what could he say to her in response?

That's all right, Janeka, I forgive you?

It wasn't all right and he didn't forgive her. He didn't know if he could. He didn't even know if he wanted to.

"I have to be with my people," she had told him, even as blood was dripping off his chin. Seven words. But they had abruptly shown Bob Carson his place in the scheme of things. Seven words. But they had rearranged the very architecture of his life.

And now, here she sat a lifetime later seeking...what? Forgiveness? Absolution?

"I meant what I said," Janeka was saying. "I am sorry. I am truly sorry. Please forgive me."

He heard a note of pleading in her voice and it pleased something small and cruel inside him that he had never known was there until just this second.

Please forgive me?

Too late, lady. Four decades too late.

He finally brought his eyes up, trying to think of some curt and humiliating way to say this. He never got the chance.

A man was standing over their table. He wore a windbreaker and had a hand in his pocket curled around what looked to be the butt of a gun, except that the gun was...pink? The man was skinny and had a bizarre haircut. He grinned at them through bruised and swollen lips, revealing a mouth full of dead things that once had been teeth.

"I've been looking for you," he said.

sixteen

Here is what Dwayne McLarty loved most about meth: It was like plugging your brain into a nuclear furnace. It gave you clarity, brought the world around you all at once into diamond-hard focus, supercharged your mind, filled it with a million new thoughts and ideas, all banging around inside like electrons in an atom or something. And it gave you this inexhaustible energy, this immunity from fatigue, this raw, electrical jolt, to put those ideas into action.

He'd had this particular idea while sitting there beneath the El in the stolen red Ford, thinking how much he needed—how much he *deserved*—this hit of Go Fast. Yes, Clarence would disapprove. Clarence always disapproved. Fuck him.

Dwayne had applied that jet of blue flame to the glass bowl of his pipe. The smoke rushed up the stem and into him and brought with it that familiar, white-heat blast of wow. And with a suddenness, he realized:

He didn't need to stake out the guy's house and wait for him. The hell with that. The guy had said he was going to lunch, right? Dwayne had heard that, right? The guy worked at a newspaper on Michigan Avenue, right? And the guy was a rich asshole, right? So no way he was going to some pizza place or burger joint like a regular guy. No, he would be in some fancy place where they served you at your table and you ate with linen napkins and metal utensils. And since he worked on Michigan, that was probably the area he knew best, probably the place he'd pick to eat.

So Dwayne would just search every single restaurant on Michigan Avenue.

That decision made, he'd sat back in his seat and took another pull on the pipe, marveling at how obvious the answer was with the magic smoke lighting up his brain.

Then he'd gone to work.

He had spent the last fifteen minutes methodically driving south from the newspaper office. Parking was a bitch in that area, so he left the truck in taxi stands and hotel driveways, ignoring the yells of consternation from valets and cabbies, marching in to restaurants past the astonished protests of maître d's and waiters. Silently, he stalked through the dining rooms, scanning each patron closely. They stared back, confused, even angry.

"What's your problem, pal?" more than one man asked.

Dwayne didn't bother to answer. He searched each restaurant quickly and efficiently, then moved on. This had been his fourth restaurant, this joint with the cow over the front door, and what did you know? There was the guy, big as life, and he was sitting in a booth having lunch with some nigger bitch. It could not have been more perfect.

God, Dwayne loved meth.

Now he stood over their table. "You're the editor, right? Bob whatsis?"

"Who are you?" the guy asked.

Hello? Dwayne was the one asking the questions. Did this asshole not see the gun? Annoyed, Dwayne pulled the butt of it a little further from his pocket, shielding it with his body so no one else in the restaurant could see.

"I'm the guy with the gun," he said. "That's who the fuck I am."

"Is that thing even real?" the guy asked.

Dwayne had forgotten his gun was pink. Now he was pissed and it was only with some effort that he was able to keep his voice conversational and low. "Why don't I shoot this bitch in the kidney and you can tell me if the gun's real," he said.

"Okay, okay," said the guy, and there was panic in his eyes that warmed Dwayne all over. "There's no need for all that. Just tell me what you want."

"I want you to come with me. Both of you."

"Leave her out of it," said the guy. "Take me."

Dwayne laughed. "Yeah, sure. So she can start screaming her fucking head off the moment we hit the door. Now come on, both of you. And put some money on the table. I don't need some asshole waiter chasing us down the street hollering about an unpaid bill."

"We're not going anywhere with you," said the woman. "What's this all about?"

He leaned close to her and whispered, "What this is all about is me shooting you in the face if you don't quit stalling, bitch."

Something flashed in her eyes like she was about to reply, but the editor guy, Bob, held up a hand to stop her. "Okay," he said, "we're coming." He reached toward his hip pocket and Dwayne flinched. "Wallet," said the guy, holding up his billfold by thumb and forefinger. "You told me to leave some money on the table, remember?"

Asshole. He didn't know how lucky he was he didn't get shot.

"Go on," said Dwayne, and the guy began fishing in the billfold for money.

People were beginning to notice them. People were staring from every corner of the room. Dwayne told himself it was just the Go Fast that made him think this way, but that didn't help. He needed to get out of there. He needed to get out. He needed to get out.

"Come on, come on, come on," he said. Bouncing on the balls of his feet, he chanted it like a mantra. He sang it like a song.

The guy put two twenties and a ten on the table. "Okay, Dad," said Dwayne, affecting a loud, nothing-to-see-here voice, "now that you finished your lunch I'll take you and—" he flinched at the next word, but no other word suggested itself "—Mom back home."

The woman gave him a strange look. "Do as he says," the guy whispered and Dwayne was happy he had that much sense, at least.

Dwayne nodded his head toward the door and Bob Whatsis and the woman stood slowly. Bob led the way and Dwayne walked close behind the woman, the pistol barrel poking her in the side through the thin fabric of his windbreaker. He put his other hand in his other pocket to make it less obvious. Still, people in the dining room stared as they passed. Dwayne tried to smile reassuringly, but that only made them turn away with expressions of disgust, so he stopped doing it.

He really needed to get his teeth fixed. Cut back a little on the Go Fast. See a good dentist.

Then he laughed softly to himself. He kept forgetting he expected to die tonight.

Out to the street. A hotel, two doors down. Some olive-skinned guy in a valet uniform saw them coming toward the Ford, which was blocking the hotel driveway, and started cursing him in some raghead language.

"Yeah, yeah," said Dwayne in a languid voice. He reached past the woman and opened the driver's side door of the vehicle. "You drive," he told her. Then he came around and opened the front door of the vehicle. "You," he told Bob, gesturing with the pocketed gun, "get on the passenger side."

Bob did as he was told. The raghead was still circling like some annoying fly, yammering in Dwayne's ear. "Get out of my face," Dwayne warned him. "Go back to Pakistan, asshole." He really felt like shooting this guy.

Now the raghead drew himself up in offended pride and spoke in heavily accented English. "I am from India, you fool—not Pakistan. And I am an American. I am American just as you are."

Dwayne snorted. "The fuck you are," he said. He *really* wanted to shoot this prick. But he let it go. Had to stay focused. Had to take care of business. So he climbed into the back door of the truck, feeling distantly grateful he'd had the foresight to steal a four-seater. He tossed the keys forward. They landed in the cup holder between the two front seats.

Dwayne freed the pistol from his pocket. "Drive," he told the female nigger.

"Where?" she asked, holding the key.

"Just drive," he told her, motioning with the gun. "Circle around."

She cranked the engine, pulled out into traffic. Dwayne was feeling very good about himself.

"What's this all about?" asked the guy. "You're the one who kidnapped Toussaint? You're the one who attacked Amy Landingham?"

Dwayne grinned. "I'm the one done a lot of things. Busy, busy, busy, that's me me me."

"What do you want from us?" asked the guy.

"Nothing from her," said Dwayne. "I want something from you."

"What's that?"

"Your name's Bob, right?"

"Yeah."

"You work for that jewspaper, right? The *Post*?"

There was a beat. Then he said, "No. They fired me this morning."

"Fine," said Dwayne, still motioning with the gun. "You worked for them til this morning. Whatever. The point is, they know you. You can get into the building. I've got a video. I want to see it on their website. You get them to post it for me." He pulled the computer disk from his pocket and flipped it into Bob's lap.

Bob lifted the disk, studying it. "They won't..."

"Bob. Trust me. Once they see what's on that fuckin' video, they'll cream their pants to put it online."

"But I can't—"

"Yeah, Bob, you can. See, that's why I'm taking your friend here. She's my insurance policy. You don't do what I'm telling you to, I'm going to shoot her full of holes. That's my promise to you, Bob."

He saw the woman's eyes flick to the rearview, watching him. "Yeah," he said, "I'm talking about you, sweetheart. Now, you drive us to the paper."

"I'm not from here," she said. "I don't know where..."

Bob touched her hand on the steering wheel. "Make your next U-turn," he said. "Ten blocks north on your left." His voice was soft, like he was trying to reassure her. She nodded.

"This your old lady, Bob?"

He didn't answer.

Dwayne shook his head. "I hate to see a white man defile himself that way. What is it about the dark meat, Bob? I mean, I can see fuckin' one because you're horny and maybe that's all that's available. But taking one out to eat? Making her your main squeeze? No, sir. Can't do the jungle boogie, Bob." Again the woman's eyes came to the rearview mirror, her gaze bright now with anger. Dwayne ignored it.

"But I guess that works out for me," he said, "her being your old lady and all. Because if she means anything to you, you will not fuck with me on this. This fucking pink pistol may look like a joke, but I am not joking. You hear that, Bob? I don't see that video online today, this afternoon, I will shoot this bitch right in the back of her fucking head."

He pressed the gun against the headrest of the driver's seat to emphasize the point and was pleased to see Bob's Adam's apple slide up and down and an expression cross his face as though he had swallowed gone-bad milk. Then, meth gave him a new inspiration. "No," he said, "better yet, I will rape her in the ass, then chop her to pieces and send them to you, one a day. You understand me? You get what I'm saying here, Bob?"

"Yes."

The woman negotiated a tight U-turn around a traffic island and for a moment, the windshield was full of cops, standing on a corner behind a traffic barricade, apparently being briefed by some other cop. Probably talking about how they were going to redirect traffic around Grant Park for the coronation of their new nigger president. Dwayne saw hope leap up in the woman's eyes at the sight of all those boys in blue.

"Don't even think about it," he told her.

And then she completed the turn and the only things in the windshield were the towers of Michigan Avenue, northbound.

"I do this, you'll let her go?" Bob was saying.

"Sure," said Dwayne, feeling magnanimous now that they understood each other. "Why would I hold onto her after that? I already told you, I ain't into the jungle boogie. That's your thing."

"How do I know you'll keep your word?" Bob asked.

"You don't," said Dwayne. "You'll just have to trust me."

"Trust you? I don't trust you. Why would I trust you?"

Fuck, thought Dwayne. The guy was panicking. He hadn't meant to make the guy panic. Dwayne tapped him on the top of his head three times with his gun hand, like a man knocking on a door.

"Listen to me, Bob. Listen. You do what I told you, you got nothing to worry about. If you fuck with me, that's when you got to worry."

"How will I know you've kept your part of the deal? How can I get in touch with you?"

Dwayne was startled. He hadn't thought that far ahead. He recovered quickly.

"You don't get in touch with me," he said. "I get in touch with you." He pointed toward a notepad in a little contraption held to the dashboard by a suction cup. "Write your number down there," he said.

Bob produced a pen and did as he was told. His hand shook as he passed the paper to Dwayne. "That's a good boy," said Dwayne, pleased by the tremors. "I see what I want to see online, I give you a call, tell you where to pick her up, and you lovebirds are reunited in time for dinner tonight. I don't see it, and you never see her again. That's the deal, asshole."

Bob touched the woman's hand. "That's it right there," he said, pointing. The building loomed on the left, just across the street. The woman brought the truck to a stop at a red light.

"It will be okay," Bob told her. He spoke with such earnestness that Dwayne knew he had guessed right. The guy had a real thing for this bitch. "I won't let anything happen to you," he told her. "I promise."

Like his promise had one damn thing to do with it.

Her eyes were moist when she turned toward him, and Dwayne could see in their faces that they both knew how impotent Bob's promise was. It made him feel powerful. It made him feel like God. Which, as far as these two assholes were concerned, he was.

"All right," he said, "that's enough. You do what I told you to do, Bob, or—"

Bob cut him off. "Yeah, I know," he said. "I know."

He opened the door and got out without waiting for an answer. Dwayne watched him melt into the rush of people trotting across Michigan.

"What now?" the woman asked in a dull voice.

What now, indeed? Dwayne knew he should get back to the warehouse. Clarence would be shitting bricks by now. But meth, God love it, had given him another idea.

The light turned. "Hang your next left," he told the nigger bitch.

Fifteen minutes later, the truck creaked to a stop over the oil stain in front of the brick bungalow where Dwayne had grown up. He pushed the back door open and got out.

"Wait for me out here," he told the woman.

When he saw her eyes, he realized his mistake.

Stupid, stupid, stupid. He was too wired. Hard to think straight. Hard to think straight. Hard to fucking think straight.

Standing at the passenger side window, he leveled the gun right at her. He knew the neighbors might see. Fuck them. "Just joking," he told the nigger bitch. "You're coming with me."

She thought about running. He could see in her face that she was calculating her chances if she just mashed her foot on the accelerator. Then something leaden came into her eyes. She knew she would never make it. She knew. The woman opened the door and came around the front of the vehicle.

"Smart choice," said Dwayne. "Come on."

She followed him as he crept toward the front door. He didn't know why he was creeping. It just felt right.

"What is this place?" she asked.

"Shut the fuck up," he told her. "This'll just take a minute."

She followed him as Dwayne pushed his key into the lock and opened the front door.

Sure enough, his asshole brother was still sitting on the couch watching ESPN. The empty bowl of cereal was on the coffee table and he was drinking a beer. Daryl looked up in surprise when Dwayne came through the door, pulling the nigger bitch behind him.

"Well," he said, "twice in one day. Guess we just won the happiness lotto. Who's she?"

Dwayne lifted the pink pistol and shot his twin brother right in that big, flapping mouth of his. Right in the mouth. A couple of his teeth went flying like tiny bits of shrapnel, blood spraying over the couch. Daryl McLarty died looking surprised and Dwayne stood there bouncing on the balls of his feet, his groin heavy with an erection that could have cut marble. It made him giggle. He'd tried, he'd really tried, to think of reasons not to shoot his asshole brother. Turned out there were none.

Oh yeah oh yeah oh yeah.

It was a moment before he realized the nigger bitch was screaming. Dwayne punched her in the mouth and she fell to the floor.

Her silence allowed him to hear a new voice, calling from the back. "What's that? What's going on out there?"

His mother. He had forgotten his mother. And he hated the idea, but what else could he do? With Earl in jail and Karen in school and ol' Daryl sitting out here having absolutely the worst day of his life, who would take care of the old lady? Besides that, she was pretty much dead anyway, wasn't she?

"I'll just be a second," he told the nigger bitch, who was writhing on the floor from the blow, still shaking her head.

He walked down the hall. Something in him made him swipe the school pictures of himself and his brothers to the floor.

"Daryl?" she called. "What's happening out there? That sounded like a gunshot."

He opened the door. She looked up in surprise, sitting there in bed, plastic tubing dripping off her face.

"Dwayne?" she said, making his name a question.

Dwayne grinned. "Sorry, Ma," he said. He raised the pistol and shot his mother twice in the chest.

She had time to look down and see that she was shot, time to look up at him with incomprehension. Then she slumped and died.

"Sorry, Ma," said Dwayne again. He closed the door behind him.

The nigger bitch had staggered to her feet and was groping toward the door when he came back into the living room. He grabbed her arm, opened the door and propelled her through. She stumbled and almost fell. Dwayne pulled the accordion security gate closed over the front door, heard it lock with a click. He hoped his brother was rotting by the time anybody found him in there.

And Ma? He thought about it for half a second, shrugged.

What the hell. Let her rot, too.

"Let's go," said Dwayne. "We got places to go and people to kill. Come on come on come on."

He was behind the wheel, the pink pistol trained on his captive, as the truck roared away, tires screeching, from the little stucco house where he once had lived.

seventeen

Eighteen years Bob had worked at this place. Eighteen years.

That meant this kid now manning the security desk in the lobby had been—what?—five years old on Bob's first day of work? Bob had nodded his way past him every morning for years. And yet here this same kid was, treating Bob like Osama bin Laden with a briefcase full of anthrax, and here Bob was, trying to be patient, trying to be rational, trying to explain to this kid that he wasn't a disgruntled employee—well, yes, he was disgruntled, but not that kind of disgruntled—come to shoot the place up. This was important. This was life or death. He had to get upstairs, and he did not have time to stand here arguing about it with some...*child*.

Not with images of Janeka in the clutches of that jumpy little animal crowding his thoughts. Yet still, like a robot in a science fiction movie, the young man kept saying the same thing: "I can't let you through without a pass, sir."

Sir. Like getting fired had made him a stranger.

Bob didn't know what to do. He felt like he was losing his mind. When Doug Perry stepped off the elevator right at that moment, he could have kissed him.

"Bob?" said Doug. "What's going on? What's wrong?"

"I need to get upstairs," Bob told him. "I've got something I have to show you all. And Jabba the Hutt here"—he jabbed a thumb back toward

218

the security guard who protested, "Hey!"—"won't let me in because he thinks I might shoot up the place."

"Something to show us?"

Bob nodded. "The guy, the skinny guy with the stupid haircut you told me about, he took us out of a restaurant at gunpoint not ten minutes ago, and gave me the disk he took from Amy."

"'Us?'"

"Janeka Lattimore." Just saying the name made Bob's eyes sting. He grabbed a breath.

"Who is...?"

"You remember the woman I told you about this morning? Sent me an email?"

"Oh yeah," said Doug with a crooked smile. "Your long lost love. I do remember."

Bob felt himself unraveling. He clenched a fist to hold himself in one piece. "Doug, you don't understand me. He's got her. That little animal has got Janeka. And he says he's going to...says he's going to..." It was no use. He could not force his mouth—he could not force his *mind*—past that point.

Doug's eyes widened and Bob was thankful to know he didn't have to. "You're serious? Come on," said Doug. "Let's go upstairs and sort this out."

Bob could have collapsed from sheer relief.

A minute later, they stormed off the elevator into the newsroom. The newsroom stopped. Reporters stopped reporting, editors stopped editing, people on the phone said, "Hold on just a minute." Bob was distantly aware of all the eyes following him, people staring the way you would if someone you knew to be dead walked up to you in the food court at the shopping mall. Let them stare.

I will shoot this bitch right in the back of her fucking head.

Let them stare.

Doug led him in long, urgent strides down the hall toward the executive suite. Halfway there, Denis Lassiter intercepted them. He got right in Doug's face, pointing at Bob. "What's he doing here?" he hissed.

"We've got a situation," said Doug, calmly. "Come on. You need to hear this, too."

Denis' eyebrow arched in suspicion. Doug didn't wait. He pushed past his boss and Bob followed. Denis was left to bring up the rear. Doug led them through the glass doors of the executive suite into a broad hallway lined with glass-enclosed offices. He paused at the secretary's desk just outside his own. "I need Hector Mendoza up here right away," he said.

Peggy Toyama took the unlikely procession in with a glance, nodded, and picked up her phone. Bob followed Doug and Denis followed them both to the end of the hall, around a corner, and into a waiting area with plush leather couches and decorative plants. On the far side of the lobby stood the glass-enclosed conference room where Bob's career had come to an abrupt end what seemed like a year ago. On the near side was Lydia's corner office, outside of which her secretary sat sentinel. Between them was a wall done up in blonde woods, with the *Chicago Post* masthead at the top. Embedded beneath that were medallions representing the six Pulitzer Prizes—two of them due to Malcolm Toussaint—the paper had won since its founding in 1901.

Lydia Barnett was standing against that wall using the Pulitzers as a none-too-subtle backdrop, speaking into a microphone held by a local TV news bunny as a cameraman recorded it all. "...and I think," Lydia was saying, "that our commitment to putting this unfortunate episode behind us can be seen in the fact that we have held the responsible parties accountable and have reprinted today's newspaper at significant cost."

"Speaking of the responsible parties," said the reporter, "where is Mr. Toussaint? Is there any truth to the reports that he has turned up missing?"

But Lydia was no longer listening. She was looking over the reporter's shoulder at the three men who had just entered the foyer. Her gaze fixed on Bob, and there was, he felt, an almost physical malice to her stare. "Denis?" she asked, gritting her teeth in an ice-cold smile, "What is going on here?"

Behind him, Bob was almost certain he heard Denis Lassiter's sphincter slam like a door. But Doug Perry, bless his heart, did not flinch. "Get rid of them," he told his publisher, nodding toward the news bunny and her cameraman. "We have a situation."

First, there was surprise. Then, slowly, like an iceberg that wanders into tropical seas, the malice in Lydia's eyes melted. She gave Doug a look that suggested they had never been properly introduced. Then she nodded toward the news crew.

"We'll have to pick this up at a later date," she said. "It appears something has come up."

Ten minutes later, they were all in the conference room, all sitting in the same seats they had occupied just that morning, including Mindy Chen at the far end of the table and Mendoza standing as he had stood that morning, against the wall with arms folded. To Bob, it felt surreal.

Mendoza popped in the DVD. The lights came down. An image of the file structure on the disk appeared on screen. There were two files, the first marked MMPR, the second marked WRA. Mendoza clicked the first. Seconds later, the conference room of the *Chicago Post* rang with a sound never before heard in those august confines, the battle cry of a 1990s children's TV show: "It's morphin' time!" And the screen was filled with young actors in bright costumes doing spin kicks and backflips, fighting against stunt men dressed as rock creatures.

Lydia glared at Bob with an expression that could have killed plant life. Bob felt his testicles crawl up inside him. He thought he might be sick. "The Mighty Morphin Power Rangers?" she said. "Really?"

"That can't be what he wants us to see," said Doug in an even voice.

Mendoza was ahead of him. He had already closed out the first file and opened the second. And there it was.

The lighting was harsh, but the image was unmistakable. It had been shot in some warehouse. Malcolm was chained to a chair. He seemed dazed and bruised. Towering over him was a massive white man in a shapeless T-shirt. He stared at the camera wide-eyed and spoke in a strangely toneless voice.

"Those who have ears, let them hear. We are the White Resistance Army. I am Sergeant Clarence Pym, under the command of Captain Dwayne McLarty."

"They're giving us their names?" whispered Lassiter. "I can't believe they're giving us their names."

"Maybe they don't expect it to matter," said Doug.

"We have captured this nigger," said Pym, "the so-called journalist that calls himself Malcolm Toussaint, who for many years has spewed his white-hating, anti-Christian poison in jewspapers all over this once-great nation, including this morning's vicious diatribe against the white men who built this nation."

"Oh, my sweet Jesus," said Lydia.

"Although the actions we take today were planned long ago, the nigger's diatribe this morning explains better than we ever could why we have felt it necessary to go to this extreme. To put it plainly: at some point, as white men, we have to call a halt, we have to say that we've had enough—or we can no longer regard ourselves as white *men*."

On the screen, the big man—Clarence Pym—cleared his throat. "To-night, there is a good chance this nation will elect a socialist Muslim nigger as its president. The nigger has been clear in his intentions. He has said he wishes to redistribute the wealth. He has said he will pay reparations to his fellow blacks. He has said this country will bow down before the false religion of Islam. The fact that a foreign-born interloper with such radical extreme leftist views might be elected president tells you how sick this country is. This tells us in no uncertain terms that the hour is late and that it is upon our heads to stand and be counted.

"We are not kidnappers. We demand no ransom. We are soldiers and this is an enemy we have captured. We are patriots who are convinced this nation cannot be cleansed except with blood. So let there be blood."

Mindy Chen's hand flew to her mouth. Doug's jaw had turned to stone.

"Dear, God, please don't tell me they're going to kill him on camera," said Bob. He was horrified and transfixed.

"We leave this document," said Pym, "as an inspiration to others so that in case we fall, they will know why we did what we did and they will pick up where we left off. Those who have ears, let them hear. We are the White Resistance Army and this is our declaration of war."

They waited, expecting to see Malcolm beheaded or shot. It was a long moment before, mercifully, the screen went black.

"Jesucristo," breathed Mendoza softly.

"'Why we did what we did?'" repeated Bob. "What in God's name are they planning to do?"

"We can't post this on our site," said Denis. He looked at Lydia for confirmation. "We can't," he said again.

Lydia pursed her lips. She did not speak. The room waited for her. Finally, she looked at Mendoza. "Run it again," she said.

Mendoza ran it again. Again, the big man spoke stiffly, delivering his manifesto against the backdrop of a warehouse. Again, Malcolm sat chained to the chair looking dazed.

When it was over, Lydia said. "Thoughts?"

Hector said, "We need to call the police."

Lydia nodded. "As soon as we're done here. And we'll be done here very quickly. Mindy," she said to the director of newsroom systems, "we're going to give them the original. There may be some fingerprint or DNA evidence on it they can use. But I want you to make copies."

"Okay," said Mindy.

"You already know what I think," said Denis. "We cannot allow our-selves to be blackmailed. You put this online, essentially at the point of a gun, and you are telling every lunatic and crank out there that we'll do whatever they want if they threaten us. Do we really want to open that door? These people are terrorists. I say we cannot negotiate with terrorists."

Doug banged a fist on the table. "For God's sake, Denis, there are two lives at stake here. They've got Malcolm and they've also got Bob's friend. It's all well and good to worry about what could happen in the future—and that does scare me, I'll admit—but let's also consider what's right in front of us. These people's lives may depend on what we decide right here, right now. You remember the Unabomber's manifesto? You remember how he demanded the *New York Times* and the *Washington Post* publish the damn thing or he would send more of his damn bombs? I'm sure they had the same concerns we do. But in the end, they did the right thing. Hell, they did the only thing they could with lives at stake."

Denis shook his head. "We have to stand firm," he said.

"Easy to do," said Doug, "when you're not the one whose ass is on the line."

Bob watched this exchange with a kind of sickened fascination, almost fearing to breathe. Then, like everyone else in the room, he turned toward Lydia for her verdict.

She looked at Denis. She looked at Doug. But her eyes were on Bob when she spoke. "We're posting it," she said softly.

Bob released a breath he had not realized he was holding. He was al-most dizzy with relief. "Shouldn't we wait to see what the police suggest?" said Denis.

"No," she said. "This is our call. These are our people."

"Respectfully," said Denis, "you're making a mistake, Lydia."

"It wouldn't be the first," she told him. "Would anyone like to hear the reasons?"

"I would," said Bob in a soft voice.

Again, she looked at him. "In the first place," she said, "I agree with Doug. If you have a chance to save someone's life, that's what you do. But there's another reason, and I am surprised no one in this room has men-tioned it."

"It's news," said Bob, still speaking softly.

Lydia nodded. "That's right," she said. "It's news. And damn it, news is still what we do."

It was an old thought that somehow hung there like a new one for a long moment. Then Lydia clapped her hands together once, as if breaking a spell. "All right, everybody, let's go. Doug, you call Chicago PD. Mindy, get those duplicates ready and post the video online."

Denis said, "Doug, you're going to want to assign a new reporter to this story, with Amy out. Maybe more than one—one to tell the main story, but also one to give readers a little context. I, for one, would like to know more about this so-called 'White Resistance Army.' Has anyone heard of them before this? Does the FBI know the name? Or the Southern Poverty Law Center?"

"I'm on it," said Doug.

"It's going to be a busy front page," mused Denis, "with election results and this. Not to mention Malcolm getting fired."

"Yeah," said Doug, "but the boss is right. This is what we do."

"Keep me apprised," said Lydia. And the meeting broke.

The next hours were insane.

The video was online within minutes. Within minutes after that, the counter onscreen showed that it had been viewed more than 20,000 times. Police detectives arrived. They questioned Bob. They questioned Doug. They drove down the street, saying they wanted to question the maître d' at Stymie's and the valet at the hotel. They came back to the paper and questioned Bob some more.

Agents from the FBI and Homeland Security showed up in the building. This was purely, they said, to observe in an advisory capacity. The local cops did not appreciate this. "Let 'em observe this," grumbled one of them to his partner, grabbing his crotch as they stormed down the hallway past Doug's office.

Doug was in the afternoon news meeting. He had allowed Bob to take refuge in his office while they all waited for the call from the kidnappers. Doug and Bob both knew Bob could have waited in what had, until this morning, been his own office. The desk was still there, the computer was still there, the phone still worked. He could have waited there, except that he couldn't wait there. So he waited here instead.

A police detective waited with him. Det. Cecil Raintree was a study in calm. He sat on Doug's couch, a tall, bronze man in a natty black suit, his long legs crossed as he silently perused that day's paper. Bob envied him his serenity. But then, he wasn't the one whose once-girlfriend had been taken by some maniac.

Bob's cellphone sat on the desk, hooked to a digital recording device. Sitting there behind Doug's desk, Bob checked the batteries in the recorder. Then he checked the volume on his ringer. Then he set the phone so that it would vibrate as well as ring. He looked at the phone, willing it to do something. It didn't.

Raintree looked at him. "I know it's easier said than done," he said, "but try to calm down. Everything that can be done is being done. He'll call when he calls."

"If," said Bob. And when Raintree gave him a quizzical look, he repeated it. "'If' he calls." Bob had begun to have a very bad feeling.

"He'll call," said Raintree, going back to his paper. Bob heard no conviction in the cop's voice.

He turned on the little television on the corner of Doug's desk and flipped between the cable news channels. On the conservative channel, a guy who hosted a radio show slammed a table and said angrily, "What if—and I'm not saying this is the case, but what if—this whole kidnapping story is actually some shameless ploy by the Obama campaign to energize the black vote? I'm just saying, I for one would not be surprised if that turns out to be the case."

On the liberal channel, a famous black civil rights activist spoke with labored solemnity. "While we certainly should not blame Mr. McCain for what has happened, we cannot, given the sort of hateful racial vitriol that has marked the Republican campaign, be surprised that people such as the young man on this video believe themselves to be under attack, and respond accordingly."

On the other channel, four talking heads in boxes argued over what the kidnappings meant and whose political ideology was at fault and whether the whole thing was a hoax or not. They talked over one another and insulted one another for a few minutes. Then the host stopped the segment and interviewed a hologram of Taylor Swift to get her thoughts. Or its thoughts. Whatever.

Bob muted the television. "Thank you," said the detective without looking up from his paper. "That crap gives me a headache."

"Yeah," said Bob. "Me, too." He picked up his phone and checked the volume setting again. He willed it to ring. It rang while he was holding it.

Raintree looked up sharply. Bob touched the green button on the screen. "Hello? Hello?"

Silence. Bob steeled himself to hear that jittery little punk on the other end. Raintree had come out of his chair, folded his paper. He watched Bob with expectant eyes. Then Bob heard a woman's voice, brimming with July sunshine and Christmas morning cheer, say, "Hello! We just wanted to let you know this is your last chance to take advantage of great sale prices on—"

Bob ended the call and somehow resisted the urge to slam the phone to the floor.

"I take it this was not him?"

"No."

Raintree sat and unfolded his paper.

A few minutes later, the door opened. A preppy-looking black kid wearing oval-shaped, wire-rimmed glasses and a banana-colored sweater vest poked his head in. He nodded at Raintree, then said to Bob, "This a bad time, sir?"

"Who are you?"

"My name's Sam Jones, sir. Doug Perry asked me to interview you for the story."

"You're a reporter?"

"Yes, sir."

"What are you, 14?"

His smile was indulgent. "I'm 28, sir."

Twenty-eight. It was getting so everybody in the building was 28. The newspaper business was slowly going over to children who could barely even remember there had once been another President Bush. Financially, Bob knew, it made sense. These Jimmy Olsens, as he had come to think of them, cost less. You could hire two of them for what it cost to hire one reporter with gray in his hair and a little experience under his belt. In this industry, which was diminishing with ever-increasing speed, this was not an unimportant consideration. So the business was getting younger. And all it cost was institutional memory and knowledge of how things worked.

"Sir? The interview?"

Bob looked up to where this...*teenager* was still waiting. "Yeah," he said. "Sure. But please, stop calling me sir."

"Yes, sir," the teenager said.

The interview lasted half an hour before Sam Jones declared he had enough and thanked Bob for his time. As he walked out, Bob checked his phone again to make sure he hadn't somehow missed the call. Then he looked at his watch and sighed. It was after 3:30. It had been more than two hours now since McLarty drove off with Janeka. Where was he? Why hadn't he called? Hadn't he seen the video online?

It will be okay. I won't let anything happen to you.

It had been a stupid promise. He had known this even as he made it. Because how could he keep anything from happening to her once she disappeared with McLarty in that old red Ford?

A stupid promise. And yet, somehow, he had meant it. Every word.

"I won't let you down," he told her now. He whispered this to himself in the silence of Doug's office. These words, too, were impotent. Yet he could not stop himself from saying them.

"You say something?" Raintree looked up from the sports page. Bob had forgotten the detective was there.

He shook his head. "No," he said.

Bob clicked on Doug's computer and looked at the paper's website. The video was on the front page. It now had more than 25,000 hits. And the message board beneath it was going crazy—a couple thousand postings. Bob began reading from the beginning.

"HumanBeing01" wrote: "What a horrible video. Though I often disagreed with Toussaint's column—and was particularly offended by what he apparently sneaked into the paper this morning—I am appalled to think this country has degenerated to the point where hostage taking and loose talk of racial war will now become an acceptable means of dissent."

"brotherwisdom" was affronted by this. "In sayin the brother 'sneaked' something into the post your only helping to further the psychosocial dynamic under which anything an african man in amerikkka does is presumed to be furtive and shifty. Your a racist."

"No," retorted HumanBeing01, "go back and re-read what I wrote. I said he sneaked it into the paper because he sneaked it into the paper. Why is everything about race with you?"

Here, "Thomas Edison" joined the conversation. "Everybody knows Knee Grows is the most racist people in America. Always playin da race card."

Bob shook his head, horrified and appalled. What planet did these people live on?

"Where do I sign up to join WRA?" asked "Speaker Of Da Howze." "I like there ideas. Get rid of all the niqqers. Starting with Barry Soetero."

"Me too," added "Whats On TV Tonight." "I would join them in a heartbeat. Time to take our country back from these long-lipped, wide-nose, buck-eyed, nappy-headed apes f-ing up everything. Send them all back to Africa. Worst mistake we ever made was to bring them over here."

"LOL," replied "GarveyXFarrakhan," "you racist crackers crack me up. Reason you can't abide Toussaint is because he speaks the truth and you can't handle it."

"You all better think twice about joining that fat guy on the video," wrote "BettySue69." "He might eat you. LOL"

"LOL," wrote "JohnD'oh!" "Guy's so fat he leaves footprints in concrete."

"He so fat, they got to grease the door frame and hold a Twinkie on the other side just to get him out of the house," wrote "Biteme."

"Guy got more chins than a Chinese phone book," wrote "Kirby11."

"Hey."

Bob looked up. Amy Landingham was coming through the door.

"Hey," he said.

"Never did get my interview with you," she said.

A rueful smile. "Yeah, something came up. How you feeling? I heard that guy really clocked you one."

Her face was bruised. She spoke through clenched teeth, her voice slightly distorted.

"I'll be okay," she said. "He broke my jaw."

"Why are you here?"

She gave him an odd look as she sat down in front of Doug's desk. "Where else would I be?"

"They put the screws in your jaw? I had that once, I wasn't any good for days."

"No screws," she said. "He wired it."

"I thought they didn't use that so much anymore."

"They don't," she said. "I asked him to. I wanted to get back sooner."

"You're a trouper," said Bob. "So I assume you heard? About Janeka, I mean? And Malcolm?"

"Yeah," she said. "I heard."

"We're waiting for the guy to call," said Bob. "Me and Detective Raintree over there."

She glanced back at the detective, who nodded without ever looking up from his paper. She turned back to Bob. "So what's that you're looking at?"

"Message boards," said Bob. "Underneath the video."

She shook her head. "You shouldn't do that. Whenever I read those things it makes me think NASA should launch a search for signs of intelligent life on Earth."

Bob nodded. "It is depressing," he said. "Look at this one: 'I'm not a racist, but it's a fact the blacks commit more crimes due to their culture and their lack of education and their lack of self control. But the liberal media covers this up because they're scared to offend the blacks due to their own cowardice.'"

"Darn that liberal media," said Amy.

"Yeah," said Bob. "Here's another: 'I don't support what these guys have done but I understand why. They have been force fed the liberal media agenda all their lives. They have heard professional victims like this Toussaint who blame all the black man's problems on the white man. And they had to ask theirselfs, Who is the real racist here? Sometimes, people just get tired. Martin Luther King even said that.'

"God," said Bob in disgust. "Makes you wonder for the future of the species. Makes you wonder if people ever learn."

"You know, I saw Malcolm this morning by the elevators," said Amy. "He was heading out, I was coming in. I asked him why he did it. Know what he said? 'I just got tired.' I didn't understand that. But I've been thinking about it all day. And I think maybe I'm beginning to."

"Yeah?" said Bob.

"Yeah," said Amy. She was watching him closely. After a moment, she said, "Bob, are you okay?"

And that was when he realized he was crying. He knocked the single tear from his cheek with an impatient swipe. "This waiting is just getting to me," he said. "I'm scared for her. All we're doing is sitting here by the phone, and I don't think this guy is going to call. They keep telling me he will, but they didn't see his eyes."

Amy leaned across the desk. She spoke in a voice just for the two of them. "So let's get out of here," she said. "Let's go see what we can find out."

He searched her face for some sign that she was kidding. He did not find it. "We can't do that," he whispered.

"Why not?" she asked in the same confidential voice. "I'm sidelined with a work-related injury. Hell, you're unemployed. We don't owe anything to anybody. We can do whatever we want, can't we? Well, what I want is to get to the bottom of this." As she spoke, she was removing her cellphone from her jacket pocket. It was the same model as Bob's. With a glance back to make sure the detective was still absorbed in his paper, she reached across, pulled out the plug linking Bob's phone to the digital recorders, and substituted hers instead. She pocketed Bob's phone. Bob felt his jaw hanging open and closed it.

"Dark-green Chrysler van," she told him in the same whisper. "Level P1. Parked right by the entrance. Ten minutes."

Then she stood, speaking in a voice that made Raintree glance up. "Bob, you take care of yourself and let me know if there's anything I can do for you. I'll be curled up around a bottle of Motrin."

She nodded to Raintree and then was gone.

Bob sat there, not knowing what to do. His eyes fell upon another posting on the message board.

"ArchConservative" wrote: "The Dems buy AA votes with welfare money while the rest of the country gos down the crapper. That's why people are mad."

"CaptainAmerica" replied; "Better watch yourself, Arch. If the libs see you revealing their scheme, they'll send you off to a re-education camp. ROTFLMAO."

Debate, American style.

Bob Carson had always been a man who followed instructions, a man who painted between the lines. His long-ago affair with Janeka was the exception that proved the rule. Other than that, Bob had always been a cautious man. He simply didn't do the kind of thing Amy was suggesting. Besides, the cops knew best.

They didn't see his eyes.

Bob checked his watch. It was after 4:00. It would soon be three hours since McLarty kidnapped Janeka. The video had been online for two hours. It was all over the Internet. All over the news. The whole world knew about it. Surely, McLarty knew it, too. Yet still, no phone call.

It will be okay. I won't let anything happen to you.

What if something already had happened? And here he sat, following instructions, painting between the lines, waiting.

Bob stood without meaning to. "I've got to go to the bathroom," he heard himself say. "Should I take my phone? He'll be expecting my voice. He hears another voice, it might spook him."

Raintree looked up, thought about it for a moment. "Yeah," he said, finally. "But if that phone rings, you get your ass back here ASAP. You got me?"

"Yes," said Bob. "I got you."

He snatched up Amy's phone and walked out of Doug's office. Raintree was watching, so he took a right toward the men's room. In the hallway, he paused a beat, then doubled back, crouched down, and peeked around the edge of the glass into Doug's office. Peggy Toyama watched him quizzically. Bob put his index finger to his lips. In the office, Raintree laid the sports section aside and picked up Metro.

Bob came to his feet and scurried past the office. He scurried down the hall. He scurried through the newsroom, oblivious to the curious eyes that marked his passage, keenly aware that he had never done anything this crazy in his entire life. He scurried onto the elevator when it came, scurried through security when it let him off in the lobby, stabbed the button for the parking elevator, and looked over his shoulder for pursuers, feeling not unlike a wanted criminal.

Amy's van was parked right where she had said it would be and she was standing at the rear bumper. She tossed him her keys when he was still six feet away and he snatched them out of the air, one-handed. "You drive," she said. "I'm in no shape."

"This is crazy," said Bob.

"Yeah, well the whole day's been crazy," she said. "Why should this be any different?"

Bob couldn't argue with that.

He beeped the van open and got into the driver's seat while Amy settled herself next to him. He started the car, adjusted the mirrors, looked over at her.

"Let's go see what trouble we can find," she said.

eighteen

Eddie even wore shades indoors. The fluorescent lights got caught in them and with his waist-length black leather coat over a black turtleneck shirt, he had the look of some dark and anonymous automaton as he paced before the group of about 20 boys and young men.

"The worst thing we can do," he was saying, "is let those brothers waste this opportunity by having just another march."

Malcolm sat in the second row of folding chairs arranged in a basement rec room in the projects.

"I'm not going to front," said Eddie. "The man made a powerful speech. One thing the man can do is talk. And his call for a work stoppage certainly has merit. But like he always does, the man pulled up short before reaching the conclusion toward which his logic was inevitably leading him. He is like a doctor who is brilliant in diagnosing the affliction, but unable to bring himself to prescribe the proper medicine to bring about a cure."

There was soft laughter under the harsh lights. Eddie waited out their amusement, the fluorescents bright and hard on his shades. Finally, he gave them a tight smile. "I mean," he said, "I heard the man say many things. I heard him tell our brothers they were deserving of dignity and I agreed with that. I heard him say that America is going to hell...and I sho'nuff agreed with that."

This brought more laughter. Again, Eddie waited it out. Then he said, "But the one thing I did not hear the esteemed Dr. King say was how the black man will climb to a position where he can stop waiting for crumbs to fall from the white man's table. The one thing I did not hear the celebrated Dr. King tell us was how the black man should seize his own destiny and show whitey we are not to be fooled with any longer. The one thing"—his voice rising to an angry pitch—"I did not hear the great dreamer say was that black people need to seize power by any means necessary—the power to control our own neighborhoods, our own lives."

Fists shook in the air at that. The man next to Malcolm said, "Tell the truth, brother!"

Eddie grinned. "They act like they don't know what we mean when we say, 'black power.' You read all these learned essays in all these highfalutin places, all asking with earnest confusion"—and here he adopted the pontificating voice of some white intellectual square—"'What does the Negro mean by power?'"

He stopped pacing. "What the hell do they think we mean?" he cried suddenly, his voice raw with indignation. "Why is this such a mystery to them? We want black power just like the white man already has white power. That means we want to control our own damn destiny. It means we want to get rid of the Memphis PD and all the Pig Departments around the country that occupy our neighborhoods and abuse our brothers and sisters. It means we want to get rid of these broken-down schools that teach our children how to be ignorant. It means we want to buy from our own people, keep our money in our own communities. Let our money be used to build up the brother man, not the other man!"

He spoke right through the cheers that erupted.

"It means we want control over our own lives and our own neighborhoods. And it means we want—no, we *demand*—a seat at the table, and if we don't get it, they have to realize we are ready to turn that motherfucker over!"

Malcolm shot out of his seat at that. The whole room did. "Yeah!" he shouted. "Yeah!" Fist punching at the air. *This* was what he wanted to hear. *This* was what needed saying.

Eddie let them go for awhile, then held up his hand. When the room settled, he spoke to them in an after-the-storm voice, a voice softened by sudden calm. "Don't misunderstand. I am not opposed to what Dr. King wants. On the contrary, on that subject, he and I are in full agreement. No, brothers, where we part ways is over tactics. I don't believe we can 'dream' our way to the so-called Promised Land. And I sure as hell don't believe in any philosophy which tells you to let some white man hit you on your head with a stick and you just sit there and take it and tell him you love him anyhow."

He took off the glasses. The eyes he showed them were bright and fierce. "Those days are over and thank God. No more of this 'nonviolent' shit. Dr. King is a brave man. But he is naïve in his tactics and foolish in his reasoning. There is nothing wrong with having a march, nothing wrong with the people coming together to speak their demands with one voice. But if whitey does not realize there is an alternative to peaceful demonstration, then all marching is going to do is wear out your shoes. A march cannot just be a plea. It has to be an *ultimatum*. Whitey must know he has a choice to make. And he has to know that if he does not make the right choice, we are prepared to escalate this thing."

He looked out over the crowd of them, allowed them to see the seriousness and purpose in those angry eyes. Then, slowly, he replaced his shades. "Now, let me tell you what we need to do," he said.

Eddie spoke for a few minutes more and when he was done, they looked to one another and grins stretched their faces and their heads bobbed and they said, "Yeah. Damn straight." They would show whitey. They would show him what black power could do.

The meeting broke up shortly afterward and Malcolm hopped on his bike to ride to work. His head buzzing with the plans they had made, he cycled northwest, out of the clotheslines and dirt-patch yards of the projects, then turned west on Crump toward the river. He had only gone a few blocks when he came upon a company of firefighters spraying water on a burning heap of wood, paper, discarded food containers, and other garbage piled in a bonfire. A crowd of Negroes stood watching with sullen eyes. Two carloads of police were there, keeping everybody back.

So many people were crowded about that they spilled into the street. Malcolm had to get off the bike and walk it through the crowd.

It was a relatively small blaze and not all the firemen were needed. Two teams with hoses sprayed water at its base. The rest stood against the truck, watching the crowd watching them. There seemed to be no great urgency. But then, garbage fires were common now in this angry city.

"Y'all need to tell Loeb to treat them men like men," cried a Negro man in a straw stingy brim, his voice sudden and loud. "That's what y'all need to do!" The cops and the firemen affected not to hear. The crowd shouted its agreement. They affected not to hear this, either.

Somebody threw an empty whiskey bottle. It arced high in the night air, then shattered at the base of the flames. The cops and firemen all jumped as if there had been a gunshot. One cop had his hand on the service revolver at his hip. "Who did that?" he demanded. People in the crowd just laughed. There was an unmistakable air of festivity to the gathering. There was also an unmistakable air of menace lurking at its edges.

Malcolm worked his way through the crowd, got back on his bike, and continued west. He was still processing Eddie's incendiary words. Demand a seat at the table—or turn the motherfucker over.

That last, he thought, was what was missing from Martin Luther King. Even as he spoke of power, he still offered the carrot without the stick. It was the same with the NAACP, CORE, all these Memphis preachers, all these tired-ass Negroes the press insisted on calling black leaders.

Leaders. That was good for a private chuckle. They'd had their day. They'd had their chance. It was time to get rid of the whole mealy-mouthed, hat-in-hand lot of them—and all their mealy-mouthed, hat-in-hand *followers*, too.

And it seemed fitting somehow as he was thinking that thought, that he rolled his bike into the hotel lobby and saw Melvin Cotter, car keys in hand, walking toward the door with Rupert Pruitt, both of them laughing. Maybe Melvin had told the white man a joke. Maybe the white man had told him one. It didn't really matter.

Melvin saw him looking. Something sour appeared on his face. He turned back toward Pruitt.

The three men passed each other like ghosts. Malcolm went through the employees-only door behind the desk, parked his bike in the closet, and pulled the mop bucket out. Another night of cleaning up after whitey began.

He cycled home the next morning in a cold and persistent rain that gave the lie to spring. His jacket plastered itself to his shirt and the newspaper he used for covering as he steered the bike one-handed soon became sodden, shapeless, and useless. After a few moments, he flung it away. Under the sluice of gray water, the city looked...forsaken.

"Child, you soaked to the bone," said Nanny Parker as he mounted the steps to his house. "You going to catch your death."

She was standing on her covered porch, one arm folded across her middle, drinking from a mug of coffee and watching the water come spitting from the sky. Even rain was not enough to drive her inside. Miss Parker practically lived on that porch.

"Morning," said Malcolm, through bitterly chattering teeth as he stood under the overhang and fumbled in his pocket for his keys.

"I heard Mozell and Sonny back there in my yard early this morning. Looked out and saw they done took all my trash down to the dump in Sonny's car. Thank them for me, would you?"

"Yes, ma'am."

"Tell me: Was you there when Dr. King spoke? Did you hear him?"

"Yes, ma'am." He had his keys in hand.

"So, are you goin' to the march tomorrow?"

This amused him and he struggled to keep it from showing. Oh, he was going to the march all right. She could damn well bet on that. "Yes, ma'am," he said.

"Me too," she said.

It stopped him. "You?" he said. "Are you sure you want to do that?"

"Oh yes," said the old woman, her eyes shining. "I wouldn't miss it."

"It's going to be a mess down there," said Malcolm. "At your age, I mean...maybe you should stay home."

She lifted the mug to her smile, gazing out over the rain. "My age ain't got nothin' to do with it," she said. "Them sanitation men doing a mighty work of God. We need to stand behind them." She gave him a meaningful look. "We *all* need to stand behind them."

"Yes, ma'am," said Malcolm. He was racking his brain for another objection, a way to tell her she shouldn't go. *Couldn't* go. But he came up empty. Then he realized he was just standing there, and she was still looking at him. "Try to march up near the front," he said. "You'll...you'll have a better view." It was the best he could come up with.

Her gaze questioned him. Malcolm pushed the door open to escape. "You stay dry, now," he told her.

It had been a moment when he should have said something, a moment when he should have done something. But he didn't say and didn't do, so it became a moment—a tiny, seemingly insignificant slice out of time—that he would live with until he died. For 40 years, the guilt of what he had not said or done, the guilt of all that happened afterward, culminating in that awful instant when he had a chance to save Martin Luther King and didn't, had sat heavily as rocks upon Malcolm Toussaint. In that one pivotal moment, he had failed his father, failed Miss Parker, failed history itself.

He supposed he'd had some inkling of his failure even then, right in the moment, as he walked into the house to escape her questioning eyes. But he had fought it down. Nerves, he'd called it.

Conscience, more like.

But Lord knew he'd had his chances, even after.

The march didn't even happen the next day as scheduled. It started to snow that same night. By the time Malcolm woke up to get ready for another night on the graveyard shift, it had been falling for hours. He washed and dressed, bundled himself in his heavy coat, grabbed his bicycle, and went out into the frozen dark. For a moment, he just stood there on the sidewalk in front of the house, breathing in cold air beneath the falling sky.

Snow. Of all things, snow. Malcolm lifted his gloved hands and watched a few flakes settle there and dissolve. They were big as silver dollars. He could not remember the last time it had snowed this late in March. Shaking his head, he hopped on his bike and rode. It was slow and slippery going, even though there was not yet much accumulation.

The snow was still falling nine hours later when Malcolm got off work. It had piled itself deep and there was no question of being able to ride his bike home. He was standing in front of the hotel with it, wondering what he would do, when Ronald Whitten came up behind him. "Come on, kid," he said. "I'll give you a lift."

Malcolm pondered turning the offer down; he didn't like being around white people any more than he had to. But then what would he do? How would he get home?

"Okay," Malcolm said, his voice stiff. "Thank you."

They walked to the lot behind the building. He lifted the bike into the bed of Whitten's old pickup truck and climbed into the cab as Whitten cranked the engine. Even for the truck, the streets were a difficult go. It slid and slipped slowly east through a world leeched of color, movement, and sound. Parked cars had become only humps of snow. Garbage heaps had become white mountains. You had to guess where the streets were because curbs lay buried.

The two men didn't speak much—what did they have to talk about? The overheated cab of the truck was filled with blue smoke from Whitten's cigarettes. Country and western music provided the background to Whitten's occasional cursing when the truck slewed sideways on the slick white surface.

There would be no march today. It was as if nature herself had intervened, had doused the trash fires, stilled the angry words, frozen all of Memphis in place.

"You've been doing good work." Whitten spoke out of nowhere.

Surprised, Malcolm glanced over. "Thank you," he said.

"Most of 'em I hire, I've got to back after 'em, check up on 'em. Never had that problem with you."

"Thank you," said Malcolm again.

"Good work habits," said Whitten. "That'll carry you far."

"Turn up here," said Malcolm.

"You learn them work habits from your daddy?"

"I guess," said Malcolm.

"What's he do?"

"Sanitation worker," said Malcolm.

Whitten arched an eyebrow. "The ones on strike?"

"Yeah."

"Bad business, that strike."

"Mmm-hmm," said Malcolm. It was the most noncommittal thing he could think of.

"They may have a legitimate beef, you know, but they're going about it all wrong."

"Right turn," said Malcolm, hoping the white man would shut up.

Whitten obeyed, still talking. "Pushing the mayor in the corner, bringing in that Martin Luther King—who does that help, you know? I'll tell you who: the communists. Now there's even talk the city may have to cancel the Cotton Carnival."

The Carnival was a Memphis tradition, a misty-eyed homage to the "good old days" of dutiful slaves and benevolent masters. It was the highlight of the city's social calendar, climaxed with the crowning of the new cotton king and queen. Whitten shook his head, miserable at the thought of cancellation. "Now what those men should do..." he began.

Malcolm cut him off. "Right here," he said. He was still three blocks from home. But he'd had enough of listening to Ronald Whitten.

The truck slid as Whitten applied the brake. Malcolm was lifting the lever on the door even before the truck came to a full stop. "Thanks for the ride," he said, opening the door.

Whitten was squinting at the sky. "Been here all my life," he said. "Ain't never seen it like this, especially in damn near April." He looked at Malcolm. "You don't make it to work tonight, I'll understand. Hell, not sure I'll make it myself."

"Yeah," said Malcolm. He slipped out of the truck, lifted his bicycle from the back, and stood there in snow that came halfway up his shin, watching as Whitten picked his way gingerly down the street, a fantail of slush spraying off his back tires.

Then he hoisted his bike and started walking. It was a tough slog, what with the weight of the bike and the depth of the snow. Malcolm's breath, ragged and loud in his ears, was the only sound in all the world. Memphis was entombed in a stillness that felt sacred. The angry city had become a blank slate, a sheet of white paper, a chance to do it over and get it right.

And perhaps it was the recognition of this that made him pause when he got home and look over to the house next door, remembering what he had not said and had not done 24 hours before. But Miss Parker was not out on her porch. She was always out there. Rain, heat, sleet, snow, it didn't matter; she sat out there all day witnessing life. But this morning, when he was looking for her, when he was half-hoping for her, the porch was empty.

Would he have said what he should have said, done what he should have done, if she had been out there? Would he have told her emphatically to stay away when they rescheduled the march? Would he have taken this second chance? Malcolm had never been able to answer the question—not then, and not 40 years later.

He stood there a moment watching the empty porch. Finally, he hoisted the bike and slogged his way up the stairs. There, he stamped snow from his feet and shook it from his body as best he could, then opened his front door and let himself in. Behind him, snow tumbled from the sky, hiding all signs of human movement—footprints, tire tracks, bike treads—beneath a shroud of forgiving white.

Except that, as it turned out, nothing would be forgiven. In the end, they would all be denied the balm of grace and mercy: Memphis, the sanitation men, Martin Luther King, Malcolm Toussaint.

The memory of it was never too far away. Especially since Marie died. He had thrown himself into work and work had thrown itself right back at him and instead of healing, it was anger that had built in him like trapped fire. He had gone to bed night after night and seen Martin Luther King die right before him or sometimes (which was arguably worse) be saved right before him. Then Donte Stoddard had walked out of that fast food restaurant, innocent of any crime on the books, but black, young, and male in an instant when those were dangerous things to be, and he had been executed for no good reason and Malcolm had written about it, had held the cops accountable (which, after all, was his job) and the same stupid fucking white racist assholes had written the same stupid fucking white racist emails they always write when things like this happen and...

and...

...and he had finally had enough of it, had more than he could bear, and now here he sat, chained to a chair in a forgotten warehouse by some fat lunatic, and he was probably going to die in some ridiculous attempt to assassinate a man who didn't even need assassinating because he was never going to be elected president, not in this racist fucking country, and it was all just...just...

Malcolm's head hung. His muscles ached. His spirit ached. He was exhausted. No, he was *spent*. Body and soul, there was nothing left.

Somewhere behind him, beyond his line of sight, lay the body of the little drunk who had almost saved him. Malcolm was only dimly aware that Clarence Pym was pacing now, agitated. For the fifth time in fifteen minutes, he checked his watch.

"After 3:00," he muttered, raking a hand back through his unruly cowlick. "Where the hell can he be?"

And it was at that moment that the man-sized metal door rolled up with a loud clatter and Dwayne McLarty stepped through, pushing some frightened-looking black woman about Malcolm's age. His jaw was swollen and purple. So was hers. The butt of a pink pistol was visible in McLarty's waistband. He looked pleased with himself.

Pym, astounded, wheeled around on his friend. "Dwayne! Where the hell have you been?"

nineteen

"Who are you?"

Malcolm whispered this to the woman. She was sitting on the floor behind him, her feet duct-taped together and her hands duct-taped behind her to the crossbar of Malcolm's chair. Pym and McLarty were paying them no attention. They stood a few feet away, excitedly bringing each other up to date.

"What the fuck happened to you?" McLarty had asked, pointing to the angry red slash on the left side of Pym's face.

"I could ask you the same question," Pym had said, pointing to McLarty's swollen and empurpled jaw.

"Yeah," McLarty had said, "but I asked you first." So Pym had dutifully, if somewhat reluctantly, shown McLarty the body of the little drunk who tried to save Malcolm and explained how he had no choice but to kill him.

"I didn't want to," he'd said in a soft voice, "but I had to."

"You didn't 'want' to?" repeated McLarty in a mocking, prissy little voice.

"No," admitted Pym.

Whereupon McLarty stretched on tiptoes and roared in his face.

"Stop being such a pussy, for Chrissake! What did you expect, Sergeant? What the fuck kind of soldier are you, anyway? We are at war with these people. In war, people get killed."

"I know that!" shouted Pym. "You don't have to yell at me, Dwayne! Stop yelling at me!"

"I'm Janeka," the woman whispered back. "You're Malcolm?"

He was surprised. It struck him that she had not used his full name, as she would've if she were just someone who recognized him from television or the newspaper. She spoke with a familiarity he didn't understand. "Do I know you?" he asked.

"Bob Carson is…" And here, there was a tiny hesitation. Then she re-phrased it. "I know Bob," she said. "We were having lunch when this guy grabbed us from the restaurant. He gave Bob some computer disk. He told him he would kill me if Bob didn't take it to his newspaper and make them put it online."

"It's a video," said Malcolm. "These two are some sort of half-assed white supremacist group. They kidnapped me this morning and recorded some kind of manifesto they want to put out to the world."

"But why?"

"They say they have a bomb and they're going to blow up Grant Park tonight. They want to kill Obama."

Malcolm had his head turned to the left, trying to glimpse the woman on the floor behind him. So he didn't even see the pistol butt that came down from the right, clouting him hard on his temple. Then McLarty was in his face, his eyes burning with fever fire, his spittle spraying Malcolm's cheek like a garden hose. "Shut the *fuck* up!" he thundered. "Shut up shut up shut up! No talking. Do you hear?"

Malcolm nodded. "Yes," he told the maddened face that filled his vision. "Yes, I hear." He was a 60-year-old man with a prostate the size of a grapefruit and a bladder the size of a walnut, and he'd had no access to a bathroom since before dawn. So Malcolm Toussaint was horrified but not truly surprised to feel sudden warmth spreading in his crotch, to look down and see the front of his pants grow dark.

He closed his eyes. He could have died, then.

McLarty staggered backwards, cackling with laughter. "He pissed himself! Did you see! This nigger pissed himself! Oh, my God! Oh, my God! Oh, my God! Clarence, get the camera! Get a picture of this!"

Pym did not reply. There was a silence. His humiliation subsumed by curiosity, Malcolm opened his eyes and brought his head up a fraction. Pym stood there with his arms folded, facing his friend. "You used," he said.

McLarty turned. "Oh, Clarence, come on."

"You used," said Pym again. "You said you wouldn't. You said you were done with that shit."

McLarty threw his hands out, one of them still clenching a pink pistol. "Yeah, I used," he said. "So the fuck what so the fuck what so the fuck *what*? Who cares? In a few hours, we'll both be dead and mission accomplished. What does it matter if I have a little fun one last time?"

"You said you were done with it," Pym said again. "You promised me." He turned and walked away.

McLarty's hands came down and he gave a great sigh of exasperation as he followed his friend. "Come on, Clarence. Don't be that way."

The argument continued over near the door.

After a moment, Malcolm heard the woman's voice whisper, "Are you okay?"

It was a moment more before he could bring himself to answer. "I'm sorry," he said, through the pain drumming in his temple, the trickle of blood on his face. "I didn't mean for that to happen. It's just...I've been sitting here for nine hours. No bathroom breaks, you know?"

"You don't have to explain anything to me," she said.

Malcolm did not reply.

"You don't," she insisted.

And this, of course, made it worse.

"So anyway," he said, needing to change the subject, "they're crazy and they want to blow up Grant Park to kill Obama."

"That's ridiculous," she said. "That will never work. The police barricades, the Secret Service, the crowds..."

"Did you miss the part where I said they're crazy? And you're right. They'll never get to Obama. But how many people will they kill in the trying? Starting with us?"

"Jesus," she said.

"Yeah," he said.

"I'm frightened," she told him. "I don't mind telling you that."

"I don't mind telling you that I am, too."

"That little one is just plain mean. He reminds of me some nasty, rabid dog. What about the other one?"

"His name is Clarence Pym. I don't know how to figure him at all. He's got some nasty in him for sure. I called him fat and stupid a few hours ago, trying to get a rise out of him. My ears are still ringing from how hard he smacked me. But then right after that, he brought me a cup of water. I'm not sure he's all there. Sometimes, he acts like this is all just a game or like he doesn't get what they're doing here. You heard him. He's all torn up because he killed some poor homeless guy who tried to save me, but then he can turn around and talk about blowing up a park full of people like it's no big deal."

"Do you think he's developmentally delayed?"

Malcolm thought it over, then shook his head. "I don't think so," he said. "In some ways, he seems intelligent. I mean, he can rattle off the box score from any Bulls game you name, especially during the Jordan era."

Behind him, the woman—Janeka—made a dismissive sound. "That's just memorization, not intelligence."

"It's more than that," said Malcolm, impatient with her for being right. "It's just...the way he puts things together, I don't think his problem is a developmental delay. If anything, he's emotionally delayed. I don't know if that's a thing, but that's how he comes across to me. It just seems like there's a lot of stuff that a normal person would get that maybe he doesn't."

"So what are we going to do?"

Malcolm lifted his arms to the rattle of chains and cuffs. "What can we do?" he asked.

"Where's the key?"

"On the table," said Malcolm. Pym had left it there after recuffing Malcolm and dragging the homeless man's body out of sight. The table was six feet away. It might as well have been on the moon.

"You can't reach it?" she asked.

"Maybe Plastic Man could," he said. "I can't."

Malcolm glanced warily to make sure McLarty was not coming up again on his blind side. The two men were still standing near the roll-up door arguing.

"Goddamn it, Clarence, you act like my fucking mother sometimes. It was just one hit, okay?"

"No. Not okay," replied Pym, voice taut with anger. "We have work to do and how are you going to do your share if your head's all messed up with that crap?"

Clearly they were engrossed in their disagreement.

"If I could get my hands on something to cut this duct tape," Janeka said in a low voice, "maybe I could get it. Or maybe go for help."

Malcolm shrugged. "If," he said.

"So it's up to Bob, then."

There was no humor in Malcolm's chuckle. "Wonderful. We need an action hero. We got Bob."

"You've got something against Bob?"

Malcolm turned back and spoke over his shoulder. "Sorry," he said. "No, I have nothing against Bob."

"I doubt you could convince him of that," she said.

"What do you mean?"

"Bob was fired this morning because of you."

Malcolm was shocked. "What? Why?" Then he answered his own question. "I used his security code to plug that column into the paper." He paused. "They fired him for that."

"Yes," she said.

"Shit," said Malcolm. "I knew I was torpedoing my own career. I really didn't care. But I didn't intend for anything to happen to Bob. They're just looking for a scapegoat. They shouldn't blame him for what I did. He doesn't deserve that. I mean, we had our disagreements, but he was a decent guy. Better than most of them, at any rate."

"Them?"

"White people," said Malcolm.

"I see," she said.

The reserve in her voice angered him. "Come on, sister. I get that he's your friend, but don't act like you don't know."

"Oh, I know," she assured him. "Believe me, I know. But I try not to think of them as, you know...'them.' Seems to me that just exacerbates the problem. Doesn't really solve it."

Malcolm sighed his concession. "Yeah," he said, "Martin Luther King once told me the same thing."

"Seriously?" she said. "We're tied up here, maybe going to be killed by these two lunatics, and you're name dropping?"

God, but she was exasperating. "I wasn't name dropping," he said. "I was—"

She cut him off. "You were name dropping. You were reminding me that you are the famous Malcolm Toussaint, author of 'A Stone of Hope,' the so-called last interview with Martin Luther King." The reference was to a story Malcolm had published in the *Atlantic Monthly* two years after King's

assassination, recounting his encounter with the great man the week before
he was felled. It was the piece that had launched Malcolm's career.

"I was just saying—"

Again she cut him off. "I wonder what Dr. King would think of what
you wrote in the paper this morning?"

Malcolm blinked. "I beg your pardon?"

"Don't get me wrong," said Janeka. "I agreed with your main points
and Lord knows I understood your anger. But your blanket condemnation?
'America can go to hell?' You didn't sound like—what was it *Rolling Stone*
called you?—'the conscience of America.' You just sounded like some old
crank venting."

Malcolm breathed consciously, working to control his anger. "Lady," he
said in a hiss, "who the hell are you to lecture me? You don't know me."

"No," she said, and anger brimmed in her voice as well, "but I know Bob
Carson and he's a good man, even if he's one of 'them.' He did not deserve
what you did to him."

Malcolm struggled to hold onto his fury, but he felt it deflate, growing
soft beneath him. He could not deny the truth of what she had said, could
he? That realization wrenched a sigh out of him. "Okay," he said, "I'll give
you that."

"Thank you," she told him, still angry. "That's mighty white of you."

He let the gibe pass. "How do you know Bob?"

"I knew him in college. We were very close. For awhile we were...well, at
the time, I thought maybe we were even going to get married."

"What happened?" asked Malcolm.

She did not answer immediately. Indeed, the silence stretched so long
Malcolm wasn't sure she had heard him. In the corner by the door, McLarty
and Pym were still going at it. Malcolm was about to apologize for asking
what was obviously too painful a question. Then Janeka said, "You're from
Memphis, right?"

"Yes," said Malcolm.

"So you remember the march Dr. King held there. The march he tried to
hold, at any rate. And you remember what happened."

Now it was Malcolm's turn for silence, guilt tumbling in his heart, memories of what he didn't say and didn't do. "Yeah," he said softly. "I remember.
I was there."

Behind him, the woman sighed. "So was I," she said. "So was Bob."

twenty

March 28, 1968 dawned overcast and a little cool in Memphis.

Malcolm, who had slept poorly all night, finally gave up trying shortly after six. He rolled out of bed, washed, and dressed. The house was empty. His father, farmer's son that he was, was already up and out, gone downtown for the rescheduled march.

Standing in the bathroom mirror preparing to follow him, Malcolm put on a black beret he had bought just for this occasion, cocking it ace-deuce til it sat at just the right rakish angle on his head. Then he slipped on a pair of dark glasses and took a look at his handiwork. The effect was startling. The man who faced him was unsmiling, mysterious, and not to be screwed around with.

Malcolm pulled a dark windbreaker over his shirt—he could not yet afford a leather jacket—and the effect was complete. He nodded in approval of the man facing him, dropped his pistol into his pants pocket, and was ready to go. Stepping outside, Malcolm saw Nanny Parker standing on her porch. The old woman was dressed in Sunday clothes, purse held in the crook of her arm, drinking her morning coffee beneath a broad black hat with pink flowers.

She saw him looking. "You walking down there?" she asked.

"Yes, ma'am."

"That's a long walk. My girlfriend Betty from church is coming to pick me up. You welcome to ride over with us, if you want."

"No thank you, ma'am. I'd just as soon head over there now."

She smiled. "You want to be with people your age. Don't want to be tied up with a pair of old biddies like us. I understand."

"I'm just eager to get there," said Malcolm. Not quite a lie, not quite the truth.

"I know what you mean," she said.

Malcolm regarded her, this woman who had given him shelter, standing there so proudly. And here was yet another chance—a *last* chance. He said, "Are you sure you should be going down there? What if things get out of hand? I would hate to see you get hurt." It was as close as he could come.

She sucked her teeth in a sound of dismissal. "Who gon' try to hurt me, old as I am? No, sir. There is no way I am going to miss this."

"Okay, then," said Malcolm, stepping down to the street. He had tried to tell her, hadn't he? He'd as much as said it outright: *don't go*. What else could he do?

Nothing, that's what. Malcolm waved at the little woman and started walking toward downtown. He told himself his conscience was clear.

It was still dark when Bob and Janeka set out for Memphis. That morning, sitting alone together in his car in front of her dorm, they had turned to one another and Bob had taken both her hands in his. He breathed a soft, simple prayer: "Protect us, Lord. Get us there safely and bring us back in the same condition."

"Amen," she said.

"Amen," whispered Bob. He squeezed her hands. Then he started the car and pulled off.

They drove in silence for the first couple of miles. Finally, Bob spoke, just to have something to say. "I'm looking forward to hearing Dr. King," he said.

She didn't answer. He glanced over. "How about you?" he asked. She seemed pensive and small in the darkness of not-yet-dawn.

"I suppose," she finally said. "But to tell the truth, my main reason for going is to show support for the sanitation men. Have you read about their working conditions? The way that city exploits those men, it's a sin, is what it is. It's just a sin."

"Yes," said Bob. "But that's why it's a good thing Dr. King is coming to lead the march. He's going to bring attention to the issue, how they've been exploiting the laboring classes. He's going to force Memphis to deal with it. And not just Memphis, but by extension, the whole country."

"I hope you're right," she said, gazing out her window to where the clouds had just begun to anticipate the sun. "I just don't want it to be the same old song and dance."

Bob glanced over at her, confused. "What does that mean?"

But Janeka just shrugged and did not answer, so Bob turned back to the road. He goosed the pedal and the car leapt toward Memphis.

A police helicopter was parked above Hamilton High School.

A brick flew toward it from the crowd below, hurled by some boy foolish enough to think his missile could reach the hovering machine. The brick arced high, then fell to earth, shattering harmlessly in a street filled with high school students who on this day would not be going to school.

A couple of the boy's classmates jeered his miss. Then, a more realistic target presented itself, a laundry truck that came trundling unawares down the street. The boys let fly with more bricks. One of them struck home. The truck's back door popped open and someone's shirts, pants, and dresses spilled into the street. It made the boys double over with laughter when the uniformed driver stopped the truck, then jumped out to throw the clothes back in. He worked quickly and nervously and kept sweeping the crowd massed behind him with wide, frightened eyes. Then he slammed the door and hustled back into the cab. A brick landed right where he had been standing. The truck took off in a rush.

Malcolm, who had attended Hamilton until just a little more than a year ago, stood across the street watching all of this. The sun had burned the clouds away and the air temperature was rising. Hard to believe snow had lain thick on the ground just six days before. He had his windbreaker folded over his arm.

The crowd of young people milled in the street. Some were dancing. Some were laughing. A white woman came driving down that street now, honking for the kids to give way. But she didn't understand, did she? Whitey wasn't giving orders here today. Black people were done giving way.

So now, more bricks flew, bouncing off the hood and the trunk of her car. Malcolm could see the white woman's face, congealed in terror. The realization that she would not be deferred to or obeyed seemed impossible for her to process. When the street opened up in front of her, she took off, tires squealing.

It was, thought Malcolm, watching her blow through the stop sign at the end of the block, a good thing to see white people frightened for a change. Lord knew black people had been frightened long enough.

And now, wouldn't you know it? Here came a garbage truck, driven by some scab, some weak-kneed, lily-livered, Uncle Tom *nigger*, driving behind a police car with lights silently flashing. Rocks, bottles and bricks flew in from all directions, making a sound like a hailstorm as they slammed against all that Detroit steel. Malcolm caught a glimpse of the scab as he drove past, his jaw set like concrete, both hands on the steering wheel, his eyes locked dead ahead.

The sight of him was a provocation Malcolm couldn't resist and didn't really want to. He cupped his hands. "You better run, you backstabbing motherfucker!" he yelled.

A boy next to him grinned. "You got that right, baby," he said.

The crowd of students was seeping like water and had begun to overflow Malcolm's position. Across the street at the school, teachers—many of them black—were in the parking lot trying to herd the kids back to class. But the kids just laughed and said they weren't going anywhere. This was a new day. None of the old badges of authority meant jack shit anymore.

"I am a man," yelled one boy to no one in particular.

"Black power!" yelled another, to the same audience.

"Fuck all you white bastards!" yelled a girl. This, as police cars swept onto the scene. More rocks and bottles hammered against more Detroit steel. There was the satisfying crunch of a windshield spider-webbing with cracks as a brick bounced off. Police came out of the cars. They wore gas masks. They raised billy clubs.

Students scattered. Some ran along side streets; some ran back toward the main school building; some ran toward police, missiles in their hands, lips curled around taunts and screams.

Malcolm ran.

Bob took Janeka's hand as they walked up Hernando toward the church where the marchers were gathering. She looked at him and he knew she was wondering if this was wise. He didn't know if it was. He only knew that he didn't really care. He only knew that he was tired of hiding. Let them look.

And they did. The crowd was a mixture of hard-faced older men and church ladies, of high school students larking about, of preachers in clerical collars and small children playing under the tolerant gazes of their mothers, and of unsmiling young men in berets. Nobody approached him and Janeka, but he felt them marking their passage.

After a moment, Janeka pulled her hand from his. She scratched her cheek, folded her arms.

They stood together in the shadow of the church. Clayborn Temple vaguely resembled a fairytale castle. It even had a tower on one end.

He was surprised there were so few white faces on hand for a march that was to be led by Martin Luther King. The few who were there stood, like him, scanning the crowd. Each white face wore the same expression—that of a person who has fallen asleep and awakened, somewhat bewildered, in a strange new place he's not entirely certain is safe. A white man nodded at him and Bob realized that in scanning the crowd, they were looking for one another, searching out another pair of blue eyes or ruddy cheeks so that they might feel a little less marooned.

It was an odd and discomfiting feeling.

"Not a lot of white folks here," said Janeka, and Bob started. It was as if she had read his mind.

"No," he said, "there aren't."

Her grin was quicksilver. "Don't worry," she told him. "I'll protect you." And she reached and took his hand once more.

"I'm not worried," he told her. But he was.

Not far away a group of black women stood comforting a white woman who was bawling that someone had stolen her wallet. Her pocketbook gaped open like a mouth. Bob was stunned and unsettled. How could these people do something so low and mean to someone who was trying to help them?

He caught himself. *These people.* Where had that come from? It wasn't "these people" who had done this. It was some pickpocket in a crowd.

The fact that he had to remind himself of this embarrassed him. Bob lowered his head, intending to offer a quick prayer of repentance. Before he could get a word out, Janeka was leading him over to the crying woman. He watched, first confused and then amazed, as his girlfriend, her own eyes brimming, touched the white woman's shoulder. The woman looked up.

"I'm sorry," said Janeka. "I'm so sorry."

Like she had done it herself. Like she had reached into this woman's purse and plucked out her wallet.

"It's not the money," said the woman, still weeping. "I only had $10. The stuff that was in there, it can all be replaced. But I just never thought, at a march like this..."

She didn't finish the sentence. She didn't need to. It finished itself in the helpless glaze of her eyes. Janeka looked up at the other black women. All their eyes reflected the same helplessness.

"Did you hear? Did you hear?" A man's voice, agitated.

Bob turned and saw him. Some scruffy black guy in a denim jacket, his eyes hot. "Did you hear?" he called again and now people were looking toward him, waiting. "They done killed some girl," he cried. "Police done killed some girl at Hamilton High School. Bashed her head in, the no-good honky motherfuckers."

He was looking directly at Bob when he said it.

No girl had been killed at Hamilton High.

At least, Malcolm didn't think so. The rumor of her death was being passed through the crowd like a virus, but he had just hiked over from Hamilton and hadn't seen anyone being killed. Certainly, there had been confusion, students running everywhere, ducking between buildings, darting through back yards, police hot on their heels. And a girl had fallen, yes. She'd even been hit by the cop who was chasing her. But she had seemed all right, after. Bloodied, a little scraped, but all right. She hadn't died.

Had she?

And he realized: he couldn't really say for sure one way or another. It made his stomach clench.

"Hey, baby, you all right?" Eddie had come up on him and was regarding him with what may have been—it was difficult to tell through the shades—concern.

Malcolm blurted, "You don't really think they killed some girl, do you?"

Eddie's smile was tight as a rusted bolt. He said, "Ain't much I would put past white police. How about you?"

"I guess not," said Malcolm. "Damn shame, though. I was just over there."

Eddie clapped him on the back. "Get yourself together. They gon' start their march soon. Time to wake these country Negroes up."

Malcolm's nod was vague and as Eddie drifted away, he surveyed the crowd. Some white nuns and priests had appeared. A group of black teachers stood together, watching as one of their number knelt down and used her lipstick to make a sign. Young men wandered through the crowd wearing jackets that said "Invaders." They were supposed to be some kind of activist group.

Malcolm spotted his father at the same time his father spotted him. The older man was perched with Sonny on a low wall across the street from the church, both holding their placards with the emphatic red lettering on a field of white: I AM A MAN. Malcolm wandered over.

"Hey, Pop," he said, removing his shades. "Sonny."

Pop said, "Mornin', Junie."

Sonny said, "Hey."

"What time is this supposed to begin?" asked Malcolm.

"About ten," said Pop. "But now they sayin' King been held up. So don't nobody know when it gon' start."

"You got a good-size crowd," said Malcolm, squinting a little as he took in the growing throng.

Pop nodded. "More of them than us," he said.

Malcolm said, "What do you mean?"

Pop shrugged. "At the beginning, this was just about us sanitation mens. Now it's about..." He paused, surveyed the crowd, hunched his shoulders again. "Hell, I don't know what it's about now."

"People just want to support you, Pop. They're standing behind you, trying to make sure you get what you deserve."

At that moment, a teenaged boy walked past, saying to no one in particular, "We're going to get us some white folks today."

Pop stared at Malcolm, his eyes questioning. Malcolm held his eyes for only a moment. Then he looked away.

There was a wrongness here.

Bob could not name it, but he felt it, deep in his bones. This was his first protest march and he didn't know what he had expected, but he knew he hadn't expected this: to find himself wondering if he was safe among the people he was marching to support.

"We're going to get us some white folks today," some passing teenaged boy said.

Bob stared after him in disbelief. Janeka reached for his hand.

"Don't pay that fool any mind," she said. "He's just some boy running off at the mouth."

Bob nodded, but he wasn't so sure. For years, he had dreamt of joining a protest march led by the great Martin Luther King. He had dreamt of this like some kids dreamt of being Mercury 7 astronauts or having a catch with Mickey Mantle. He had watched, breathless, the nightly news coverage of King's great protests in Birmingham, St. Augustine, Selma, and he had wondered—barely an adolescent, not even shaving yet, but he had *wondered*—if he had what it took, if, when the moment came, he would be strong enough in his faith to stand there and take it while some mob of vicious racists kicked him and punched him and called him every dirty name in the book, yet not raise a hand back to them and, indeed, pray for them even as they harmed him.

His perplexed parents called him "tenderhearted" when he complained about the injustices the Negroes had to endure. Oh, they agreed that, as his father once put it, the Negroes got a "bad deal down there," but they didn't see why he felt that he, personally, had to do something about it. They didn't see why he couldn't just send some of the money he earned working part-time to the NAACP or some such group and be done with it. They didn't see why he insisted that he needed to do more, much less what that sense of obligation had to do with being a Christian.

But then, he had long since realized, to his mild disappointment, that his parents defined that word differently than he did. They were willing enough to spend Sunday mornings in church, to put a little extra into the poor box at Christmas, and to donate one of Estelle Carson's famous lemon pound cakes for the annual church picnic. But the idea of faith as an activist thing, the idea that it could require one to give one's own body in sacrifice for a good cause, struck them as, well...*extreme*.

So they had watched their oldest son with a kind of awed fascination and inchoate fear as he bubbled over in his enthusiastic admiration for John Lewis, a Negro college student whose skull was fractured on a bridge in Selma, or Jim Zwerg, a white college student who had his back broken at a bus station in Montgomery. Not that he wanted to be hurt like them, he had explained quickly, but he wanted God to test him as He had tested them. He wanted to know that he could pass that test, that he had the courage to put his faith into action.

Concerned, Bob's parents had asked their pastor, Oliver Purvis, a mild, bespectacled Presbyterian who owned a used car lot in town ("A Fair Deal—You Have My Word On It") to talk to their son. Reverend Purvis had dutifully tried to convince Bob that it was enough simply to want better for the Negroes and all of God's mistreated children, to send money and prayers to help them and that it wasn't necessary to bleed for them.

Bob had listened politely and when the preacher was finished he said, "Yes, sir, but Dr. King says that if a man hasn't found something he's willing to die for, he's not fit to live. Don't you believe that?"

Purvis had swallowed hard and said, "Well, yes, I do, but this isn't your fight, now is it?"

And Bob had said, "Yes, but what about where the Bible says, 'Do we not all have one father? Has not one God created us?'"

Fifteen years old and staring earnestly at the man who had once sprinkled water onto his face and pronounced him baptized. Reverend Purvis had given him a strange look. Then he said, "Well, you know, Bobby, you've given me a lot to think about." And he excused himself, and did not return.

So Bob had continued to dream of this moment, of one day having the opportunity to march behind Martin Luther King.

But he had not dreamt it would be like this.

There was an anger here he had not expected. It wasn't just the loud brashness of some kid. No, you could sense it, you could smell it, you could see it.

He looked around at the young men in the berets, their eyes behind dark glasses.

He looked at the high school kids making their own makeshift signs: FUCK MAYOR LOEB said one. LOEB EAT SHIT said another.

He looked at the preachers looking at their watches and assuring everyone within earshot that Dr. King would be here soon.

He looked at the students, laughing and joking and yelling out the names of their schools like some kind of challenge—or threat.

He looked at the marshals with their yellow armbands, trying to get the students to pipe down, line up, behave.

He looked at the white people, still scanning for other white people.

He looked at the men, the sanitation workers who stood together in their ill-fitting coats and shiny pants, with their faces carved and eyes squinted by endless years of riding on trucks and toting garbage through sun and cold, the men who seemed somehow shrunken, lost, and even forgotten in this crush of disparate people gathered in their name.

A boy paraded through the crowd holding high a tree branch. From it dangled two objects. One was a noose. The other was a sign that read, LOEB'S HANGING TREE. "Oh yeah," the boy said through a broad grin, "this here is gon' be a nonviolent, peaceful march. Yes, sir!" He rolled his eyes. All around him, young people shrieked with hysterical laughter.

Bob stood there watching this confusion on Hernando Street in front of the Clayborn Temple and heard himself whisper his doubts to the bright morning air. "I don't know about this," he said. "I really don't know."

The crowd was growing. A police helicopter chopped its way through the air above. And it was getting hot. The sun, having burned its way through the morning clouds, was making up for lost time.

Off came jackets and coats. Newspapers and leaflets fluttered beneath shining faces, having been pressed into service as impromptu fans.

"Fuck nonviolence," a rangy, dark-skinned man was saying. "One of them crackers bust me upside my head, I'm gon' put that bastard on the ground. You best believe that."

Malcolm felt his father tense and he knew Pop was about to confront the man. He was thankful when some preacher got there first. "Brother," he said, "I appreciate your feelings, but this *is* a nonviolent march, and if you can't accept that discipline, then we just ask respectfully that you do not participate."

The man's mouth worked for a moment as he regarded the man in the clerical collar. "I'm just sayin'," he finally said. "That's all."

"I understand," said the preacher. His voice was all reason and calm. "But we still ask that you do not disrupt what we are trying to do. Can I count on you for that?"

The man glared. "Ain't disruptin' nothin'. Just sayin'."

When the preacher didn't respond, the man flung his hands in a gesture of dismissal and walked away. The preacher shook his head, then glanced at his watch as he wandered off through the crowd. "Everybody be cool," he was saying. "We'll be starting in a minute."

"Glad he got rid of that fool," said Pop. He nudged Sonny. "Ain't never lifted a tub a day in his life. What the hell he doin' here? What make him think he got the right to run his mouth?"

"You could say that about a lot of them," said Sonny.

"You think you could do it, Pop?" asked Malcolm.

"Do what?"

"Stand there and take it while some whitey beats on you?"

Pop pursed his lips. "I don't know," he said, after a moment. "But I'm willing to try."

"Lord have mercy," said Sonny. "Look at this fool." He was pointing toward a man who stood unsteadily in the street near a group of high school students, hoisting a bottle of cheap wine. The students' laughter was harsh and loud.

"Don't bogart the whole thing, Pops!" one boy yelled.

"Yeah, save some of that for me!" another cried.

"You gon' drink after him?" some girl asked, scandalized.

"Hell, wine's wine," said the boy and the ugly laughter renewed itself.

There were, now that Malcolm looked, a number of disheveled men drifting through the crowd. There were pimps in flashy suits, hair straight as a ruler and gleaming with congolene. There were hustlers in straw stingy brims and pencil moustaches, eyes always on the make, sizing up the crowd. The shifty dregs of Beale Street, on the way home from their nighttime revels, had detoured by to enjoy the spectacle.

There were so many people out here. Thousands. Easily, thousands. Where had they all come from?

"You right," said Sonny. "Ain't even our march no more."

"You know, Miss Parker said she was coming," said Malcolm. "I don't like the idea of her being out in the middle of all this." He had to raise his voice as the orbit of the police helicopter brought it right overhead.

Pop had little use for Nanny Parker. Her very existence was a reminder of the bad times, all the days Malcolm had sought refuge over there. But even he shook his head now and said, "No, that old lady got no business being out here. Too many people, too much confusion."

A man was passing out placards with sticks attached so the signs could be hoisted into the air. MACE WON'T STOP TRUTH, they read. One girl read this without apparent interest. Then she flipped the sign over and pried the stick off. As the placard fell into the street, she lifted the stick for her friends to see. "Look!" she cried.

Moments later, placards littered the street and sticks, like pine wood swords, began to wave high above the crowd.

It was about eleven when the white Lincoln Continental finally came gliding down the street. The young people in the crowd pressed themselves against it, slapping at it, pounding on it, or just touching it, laying hands on it as though they might draw some magic, some knowledge, some valuable essence, just from contact with the metal.

The car nosed its way through the people and finally stopped, unable to move any further. The crowd had simply congealed around it.

Bob climbed atop a low stone wall next to some sanitation men. He reached down and gave Janeka his hand so that she could come up as well. It gave them a perfect vantage point.

What they saw was chaos.

The people—and most of them were children, laughing, giggling, giddy—were mashed so heavily against the car that the doors could not be opened. "Hey, Dr. King," they sang out. "Hey, Martin!"

"Move back!" cried one of the marshals.

"Give them some space!" cried another.

They were trying to shove the young people off the car, but there was nowhere for them to go, so tightly was the crowd massed.

"People in the back, move back!" cried a man in a clerical collar. "Give them some room!"

"This is a mess," said Bob.

"You got that right," said the sanitation man standing on his left.

It took a long time. The men inside the car were trapped there until a group of ministers linked arm in arm bulled their way through the crowd. A window came down and one of the ministers, a stocky man with a large, square head, leaned in for what looked like urgent consultation with the men inside.

Still the crowd jostled and pushed. Bob was grateful he'd had the foresight to seek sanctuary on this wall off to the side. "I didn't think it was going to be like this," he told Janeka. It felt almost like an apology.

After a moment, the preachers managed to push the crowd back far enough for the door to swing open. A dark-skinned man with blunt features stepped out first, and Bob recognized him as Ralph Abernathy, King's best friend and second-in-command. He buttoned his coat as he looked over the crowd. He did not seem pleased.

Then another man stepped out of the car and this, finally, was Martin Luther King. The crowd went wild. They surged forward, straining to touch him, reaching to lay hands on the top of his head, his shoulder, his hand, the hem of his garment.

Like they reached toward Jesus, thought Bob. The thought was unnerving.

"My Lord," said Janeka, reading his thoughts yet again, "you'd think it was the Second Coming."

The ministers staggered under the onslaught, but the line held and they surrounded King and cleared a path to the front of the march. Martin Luther King was not a big man. Rather, he was on the short side, with a stocky build going over to outright fat. But in the midst of that crowd he seemed smaller still, flotsam bobbing on a tide of human passion. Pushed and shoved and yanked about, people screaming and shouting, a police helicopter beating the air above him, he looked anxious, even scared.

Bob looked closer, then, and realized there was something else in those eyes. Exhaustion. A grinding fatigue. Martin Luther King was so tired he could barely stand.

The phalanx of ministers almost carried him through the crowd.

"Give way!" they shouted.

"Clear the way!"

A flatbed truck stood at the intersection, mounted with news cameras. One of the ministers shouted, "Get the sanitation men up front with Dr. King!"

"Guess that's us," said the man next to Bob to a friend on the other side.

The two men stepped down from the wall and began making their way toward the front. A boy came up from behind, elbows high, pushing his way through the crowd. He caught the taller man in the chest and almost knocked him down. The boy didn't stop, didn't even pause.

"You all right?" asked the taller man's friend.

The taller man just shook his head and spoke in a bitter voice. "Like I told you: more of them than us."

Malcolm watched as the mob—it was difficult to think of this unruly mass as a march—stretched itself down Hernando and then, far up in the distance, swung left on Beale. His father, he knew, was somewhere up in the front with the other sanitation men, jostled and pushed by high school boys trying to get close to Dr. King. Now Malcolm, who had hung back, brought up the rear, walking in an assemblage of young men with sunglasses, T-shirts, and Invaders jackets.

He was thinking about his father, whom he'd watched shoved aside by some boy running to see King.

The truth was, he felt sorry for Pop, for all the sanitation men whose great march was being taken from them by unruly children. Even now, a trio of teenaged boys was running up and back on the sidewalk along the sides of the mob—the *march*—laughing and giggling like they were at the state fair. At 19, Malcolm was only three or four years older, but it felt like a gulf of decades.

It wasn't fair to the sanitation men, what was happening. Much less what was going to happen.

But, he reminded himself, it *needed* to happen. All of it needed to happen. These men needed to learn that Martin Luther King was not some savior with magic powers and a fancy suit. This city and this country needed to learn that henceforth, they would have to deal with a new movement that was impatient by design, that would not be mollified by marches and pretty speeches, that would demand—and take—what black people were rightfully owed.

From far ahead, the sound of singing drifted back on the warm morning air. "We shall overcome," the voices caroled, the melody stately and yet from this distance, somehow insubstantial and frail.

"We shall overcome," they sang. "We shall overcome, someday."

Pulling at the last syllable, running it up and down the scale, through colorations of want, need, and hope.

Someday. A pathetic word, freighted with too damn much patience. Why couldn't they see that? What was it about getting old that leeched the fire from your bones and made you content with singing hymns to maybe, possibly, and tomorrow? Malcolm didn't understand and hoped he never would. All at once, he was reminded of a rock song this white boy at his college used to play in the dorms over and over again.

"Hope I die before I get old," the singer sneered. Amen to that, amen to that.

"Down with Loeb! Down with Loeb! Down with Loeb!"

This chant rose full and lusty from somewhere in the middle of the mob ahead, contrapuntal with the sweet, patient lyric being sung in the front. It made him grin. "Now that's more like it!" he cried to no one in particular.

"You got that right, baby," said the man next to him.

If it wasn't fair the sanitation men's march was being overtaken, overrun by kids, well, life itself wasn't fair. And maybe the kids knew something the old folks didn't know or, being old, had allowed themselves to forget: the squeaky wheel gets the grease. Too much patience only gave whitey permission to ignore you. No, what you had to do was make yourself impossible to ignore.

"Black power!" he shouted. It came from out of nowhere and it felt good. He liked the urgency and the immediacy of it, the implicit reminder that "someday" was not nearly soon enough. So he shouted it again. "Black power!"

A group of them picked up the chant, bringing up the tail end of the march. "Black power! Black power! Black power!"

Beale Street was just ahead.

The crowd was moving too fast.

Bob had always imagined that a protest march maintained a dignified pace, the better to emphasize the long suffering that motivated it and the righteousness from which its power sprang. But this march was moving at a quickstep, pushed along from behind by young people, still cutting through the crowd, still running along the outskirts, trying to get close to Martin Luther King.

King seemed to be getting the worst of it, at least as far as Bob could tell from his vantage point several rows back. His head lolled on his neck from time to time and the men to either side of him seemed less to be marching with him than simply holding him upright.

Bob stumbled as some student shoved past on his left, yelling over his shoulder. "There he is! There King right there!"

"Watch it!" yelled Bob, his voice sharp.

The boy didn't even notice. It made Bob fume. This was not how it was supposed to be.

He remembered Janeka, then, and worried, because she was a small woman and could easily be hurt if this march, this *mob*, got much more out of hand. "Are you all right?" he asked her.

"I'm fine," she said in a voice that quivered slightly and did not convince him at all. Her hand clung to his as another impatient teenager tried to push between them.

"You don't look fine," he told her as the teenager finally gave up and went another way. Her eyes were round and mostly white.

"I'm fine," she repeated, trying for definitive emphasis, but not quite getting there.

"Maybe we should go," said Bob. "These people are getting out of hand."

She arched an eyebrow. "These people?"

It irked Bob. "You know what I mean," he told her. "Don't start that. I'm just saying this crowd could be dangerous. Maybe we should get out of here while we can."

"And how would we do that?" she asked.

This, Bob was forced to admit, was a good question, hemmed in as they were on all sides by walls of humanity. Getting out would require hacking his way through with one hand, Janeka trailing behind holding onto the other. It was possible, but it would not be easy. Not at all.

Bob was still trying to figure out what to do when he heard the sound. Everybody looked to everybody else. "What was that?" asked Bob.

But he already knew.

The pine sticks that had been designed to hold the placards high in the air were thin and so, made poor cudgels. The boys had to hammer the clothing store window several times before it finally broke, caving in on itself in a cascade of glass that chimed and tinkled like some devil's xylophone.

A cheer went up. Fists went up. "Black power!" someone cried. "Black power!"

The store had been breached; the remains of the window hung in jagged shards, but no one even bothered to go inside. Malcolm watched, frozen in amazement, as a couple of boys grabbed items from the broken display case—a man's hat and a pair of shoes—and then ran, holding the items above their heads like trophies. Looting the store, he realized, this wasn't the point. No, the point was the breach itself, the line crossed, the barrier broken, and whitey forced to see that this was a new day and nobody was taking his shit anymore.

"Black power!" they cried.

And the cry echoed and doubled back upon itself. "Black power! Black power! Black power!"

"Damn it! They're breaking windows back there!"

This is what one of the sanitation men cried as the march leaders paused, looking back toward the sound.

"They're ruining the march!" cried a minister right next to Bob.

Another minister—Bob recognized him as the same stocky man who had conferred with King when the white car pulled up—took a bullhorn and started walking toward the back of the march. "You are hurting the cause," he called out. "This is a nonviolent campaign."

There was the sound of another window breaking.

Bob still had Janeka's hand. It was small and sweaty in his.

"What about you, brother? You just going to watch?"

This was Eddie, coming up behind Malcolm, sweat beading on his brow. And Malcolm realized he had indeed just been standing there transfixed, as the second window caved in and another cheer went up. Somehow, he felt sickened and exhilarated all in the same instant. He did not know how that was possible, but it was.

"Well?" demanded Eddie. "What you gon' do?"

Malcolm looked at him. He felt himself teetering, as if on the deck of a ship rolling across the waves. He felt himself balancing as if on a tightrope between the life he had lived all these years until this very moment and everything that would come after.

On the ground was an abandoned stick from one of the placards. With a nod to Eddie, he reached down and snatched it up. He held it high as he charged forward like some soldier in a forgotten war. Screaming some cry beyond words, he brought the stick down hard upon the head of the rapist Rupert Pruitt, upon the head of a white cop with a can of Mace, upon the head of a long-haired white college professor who had once patronized him with a smile and asked him to describe to a class of earnest white faces what it was like "for our black brothers in the ghettoes"—and upon the window of a pawnbroker notorious among black people in Memphis for miserly loans and usurious rates.

He broke the glass with one fury-driven blow. The sound of it shattering was symphonic.

Malcolm heard himself laughing, joyous in madness.

———

With the exception of the helicopter hovering overhead, there had been no real police presence. The apparent absence, Bob assumed, had been a tactical decision to avoid unnecessary provocation.

That all changed now with a suddenness.

Behind him, he saw police pouring out from side streets, batons high, Mace cans in hand.

"Oh, my God," said Janeka.

Martin Luther King's men saw it too. One of them said, "We've got to get you out of here, Doc."

King shook his head. "No," he said, "we must get this under control. If I leave now, they'll say I ran away."

The other man was exasperated. "Martin, it is not safe for you to be here."

Something pained showed on King's face. "Perhaps we can talk to them. Get them to settle down."

The other man swept his hand toward the other end of the street, where police could be seen chasing teenaged boys in and out of buildings, nightsticks flashing. "Does that look like something we can settle down?"

Another man spoke to Abernathy. "I understand Martin's concerns," he said, "but you need to get him out of here."

King surrendered with a palpable reluctance. Bob watched as two of his men linked arms with him and led him down a side street. There, one of the men flagged down a white Pontiac. Moments later, it roared away with King and Abernathy inside.

Watching this, Bob felt...abandoned.

This was his hero? This was the great Martin King, this stocky little man being hustled away to safety as all hell broke loose around him?

For a long moment, Bob just stood there, chaos swirling around him. The police helicopter hovering above. Someone yelling, "Go back to the church!" The sanitation men dutifully obeying, turning around and walking in a group back toward the temple. A police officer yelling, "Get back here, you black son of a bitch!" as some fleet-footed young man outdistanced him. Glass breaking. People running every which way.

He was still holding Janeka's hand. Now he looked down into her face and saw his own fear reflected. "We've got to get out of here!" he told her.

He didn't wait for her response. They took off, running.

———

Now the looting began in earnest, people clambering through broken windows, taking whatever there was to take.

Malcolm stood breathing heavily by the broken window, still frozen by the wonder of what he had done, until Eddie clapped him hard on the back, breaking the spell. "Come on, fool. Stop daydreaming and get your ass on in there. You the one broke it. You get first pick!"

Malcolm didn't want first pick. He didn't want anything. The triumph that had sizzled through him an instant ago, the righteous vindication of watching that window cave in on itself, had dissipated like fog under the sun. All he felt now was an abrupt wrongness, a deep unease that bubbled like nausea in his gut.

But how to say this? What words might encapsulate it, especially in this moment where there was no time for words because everything was moving so damn fast?

Malcolm didn't even try to say it. He didn't resist. How to resist? Everywhere you looked, everybody you saw was climbing in a window, coming out with sport coats and whiskey and toy trucks and trumpets and women's hats. The windows were down, the barriers were crossed, the rules no longer applied.

"Yeah," said Malcolm, "all right." And he joined the crowd pouring through the window into Johnson Brothers Pawnbrokers.

Bob and Janeka ran hand in hand back down Beale Street.

It was dangerous going this way, but they had no choice. They did not know the city and Bob was scared of getting lost in this madness if he tried to improvise a new route back to his car. So the only thing he could think to do was run straight back the way they had come, through the heart of the madness.

And it was, indeed, madness. Boys with rocks squaring off with police. A violin sitting broken and useless right in the middle of the street. Some boy, for no apparent reason, heaving an empty whiskey bottle so that it struck an older black woman in the back of the head, driving her to her knees. Now, teargas canisters were hitting the asphalt with metallic clinks, hissing their noxious fumes into the air.

It burned. Bob buried his mouth and nose in the crook of his forearm. Then he thought about Janeka. "Are you all right?" He tried to yell this, but his voice was muffled and she didn't answer. He lifted his head and turned to look behind him, still running. "I said, are you—"

Bob never even saw the fist that came from out of nowhere then and landed flush on his jaw. He had been running at top speed and now, like something out of a Warner Brothers cartoon, his legs ran right out from under him. He landed hard, banging his head on the sidewalk, skidding on concrete littered with broken glass.

Before he knew what had happened to him, a man came down hard on his chest and started pounding him with a manic glee.

"White motherfucker!" he cried. "Hate all you bastards!"

Malcolm had picked up a little transistor radio, just to be picking something up, just to make Eddie stop haranguing him about taking first pick of the merchandise. Now, they were the last two stepping through the broken pawnshop window. Eddie's arms were loaded down with a bizarre assortment of loot: suits and a typewriter and a guitar and a vacuum cleaner.

He was grinning derision at Malcolm. "All that shit in there, I don't know how you end up with a little cheap-ass radio," he said.

Malcolm never got a chance to reply.

"Freeze!" the cop cried. Just like on television. And just like on television, he had the drop on them, stood with gun drawn and ready to fire.

Malcolm's hands went up. Eddie dropped his stuff and was raising his own hands.

Their salvation came in the form of a brick. It arced in from across the street and struck the cop hard on the back of the head. He was wearing a riot helmet, so it didn't hurt him, but he staggered from the blow and turned automatically to see what it was. Too late he realized his mistake.

Before he could turn back, Eddie had taken him to the ground and they were wrestling for the gun. The cop was fending Eddie off with his forearm, trying to yank his gun hand free from Eddie's grip. "Officer down!" he cried. "Officer down!" Then Eddie punched him, two hard kidney shots that brought the cop's forearm down to protect his side. Now Eddie went for the hand that held the gun, sinking his teeth deep into the white man's thumb. He cried out, his hand came open, and the gun clattered free. Eddie snatched it up and sprang to his feet. His sunglasses had come off in the struggle and his eyes were twin dots as he pointed the weapon at the police officer lying at his feet. Eddie's triumphant grin showed bloodstained teeth.

The cop's hands came up. "I've got kids," he said in a slow, careful voice. "Ezra and Sally."

Eddie just grinned. And without even knowing he was going to do it, Malcolm put himself between the cop and the gun.

"Get out the way, brother," Eddie told him. In contrast to his mad eyes, his voice was deliberate and calm.

"Don't do this, man!" cried Malcolm.

Eddie sneered. "Come on, baby. What you care about some whitey? Some cop at that?"

And how to explain?

It was one thing to be mad at whitey. Who wasn't mad at whitey? But it was another thing to watch a *man* about to be killed right in front of you, to see his hands come up as he spoke his children's names, to look in his frightened eyes and see reflected there the terrible realization that everything he was and everything he would ever be had reached an end. This was an awful thing to see, no matter what color the man you saw it in.

But he did not know how to say this, so he said instead, "This ain't black power, brother. This is just murder."

Eddie didn't answer. A forever crept by in silence, Eddie staring down the length of the revolver to the man lying so still on the sidewalk.

All at once, the mad eyes softened. Eddie raised the gun to menace only the sun. Then he tucked it in the small of his back.

"Fine," he said. "You like this pig so much, you can have him, 'brother.'"

He put something nasty on the last word, something that made the word contradict itself, even hate itself. He smiled. And then he left. He did not run away. He strolled. Malcolm watched.

"You saved my life."

It was the police officer, his voice shaky. Malcolm had forgotten all about him. The cop had come to his feet and his outstretched hand was the first thing Malcolm saw when he turned. Malcolm took it automatically, because what else do you do when a man offers you his hand? Then the officer lifted the riot shield on his helmet and for the first time, Malcolm saw his face. He froze.

Who...?

He knew this face, but he could not place it.

And then he could.

He had seen this man on Main Street two blocks south of City Hall a little over a month ago. The man had sprayed him in the face...

(like a damn roach)

...called him a nigger and told him to go jump in the river.

He pulled his hand back. He could see the cop wondering why. Malcolm tried to speak. He laughed instead. It was a bitter sound, but he could not make himself stop. The cop was still staring in confusion.

Malcolm's mouth laughed until his eyes wept.

"Get off of him!" Janeka was screaming.

She seemed far away, her voice barely audible behind the blood roaring like rapids in Bob's ears. Presumably, the man who sat straddling him could hear her just fine, but if so, he ignored her cries, concentrating instead on battering Bob with his heavy fists.

"Leave him alone!" Janeka said, still screaming.

The man on top of him snarled, apparently intent on holding Bob accountable for the sins of every white man since Columbus.

Bob managed to get his forearms up, turning his head this way and that, trying to dodge the blows. But the fists kept coming down like pistons.

Then, all at once, there was a sound like an axe makes when it splits a log and the blows stopped. Bob squeezed one eye open. He saw the man on top of him sway like a palm tree in a Hawaiian breeze, his eyes rolling up like a broken slot machine. Then he slid off Bob and fell onto the curb, insensate.

And Bob saw his girlfriend, his partner in the struggle for nonviolent social change, his colleague in a group whose middle name was "unarmed," standing there with a broken, bloodstained chunk of masonry so big she had to use both hands.

Janeka threw the masonry down and extended her hand. "Come on," she said. "Can you walk?"

She braced him and he climbed through levels of dizziness and pain until he found his feet. "Lean on me," she said and he did and they made their way down the street as police officers trotted past them. A child stood in the middle of Beale Street screaming for his mother and a policeman stood dumbfounded as some man on the other side of the street laughed crazily and then began to cry.

"We've got to get you to a hospital," said Janeka.

He shook his head, and this brought a new explosion of pain. "Home," he said. "You drive."

"Bob, you might be hurt. Something might be broken. You have to see a doctor."

"I will," he said. "Just not here. Take me back to school. We'll call an ambulance from there."

"Bob," she began.

"Home," he said. "Please."

So they walked. Beale to Hernando, down past the temple where sanitation men stood congregated, watching the disorder at the other end of the street. Some of the men looked toward them with concern as they passed on the far side of the street.

"Y'all okay?" one man yelled. "Y'all need help?"

Bob just lifted a hand and shook his head. He didn't want their help. He simply wanted out of Memphis. Two blocks later, they turned onto the side street where his car was parked. Janeka fished his keys out of his front pocket and opened the passenger side door for him.

By the time she started the car, he was unconscious.

Bob awoke to the sound of Janeka asking a gas station attendant for directions to the nearest hospital. He touched her arm and she looked around. "I don't want to go to a hospital here," he said. "Just take me back to campus."

"Bob, we're in a city. Why would you want to go to some country doctor down in the boondocks?"

"I don't want to go to a doctor *here*," he said. His jaw had swollen and talking was difficult. "Take me back to campus. Will you do that? Please?"

With tears in her eyes, she nodded.

Bob slept again and this time when he woke, the car was parked in front of a diner on a dirt road he recognized. They were maybe five miles from campus. He craned his head to the right and saw Janeka in a phone booth. He touched his jaw. It was a grapefruit. He touched his temple. It was still tacky with blood.

Janeka saw him looking. She hung up the phone and got back in the car. "You got your wish," she said. "We're back near campus. But I had to call for an ambulance. I have no idea where the nearest hospital is." There was a note of reproach in her voice.

"I'm sorry," he said. The voice that came out of his swollen and injured face was heavy and slow and sounded nothing like his own.

"I still don't understand why you couldn't have just gone to a hospital in Memphis," Janeka said.

"Memphis is insane," said Bob in his new voice. "I just wanted to get out of there."

She said, "A man on the radio said they're probably going to bring in the National Guard."

"Good," said Bob.

"From what he said, it sounds like they're already blaming Martin Luther King for the riot."

Bob turned his head. He didn't answer.

"Did you hear me? I said—"

Bob was watching as some white girl with a Confederate flag emblem on the back pocket of her jeans got out of a truck and went to the phone booth Janeka had just used. "I heard you," he told Janeka without turning. "He didn't start it—but he didn't do anything to stop it."

"Bob, what do you mean?"

Now he turned his ruined face back toward her. "He ran. He abandoned us."

"But what could he have done? You saw that crowd. They were out of control."

"I don't know," he admitted. "I just know I expected better."

She shrugged. "Maybe you expected too much," she said.

"What do you mean?"

"Don't get me wrong," she said. "I respect the man and all the things he's done. But at the end of the day, he is not Jesus, he does not walk on water, and he does not have all the answers. I get tired sometimes of people acting as if he does."

This stunned him. After a moment he said, "So you don't believe in Martin Luther King?"

Even as he said it, he realized he was speaking in the exact tone of wonder and disbelief he'd have used to ask if she no longer believed in Jesus. The little smirk that twisted her lips just then told him she had heard the same thing.

"I'm just saying," said Janeka, "maybe it's time to try something new. Some new philosophy, some new approach. I don't know if he's the right man for these times."

The injury to his face prevented Bob's jaw from dropping. But his mouth came open and he stared at her. He could not believe what he was hearing.

They sat in silence for long minutes. The girl with the Confederate flag patch finished her phone call, got back in her truck, and peeled out in a great cloud of dust. A moment later, Janeka said, "There's something else I need to tell you."

And for some reason, Bob felt his heart lurch sideways.

"What?" he asked. There was a slight tremble in his voice. From a distance, he could hear the cry of the ambulance siren.

"I've been thinking about this for a long time," she said, "but today, all this sort of made up my mind for me."

"What?" he asked.

"It's not about you. I want you to know that."

"What?" he pleaded. Tears were already in his eyes. They slid down, stinging the cuts on his cheek.

"Bob, don't," she said.

"What is it?" He needed to hear although somehow, he already knew. The siren was growing louder.

"I'm leaving school, Bob. I just...I don't want to be here anymore."

"But why?"

"I just don't," she said.

"Because of me? Because of us? Did I do something?"

"Everything is changing, Bob. The whole country, the whole world, everything is changing. I just don't think this is the right place for me anymore."

"'The right place?'" He tried to laugh, but something strangled and desperate came out of him instead. "What is the right place, Janeka?"

She sighed. "I want to go to a black school," she said. "Maybe even an all-girl school like Spelman."

"What about us?"

"I don't know," she said, looking away. And he heard it for the lie that it was. She knew, all right. She just could not make herself say.

And she still had not answered the most important thing. "But *why*?" he asked again.

The siren grew louder, grew until it filled all the spaces, and then abruptly shut off as the truck pulled next to them in a crunch of tires on dirt and rocks. Janeka sprang from the car as if escaping it. Bob heard her tell the

attendant, "He's right here," and then two young white men in white uni-
forms were looking through the car window at him.

"What happened to you, bud?" one of them asked.

"He was in Memphis," said Janeka, and at that, he saw one of the white
men shoot the other one a look. "We were both in Memphis," she corrected.

"Can you walk, bud?"

The attendant opened the car door and put a hand on Bob's upper arm.
He came out stiffly. His eyes never left Janeka.

"Why?" he asked her again.

She pretended not to hear. "Some big guy jumped on him and beat him
pretty badly," she told the attendant, who was leading Bob toward the back
of the ambulance.

"Yeah," replied the attendant in a dry voice. "I can see that."

"Why?" Bob asked, still staring at her.

"Seems like he's asking you a question, miss," the attendant said.

She said, "Bob, we can talk more later. I still have your keys. I'll park
your car at the dorm and leave them with the monitor."

They were helping Bob into the back of the rig. He climbed in with the
painful, uncertain steps of an 80-year-old, turning slowly and sitting on the
stretcher. Janeka stood there, looking small. The attendant put an icepack in
Bob's right hand, then lifted Bob's hand to Bob's temple. Bob hardly noticed.
He made his strange new voice as loud as he could, as emphatic as he could.

"Why?" he demanded. "Why? *Why?*" His eyes had filled again with
tears. Blood dripped from a reopened cut on his chin. The ambulance attendant was strapping a blood-pressure cuff on Bob's forearm. Now, like Bob, he
paused and waited.

Janeka came closer. She leaned into the rig, put her mouth next to his ear.

"I understand," she whispered, "that you're hurt and that you're angry.
But you know this is for the best. Everything is changing, Bob. Nothing is
the way it used to be even a year ago. You saw that today, didn't you? The old
ways, the old stuff, it just doesn't mean anything anymore. It doesn't work
anymore. Maybe in another place and time, you and I would be...could be..."
She gasped, unable to go on. She tried to step back, but he grabbed her hand.

Her eyes met his. "Don't," he said. "Please."

She gave him a look he would carry to his grave—pain sorrow resignation pity. Maybe even love. Maybe. And she leaned in again and whispered
in his ear.

"I have to," she said. "I have to be with my people."

She pulled back. And Bob heard himself whisper, "I thought I was your people, too."

He didn't know if she heard him. The ambulance door closed in the same instant he said it.

And just like that, she was gone.

twenty-one

Pop and Sonny straggled through the door of the little house a few minutes after Malcolm did, dragging the signs that proclaimed their manhood. They looked stunned.

Malcolm was sitting in Pop's chair in front of the television. He got up without being asked and Pop sat down. Malcolm and Sonny sat side by side on the ratty couch. No one spoke.

The television screen was filled with bedlam—police firing teargas, rioters throwing bricks, kids running past the broken windows of downtown stores. Pop watched this for a moment, listened to the reporter narrating the disaster. Then he reached across and turned off the television. The silence was fat and heavy.

"You was out there in all that mess?" As if he were just waiting for Malcolm to deny it.

"You know I was there," said Malcolm. "You saw me."

"You know what I mean," said Pop. "Was you out there throwin' bricks and breakin' windows? Was you one of the ones done that?"

"He was out there, all right," said Sonny. He spoke in a voice of low menace. "I can see it in his eyes."

Malcolm was yanked to his feet as much by guilt as true indignation. "You don't see shit, nigger!"

Sonny stood more slowly. He faced Malcolm. "Call me out my name again, boy."

So much churned inside Malcolm Toussaint then. So much anger, so much shame, so much confusion. He had broken a store window. He had faced down a brother. He had saved a whitey he hated. And now there was this: his space invaded by this garbage man of impotent dreams. He said emphatically, "What you gon' do about it, *nigger*?" And braced himself to fight. *Wanted* to fight.

But Pop spoke. "Bunch of young fools ruined our march. We out there tryin' to show manhood. We out there tryin' to show dignity. And all that get throwed away 'cause of a bunch of hard-head, dumbass young mother-fuckers. So I ask you again, June, was you out there in all that riotin'? Did you have anything to do with it?"

Malcolm looked at his father. Pop's eyes were cold with fire.

He heard himself say, "I took a stick, okay? I broke a window."

And all of a sudden, he was sprawled on the couch, his hand cupping the pain in his jaw. His father had knocked him into the cushions and now stood over him, index finger cocked like a gun, voice coiled with fury.

"You took a stick. You broke a window. And I think you halfway proud of yourself for that."

"Ain't proud of—"

His father bulldozed the interruption like a locomotive through a snow bank. "You took a stick. You broke a window. You turned our march—*our* march, goddamn it—into a riot. And you ruined every goddamn thing we worked for. You and all the rest of them young punks." He turned away, one hand plowing through his short-cropped hair. "I hope you happy, June. I hope you real happy."

"We were trying to help." Malcolm came fearfully to his feet, one hand massaging his jaw.

He flinched when his father wheeled around. "Help? Is that what you call it?"

Sonny shook his head. He even laughed. He said, "You know, boy, I used to admire you. You whip-smart and you done read all them books and you know a whole lot of shit. Here I am, a grown-ass man"—another laugh, sour as lemons—"but I used to look up to you. I used to think you was really somethin'. But now I come to realize: you ain't shit, is you, nigger? You really ain't."

"So what are we supposed to do?" demanded Malcolm. He had had enough of them. Both of them. "You want us to march up and down the street singing 'We Shall Overcome' like y'all do? You want us to kneel and pray to blue-eyed Jesus while white folks beat the shit out of us? Is that your plan? Is that what your Dr. King tells you all to do?"

"It's called nonviolent protest," said Sonny.

"It's called cowardice," Malcolm said evenly. "But I guess that's what you got to expect from a bunch of handkerchief-head, plantation *niggers*. The rest of us, we don't believe in that Uncle Tom bullshit no more."

"You think we Uncle Toms? You think we cowards?" Pop's eyes were livid. "Marchin' in that street? Tellin' them white folks they got to respect us now? That make us *cowards*?"

Malcolm met his eyes. "You think it makes you brave? You think it makes you men?" A tiny smirk hooked one corner of his mouth. "Some of us, we don't need no goddamn signs to know we're men."

And at that, the room went cold and still. Pop's face changed. He stared at Malcolm hard, stared as if he did not know him.

Malcolm wanted to say something else, desperately felt the need to say something else, something that might wave away the terrible words as you would a stink in the air. But he couldn't think of anything.

"Pop," he began.

And then there was a knock at the door.

Sonny was closest. He threw one last look at Malcolm, his eyes furious. Then he opened it. Melvin Cotter stood there.

You could see in his face that he knew he had walked in on something. His wide eyes went from Sonny to Pop and, finally, to Malcolm, who said, "What are you doing here?"

Melvin said, "I thought you should know. The old lady got hurt."

Something cold thumped Malcolm's breastbone from the inside and it was a moment before he realized it was his heart. His fists fell open. "What?"

"Miss Parker," he said. "I seen her. She was out there when all that mess started. She was yellin' for 'em to stop, but ain't nobody paid her no mind. Then she just kind of keeled over. I think it was a heart attack or somethin'. They put her in the ambulance. She didn't look good, Malcolm. She didn't look good at all."

All at once, Malcolm could not suck in enough breath. "Where is she?" he demanded. "Where'd they take her?"

"St. Joe's."

St. Joseph's hospital was about eight miles north. He could be there in under an hour, easily. Malcolm reached for his bike.

Melvin did not bother hiding his surprise. "Are you crazy? You gon' take your bike over there?"

"I got to go," said Malcolm.

"You don't understand," said Melvin. "It's wild out there. Cops still out there bustin' up everybody black they see. Done already killed some boy. Way I heard, he wasn't even armed, and they shot him."

"I got to go," said Malcolm.

Pop spoke. "Fool," he said, "ain't no sense in you goin' out there, 'specially on no bike. Ain't nothin' you can do for that old lady. How it gon' help her if you get your head busted in?"

"I got to go," said Malcolm. "I got to see about her."

He pushed the bike through the door without another word as his father stood there, too dumbfounded by his defiance to protest it. Malcolm rolled the bicycle down from the porch, hopped astride in one smooth motion, and took off for the hospital without a backward glance.

The pain he felt was almost a physical thing. He could have stopped her. He could have stopped her. He could have stopped her.

Instead, he had allowed her to walk, in her church dress and her flowered hat, right into the middle of a riot that he had known was going to happen—that he himself had helped engineer. His reasons had been noble, hadn't they? His reasons had been unselfish. All he had wanted to do was help the garbage workers, right?

Black power, right? Black power. Black power.

Malcolm felt as if he might vomit. He was dazed with guilt.

He rode north around trash fires, down streets of broken glass, past phalanxes of Memphis cops. He rode across an angry city tearing itself apart, but he was lucky: no one stopped him, no one challenged him. He rode to the hospital and made his way to the nurse's station on Nanny Parker's floor.

He asked for her and the young white nurse on duty asked who he was. The lie sprang readily to his lips. "I'm Malcolm," he said. "I'm...I'm her grandson."

The woman consulted a clipboard. "I'm afraid your grandmother had a heart attack, Malcolm. Poor thing. Apparently, she got caught up in that melee down on Beale."

Melee. It almost made him laugh. It had not been a melee. It had been a riot. It had been a brawl. And he had been one of its main actors.

The nurse showed him to Miss Parker's room. At the sight of her, lying there unconscious but, thank God, *alive*, he collapsed on the chair next to her bed, undone by grief and relief, but most of all, by an awareness of his own culpability.

The nurse was still looking at her clipboard. "Is there any other family?" she asked.

"No," said Malcolm. "She had some friends with her. They went down to the...to the march together. Do you know what happened to them?"

The woman shook her head, still consulting the clipboard. "She was alone when the ambulance got there. Perhaps they got separated. I understand it was crazy down there."

"She goes to a church," insisted Malcolm. "My Hope Baptist. I don't know the pastor's name, but maybe somebody can look it up and you can contact him?" He hated the idea of Miss Parker lying here, unknown and all but alone.

It must have shown on his face. The nurse gave him what was meant, he supposed, to be a reassuring smile. Then she disappeared from the door. Malcolm took Miss Parker's hand. It was bony and cool to the touch.

The room was a double, but the second bed was unoccupied and for this, Malcolm was grateful. It meant there was no one to throw him wondering glances, no one to ask him questions for which he had no answers, no one to see the tears straggle down his cheek.

She lay in this bed looking far too small, far too frail, her long gray hair stark against the crisp white sheets. She had no idea he was there, but Malcolm sat with her anyway, sat with her for hours as outside, shadows marched across Memphis and evening settled in. He didn't want her to wake up in this strange place and find nobody there.

Malcolm felt he owed her at least that much, owed it to her to be there.

At some point, he slept.

"June?"

The sound of it drew him out of himself. Malcolm's eyes blinked open.

"June?" Her eyes were open. Her voice was a small, fluttery thing.

"Yes," he said. Hope all but strangled him.

She tried to lift her head, failed. "Where am I?"

"At St. Joe's," he said. "You had..." He swallowed something dry and withered that had died in his throat and tried it again. "You had a heart attack."

Her glittery, luminous eyes seemed to struggle to take this in. Then they flared with remembrance. "The march," she said. "Young people started breaking windows?"

"Yes, ma'am."

"Why would they do that?"

Malcolm's face was wet with tears he knew nothing about. Guilt gnawed him like some small, mean animal trapped in his gut. "It was me," he said.

She looked confused. "What?"

"It was me. I was out there with them. I broke a window. I'm sorry, Miss Parker. I am so very sorry. I should have told you. I should have warned you."

She studied him for a long moment. A long moment. Then, all at once, she smiled and her face glowed with beatific certainty. "No," she assured him in a tender voice. "You wouldn't do nothing like that. You're a good boy."

"Miss Parker, please..."

"A good boy," she said again. She patted his cheek. Her hand was as dry and weightless as a dead leaf. "I know you," she said. "You wouldn't do that." There was a pause. Then she said, "Lord, I am so tired." And she closed her eyes. She was still smiling.

"There's a curfew," the nurse was saying. She had a pleasant, sympathetic face. "You all have to be off the streets by seven, can't go out again til five in the morning unless you have a police permit."

"We all?" Malcolm doubted even Henry Loeb would have imposed a curfew that applied only to blacks. But then, this woman was probably right about the spirit of the thing, if not its exact wording.

She shrugged now, helplessly. Malcolm checked his watch. It was 9:05.

Nanny Parker had died an hour and a half before and he still felt drained by grief. The doctors and nurses had pushed him out of the room when she coded. He had paced the hall talking to a Jesus he hadn't spoken to since his mother died. It had not helped. They had come out of the room half an hour later and a doctor had said, "I'm sorry, son. We did our best but we couldn't save her." They had pulled the sheet over her and allowed him to sit with her until two orderlies came and wheeled her—wheeled the *body*—down to the morgue.

Now Malcolm stood there, lost. He did not know what to do. He could not go home. He simply could not. But he didn't want to go to work either.

Besides, if this white lady was right, he had no way to get wherever he was going anyway. Not if the whole city was under curfew. Malcolm shook his head. He had not known a worse day since his mother died.

The woman saw him. "Would you like a ride?" she said. "I get off in an hour. You could maybe lie down on the floor in the back of the car and I could cover you with a blanket. They won't bother me."

His incredulity must have shown on his face because she added quickly, "You seem like a nice young man. I'd hate to see you get in trouble because you were visiting your grandmother. Especially with...you know... what happened."

"Thank you," he said, and then he had to stop. He regarded her, this white woman—late 20s, he would guess, brown hair pinned back beneath a white nurse's cap—offering him, this unknown black guy, safe passage through the city on this day of all days. You never knew about people. You just never knew.

"Thank you," he said again, "but I'll be all right."

He spoke with a confidence he did not feel and he saw the doubt in her eyes, but she only nodded and said, "Well, okay. If you're sure."

Malcolm said he was, even though he wasn't. But then, he wasn't sure of anything anymore.

Moments later, he was downstairs near the hospital entrance, unchaining his bicycle from the rack to which he had locked it. He straddled the bike and began pedaling slowly toward the hotel on the river.

Memphis lay largely silent that night, largely still beneath a haunted absence of cars, people, movement. No one was out and Malcolm had the city to himself, but for the occasional police car sliding past, lights flashing in silence. When Malcolm saw them coming he found shadows and doorways in which to hide.

In this way, he worked slowly west toward the river, figuring to ride along the bluff and come upon the hotel from behind. Most police and National Guardsmen, he figured, would concentrate their patrols in the center of town and in the areas south of that where black people lived.

But there was no way to avoid City Hall, which sat just a couple blocks off the river with its back to the water. That area, he thought, would surely be heavily patrolled.

Malcolm rode with caution, eyes and ears alert, avoiding streetlights. He kept to the alleys, slipped down North Front Street, and zigzagged through the backhoes and bulldozers of the construction zone where a new bridge was taking shape. It struck him that elsewhere in Memphis, families were settling in for an evening of television. It was Thursday night. That meant *Bewitched, The Flying Nun, That Girl, Dragnet*—a TV universe of white people in foolish situations, white people keeping the peace, white people running things. It seemed impossible that Sister Bertrille could be soaring above the convent San Tanco on some silly errand or Samantha Stephens twitching her nose to turn some man into a frog in the same world at the same time as Malcolm Toussaint was ducking through shadows in fear of being seen.

The heavy rumbling of the engine yanked him from his reverie. Malcolm whipped his eyes around to downtown Memphis on his left. He was passing abreast of City Hall. The building was ablaze with light and he felt distantly pleased to know the city government found it necessary to work so deep into the night. Then he saw what had made the sound: an armored personnel carrier came lumbering down Adams Street on the south side of the building, asphalt crunching beneath its treads. He could see the shadows of the helmeted men in the vehicle, tense, ready, scanning every direction.

Malcolm froze. The heavy green carrier seemed to be coming right toward him, as if it could smell him, as if it knew exactly where he was. It came closer, crossing Front Street, moving down the bluff toward Promenade Street. Here it paused, and it seemed to Malcolm as if whoever was driving the thing must be staring directly at him. He was so close that he could make out voices and hear the squawk of a radio, though he could not decipher words. Malcolm did not breathe. He made himself a shadow. The decision to spurn the white nurse's help suddenly seemed a very foolish one, indeed. He began to think of what he would say when he was arrested.

Then there was a sound of gunshots. Two of them, echoing faintly off the buildings somewhere to the east. A moment. Another moment. Then, abruptly, the vehicle reversed itself, swung around, and climbed east on Adams, looking for the shooter.

Malcolm almost collapsed from relief. It was a minute before he could gather himself and when he did, he pedaled on shaky legs toward the Holiday Inn, still far in the distance. He hugged the river, using the bluff as cover, racing through a park named for Jefferson Davis, in the shadow of another park high above that was named for the Confederacy, under the glare of cotton brokers' offices—all these symbols of whiteness and power and the

Old South, co-opted as cover on this night by a frightened black man, sweat streaming on his brow, heart hammering within his chest.

Voices.

Malcolm stopped. High above him on the sidewalk, he saw the shadows, saw the orange-tipped glow of a cigarette. Two cops walking along in the opposite direction.

"All this shit over one man," said the first.

"Ol' Martin Lucifer Coon," said the other with a soft, nasty laugh. "He gets the shit started, then runs away."

"Yeah," said the first. "Mr. Nonviolence. I don't know about you, but what I saw today looked pretty violent to me. Got these niggers all riled up."

"Somebody ought to put a bullet in his ass."

"Would not break my heart at all."

Malcolm waited until they were gone. He waited five minutes more. Then, his breath loud and ragged in his ears, he hoisted his bicycle and carried it across the uneven cobblestones that had been laid into the riverbank a hundred years before. It was hard going. He tried to listen above the sound of his own breathing for more voices. Finally, hearing none, he chanced it. He climbed the bank to the sidewalk, hopped astride his bike, and pedaled as fast as he could, all attempts at stealth abandoned. Moments later the hotel rose before him.

Malcolm's shift began at 11:00. He walked into the hotel a few minutes after 10. The white girl at the counter glanced up at the sound of his entrance. Her eyebrows leapt and he knew she was surprised to see him. Malcolm wheeled his bike to the closet off the hallway behind the desk and stored it there. Then, with nothing else to do, he sat in the lobby.

The lobby was much like the city—wrapped in a dead silence. The lounge seemed busier than usual, though. From behind him, Malcolm heard the clink of glasses, the muted hum of chatter, the occasional music of a woman's laughter. With nowhere else to go, the hotel's guests had apparently decided to amuse themselves by getting drunk in the bar.

Ronald Whitten came through the lobby doors at 10:30. He stopped when he saw Malcolm. "Didn't expect to see you here," he said. "Did you get a police pass?"

"No," said Malcolm.

"You just drove through the curfew?" Whitten seemed impressed.

"Yes."

An approving nod. "Well, that shows some real dedication, son."

"I don't have my work shirt," said Malcolm, meaning the shirt with his name in a little oval on his left breast pocket. "I wasn't able to get home to get it."

Whitten waved it off. "Are you kidding?" he said. "It's enough that you made it in. I'll see about getting you a police pass for tomorrow. Why don't you just punch in now, since you're already here, and you can take out the trash in the bar. Evening shift was down a man—he got arrested for rioting—so I expect you and me are going to have a lot of slack to pick up."

He took a step, stopped, then turned back to Malcolm. "Real glad you made it in," he said. A tight nod, and he was gone.

Watching him walk away, Malcolm almost laughed. Somehow, on this godawful day, he had managed without trying, without even really caring about it, to impress his boss. Ronald Whitten had mistaken having nowhere else to go for initiative. Life was funny sometimes. Malcolm sighed and got up from the couch.

Moments later, he was bear-hugging a barrel of empty liquor bottles through the kitchen when he saw Melvin standing there in his white busboy's uniform, scraping food off plates before washing them. He looked up. "You made it," he said.

"Yeah," said Malcolm, remembering the personnel carrier and the police on the sidewalk. "Barely."

"How's the old lady?"

"She died." Malcolm lowered the trash barrel.

"Oh, man."

"Yeah."

"I'm sorry to hear that, Malcolm. She was a nice old lady. I know she meant a lot to you."

"Yeah."

Melvin regarded him for a moment. He said, "Look, Malcolm, I been thinkin': you been my ace boon coon since we were little fellas. Don't hardly seem right for us to be walkin' 'round here not talkin' to each other 'cause of Pruitt's fat ass. Yeah, he's a bastard, but you know well as I do, sometimes you got to—"

He stopped. Malcolm was crying. "Malcolm?" he said.

Malcolm said, "I killed her, man. Killed her as sure as if I put a gun to her head. I knew what was going to happen down there, I knew what they planned. I should have told her to stay home. I should have made her stay home."

Melvin said, "Brother, you can't take that on yourself. She had a heart attack. Ain't no way you could have stopped that."

Malcolm looked at him. He wanted to believe. He wanted to be comforted, desperately so. But he could not—and he was not. There was no escape from the awful thing he knew he had done. The simple truth, the truth he would bear like a weight through the rest of his days, was that Melvin Cotter was wrong. Malcolm could indeed have stopped it, could have prevented what happened to the old lady who had been like a mother to him. He could have, but he didn't.

So Melvin's words of intended comfort fell on him like rain on a sidewalk. They did not sink in. They made no difference. Without a word, Malcolm hefted the barrel and took it out back to empty it into the Dumpsters. The private haulers the hotel had contracted would take it away to the dump.

Melvin called after him. Malcolm did not reply.

The next hours passed in a routine whose very mindlessness made him grateful. He did work that, even after only five weeks on the job, he felt he had already done a million times—clean the bathrooms, empty the ashtrays, run the buffer—but he gave himself over to it gladly, willed his entire self to be concentrated into the task of picking soggy cigarette butts out of a latrine or rubbing a shine into a heavily traveled floor.

It was tough, thankless work. But it was easier than thinking.

Malcolm had been working for a few hours when Whitten happened by, carrying an armload of paper towels for the lobby-level restrooms. He stopped to appreciate the mellow gleam of the floor in front of the bank of elevators. "Good work," he said with a nod of approval. "You keep it up, you're going to have my job some day."

The words jolted Malcolm. He realized suddenly that he could see this happening. A month ago, this had been a temporary stop, a brief respite on the way to whatever his destiny might be. But now, it seemed almost a more welcome and, certainly, a safer thing: something to do where you didn't have to think. You could collect a check, put food on your table, and not have to ponder anything beyond the next task. You could simply be. In this moment, at least, something about that seemed very attractive.

"It's after two," Whitten was saying. "Don't you usually take a break long about now?"

"Yes, I usually do," said Malcolm. He had gotten lost in the work. He hadn't realized so much time had passed.

"Go ahead," the white man encouraged him with a nicotine-stained smile.

"Okay," said Malcolm. "Thank you." And he powered down the machine.

Malcolm stopped through the kitchen of the sleeping hotel and plucked a couple of hard-boiled eggs from the big refrigerator, took a salt shaker and a paper towel, popped a bottle of Coke with an opener, and went to stand out back by the Dumpsters to watch the river meander past him in the darkness.

This, too, he had done so many times in just a few weeks that he did it automatically, did it without thinking—or seeing. So he was right up on the man before he even realized he was there. The stranger stood in shirtsleeves contemplating the endless river, a cigarette burning low between two fingers of the same hand that meditatively swirled a shot glass half full of some brown liquid.

The man turned at the scrape of Malcolm's feet and for an instant, they stared at each other in mutual surprise. Then Martin Luther King said, "I'm sorry I startled you. I didn't think anyone else would be out here this time of night." It was the voice Malcolm knew from a hundred newsreels, the same great baritone with the same soft Georgia drawl, but it was different somehow, too—less solemn, less portentous and formal. It was an off-duty voice, an after-hours voice.

Malcolm coughed, trying to find his own voice. "I work here," he managed. "I usually take my breaks out here."

King dropped the cigarette and ground it out beneath the toe of his shoe, lifted his glass in a salute and said, "Well, then, I'll leave you to your solitude."

"No, no," said Malcolm. "That's okay. I mean, I can go somewhere else if you're thinking or praying or something."

"None of the above," said King, lifting the glass again—this time as an explanation, not a salute. He smiled. "I'll tell you what, my man. It's a big river. Why don't we just share it?"

"Yes, sir."

Yes, sir?

Malcolm's brain was screaming at him to say something more, but that same brain was locked tighter than a bank vault. It would not open, would not give him anything. There he was, right in front of him, the man he had scorned, the man he had mocked and called "De Lawd." There he was, that ponderous, prayerful, far-too-patient preacher so joyfully rebuked by younger men like Malcolm who said what they meant and damn well meant what they said when they lifted clenched fists and yelled, "Black power!"

And he was yes-sirring him?

Martin Luther King reached across. "I'm Martin," he said.

"I know who you are," said Malcolm, taking King's plump, soft hand in his own.

"Yes," said King, "but I am afraid I cannot say the same."

"I'm Malcolm," said the former Mozell Wilson, Jr., shaking a hand he had never expected to shake. "Malcolm Toussaint."

King's eyebrow lifted. "Toussaint? Like Toussaint L'Ouverture?"

"Yes," said Malcolm. "It's not my real name. I mean, it is my real name—I had it legally changed—but it's not the name I was born under."

"I see," said King, taking a sip of the brown liquid. "Why did you change your name, then? And why Toussaint?"

"Because he was a revolutionary."

"Aha. So 'Malcolm' is..."

"For Malcolm X, yes. And my middle name is Marcus, after Garvey."

"Three revolutionaries," said King.

Malcolm was stunned by what he heard himself say next. "I believe in black power," he announced to this preacher who in recent months had been chased from one end of the country to the other by angry young men shouting that very thing.

Malcolm feared the man might be angry. But Martin Luther King only smiled. It was a smile filled with mystery and sorrow. "I believe in black power, too," he said.

And apparently, although his brain was still locked, Malcolm's mouth was open for business. "No you don't," it said in a voice both scandalized and incredulous. Hearing himself, Malcolm brought a hand up, but of course, the hand was too late. The words were already out.

King only watched him from the shadows of that smile. "Yes, I do," he said. "Black power is a call for black self-determination, isn't it? It means economic and political power, doesn't it? It means men demanding to be treated like men, right? Isn't that what black power means?"

"Well," said Malcolm, flustered, "yes."

"Then yes," said King, "of course I believe in black power. What else have I been fighting for?"

Malcolm gaped. "But then, why...?"

King got there first. "Why do I oppose the slogan?" Something melancholy came into his face then. "Every word has two meanings, Malcolm, the denotative meaning and the connotative meaning. The denotative meaning is—"

"The denotative is what it denotes," interrupted Malcolm, "what it actually means. The connotative is what it connotes, what it implies or suggests."

It was King's turn to look surprised. "Yes," he said, "exactly. And while the denotative meaning of the words is quite clear and unassailable, the connotative meaning is another matter. A white man—or any man, for that matter—who hears you cry out for black power is going to hear it as a threat, a call for violence and black supremacy. Is that what you want, Malcolm? You want to dominate white people?"

"No," said Malcolm. "I just want them to leave us alone."

King sighed. "Well, you're hardly alone in that," he said. "Our people are saying that same thing all over the world. They want to be left alone. They want their freedom and they want it now."

King regarded Malcolm for a moment, then said, "But have you ever noticed: Jewish people have gained power in this country, but you never heard them cry, 'Jewish power!' The Irish man gained power, but he never cried, 'Irish power!' You see, they had a strategy for achieving that power and they followed it. But our people—our young people, at least—have fixated on a mere slogan that has no strategy whatsoever."

Abruptly he stopped. "Aren't you going to eat that?" he said, pointing.

Malcolm's eyes followed King's index finger to the boiled eggs and Coca-Cola bottle he had forgotten he was carrying. "Would you like one?" he asked.

King accepted the egg with a grateful nod. "I can't remember the last time I ate," he said. "It's been a long day." There was a low stone wall overlooking the river. King nodded toward it. "Brother Malcolm, let's sit and eat while we talk." So the janitor and the Nobel laureate moved to the wall, sat down next to each other, and began peeling hard-boiled eggs. Some part of Malcolm was watching this happen and did not believe what it was seeing.

"Would you like me to get you another egg?" he asked. "There're plenty in the kitchen."

"No, this is fine," said King. "I just needed a bit of nourishment, is all."

His face was puffy. And there was, now that Malcolm looked closely, a mourning in his eyes that seemed to go down for miles. Malcolm was suddenly concerned. "Are you all right, Dr. King? You look tired."

"That's because I am tired," said King, working his thumb beneath the shell of the egg. "I'm exhausted, to tell you the plain truth, but I can't seem to rest. Andy Young says I'm fighting a war on sleep." A melancholy chuckle. "Too many things pulling at me, I suppose. I'm sure you saw what happened out there today? All that violence?" He winced. The word itself seemed to pain him.

Malcolm nodded. He felt the guilt rising in him like floodwaters.

King made a sound of mild disgust. "The press is going to have a field day with that in the morning." Shaking his head, he waved the thought away as if shooing a fly. "Enough about that." King sprinkled salt from the shaker Malcolm had sat between them onto his egg and said, "Tell me about yourself, Malcolm."

Malcolm lowered his head. "There's not much to tell."

"Are you from here in Memphis?"

"Yes, sir. Born and raised."

King took a bite from the egg. "You've been a janitor for a long time?"

"Only a few weeks," said Malcolm. "I was in college until last month."

"You dropped out?"

"Yes. I mean, sort of."

"Did you run out of money? It's nothing to be ashamed of, if you did. That's a problem many of our young men have to deal with."

"No, sir. I had a full scholarship."

Confusion narrowed King's eyes. "Then, why did you drop out?"

"Well, first they put me out. They put me on what they call administrative leave, but they said I could reapply to come back next semester. I'm not going to do that, though. College is not for me."

"Why did they put you out?"

"For protesting."

"Protesting?"

Malcolm sighed, embarrassed. "Well, for painting protest graffiti on the side of the administration building."

Martin Luther King stared at him. Slowly, he began to shake his head. "Malcolm," he said, "do you have any idea what a waste that is?"

"I disagree," said Malcolm. "Dr. King, I want to help my people. And I don't see how getting some sheepskin from some white man's college is going to enable me to do that."

"Malcolm," said King, "science isn't white. Mathematics isn't white."

"Yeah, but Shakespeare is white. The history they teach us, that sure is white."

"Then change it," said King. "Demand that they broaden the curriculum to include the black man's literature and the black man's history."

"I'd rather just leave," said Malcolm, pulling a piece of shell off his egg and flinging it toward the river.

"Yes, but think about what you're throwing away."

"Are you saying there's something wrong with me just being a janitor?"

King shook his head, chewing thoughtfully on a mouthful of egg. "Of course not," he said. "There is no shame in any honest work. The shame is in wasting an opportunity. Education is the key to much of what troubles our people, Malcolm. Education is the solution to joblessness and hopelessness. Education is the solution to the ghettoes and the slums. You say you want black power? Education is the *source* of black power. There are young men who would give anything they had to get an education. And they've given you one for free and you throw it away? That's the waste, Malcolm."

King paused. He considered Malcolm with a gimlet eye. "I'm curious," he said. "What was the 'protest' graffiti you wrote that got you put on leave?"

Malcolm looked down. "I'd rather not say."

"Oh, come now, brother Malcolm. There's no one here but you and me and the Mississippi River. What did you write?"

Malcolm felt ten years old. "I'd rather not say it to *you*," he clarified.

King laughed. It was a rich, homey sound. "Brother Malcolm," he said, "you wrote it on a wall for the whole world to see. Surely, you can—"

"'Fuck the system.'"

"Beg pardon?"

"'Fuck the system.' That's what I wrote on the wall."

"I see," said King. "Yet despite your vivid scorn for it, the system still stands unchanged, doesn't it?"

"Yeah," conceded Malcolm.

"The only thing that was changed was your circumstance. You had been a student studying toward a goal of helping your people. Now you are a janitor working a graveyard shift."

King sighed, ate the last of his egg. "Sometimes, if you're not careful, Malcolm, the thing that makes you feel empowered can be the thing that destroys you. You do something to satisfy your immediate longing to strike back without giving any thought to how that might damage you in the long term. Unfortunately, that's what happened yesterday on Beale Street."

And at last, Malcolm could not take it anymore. "I broke a window," he heard himself say. He spoke in a small voice and he wasn't sure King had heard him. Then he saw surprise widen the great sad eyes and he knew King had heard him just fine.

"I see," said King.

"I'm sorry," said Malcolm. "I ruined your march."

"Well, you had help in that regard," said King mildly. "It wasn't just you."

"But still," said Malcolm, "I was part of it."

"Why did you do it?" asked King.

Malcolm's eyes met King's. "You want the truth?"

King nodded.

Malcolm steeled himself and said, "Because your way is too slow. I get tired of begging white people to give us what we should have had all along. I want whitey to pay attention. I want them to hear what we're saying. That's why."

King didn't speak all at once. He took a sip of the amber liquid, giving Malcolm's words space to breathe. When he did speak, some indefinable hardness had crept into his voice.

"Do you think you're the only one who is impatient, Malcolm Marcus Toussaint?"

"No, but—"

"How old are you, man? Nineteen, maybe? I am 39 years old, Malcolm. So I am 20 years more impatient than you. I am 20 years more frustrated. And I am 20 years more exhausted. Especially tonight, after seeing what happened and knowing what white people—some white people, at least—are going to say about it."

He paused. He sighed. "You say you want them to hear what you're saying? Violence is not a language that encourages people to hear you, Malcolm. It's a language that encourages them to *fear* you."

"Maybe I want them to fear me. Maybe that's a good thing."

"And then what, Malcolm? They'll give you better schools? They'll provide more job opportunities? No. They'll simply call out the army to lock you down in your own neighborhoods. Violence only begets more violence. Look at what is happening in Memphis as we're sitting here, tanks and troops patrolling the streets, people forbidden to leave their homes. That's what violence does. And the cycle won't end until you end it, until you reach the place where you're willing to meet physical force with soul force."

Malcolm made a derisive sound. "You mean, let those crackers whip me upside the head and I don't hit back? I'm sorry, Dr. King. That's not going to happen."

"So you hit them back."

"Damn right."

"And then what?"

"How do you mean?"

"I mean, they just hit you and you just hit back. What happens, then? They call the police?"

"Probably."

"And let's say the police officer hits you and you hit him back. Then what happens?"

Malcolm could see where this was going. He conceded the point with a sigh. "Probably, they pile on me and kick my ass."

"Maybe they *kill you.*"

"Maybe. But at least I die knowing I stood up for myself. I didn't let someone just walk all over me."

"And then what?"

Malcolm shrugged. "And then nothing. I'm dead."

"Yes, brother Malcolm, you're dead. And nothing has changed. And the system is still in place. So your death is a futile act that accomplishes nothing. Just like writing graffiti on a schoolhouse wall."

Malcolm shook his head. "I'm sorry, Dr. King," he said. "I know you believe in nonviolence. But I just don't. I can't. I'll never give the white man permission to believe he can do anything he wants to me and I won't hit back."

"'The white man,'" repeated King. "You speak as if they were all one. They are not, you know. Viola Liuzzo was a white woman. She died for our freedom. James Reeb was a white man and he did, too. Jim Zwerg had his back broken in Montgomery for our freedom. White people are not all alike, any more than we are all alike. We seek to reach the ones who can be reached, to persuade the ones who can be persuaded. Violence can never do that. Only nonviolence can."

Malcolm lowered his head. He found himself remembering the nurse at the hospital. He didn't even know her name. All at once, he felt a sorrow welling in him. Somehow, it expressed itself in a smile. "You know," he said, "I saved a white man's life today. I don't know how it happened."

Malcolm glanced up. King's eyes were steady on him. "He was a cop," he heard himself say. "And this guy, this brother, had got his gun and was about to shoot him and for some reason, I jumped in front of the gun. I don't know why I did that."

Malcolm's voice trembled. He was surprised to feel a tear overflow his right eye. "I saved his life, but this old woman who lived next door to me, she went out in the middle of that mess and had a heart attack. She died tonight, right before I came to work. And I could have stopped her, Dr. King. I could have told her what was going to happen, could have told her to stay away, but I didn't."

He brushed impatiently at the tears sliding down his cheeks. "She was like a second mother to me and I didn't save her, even though maybe I could have. But this guy I did save, he was a white cop. And what's worse, when I got a good look at him, he was the same white cop who sprayed Mace in my eyes last month and told me, 'Nigger, go jump in the river.'"

King spoke softly. "Life is cruel sometimes. Unforgiving and cruel and filled with tragic paradoxes like this. You must try to learn to live with what happened today and your role in it, Malcolm, just the same as I. It won't be easy, but you must. You cannot change what has already happened. But you can use the lessons learned from it to change the future. Do you understand what I'm saying?"

Malcolm nodded. "I think so."

"You're going to have to forgive yourself, Malcolm. God will forgive you if you ask him. But you must also forgive yourself."

Malcolm shook his head. "I don't know if I can. Ever since the day that cop sprayed that Mace on me, I've just been *angry*. Sometimes, I feel like I can hardly breathe. I bought a gun and I've been carrying it ever since, because I said I'd never let that happen again, never let whitey treat me that way again."

Malcolm looked back up into those eyes, still steady as high beams. King said, "A gun won't give you comfort, Malcolm. A gun won't ease your pain."

"But they have to know they can't keep pushing us around." Malcolm's voice was a plea. "They have to know we're ready to fight back."

There was a moment. Then King said, "You want to give up on white people, don't you? All of them."

Malcolm nodded. "Yeah," he said. "Especially lately."

King smiled that sad smile. "Yes," he said. "Sometimes I do, too. Sometimes, they can be bitterly disappointing—even our white liberal allies have their moments when they just don't seem to understand, when they just don't seem to hear what is coming out of their own mouths. But you know why I don't give up on them?"

Malcolm looked up. "Because of Viola Liuzzo and James Reeb and that other guy, Zwerg?"

"Well, yes," said King. "But also because I can never figure out what happens next."

"What do you mean?"

King regarded him for a moment. Then he said, "You've named yourself after three revolutionaries. Well, Toussaint fought a war. But we're not going to fight a war—22 million Negroes against 176 million whites? Even if I believed in violence, I would not like those odds. Garvey wanted to go back to Africa. How are you going to move 22 million Negroes—assuming they all wanted to go—to Africa? And why should we go to some developing nation to start all over again when all our claims are here, when our ancestors cleared this country's fields and fought its wars? That leaves Malcolm X, and we both know black supremacy is no more of an answer than white supremacy. He himself said as much before he died. So if we're not going to fight a war, and we're not going away, and we're not going to set up our own black supremacist government here, what other options do we have, Malcolm?"

The question was not rhetorical. King was looking hard at him, waiting for an answer. Malcolm lowered his eyes. He had none.

"Exactly," said King. "So the only thing we are left is to wrestle with white people, to contend with them, try to make them see what they can't see or won't see. We have to trust that something in our humanity will touch something in their humanity so they'll finally be able to recognize us as brothers. That's really our only option. We can't give up on white people, Malcolm, because if we do, we give up on ourselves. We might as well stop struggling and just accept our lives the way they are. No, we have to believe they can be redeemed—and we have to struggle until they are. We have no other choice."

"That's easy to say," said Malcolm.

"We have no other choice," repeated King.

"I don't know if I can do that," said Malcolm.

King looked at him. "We have no other choice," he said.

Malcolm sighed. "I'll think about it," he said. "Maybe you're right."

"Maybe I am."

Malcolm started to push up from the wall. "I should probably be getting back to work."

"Malcolm?"

He paused. "Yes?"

"You are a bright young man with a sharp mind. Don't waste these gifts. You say you want to help our people? You say you want to change the system? Go back to school."

"I don't know if—"

One last time, King got there first. "Yes you do," he said. "Go back to school."

There was a moment. Then Malcolm said. "I'll think about it."

"That's all I ask," said King.

Malcolm was about to reply when a voice behind him said, "There you are. Been looking for you. Break time's about over, ain't it? Still need you to—"

Ronald Whitten's next words died as he came closer and saw who it was Malcolm was talking to. "Oh," he stammered. "Oh. I...I..."

King stood up with a gregarious smile. "Please don't chastise the young man on my account," he said. "I'm afraid I am the cause of his tardiness. I asked to him to sit and talk with me and I guess we both just lost track of the time."

"No, sir," said Whitten, still struggling to piece words together. "No, that's...that's...fine. It just...I just..."

"Yes," said King. "Please excuse me, I have to try to get at least a little sleep. I expect that this is going to be a very demanding day."

Its job done, the gregarious smile faded like morning mist. King looked tired. Indeed, in that moment, Malcolm thought this might be the most thoroughly exhausted man he had ever seen. He stood with Whitten and watched as Martin Luther King walked alone into the sleeping hotel, absently swirling the glass of brown liquid in his hand.

twenty-two

Bob's cellphone chirped.

When Bob answered, Doug Perry spoke without preamble, "Where the hell are you?"

Bob sighed. "He's not going to call."

"You don't know that."

Bob braked to a stop at a red light. He said, "It's been what, three hours now? Plenty of time for him to have seen the video online. Heck, look at the comment board. I saw hits from Limoges, France and Sao Paulo, Brazil. This thing has gone global. You can't tell me this guy in Chicago, USA doesn't know it's there. He's not going to call. He never had any intention to call."

"I've got a building full of cops who are very pissed at you just now."

Bob's laugh was bitter. "That is so far down on my list of pressing concerns that I can't even see it from here. You tell them if that animal does call—which he won't—I'll make sure they know. But I can't just sit around waiting."

"Your car is still parked downstairs. You can't have gone far. We know that."

"Amy gave me a lift."

Doug made a disgusted sound. "So what is it you and Amy think you're going to do that the cops can't? You're going to ride around town rousting perps and hassling informants til you get a bead on these guys? Who do you two think you are? Starsky and Hutch? Batman and Robin?"

"Woodward and Bernstein," said Bob. "We're *reporters*, remember? We're going to see what we can find out."

"This is a bad idea. I've got a bad feeling about this."

"I told her I wouldn't let anything happen to her. I *promised* her. But she's probably already...probably already..."

He couldn't say it. Even in his mind, he couldn't say it. He was conscious of Amy looking over to make sure he was okay. Then he realized the light had turned green without his noticing. Bob accelerated, but a little green sports car cut him off without signaling and he had to brake sharply to avoid clipping it.

"Idiot," he muttered.

"Beg pardon?"

"Doug, I've got to go. I'm driving. I'll let you know if we find anything."

He clicked the phone off without waiting for a response. Amy said, "They're not very happy with you, I take it?"

Bob shrugged. "What are they going to do? Fire me?"

"They never should have done that in the first place," said Amy.

"That's also not very high on my list of concerns right now." He made a left onto the expressway.

"I understand, but I'm just saying."

"It's about appearances," said Bob. "They needed to show that they took decisive action. Zero tolerance and all that."

"They needed a scapegoat, is what they needed."

"I'm fine with that," he said. Bob sensed her eyes on him when he said that. He looked over. "Really, I am. This morning, I'll grant you, I was about ready to take hostages. But as I keep saying, my priorities have changed since then."

Amy nodded. "Doug told me the woman they're holding hostage is someone you knew in college?"

Bob nodded.

"She must be some kind of woman."

Bob was about to reply when the telephone chirruped again. He glanced at it and it felt as if something had rabbit punched his heart: the caller ID came up, "Unknown."

He pressed the button to accept the call. "Yeah?"

"Bob?"

It was a man's voice Bob didn't recognize. He was distantly aware that Amy was watching him with anticipation and he knew the hope and fear he was struggling not to feel must be plastered all over his face.

"This is Bob," he said.

"Bob, this is Cecil Raintree. I got to say, buddy, that wasn't the smartest thing, skipping out on us like that."

Bob's hope and fear deflated down to a little pebble of disgust. All at once, he realized that he was clenching the steering wheel so hard his knuckles ached. He loosened his grip, flexed his fingers. "Look, Detective: I appreciate your position, but I don't think you appreciate mine. That woman he has is a friend."

"Maybe a little more than a friend, the way I hear," said Raintree.

Bob counted a silent ten. He tried not to think of that Ford truck driving away from him, Janeka all alone with that jumpy little...*monster* and his ridiculous pink pistol. "Yeah," he finally said, admitting it as much to himself as to Raintree. "Yes, she was. Yes, she *is*."

"Then *think*, Bob. You really don't want to do anything that's going to get her hurt. How could you live with yourself?"

Bob thought about this. He really did. The fear that he might do some bumbling thing that got Janeka hurt had been ever present since he and Amy had left the building. Who was he to figure he knew better than the police?

"I can't just sit around there waiting," he said. He was aware that a pleading note had come into his voice.

"I know it's hard," said Raintree, "but that's exactly what you have to do. It's the best thing if you want to see this lady alive again."

Bob felt his resolve crumbling beneath him like a sand fort when the tide comes in. "I don't know," he said.

"Well, I do," said Raintree, sensing his advantage. "Look, Bob: you're an editor, right? That's what you do, right? I wouldn't presume to tell you how to do your job. I wouldn't know the first thing about it and if I tried to do it for you, we both know I'd only screw it up. Well, this here is *my* job: catching bad guys. I know how they think and how they behave. So I need you to get out of the way before *you* screw it up. Let me do my job, okay?"

It was a persuasive argument—and especially so for Bob Carson who, all his adult life, had followed instructions, respected authority, colored within the lines. He pulled the van to the side of the road. Rush hour traffic moved sluggishly past them. Amy stared at him, her eyes full of questions. He ignored them.

"Bob?" Raintree asked. "You still there?"

"Yeah."

"So you're going to turn around and come back, right?"

"If I do that, can you promise me you will find her?"

"Bob, you're not being real fair here."

Bob knew that. He didn't give a damn. "Can you guarantee that if I come back, you will find Janeka and get her out of this alive?"

"Bob, you know I can't do that. You wouldn't believe me if I did."

"Because we both know she's probably already..." Again, the word choked him, glued itself inside his throat. But this time, he gritted his teeth and made it come out, some masochistic impulse needing to hear it, needing to hear himself say it. "...probably already dead." His voice was ashen.

Raintree said, "Bob, listen..."

Bob was done listening. "Don't call again," he said. And he clicked off the phone.

Amy was looking at him. "You okay?" she asked.

"No," said Bob. He nosed the van back into traffic.

He didn't speak for a few moments. Amy respected his silence. Bob was grateful for that. Finally, he said, "So, where are we going? You find anything for either of these guys?"

"No telephone listings," said Amy. She was poring over a laptop computer. "I still can't believe they used their actual names on the video."

"They must think it won't matter very long," said Bob.

Amy glanced up. "You're probably right," she said, "unfortunately. There were some possibles on Facebook, but too many to narrow down quickly. Same for MySpace and Twitter."

Bob was confused. "Wait," he said, "what's a Twitter?"

"It's a social networking website where—never mind. The point is, I don't think we'll find them there. At least not quickly. But I also did a public records search on LexisNexis," she said, and Bob did recognize the name of the online database used by every journalist everywhere.

"What did you find?" he asked.

"Well, I didn't have birthdates or social security numbers to confirm, but on the other hand, they both have fairly distinctive names. On the big one, Pym, there's nothing. As near as I can tell, he's never even had a parking ticket. But the other one, the one you and I dealt with, he's a different story. He's been popped a few times—one or two assaults, but mostly drug possession. Meth. I found a last-known address."

"Give it to me," said Bob.

She did. For the next few minutes, they inched toward the address in silence. Bob kept expecting the phone to chirp again. Maybe the next appeal would come from Lydia or Denis. Or maybe they'd find his son and get him to call.

We need you to talk some sense into your old man, kid. He's gone off the deep end. He's not acting like the good old Bob Carson we used to know.

But the phone made no sound. Bob gave thanks for this small mercy.

"Are you going to tell me about her?" Amy had apparently had enough of silence.

"Not a whole lot to tell," he said. "It was a long time ago."

"That's why we're on the run from the cops, hunting down bad guys? For somebody you kind of knew a long time ago?"

"Look, she's a friend, okay? We went to college together. We dated for a few months."

"Bob, give me a little credit. I'm a better reporter than that."

"Oh. Is that what you're doing here? Reporting?"

"Well, you did promise me an interview, remember?"

Surprised, Bob glanced over and son of a gun if she didn't have her digital recorder running and notepad at the ready. "Tell me about her," she said.

"I thought the interview was supposed to be about my getting fired."

"Tell me about her," said Amy again.

Bob swallowed. He cleared his throat. He heard himself say, "I loved her." And all at once he couldn't see for the tears. He mashed impatiently at his eyes, sniffled up the salty water. "I loved her," he said again. "And I suppose I still do, much as I've tried to deny it to myself all day. I guess I always will."

"She's African American, right?"

"Yeah."

"Was that part of the reason you all broke up?"

"It was the only reason, as far as I can tell. She dumped me."

"Why?"

Bob glanced at the impossibly young woman sitting next to him. "You know anything about the civil rights movement?"

Amy waggled her hand. "Birmingham, dogs and hoses, Rosa Parks, and like that," she said.

Bob sighed. "In the spring of '68, Martin Luther King came to Memphis to lead a march by striking sanitation workers. The march turned violent. Janeka and I, we were there. We barely made it out in one piece. Me, especially. We were trying to get away from the fighting when some black guy coldcocked me. He had me on the ground and was trying to beat the life out of me til Janeka bashed him in the head with a piece of masonry."

"Why would the black guy do that?" Amy asked, astonished. "You had been part of the march, right? You were on their side."

So young.

"Because I'm white," said Bob. "It was a bad day and a bad place to be white. Anyway, they took King out as soon as the trouble started. He didn't want to go, but they made him. I was angry with him for that. I was angry about a lot of things that day, to tell you the truth—not the least of which was that some guy had beat the heck out of me just because I happened to be handy and white. But I think one of the things I was angriest about is that she didn't seem angry enough. Or maybe we were just angry about different things, I don't know. We argued about it."

"So what happened?"

"She left. That very day, she told me she was transferring to a black school—an HBCU, we'd call it now. She said she needed to 'be with her own people.' I was sitting in an ambulance, beat all to pieces from trying to help her people. So, it hurt. Hurt then, hurts now."

He fell silent, suddenly out of words. An endless line of brake lights stretched before them. The shadows had lengthened, the sun deep into its long fall toward twilight.

"You held that against her," said Amy.

"Do you blame me?"

Amy gave this some thought. "No," she said, after a moment. "But you ever think about why she did it? You ever wonder what it must be like to be them? Black, I mean?"

"I'm not sure I follow," said Bob.

Amy hunched her shoulder. "Maybe it's just the concussion talking," she said, "but I've been thinking about this ever since I ran into Malcolm this morning. Sometimes, it seems to me there's this whole other world, this whole other America they live in that you and I know nothing about. And maybe sometimes that's the reason they do things or behave in ways that, to you and me, don't seem to make much sense."

"You're romanticizing."

"Maybe I am," she conceded. "Maybe I'm just another white liberal with an advanced case of good intentions and guilt. All I know is that when I read Malcolm's column this morning, it really took me by surprise."

"You were surprised how angry he sounded?"

Her eyes, which had been fixed on the laptop, came up. "No," she said. "I was surprised how sad and *hurt* he sounded. He sounded like someone who'd given up."

"Given up on what?"

"On us, I guess. White folks."

"That's absurd," said Bob. "I never did anything to Malcolm, did you?"

"No," said Amy, "but maybe it's not about you and me. Maybe what he's given up on is the idea that he can ever make white people in general understand."

Bob was getting impatient. "Understand what?" he asked.

"How it feels when you're not white."

She looked at him. He looked at her. He returned his eyes to the road and took the next exit.

Dwayne McLarty lived in a house of ramshackle neglect on a street two blocks from the railroad tracks. The buildings were jammed so close together you almost had to turn sideways to walk between. Bob parked the van and for a moment, they just sat there looking at the place. Then he said, "Come on," and they got out and went up the walk together.

Amy thumbed the doorbell. There was no answering chime from inside the house. "Broken," said Bob. Amy reached through the accordion security gate and knocked at the door. They waited. There was no answer. She knocked again.

"Are you more police?"

A woman, trailing a little girl on a Big Wheel, was calling to them from the sidewalk. "Beg pardon?" asked Bob.

"I asked if you were more police."

"No," said Bob. He stepped down from the porch. "We're reporters. I'm Bob, this is Amy. You said, 'more' police. They've already been here?"

She nodded. "Yeah. They were looking for Dwayne. Apparently, he's posted some crazy video on the Internet."

"Yes," said Bob. "I know. So he does live here?"

"No," said the woman. "Like I told the detectives earlier: he moved out maybe three months ago. Some big fight with his brother, the way I hear. There was always some kind of commotion when he was around. Good riddance, I say."

"He wasn't your favorite person?" Amy had come up behind Bob. She had her notepad and digital recorder out.

The woman glanced down at her daughter, who was singing a nonsense song and driving a loop around her mother's legs. "No," she told them, "he was an..." And she mouthed the word "asshole."

"Do you have any idea where we might find him?" asked Amy.

She shook her head. "He was here earlier today," she said. "Noontime, or thereabouts. Snapped at Bethany here just for looking at him when she rode by. I ask you: what kind of man snaps at a child for riding on a sidewalk?"

"A nasty one," said Bob.

"Exactly," she said.

"What about his family? You mentioned a brother?"

"Yes," the woman said. "His brother Daryl and their mother Edith live here. I guess they're out. Maybe a doctor's appointment or something. That's pretty much the only time she leaves the house the last year or so. She's got emphysema, you know."

"That's terrible," said Amy.

"Yeah," said the woman. "She's had a pretty hard time of it."

Amy gave the woman her card and got the correct spelling of her name, Lucinda Vasquez. She finessed the inevitable question about when the story would appear in the paper, thanked the woman for her time, and then stood with Bob watching the woman walk off, following the little girl on the Big Wheel and patiently explaining to her that, no, she could not have ice cream for dinner.

"So," said Amy, "we just drilled ourselves a dry hole. What do we do next? I don't know about you, but I'd hate to have to toddle back to the building with our tails between our legs."

Bob was tugging on his bottom lip. He didn't answer.

Amy said, "Maybe we could just wait out here and see if they show up. If the mother's got emphysema like the lady said, she probably won't be gone too long. Probably can't be."

Bob looked at her. "Or, we can break in."

Amy laughed. "Right," she said. "Let's just kick the front door open." Then, whatever she saw in his face made her realize he was not joking. "Bob," she said, "you can't be serious."

He didn't answer.

"For God's sake," she said, "We're reporters, not...home invaders."

"*You're* a reporter," said Bob. "I'm just a desperate man trying to track down the animal that took the woman I love. And if McLarty lived here til just three months ago, maybe he left behind some clue to where I can find her. Maybe it's in there right now, waiting for me."

"Bob, think about it. Even if it was a good idea, which it isn't, how do you propose to get through that?" And she pointed to the door, over which the accordion gate was closed.

"I don't know," he said. "I'll have to figure something out. Look, Amy, you've got a career to think about. Get in the van and drive away if you want to. Call the cops if you feel like you need to do that. I won't be angry with you. But I *have* to find her. And right now, this is the only idea I've got."

He started back toward the house without another word. After a moment, Amy followed.

He rattled the iron security gate on the front door uselessly. He peered through a similar gate that covered the windows. The curtains were drawn and he couldn't see a thing. Amy kept looking nervously behind them.

"I already told you," he said, "you can bail if you want. I won't be mad at you."

"This is insane," said Amy.

"Yep," said Bob, hopping down from the porch.

Still, she followed as he made his way down the tight passageway on the west side of the house. Halfway down, he stopped and pointed. Above them a curtain billowed lazily from an open window.

"I know you're not thinking what I think you're thinking," she said.

Bob had already leapt up and caught the windowsill and now dangled there. "I just want to see inside," he told her.

"Yeah, and what if what's inside is a man with a Glock wondering who this is climbing through his window?"

"Look," said Bob, "if you're going to stay around, could you at least make yourself useful?"

He heard resignation in her groan. Then she put a shoulder under his backside and pushed. He pulled himself toward the open window, legs scrabbling for purchase on the bricks.

"Watch your feet!" she cried out from below. "If you kick me in my broken jaw, I'm going to be very pissed at you."

"Sorry," said Bob.

He got first his right elbow wedged inside the window, then his left. Bob levered himself up until he got his head through. And then he saw. And then he stopped. His body went limp and he nearly fell from the window before he caught himself.

"Bob?" Amy was hissing his name from down below. "What is it? What do you see?"

Bob coughed. His throat seemed clogged with dead leaves and yellowed grass.

"There's a woman," he began.

Amy could not make out his dead leaves and yellowed grass whisper. "What?" she asked.

Bob coughed again. "There's a woman," he said. "She's dead. His mother, I think. She's been shot."

"What? Are you sure?"

Edith McLarty's head sagged upon her chest, eyes open, face frozen in confusion, and the front of her looked as if it had been splashed in red paint. The blood was still wet. It came from two small holes that had been drilled right through the center of her chest.

"I'm sure," he said.

"That's it. I'm calling the police."

"Wait. Give me five minutes to go through the place first."

Without waiting for an answer, Bob hauled himself through the window, landing in a heap on the floor next to the woman's bed. "Bob," called Amy from outside, "don't mess with anything. That's a crime scene."

"I won't," said Bob. But he was pawing through the detritus on the dead woman's nightstand as he spoke. Matchbooks, lottery tickets, receipts, expired coupons, catalogues from the spring of 2005, an instruction manual for the oxygen tank on the floor by the bed. He felt panic burning in his gut like an acid. The sense of wrongness was palpable. Amy was right, he was violating a crime scene. He was desecrating the sanctity of death. He was rifling through a dead woman's lingerie drawer as she sat not five feet from him, a remote control still clenched in her right hand, pointed toward a television that showed a soundless picture of Barack Obama playing basketball with some of his aides.

And he was finding nothing.

And he was accomplishing nothing.

And he was leaving evidence of his presence at a murder scene all over the place. CSI—assuming that was a real thing and not just something on television—would have a field day.

And meanwhile the mad dog who (he was sure of this, he was so sure) had done this thing still had Janeka, could at any moment do to her what he had done to his own mother. Maybe already had.

That's enough.

Maybe already had.

Focus. Concentrate.

"Bob?" Amy's uncertain voice came through the open window. It seemed far away and Bob ignored it. He opened the bedroom door (leaving DNA and fingerprints all over the doorknob, warned a small voice) and found himself in a hallway. Two bedroom doors on his left, another bedroom and a bath on the right. Bob entered the bedroom on his right.

He didn't find much. Clothes bulging from a dresser, a mattress on the floor, a stack of pornographic magazines lying next to the mattress, but nothing that gave him a hint about who Dwayne McLarty was or, better yet, where he might be. Panic was eating him now. Indeed, panic was corkscrewing its way through him like a worm chewing through a rotten apple. His mind was infested with unthinkable thoughts.

He crossed the hall. He tried the second bedroom. The door was locked. He thought about trying to break it down—maybe it was locked because it had belonged to McLarty and he was no longer in residence—but abandoned the idea. Instead, he entered the last bedroom. And stopped.

Oh, my God.

His cellphone chirped. He didn't hear it.

Oh, my sweet Lord.

His cellphone chirped again. He answered it without looking.

"Yeah?"

"Bob?" Amy's voice. "Are you all right? You've got to get out of there."

"He's crazy." Bob's voice was a whisper. "I found his room."

"Bob, get out of there."

"In a moment. Hold on. I'm close."

The room was a dingy hole, lit by the seepage of light from a torn window shade. But even standing there in the shadows, Bob knew he had found McLarty's bedroom. It was a citadel of loathing, a temple of hatred.

He flicked a light switch. A naked bulb came on overhead and the room leapt into sharper view. Bob gasped.

Adolf Hitler commanded one wall. He faced the room with a stiff-armed Nazi salute, eyes fixed on some middle distance of purpose and racial purity. The legend on the bottom read, "He Tried to Tell Us!" From a second wall, what appeared to be an authentic Ku Klux Klan hood watched the room with sightless eyes. From the facing wall, Timothy McVeigh stared the Klan hood down with a gaze of steel and determination.

But those were just the highlights. Every surface of the room, every wall, nightstand and dresser top, was covered with paeans to racial hatred. There were racist publications with headlines like "The Coming Nigger-ization of America," "Ten Lies of the Nigger Obama," "The Holocaust Did Not Happen—But It Should Have," "Nigger Kills, Rapes, and Disembowels White Co-Ed," and "Mongrel Nation: The White Man's Guide to Survival in the New Order." There were figurines—fat black mammies in kerchiefs, long-limbed, red-lipped street hustlers, a Jew with goat's hooves. A Confederate flag depended from the ceiling. From a poster on a wall, a morbidly obese black woman crouched nude on a chair, hands splaying her massive backside as she looked over her shoulder with a leering, gold-toothed grin.

Bob gaped. He had known this kind of thing was in the world, yes. But there was a vast difference between knowing it in some distant, abstract sense and standing right in the middle of it, bearing personal witness to hatred so venomous and pure as to render coherence impotent. In some far corner of his mind, he was aware that he was wasting precious time. But he couldn't make himself stop looking. He was frozen. Everywhere he turned, some new obscenity blasted his eyes.

There was a stack of books on a desk. *The Coming Race War. Will an Illegal Take Your Job? The End of White America. Victim: Facing Up to Black Racism*. And many, many more.

Focus. Concentrate.

There were CDs filed neatly in a rack. *Music of the Reich* by Storm Trooper. *I Have a Dream* by Bobbi Jean and the Klan. *Niggers and Flies* by Johnny Rutherford and his Tennessee Rednecks. *If the South Woulda Won* by Hank Williams, Jr.

Focus! You're wasting time!

There were video games. Bob examined a few of the discs. One was a first-person shooter in which the object was to guard the border against illegals. One was a strategy game in which the object was to help Germany win the Second World War. Another refought the Battle of Gettysburg, but gave the South machine guns and tanks.

Come on, come on.

There was a poster of three African Americans with rifle sights over their faces. Martin Luther King. Malcolm X. Barack Obama. The legend read: "Two Down. One to Go."

There were phone numbers.

Wait.

There were phone numbers!

They were written on the wall at the head of the bed in pencil—dozens of numbers, dozens of names. Bob turned on a lamp on the nightstand, sat on the edge of Dwayne McLarty's bed, and scanned them closely. His lips moved as he read each name out loud. His mind said the same thing over and over again, "Please, God. Please, God. Please, God."

And then he saw it: "Clarence," it said, followed by a number.

Bob hardly dared to breathe. He hardly dared to hope. He whipped out his cellphone and took a picture of the number on the wall. Checked the image to make sure. Took another shot, to make doubly sure.

He called Amy.

"Bob?"

"I got it," he said. "I'm coming out the front."

He clicked off without waiting for her to answer, stood from the bed, and took one last look around this chamber of hatred in which McLarty had cocooned himself. He tried not to think of the fact that the man who had slept here now had Janeka in his clutches. Bob turned off the lamp. He turned off the bare bulb. He closed the door behind him and turned left down the hallway.

He stepped over a bunch of pictures that for some reason were lying in the middle of the floor. He reached the living room. And he saw.

This must be McLarty's brother. He sat with his head back, mouth a pulpy ruin, the couch pillow against which he rested sodden with blood.

Bob's hand came up to his mouth. His stomach bubbled like a cauldron. He felt a powerful disgust unlike anything he had ever felt—or known it was possible to feel—for another human being. What sort of man was this Dwayne McLarty?

He had told Janeka—he had promised her—that nothing would happen to her, that he would save her.

But he hadn't known...how could he have known...?

Enough. Move.

He crossed the living room, inadvertently kicked something small and white, and looked down in time to see one of the dead man's teeth ricochet off the leg of the coffee table. An empty cereal bowl and a box of children's cereal sat on top.

"Oh, my God," said Bob. He shook his head, willing his thoughts into stillness, willing his fears into silence. He opened the front door, unlatched the security gate, and stepped out. It was nearly dark. The air had cooled noticeably. It felt like the very kiss of God on his sweating brow.

Amy was standing there. "So?" she said. And then she saw his face. "God, you look like crap."

"Yeah," he said. "I'm sure I do. Come on, let's go. We've got work to do."

twenty-three

"Raintree?"

"Yeah," said the voice on the other end. "Carson?"

"Yeah," said Bob.

"Did he call? Where are you?"

Bob braked at the end of McLarty's block and looked to Amy for instructions.

"Right turn," she told him after consulting her phone.

"Carson? You still there?"

"Sorry, driving." Bob navigated the turn with his left hand, holding the cellphone with his right, straining to make sure no traffic was coming.

"I asked you if he called."

"No," said Bob. "But I've got something for you."

"I'm listening." Raintree's voice had gone sour with skepticism.

"I assume you sent detectives to McLarty's last known address?"

"Of course. There was nobody home. A neighbor told my guys he doesn't live there anymore, which screws us up on PC. We're trying to get a warrant anyway. Should have it any minute."

"I've got your PC," said Bob. "I broke into the house—me all by myself, by the way. Amy had nothing to do with it."

"Noted," said Raintree. "And you realize, don't you, that you just confessed a Class B misdemeanor to a duly sworn officer of the law?"

"Do you want this or not?"

"Go ahead," said Raintree.

"They're dead," said Bob.

"Who's...?"

"McLarty's mother and brother. I found them both, shot. Looked fairly recent, though of course, I'm no expert. He killed them."

"Uh-huh. And how do I know you didn't kill them yourself? Maybe you got into a struggle with them when they caught you breaking in. Maybe you went berserk because they couldn't—or wouldn't—tell you where McLarty is and now you're trying to cover your ass. In which case, your misdemeanor just became a felony. Murder two, I'm guessing."

"Give me a break," whispered Bob.

"Unfortunately," said Raintree, "these are the kinds of questions I have to consider, since I'm dealing with some lunatic amateur running around my town trying to do my job. At the very least, you traipsed all over my crime scene, which does not make me happy."

"You want to be serious here?" Bob was so exasperated he almost missed a turn Amy was pointing him to. He had to brake sharply, which earned him an angry blast from the Toyota behind him.

"I am serious," said Raintree in a voice that, as a matter of fact, held not a scintilla of humor.

"Fine," said Bob. "Arrest me if you want. You'll see me soon enough. In the meantime, maybe you'll send somebody over there to take a look." He marveled, distantly, at his own boldness.

"I might," said Raintree. "Now, why don't you tell me whatever it is you found in there that you're not telling me about?"

This surprised Bob enough that he hesitated. "What do you mean?" he finally managed.

"You ever read Spider-Man comic books when you were a kid, Bob? You know how he has that spider sense? Well, me, I've got cop sense. And it tells me you're holding out. Now, why don't you be a good boy and come clean?"

"I don't know what you're talking about," said Bob.

Raintree sighed in mild irritation. "Yeah, I'm sure you don't."

"I'll call you back," said Bob. They both knew there was nothing more to say.

"Bob?" Raintree's voice had shed its edge. He sounded concerned.

"Yeah?"

"You're playing a dangerous game here."

"Yeah, I know," said Bob. He broke the connection.

Amy glanced over. "He wasn't impressed that you found them dead?"

"He was," said Bob. "He was just being a cop. Said he might arrest me on suspicion of killing them myself."

"He had to be joking."

"Trying to rattle me," said Bob, "get me to head back to the office."

"I see," said Amy. "Well, thanks for telling him I had nothing to do with it."

"Sure thing," said Bob. "Just promise you'll come visit me at Stateville."

"You bet," said Amy with a grin. "I'll bake you a cake with a nail file in it."

Gallows humor. And that, more than the nervous ticking of his heart or the bigness of Amy's eyes, told Bob just how frightened they were. This was uncharted territory for both of them.

Amy was watching addresses go by. "Right here," she said, pointing.

Bob pulled up in front of a small, neatly tended bungalow, the walk-way flanked by low shrubs and autumn flowers. On the small porch, a wind chime turned idly, stirred by the occasional caprices of the air. A pair of rat-tan chairs sat on either side of a round-top table that would have cried out for a pitcher of cold lemonade and two glasses had this been a balmy twilight in summer and not a chilly one in early November. There was a quiet elegance to the house. It looked, Bob thought, like Martha Stewart on a budget. "Hel-lo, Irene Funicelli," he whispered.

When they had plugged the phone number from McLarty's wall into the backwards directory, they'd gotten a surprise. The address came back, not to Clarence Pym or anyone else named Pym but, rather, to this lady whose name they had never heard. "I wonder who she is?" said Amy now.

"One way to find out," said Bob, climbing out of the van.

Amy followed him up the walk. Bob pressed the doorbell once and heard a three-tone chime from within the house. Seconds later the door opened and a small woman wearing a long, summery dress and a pearl neck-lace was peering quizzically up at them through oval glasses.

"Yes," she said. "May I help you?"

She was about 60, gray hairs just beginning to streak the brunette fall that framed her face. She had a nice smile and deep dimples and you could tell that, once upon a time, she had been a traffic stopper. This had to be a mistake. What could this woman possibly have to do with the monster on that video?

All at once, Bob realized both women were waiting for him to speak. He cleared his throat. "Beg pardon," he said. "My name is Bob Carson and this is Amy Landingham. You are Irene Funicelli?"

She was hesitant. "Yes, I am," she said. "What's this about?"

"Ms. Funicelli, we're reporters for the *Post* and we're doing a story on a man named Clarence Pym. We ran his telephone number and it came back to this address. We were wondering if you knew him."

"Clarence is my son," she said. She was looking at him hard now. "What could you possibly want with Clarence?" she asked.

Bob looked to Amy for help. She said, "Ma'am, do you have a computer?"

Her face clouded. "I'm afraid I'm not much for computers. Clarence has one, but he has it with him. Why would I need a computer?"

"Well, I can probably show you on my cellphone," said Amy. "Is it all right if we come in?"

And this was when Irene Funicelli noticed for the first time that Amy's mouth was wired closed. "My goodness," she said, "what happened to you?"

Amy said, "I got punched in the mouth today by a man named Dwayne McLarty. I suspect you know him, too. Am I right?"

The dumbfounded woman nodded.

"May we come in?" repeated Amy. "I can show you on my cellphone."

She regarded them for a wary moment. Finally, with a dubious nod, Ms. Funicelli stood aside to admit the two strangers to her home. Inside, she offered them her couch. Amy sat and began bringing up the *Post*'s website on her phone. Bob sat next to her and took the opportunity to look around.

The inside of the house mirrored the outside. The furniture was traditional, not expensive but not cheap, either. In one corner stood a lighted display case full of porcelain figurines and whatnots caught in frozen capering and soundless laughter. Through an archway Bob could see the dark wood of a dining table, watched over by a cabinet full of china and wine glasses.

On the mantel there were perched, in chronological order, a series of school portraits tracing the growth of Clarence Pym. In each picture he was the same, a doughy-faced boy facing the camera with a dour expression—indeed, facing it as a condemned man might face a firing squad. As the pictures marched across the mantel, he grew older and bigger but never any happier.

Above the mantel hung a large framed portrait of mother and son, dominating the room. Irene Funicelli stood behind the seated Pym, arms crossed protectively in front of him. She was glowing as if lit from within by candles. Pym seemed no happier in this photo than in any of the others.

Ms. Funicelli caught him looking. "That's my Clarence," she said.

"Yes," said Bob, "I know." And then, because saying something else seemed somehow necessary, he added, "You have a very nice home."

"Thank you, Mr. Carson," she said, "but I must confess I'm still confused as to why you've come here. What interest could two newspaper reporters possibly have in Clarence?"

Amy's phone started speaking then and it answered the question. "Those who have ears, let them hear," said Clarence Pym, as Amy passed his mother her phone. "We are the White Resistance Army." Irene Funicelli's right hand clamped itself over her mouth as the video played. By the time it was done, two minutes later, that hand was damp with tears.

She looked from one to the other and the expression on her face was so naked in its needfulness and helplessness that Bob almost turned away. "Is this real?" she asked. She stared at the phone, then remembered belatedly to return it to Amy. "This can't be real. This can't."

"It's real," said Bob.

"Oh, sweet Jesus," she breathed. "Oh, God, help my poor son."

"We're sorry," said Amy.

"When was this done?" she asked.

"This morning, apparently," said Bob.

"Where is he? Can I talk to him?"

"We were hoping you'd be able to tell us."

She shook her head and began moaning again. Finally, Bob did turn away. This was getting them nowhere. He gave Amy a let's-go look. She gave him back a look that told him to wait. Bob sighed and tried not to think of Janeka.

Ms. Funicelli was sitting across from them. Amy reached to touch her knee and said, "Tell me about your son."

There was something of gratitude in Irene Funicelli's eyes when she looked up, and Bob guessed that after the video, this mother was simply grateful someone was willing to listen to her explain that her son was not a monster. Although, of course, he was.

"He's always been a good boy," she said in a wondering tone. "Always a good boy."

"So you're surprised by this?" Amy was leading the woman gently.

"He's a good boy," she insisted.

"Then how did he get mixed up in all this?"

"It had to be that other one, McLarty." Ms. Funicelli spat the name as though it had a foul taste. "He came to stay with us a few months ago. He sleeps in Clarence's room. Clarence said he got turned out by his family and had nowhere else to go."

She grimaced as if the memory of it brought her pain. "It was against my better judgment," she said. "I didn't like him. Something about him just seemed bad. He was nice enough to me, very polite, but sometimes you get these feelings about people, you understand?"

Amy nodded that she did. Somehow, she was taking notes without her eyes ever seeming to leave Ms. Funicelli's. At some point, without Bob even noticing, she had set up her little digital recorder on the table.

Unfortunately, none of this was getting him any closer to finding Janeka.

"So," prompted Amy, "you let him stay here even though you didn't like him."

"Clarence likes him," she said. "And more importantly, he seemed to like Clarence. They sit in that room til all hours, laughing and talking together." She hesitated. Then she said in a confiding tone, "Clarence has never had many friends."

Amy spoke carefully. "Is that because of his size? Kids teased him, I assume?"

Ms. Funicelli nodded. She said, "Have you ever heard of gigantism?"

The hand that was somehow writing without Amy appearing to look down froze now, midstroke. Then it went back to work, furiously. "Yes," she said. "I think I have heard of it. That's that condition where the body doesn't stop growing, correct?"

"Yes," said Ms. Funicelli. "It's a disorder, a tumor on the pituitary gland that causes people to just keep on growing. Clarence has that."

"That's very rare, isn't it?"

"It's not rare enough," Ms. Funicelli said.

"And I assume that when he was in school, the other children were not very understanding."

Ms. Funicelli gave her a cutting glance. "The other children were *cruel*," she said. "But of course, you already knew that."

"It's an old story," said Amy.

"Perhaps. But that doesn't make it any easier to bear when it's your child. You have children, miss?"

"Yes."

"Then you know."

"He and McLarty met in high school?"

Ms. Funicelli nodded. "I was so happy Clarence had a friend. I suppose that's why I overlooked what my instincts told me about him. Sometimes, I would overhear him say disparaging things about the blacks or the Jews, using the kind of words I don't allow in my house. I told him I didn't appreciate that sort of language, but I didn't think any more of it. I see now that I should have listened. Sweet Jesus, what has he gotten my son mixed up in?"

"You blame yourself." Amy didn't bother making it a question.

"You have to understand. Clarence was such a lonely boy. He spent hours in his room, just him and his books, him and his video games and his basketball trading cards. I wanted him to know what it was to have at least one good friend before he died."

Amy's gaze sharpened. "Beg pardon?"

"I thought you knew," Ms. Funicelli said. "Some people with gigantism, they can remove the tumor. But Clarence's is inoperable. This means he will simply keep growing. Six feet, seven feet...one poor man was almost nine feet tall. The disease itself is not fatal. But the stresses it puts on the body—enlarged organs, heart disease, joint ailments, diabetes, weakness—eventually, it just wears you down. They tend to die relatively young."

"I'm sorry," said Amy.

And somehow, for Bob, that was finally too much. "Do you mind if I have a look in his bedroom?" he asked. The question was abrupt, he knew. He didn't quite care. He would not sit here and feel sorry for one of the men who had kidnapped Janeka and Malcolm.

Ms. Funicelli looked startled. Then she said, "Well, I don't know..."

Bob was standing now. "I just want to see where he lives, get a sense of what sort of man he is. We're not the police, Ms. Funicelli. We're just two reporters looking for information that will help us humanize your son when this story comes out."

Humanize. He had chosen the word quite deliberately, certain that a distraught mother desperate to show people her child was not the racist, mastodonic freak he seemed would cling to it like debris in a flood. Sure enough, her face brightened. "Well, it's right through there," she said, pointing to the dining room. "Down the hallway, second door on the right."

"Okay," he said, "I'll go take a look while you and my colleague finish chatting."

His eyes snagged Amy's then, and he thought he saw some faint accusation. But that was probably just his imagination. Or maybe it was his conscience.

Whatever it was, Amy quickly returned to her interview. "So," she said, "I notice you and your son don't have the same last name. How did that come about?"

Bob was out of the room before Ms. Funicelli began to answer. Down the hall, second door on the right, and he entered the room. And stopped. He did not know what he had expected, but whatever that was, this wasn't it.

The room seemed *not* the lair of a crazy person. Granted, the decor was a little on the young side for a man who had to be in his 20s. You wouldn't expect a man that age to have a family of action figures posed on top of the desk, or a poster of Michael Jordan on the wall, tongue wagging as he dunked on some hapless defender. And the furnishings had all been chosen—probably custom made, Bob decided on second thought—to accommodate Pym's prodigious frame. The bed crowded the room. The desk chair was big enough for an NBA center to repose comfortably.

In fact, the entire room, now that he looked, appeared to have been remodeled for Pym's comfort. The ceiling was higher than elsewhere in the house and the room itself seemed larger than you'd expect in an otherwise modest-sized bungalow.

Irene Funicelli had spared no expense to provide her son with one space in the world where he might be at home. Still, the room was, for Bob at least, disappointingly ordinary after the pit of hell where McLarty had once slept.

The books shelved neatly in a tall case at the foot of the bed included *The Catcher in the Rye, 1984, The Shining,* and *Of Mice and Men*—a far cry from the literature of bigotry that crowded McLarty's room. The poster of Jordan—sweat gleaming on his unmistakably dark skin—suggested that whatever racial hatred McLarty had managed to inculcate in his pupil's mind was selective at best.

Bob kept looking. He paged through a sheaf of pamphlets and magazines on the corner of the desk. This, too, was not incriminating: Marvel comic books, copies of *Playboy* and *Sports Illustrated*, pamphlets on gigantism. He examined the figures on the desk. They were all of Action Jones, a superhero character whose TV cartoon had been briefly popular in the greater Chicago area in the late 1970s, but who never caught on nationally. "It's time for Action!" went his uninspired and uninspiring battle cry. It was surprising that a character so forgettable had merited an action figure.

Bob sighed.

There was nothing. Still, he kept looking. What else could he do? He rifled through mail on the desk. Most of it was junk, not even bills. That made sense, he supposed. Given his condition, Pym likely couldn't work, so his mother probably paid his cellphone and cable bills. It was, he reflected, a miserable existence.

Bob opened the closet. It was filled mostly with shapeless, oversized T-shirts and jeans of the type Pym had worn in the video. More from a sense of morbid curiosity than any expectation it would prove helpful, Bob checked the waist size on one pair of pants. Fifty-four.

On the closet floor was an open suitcase, which likely belonged to McLarty. This made Bob briefly hopeful, but upon a quick examination, he saw that the suitcase contained only clothes. Indeed, it and an air mattress leaning against one wall were the only signs McLarty even resided in this room. After cocking an ear to make sure Amy and Irene were still talking in the living room, Bob went quickly through Pym's underwear drawer. He felt he owed as much to McLarty's mother, given that he had subjected her to the same indignity.

Not that it mattered. Once again, the search proved fruitless.

Bob was defeated and discouraged by the time he wandered back through the house to the front room. Both women looked up as he entered. "Did you find anything helpful, Mr. Carson?" asked Mrs. Funicelli.

Bob shook his head. "No," he said, "I'm afraid not."

He implored Amy with a look and was gratified when she nodded and closed her notepad. "Well, Mrs. Funicelli, thank you very much for your time," she said, extending her hand.

The woman grasped it like a lifeline. "Please, Miss Landingham," she said, "try to understand: I know how awful that video is. But my son is not a monster. At least, he wasn't before he met that other boy. Promise me you will remember that when you write this story."

"Yes, ma'am," said Amy, "I will." Her voice was grave, and Bob realized with a sour jolt of consternation that she wasn't just saying this to placate a distraught mother. She meant it.

The older woman gave one last penetrating look and apparently came to the same conclusion, because she finally returned Amy's hand. "God bless you," she said.

Moments later, Bob and Amy were standing together on the porch, the door having just closed behind them. Bob said, "Please tell me you're not going to write some tearjerker about the poor, misunderstood giant."

Amy's glance speared him. "I understand how you feel. But this woman and her son have a story, too."

"Oh, my God," he said, "you're going to do it. You're going to write some touchy-feely garbage about this. You're going to ask people to feel sorry for this guy."

"I'm going to tell the story," said Amy in a measured tone. "That's the job description, remember?"

"And we wonder why people hate the media," said Bob. He felt anger growing large in him, couldn't make it stop. Didn't even want to. "He's got a bad disease? Boo hoo. That's tough. Can't you see that if you use that as an excuse, you perpetuate a mindset that says nobody is ever responsible for their own actions? It's *always* a bad childhood or a mean father or some terrible illness that's to blame, and we're supposed to sympathize with them because they've had this hardship. And never mind that a million other people go through the same hardships and worse, but somehow, they never end up joining some white supremacist gang or kidnapping innocent people who never did a damn thing to them! I don't blame people for hating us when we do this kind of shit! I'd hate us, too! This story you say you want to write? It's *crap*, Amy! It's pure, unadulterated—"

He stopped all at once, surprised to hear himself yelling. *Screaming.* He looked at Amy. Amy looked at him. Abruptly, Bob pivoted on his heel, stormed off to the van and slammed the door behind him. It was a moment before Amy joined him. She didn't say a word. They sat in silence, both staring straight ahead as twilight gathered itself.

Then Bob said, "I'm sorry."

"Forget it."

"No, seriously," he said. "I apologize. I don't know what that was about."

"You're scared."

"I'm terrified," he corrected.

"I understand that," she said.

"Thank you for that, then." Bob blew out a defeated breath. "So," he said, "where to?"

"I was hoping you might have some idea," she told him. "I take it you really found nothing in his room?"

Bob shook his head. "Except for the fact that everything in it is scaled for a giant, it's a perfectly normal room. At least, it'd be a normal room for a 16-year-old boy."

Amy questioned him with a look, so Bob briefly described the Michael Jordan poster and the figures of Action Jones. She knew Jordan, but had never heard of Action Jones.

"Cartoon hero," said Bob. "Real big on local television for a year or two back in the late '70s. My kid was crazy about him."

Amy's brow wrinkled. "Late '70s? Pym is 26, according to his mother. Why would he know or care about some second-rate cartoon that was cancelled before he was born?"

Bob shrugged. "Good question," he said.

"Well," said Amy, "I'm afraid I came up pretty empty myself, at least insofar as anything that might help us find this guy."

"Let's hear what you got."

She cut him a glance. "You sure? Most of it's touchy-feely crap."

"Yeah," he said through a smile full of regret. "Not like I have a bunch of other ideas."

Amy referred to her notepad. "Okay," she said, "well, let's see. You heard all the stuff about the other children taunting him and McLarty befriending him. Mom is originally from Lawrence, Kansas. Came here after college, found work as an executive secretary at a law firm. That's where she meets her first husband, Darrin Pym, and she thinks she's hit the husband lottery, snagging herself an honest-to-God lawyer. But it turns out he's a lawyer on the fast track down, a loser whose career is in the toilet, the firm just waiting for an excuse to get rid of him. They get their chance when he's arrested for a hit and run and it comes out he's heavy into drugs and alcohol. He's been shopping resumes for weeks without a nibble when she learns she's pregnant with Clarence. This does not please Mr. Pym, whose mood only grows more sour as the job offers continue to not come in and Clarence gets older and becomes this abnormally large little boy. Mom says dad used to beat the boy like an animal over the slightest thing. Hated to see him eating, insisted the boy be put on these starvation diets, little more than leaves and berries, by mom's accounting. Apparently, he had a real issue about Clarence's weight. He nicknamed him Glutton. Then, when Clarence is 11, his mother takes him to see a specialist and they learn the weight is not just a self-control thing, but this actual, serious illness. That same week, Mr. Pym decamps for his native Canada. Divorce papers arrive in the mail shortly after. Mother and son have heard nothing of him since. Not so much as a postcard."

"Mr. Wonderful," said Bob.

"Right," said Amy. "And husband number two is no prize himself. Giuseppe Funicelli—Joe to his friends—works for his father at the family toy company. Chases every skirt from here to Ohio, verbally abuses the boy when he's not ignoring him altogether. Finally abandons them both when Clarence is 18 for some stripper in Cleveland. The one bright spot is that Joe's father has taken to the boy. When Joe abandons his wife and stepkid, the grandfather is so embarrassed that he denounces his own son and provides Irene with a stipend to help support her and Clarence. It continues til the old man dies a couple years later. Then Joe swoops back into the picture and he and his siblings abruptly cut Irene off. That's apparently the last thing the siblings ever agreed upon. The old man's kids have been embroiled in some big fight over his assets ever since, although Irene says—"

She paused when Bob held up his hand like a traffic cop. "Wait a minute," he said. But he didn't say anything else. He sat there, frozen, thoughts racing. All at once, he started the van, threw it into gear, and took off fast.

Questions crowded Amy's eyes. "Bob?" she said.

Bob glanced over. He had almost forgotten she was there.

"I think I know where they are."

twenty-four

It was dark inside the warehouse now, the only illumination coming from a crescent of moon and the pale orange glow of the sodium lights from the highway above. Otherwise, the room was enveloped by shadow.

McLarty had moved the van up to the rollup door. Now, he and Pym were using a dolly and a makeshift ramp to load the metal drums into the back, working by the light of two halogen lanterns clamped to the door frame. They still didn't seem to be getting along very well—muttered curses occasionally reached Malcolm's ears. McLarty had become increasingly peevish under Pym's hectoring, but apparently, they were getting the job done.

"They're going to kill us. We've got to get out of here." This was Janeka, whispering behind him.

Malcolm didn't answer. What was the point? What was he supposed to say? He had been tied to this chair for thirteen hours. He was spent. His joints were stiff, his ribs ached, his skull throbbed, his head hung like a weight, and his trousers were still cold and damp with his own urine.

"Malcolm, come on. Think of something."

"You think of something," he told her. He tried to muster anger, but even that was beyond him. His voice felt like a dead thing lodged in his throat. Malcolm was simply ready for all of this to be over, one way or another. He didn't much care how.

"You think I'm not trying?" hissed the woman behind him. "Come on, you can't give up. If we could just figure out a way to cut this damn duct tape, I could get that key and we could get out of here."

If.

It reminded him of something his father used to say: "If worms had machine guns, the birds would stop fucking with them." Because "if" was the most useless word in the entire English language. Malcolm shook his heavy head. "It's no use," he said. "There's no way."

"So we should just die?"

He sighed. She was determined to have an argument. Intellectually, he understood what she was doing. She was trying to jolt him, fire him up. But Janeka Lattimore hadn't been sitting here since dawn. What was he supposed to do? Was he supposed to dislocate his thumb and slip it out of the cuffs like some action hero in a movie? He wasn't an action hero. He was a 60-year-old man who had spent his entire professional life sitting on his ass typing at a keyboard, a man who had seldom in all those years done anything more demanding than take the stairs. And she was expecting him to save them?

No. There was nothing he could do. Nothing *they* could do. There was no way they could get out of there. There was...

All at once, the litany of anguished thought stopped. His mouth fell open. For a moment, Malcolm could not move. Then he shook his head. He almost laughed.

Lord, the answer was right in front of him. It had been there the whole time. Literally, right there in front of him.

"Come on, Malcolm," said Janeka. "You can't give up. You can't—"

He cut her off. "I've got an idea."

"Bob, slow down!" cried Amy through her gritted teeth.

Bob was driving like a crazy man, hurtling the van down the expressway, riding close on the bumpers of cars that made the mistake of being in his way. He darted in and out of traffic with bare millimeters of space to spare. Now he was bumping along the shoulder of the highway to get around a clump of cars poking along at 65 miles an hour.

"Can't slow down," he told Amy, ducking back into the flow of traffic and hammering the accelerator. "I think I know where they are."

"So you said. But where?"

Bob didn't answer. He glanced at his sideview mirror, then jerked the wheel hard to his left. The sudden lane change forced the driver of an 18-wheeler to jam on his brakes. That driver expressed his displeasure with the angry blatting of an air horn.

"Look," said Amy, "if you don't care about your life—or mine—you might want to at least think about the fact that Raintree has probably put an APB out on this van. You think none of these drivers has a cellphone?"

Bob chanced a quick glance at her. She made sense. He hated it, but she did. "All right," he said. And he eased up fractionally on the gas.

"Now, where are we going?" asked Amy.

"It's just a hunch," said Bob.

"Fine. What is this hunch you're willing to kill us both for?"

"You remember the backdrop on the video? Seemed like it was shot in some industrial space, right?"

"Yeah. So?"

"You asked how Clarence Pym could have ever heard of Action Jones, this obscure cartoon that came and went before he was born. And how he could have cared enough to have a complete set of Action Jones dolls."

"Yeah?"

"Think about it," said Bob. "That's not something anybody would have bought for him. It's something they *couldn't* have bought him, since by the time he was born it wouldn't have been on the shelves. So those toys had to have been given to him by somebody who already had a bunch of them. It's the only way he could have gotten them."

"You mean, like, by some collector?"

Bob shook his head. "No. I mean, by the manufacturer. Probably out of the overstock."

He saw understanding dawn like sunlight in Amy's eyes. "His grandfather—stepgrandfather, I mean—was a toymaker."

"Exactly," said Bob. "Ben Funicelli. Funn Toys. They went out of business a few years ago. But the thing is, they had a headquarters about a mile off Michigan. It's been empty since the company folded. I remember because there was some talk a while back about a redevelopment project in that area. They had plans to put in a movie theater, some restaurants and shops, make it a real date-night promenade. Most of the property owners around there were all for it, but the deal was held up when the developer couldn't come to terms with one family."

"The Funicellis."

"Right. The developer eventually gave up on the idea and moved on. I remember we did an editorial about it, blasting the family for their greed."

Amy was nodding. "You might have something," she said. "The building is in his extended family. Even though his mom is on the outs with her in-laws, it wouldn't be that difficult for Pym to get access. Maybe he even had a key from when the grandfather was alive."

"Exactly. Or maybe he just broke in. A little 'screw you' to the stepfather and the in-laws who treated him and his mother like garbage. It can't be that hard to get into one of those old places. And it's not like anyone would notice."

"I think we should call the cops," said Amy.

"We will," said Bob. "But first, let's make sure I'm right about this. As pissed off as Raintree is, the last thing I need to do right now is waste his time on a wild goose chase."

Amy gave this some thought. "Okay," she said finally. "But if you're right, we call him right away. No trying to take matters into our own hands. Agreed?"

"Definitely," said Bob.

And at the time he said it, he meant it.

If he got out of this—still a very big if, as far as he was concerned—Malcolm had decided he would learn the name of the little homeless man who had given his life in a futile rescue attempt and find some way to honor him. A plaque on a wall. A statue in a park. A scholarship in his name. Something.

He had come running across that room holding a broken ceramic toilet tank lid overhead and he had looked, for just that instant, not like what he was—a ruined little man wielding an absurd weapon—but, rather, like some knight of old charging into battle with his broadsword held high, ready to deliver a killing stroke. It had been a gloriously brutal sight. He had raked Pym's face with the jagged edge of the thing. And then, moving with a war-rior's grace, moving with the confident surety of some long ago action his bones still recalled, he had pivoted, even as Pym bellowed, and brought the weapon down again, emphatically, breaking it upon the crown of the giant's skull. And the big man had fallen like a tree.

Success had been short-lived, of course. But maybe that death had not been in vain. Because the broken pieces of the ceramic tank lid still lay on the floor, the closest one just two tantalizing inches beyond the foot Malcolm was now desperately stretching to reach it. The handcuff bit into his ankle as he extended his foot as far as he could—*further* than he could, yet still, not far enough. The thing lay in a pool of moonlight as if placed there by God's very hand, escape, salvation, redemption, all wrapped up in a shattered ceramic shard from some old office crapper.

Reach, goddamn you. Reach!

He reached. With everything in him, he reached.

"Have you got it yet?" Janeka was peering over her right shoulder, trying to see.

Malcolm didn't answer her. He grunted with the effort, his flaccid, 60-year-old tendons popping and creaking from the unaccustomed exertion. The entirety of him was focused on this one task, the toe of his pricey athletic shoe hovering so close, so close...

"Malcolm?"

He ignored her.

Come on, man. Reach! Reach!

"Malcolm, why don't we just move the chair?"

Come on, Malcolm. Almost there. Just reach, and...wait. What? Move the chair?

She seemed to hear the thought. "We could bump it forward, couldn't we? You've got a good six inches, maybe even a foot of give in those handcuffs. Wouldn't that work?"

"Uh, yeah," he said. "It might."

Move the chair. Of course.

"Okay," he said, "on the count of three, try to lift up and scoot back. And be as quiet as you can, okay?"

She said okay. He counted to three.

It was a difficult and awkward maneuver, requiring Janeka, with little leverage and with both hands and feet duct taped, to lift her backside and push the chair, with Malcolm in it, forward as Malcolm stretched his legs out as far as he was able—which wasn't very far at all—using his feet to pull the chair forward. His exhausted body groaned in protest. Behind him, Janeka grunted a curse as she put her weight behind the chair. Through the open door, he heard McLarty reading to Pym what sounded like bomb-making instructions.

Malcolm felt the chair totter beneath him. "Come on," he said softly, "come on, come on." But it was no use. The leverage was all wrong, she wasn't strong enough, it wasn't going to work.

And then, with a harsh scrape of wood on stone, the chair moved. The sound was so loud, Pym and McLarty had to have heard it. Malcolm didn't breathe, straining his ears for the sound of one lunatic or the other coming to investigate. Instead, he heard McLarty mutter, "OK, that's the last one. Now you start mixing up the Kool-Aid while I get to work on the wiring."

Kool-Aid? Malcolm didn't even want to know what that meant.

Behind him, he heard Janeka gasping heavily. "Did that do it?" she asked.

Malcolm reached his foot out. It hovered easily over the broken ceramic. "Yeah," he said.

With his foot, he drew this makeshift knife closer. When he had it centered right in front of him, right between the legs of the chair, he said, "Here it comes." And then, with a flick of his ankle, Malcolm sent the thing skidding back for Janeka to catch it.

"You got it?" he asked.

There was a moment. Then she said, "I got it."

Malcolm felt himself breathe for what felt like the first time all day. "Then get us out of here," he said.

The van had been a gift from his Grandpa Ben, who was not his real grandfather at all, but who, for a time, had been the only person besides his mother who treated Clarence Pym like a human being with human feelings. It had been one of the fleet that Funn Toys salesmen drove all over the upper Midwest hawking his grandfather's products.

When the business went under and all his assets were liquidated, the old man had held the van out and given it to Clarence. Clarence had been delighted. Designed for commercial use, it was big enough to accommodate his size. Clarence had learned to drive in this thing. When he got his license, he'd had the Funn Toys slogan ("It's Ben Funn!") and phone numbers on the sides painted over and he'd used the thing to go everywhere—to Bulls games, where he had to sit in folding chairs in a spot designated for cripples in their wheelchairs, or to baseball games and movies, where he watched standing up behind seats he could not wedge himself into. People stared, but he told himself that was okay. It was worth it just to be out on his own like a normal guy.

Clarence had loved this old van. After a childhood spent largely in classrooms, doctor's waiting rooms, and his bedroom, it had given him something he'd never had before: freedom. Now here he was, turning it into a bomb.

Sitting in a chair behind the old van, Clarence stirred a mixture of ball bearings, nails, and bolts into small plastic tubs, each already half full of something Dwayne had dubbed "Kool-Aid,'" a foul-smelling sludge of piss, liquefied dog shit, ammonia, roach spray, and rat poison. These tubs would sit on top of the larger drums that constituted the bomb itself.

Anybody who survived the initial explosion would be in for something almost as bad, Dwayne had said, when they found their wounds infected with shrapnel coated in that nasty concoction. He had giggled at the idea like a little girl and told Clarence he wished he could see the faces of the doctors and the CSI types when they realized what all manner of nastiness coated that shrapnel. They would go absolutely apeshit.

Maybe they would, thought Clarence, face congealed in a frown as he ran one of his mother's cooking spoons down into the filthy concoction and stirred. But in the meantime, he was the one who was forced to deal with the stuff. He felt as if he were about to be sick to his stomach,

Dwayne saw. "Cheer up there, Sergeant," he said as he sat inside the back of the van, braiding copper wiring together. "Just think of all the niggers and nigger-lovers and Jews that shit will kill. Hell, maybe a nail from that very batch you have in your hand will go right through Barry Obama's fucking eye, huh? Got to look on the bright side."

"Yeah," said Clarence without conviction as he closed the lid on one of the nasty tubs.

Dwayne's face puckered. He had been trying without success to jolly Clarence into talking ever since returning to the warehouse stoked to the gills on meth. It wasn't that Clarence wanted to stay angry about it. Hell, Clarence had been trying to look past it, get over it, or just forget it ever since it happened. He really had. But nothing had worked. Now Dwayne spoke sharply. "Something wrong there, Sergeant?"

"No, Captain."

"Sure as hell better not be. We're on the verge of our greatest triumph here. It doesn't look right for you to be moping around. Get your head in the game, Sergeant. That's an order."

"Yes, sir." Clarence spoke automatically, without even bringing his head up from what he was doing. Truth was, he didn't particularly feel like taking orders from Dwayne McLarty just now.

Dwayne smacked him in the back of the head so hard he dropped the spoon. "Ow!" cried Clarence, more surprised than hurt. He lumbered to his

feet and wheeled around, one massive hand palming his head where Dwayne
had hit him. "Why the fuck did you hit me?"

Dwayne was ostentatiously unimpressed. His gaze was level, his voice
even as a ruler. "Shape up, Sergeant, or there'll be more where that came from."

At that, Clarence could only stare, his incredulity warring with his rage.
"Shape up? You're telling *me* to shape up? I'm not the one who came back
from a mission all fucked up on meth, 'Captain.'" For the first time since
they had formed their army, he pronounced the rank with air quotes around
it, like something ridiculous, something made up, something dumb.

It got Dwayne's attention. He came off the back of the van, all pre-
tension of indifference forgotten, and drew himself up to his full height—
which brought his nose to somewhere beneath Clarence's sternum. "Look,
Sergeant," he said, and he pronounced the rank with definitive emphasis, as
if to reclaim the whole idea of rank from Clarence's ridicule, "I don't answer
to you, understand? It's not for you to question what I do. That's what the
chain of command is all about."

Clarence regarded his friend for a long, cool moment. Then he said,
"Fuck you, Dwayne." And he turned his back and walked away.

He did not go far. Just a few feet. Just far enough to put distance between himself and the idea of wrapping his hands around Dwayne McLarty's
scrawny neck and squeezing until his eyes bulged and his neck cracked and
he gurgled and flailed helplessly and his breathing stopped. Why not? He
had done it once already, hadn't he? No going back from that.

And unlike the little homeless nigger whose body lay discarded like
trash in a corner of Grandpa Ben's old warehouse, maybe Dwayne actually
deserved to have the life choked out of him. He had used. He had fucking
used. After all the promises he had made, after all Clarence had told him
about how he hated that shit and *why* he hated that shit, he had gone first
thing and hit that fucking pipe.

They were white men. Dwayne had preached to him a hundred times,
a thousand times, how that meant they were heirs to the great warriors of
Europe, cosigners of the great documents that had lifted humankind out of
the cave, copainters of the great works of art that hung in the great museums
of European capitals, codiscoverers of the great advances in science that had
brought light, flight, and microwave ovens to a waiting world. Theirs was
a proud and noble legacy unmatched by the woolly African niggers or the
slopes or the spics or the Jews or the redskins or any of God's other rejects.

They were white men. This meant they were better.

Except how could they call themselves better if Dwayne was sucking on that fucking pipe? That pipe made a lie out of everything he ever said, all the great glory he ever claimed. Why could he not see that?

"Look, Clarence..."

And now, predictably, here came Dwayne, his voice contrite. "I apologize, okay? How many fucking times do you want me to say it? How many fucking times how many fucking times how many fucking times?"

Clarence spoke without turning around. "You're doing it again," he said.

"Doing what? What am I doing? Doing what?"

"That thing you do when you're high where you say everything three times."

"No I'm not no I'm not no I'm not."

"You just did it."

"When?"

"Just now."

"Really? Shit shit shit. I didn't mean to."

"Yeah, that's what they always say," said Pym. "People who use that shit, they always tell you they don't mean to say the things they say or do the things they do. They always say they don't mean to treat you like crap and they always promise they'll never do it again. But somehow, that never stops them from doing it. Gets to the point you can't even stand to listen to it. Gets to the point you don't believe a goddamn thing they say anymore."

"Clarence Clarence Clarence..."

Clarence turned. "When you use that shit, it makes you mean and nasty just like he was. I promised myself when I was a kid that the one thing I wouldn't do when I got grown, I wouldn't put up with being treated like that ever again. I'd rather die first. I told you that, right? I'd rather die."

Something flickered in Dwayne's berserk eyes. "Yeah, partner," he said, softly, "you told me."

Cautiously, Dwayne came closer. Clarence was embarrassed to feel his eyes welling. He smacked at them with his large hands, angry with himself for allowing this emotion, this *weakness*, to leak out of him. Dwayne was touching his shoulder. "I let you down," he said. "I get that. I broke my promise."

"You don't hit me again," Clarence said. He leveled his finger. His voice was hard. "You don't ever lay a fucking hand on me again. You got that?"

"Yeah," said Dwayne, solemnly. "I got it."

"You never did that before. You never treated me like Darrin before."

Dwayne nodded. "Yeah, that was the first time," he said. "But you know something?"

Clarence was curious, even though he didn't want to be. "What?" he asked.

Dwayne's grin was Cheshire. "At least you know it's also the last."

Clarence barked a short laugh without meaning to. "Yeah, I guess you're right about that," he said.

"So what do you say, Sergeant? You ready to help me complete this mission?"

It took a moment. Then Clarence nodded. "Right behind you, Captain," he said.

"You making any progress back there?" whispered Malcolm.

"Yes," said Janeka. "I'm making great progress in cutting my fingers to ribbons. The other kind, not so much."

"Damn," said Malcolm.

"I'm doing my best," she said.

"I'm not blaming you," he said. "I'm just worried. I don't know how much time we've got."

"I've got no leverage," she said. "Nothing to brace this thing against. And with my wrists taped together and not being able to see what I'm doing, it's not the easiest thing in the world to do."

"Keep trying," said Malcolm. "It's not like we have any other options."

"I still can't believe they think they're going to kill Senator Obama," said Janeka.

A snort of laughter escaped Malcolm. "Waste of time even if they could," he said.

"What do you mean?"

"They're trying to stop him from being elected president, right? They could have saved the effort. The American people are going to do that by themselves."

"That's right. You said that in your column this morning, didn't you? You think he's going to lose."

Malcolm corrected her. "I *know* he's going to lose," he said.

"You do know that I work for the senator, right?"

"No, I didn't," admitted Malcolm. "Not that it would change my opinion. I'm sorry to burst your balloon, but tomorrow you'll still be working for the senator and some bright and shiny white Republican with a flag pin in his lapel will be working for the president-elect."

"Well," said Janeka, "I've seen the polling and the polling disagrees with you."

"Come on, sister," whispered Malcolm. "We both know there are some things those polls are never going to capture, some things white folks aren't even going to know they feel until they're all alone in that voting booth."

Malcolm heard a gust of anger blow out of the woman behind him as the soft sound of ceramic scratching against duct tape continued. "You know," she said, "you really have a way of pissing people off."

"It's a gift," said Malcolm. "Keep sawing."

With a grunt, Clarence lifted the last of the Kool-Aid tubs into the van. Dwayne was inspecting a blasting cap.

"That's the last of it," said Clarence.

"We've still got to paint the armor."

"Yeah," said Clarence, "I know." He dragged a forearm across his brow. It came away muddy with dirt and sweat.

"Why don't you check on the prisoners, Sergeant? They're mighty quiet back there. I don't trust niggers when they're quiet."

"Yes, Captain."

"I got it," whispered Janeka. Malcolm heard the adhesive tearing even as she spoke. Adrenaline drove a spike through his chest.

"Hurry up, then. Get the key so we can get out of here."

"What am I supposed to do?" she hissed, "walk over there on my hands? Let me get my feet loose first."

It was as she was saying this that the sudden harsh white light fell upon them, its brightness so punishing it was like looking into an electronic sun. Malcolm squeezed his eyes shut. He tried to bring his hands up, but the chains prevented this.

"What's going on here?"

It was Pym, though Malcolm only knew this by the sound of the voice. Had he heard them? Malcolm decided to believe he had not. "We're having a picnic," he answered in an acid voice. "What do you think is going on? And get that light of my eyes, would you?"

Pym gave a sour chuckle. "Funny nigger til the end," he said. But he moved the powerful battery-operated lantern to one side and Malcolm, blinking hard, was able to make out the shadow of him, looming high above like a mountain.

"You and your friend come to your senses?" asked Malcolm. "You're here to apologize and let us go?"

"Hee-fucking-larious as usual," said Pym. "You're just a regular Chris Rock, huh?"

Without waiting for an answer, Pym took his lantern and went to check on Janeka. "What about you, lady? You all right back there? You want some water or something?"

"She wants you to try a new mouthwash," said Malcolm. He had to goad the giant, provoke him, keep him from inspecting too closely and seeing that Janeka's hands were free.

"Keep it up, funny guy," said Pym. "We'll see who laughs last."

"I'm fine," Malcolm heard Janeka say.

Pym told her, "I'm sorry about this, by the way. It wasn't supposed to go like this. He wasn't supposed to involve anybody else."

"Uh-huh," she said, "so now I guess you're going to kill me, too?"

"It's not like it's something I want to do," said Clarence. A wounded, faintly defensive note had crept into his voice.

"Won't matter to me much if it's something you wanted to do or not," said Janeka. "I'm dead either way. I don't want to die, Clarence. I haven't done anything to deserve to die."

"Nobody deserves what they get," said Pym, "and damn few get what they deserve."

He sank down to the metal chair he had used earlier in the day. The giant suddenly seemed tired in some way that went far beyond the merely physical.

"You look exhausted," said Malcolm.

"Yeah."

"Hard work, being a homicidal psychopath."

"Would you just, for one minute, shut up and leave me the fuck alone?" Pym pleaded.

Malcolm was about to answer when McLarty yelled into the darkness. "You all right in there, Sergeant?"

"Yeah," called Pym with a sigh.

"Taking you a long time just to check on a couple niggers."

"I'm tired," called Pym. "Taking a break."

"Is that so?" A moment later, McLarty appeared, walking in a semi-crouch, his own lantern held high, the ridiculous pink pistol clutched in his fist, turned sideways like something from a rap video. When he saw Pym, he straightened and shoved the gun into his belt. "Thought they might have gotten the drop on you," he said. "Can't be too careful."

"No," said Pym. "I told you. I'm just resting."

"So I see."

Pym nodded toward the weapon. "That's your mom's gun, isn't it?" he asked.

For no reason that Malcolm could see, McLarty giggled. "Yeah," he said. "It's hers all right. She doesn't mind if I use it."

"But what happened to the Luger?"

"Long story," said McLarty. "Come on come on come on, we got to get back to work. Got to finish wiring the bomb, paint the armor."

"In a minute," said Pym.

At that, Malcolm saw an unmistakable irritation flash in McLarty's eyes. He struggled visibly to master it. "All righty then," he said in a magnanimous voice, "we'll take five."

Then his gaze fell across the computer, sitting dark and quiet on the table, and he snapped his fingers. "Holy shit," he said. "I clean forgot to look for the video. Been so busy getting ready for the big event it slipped my mind." A glance toward Janeka. "Bet your boyfriend's shittin' bricks, huh?" She didn't answer him and he didn't wait for it, nodding instead toward Pym. "Why don't you fire it up, Sergeant?"

With a grunt, Pym came around on his chair, turned the computer on, and started banging at the keys. Moments later, McLarty emitted a cackle of delight that banged off the walls of the old warehouse as the image of Pym, massive and sullen, came onscreen, reciting their manifesto while Malcolm sat in front of him, dazed and disheveled, grimacing in pain and not quite in the world.

"There it is," cried McLarty, as if they could not see. "He did it! Good going, Bob. They know we're serious, by God. The white man has taken all he's going to take!" Another laugh as he slapped Pym's broad back. Pym allowed himself a grin of satisfaction at the sight of himself on the screen.

"Look here," he said, pointing to the counter beneath the image. "Over 60,000 hits."

"I told you, didn't I? I told you!"

"You told me," agreed Pym, still grinning, fatigue apparently forgotten. "This is so fucking cool."

"You know what I'm going to do?" McLarty had whipped a piece of scrap paper from his pocket. "I'm going to call this chick's boyfriend. Poor sap's been waiting for hours. Told him I would let her go if he got the video posted online. Lend me your phone, will you? Mine's busted."

Clarence passed the phone across. "So, you're going to do it? You're going to let her go?"

McLarty, the scrap of paper in one hand as he punched numbers in with the thumb of the other, looked up with an incredulous grin. "Are you kidding? Fuck no fuck no fuck no. She dies like everybody else."

They had covered the last block on foot so the sound of the van's engine would not alert Pym and McLarty to their presence. That is, assuming Pym and McLarty were even there.

This was, Bob had come to believe, a very big assumption. He had reached a conclusion based on conjecture and hope, a need to be doing something other than just passively waiting while other people decided his fate—and Janeka's. But he'd had time to think about it while navigating his way here, first barreling through traffic, then creeping along as they got closer to the area, and he had concluded he was probably wrong.

Who did he think he was? Spenser? Mike Hammer? What he'd done wasn't deduction. It was the glorified hunch of a man who desperately needed it to be true, and for that reason it was as unreliable as the stock market. Raintree was right. This was work best left to people who knew what the hell they were doing, not some clumsy amateur driven by four decades of carrying a torch for a girl he knew in college.

Bob had almost turned back. But what the heck? He was so close, he might as well follow through. At this point, what could it hurt?

He came creeping around the side of the building, Amy behind him, feeling like some kind of fool, eager to just get this over with. He peered around a corner into what turned out to be a short, narrow alley with no exit, closed on the far end by a brick wall.

There was a white van parked there with what appeared, in the light from the street lamps, to be metal drums in the back. And parked behind it was a red pickup truck.

"Holy shit," said Amy, gaping from behind him.

"Yeah," said Bob.

His gaze went again to the van and the drums inside. He wondered why the sight sent a coldness radiating through him. And then he knew. Bob hardly dared to breathe. "I think they're building a bomb," he whispered.

Amy said, "Shhh. Listen."

She was pointing toward an open rollup door he had not noticed before. Through it, he heard Dwayne McLarty say very clearly, "I told you, didn't I? I told you!"

Another voice—Pym, he assumed—agreed. "You told me. This is so fucking cool."

It was them. He had done it. He had actually found them. And maybe Janeka was in there, alive and unharmed. Bob's heart hammered like a carpenter.

"Bob?" whispered Amy.

"Yeah?"

"We've got to call the cops, remember? Get Raintree down here."

"Right!" He grabbed his cellphone off the holster on his belt and brought it up to the light so he could look for Raintree's number.

And right at that instant, the phone chirped.

Loudly.

"Oh shit," said Amy.

McLarty's voice said, "What the fuck? You hear that?"

"Yeah," said Pym. "Somebody's out there." Then he yelled. "Who's out there?"

"Run!" hissed Amy.

They ran. They ran as fast as they could. It was not nearly fast enough.

Bob, who hit the gym on a regular basis, was still in good shape for a man of nearly 60 years, and he might have had a chance if he had been alone. But he wasn't. Amy was body sore, still half concussed, and by all rights, should have been curled up on a couch with a teddy bear and a bowl of chicken soup. Bob grabbed her hand and tried to pull her along, but it was no use.

She stumbled after him as best she could, but together they were no match for the speed at which the hopped-up little meth freak came tearing out of the old warehouse, waving that absurd pistol and yelling "Stop, motherfucker! Stop, or I'll shoot!"

Bob looked back at Amy. She knew what he was thinking. "Don't you stop," she told him. "Leave me here! Get help!" She tried to wrench her hand free of his.

Bob stopped.

An instant later, McLarty was on them. "All right," he snarled, "you got, like, two seconds to tell me who the fuck you are and—" Then he squinted in the pale light, recognition brightening his face. "Bob?" McLarty laughed. "Bob, is that you?"

"Yeah," said Bob. "Small world."

"And you." He looked closer at Amy. "That crazy bitch who slugged me. Ought to pop you right now." And holding the gun sideways, he pressed the muzzle hard against Amy's temple, pushing her head back. Her hands came up and she jammed her eyes shut and Bob tried to think of what to say, what to do, because this could not happen in front of him, it simply could not. But his mind was as empty as an abandoned house.

McLarty grinned. "Nah," he said, pulling the pistol away. "I'm just fuckin' with you. We got plenty time for that later." He confiscated their cellphones and motioned with the gun. "Come on inside. Let's get acquainted."

And what else could they do? Bob lifted his hands like the captive in some old TV western. He and Amy walked back toward the building and stepped through the rollup door. It took Bob's eyes a moment to adjust when they entered the warehouse. Two lanterns punched blinding holes in the darkness and he had to shield his eyes.

"We got visitors," announced McLarty merrily. "This here is Bob. And this other one here is Amy. They're the ones work for the jewspaper."

"Bob?"

"Bob, how...?"

The second voice was Malcolm's, but Bob barely heard it. Because the first voice that reached him from out of that darkness had been Janeka's. He had been so frightened. He had been so *terrified*. "Janeka, are you in here?"

"Yeah, she's here," growled McLarty. "Where else she going to be? Now all of you shut the fuck up."

"How'd they find us?"

Bob's eyes were adjusting themselves to the light and he could make out the shape of the mammoth man who asked the question. He was the same one who had read the manifesto on the video.

"I don't know," answered McLarty in the same carefree voice. "Why don't you ask 'em, real nice-like?"

"How'd you find us?" demanded Pym.

The big man stood above him. Lowering his hands, which had been lifted all this time, Bob fixed his gaze on Pym as best he could. "Your mother says hi," he said.

Pym's eyes squeezed down to mere slits. There was, Bob noticed, a vivid, angry scar that had not been there on the video. "What do you know about my mother?" demanded Pym.

"Irene Funicelli," said Bob, affecting a nonchalant shrug. "We just left her. We showed her the video. She's very concerned about you."

Panic lit Pym's eyes. "You leave my mom out of this," he said.

"I'm just telling you what she said," said Bob. "It broke her heart, that video."

"She wasn't supposed to see that."

"How did you think she wouldn't see it? The whole world has seen it."

Now Pym simply looked helpless, like a child. "*She* wasn't supposed to see it," he repeated. He looked at Bob. "How'd you even find my mother?"

Bob thought of saying that he had gone to McLarty's house first and found Pym's number scrawled on a wall, but the jumpy little rat with the gun would know what else Bob had seen there. No telling how that might play out. So instead, he just shrugged. "We're reporters. That's what we do, we find stuff out."

McLarty was scratching his chin thoughtfully with the muzzle of the gun. "Seems to me there's a bigger issue here, Sergeant," he said. "Fuck how they found your mom. We need to know how they found *us*."

Again, Bob shrugged. "Irene Funicelli, Ben Funicelli, Funn Toys. It's a simple connection. I'm sure the cops will make it soon enough themselves."

Pym's frightened eyes shot McLarty a question. McLarty said, "Nah, don't worry about it, Sergeant. They got lucky is all. One in a million shot. Hell, if it was that easy to make the connection, cops would be all over this place right now." With a theatrical gesture, he cupped a hand to his ear. "I don't hear no sirens."

"I guess you're right." Pym didn't sound convinced.

"Of course I'm right. Of course I'm right. Of course I'm right. The problem we have right now is this: We've got work to do and we have too many fucking hostages to keep an eye on while we do it. It's time to cull the herd, Sergeant."

"What do you mean?"

But Bob already knew. Icebergs swam through his arteries. He could not feel his legs beneath him.

"I mean, we got to kill them," said McLarty, as if amazed by his friend's obtuseness.

"Kill them?"

"Sure," said McLarty. "Let's see who's first. Eenie meenie minie moe." He bobbed the gun in time to the old children's rhyme. With the last syllable, it fell on Janeka. She was still sitting on the floor with her back to them, craning her head, trying to get a view. Bob could only see one eye and it was round with terror.

Now McLarty went to her, racked the slide and pointed the pistol at her forehead. "Sorry, babe. Any last words?"

Bob roared. "*No!* Leave her alone, goddamn you! You fucking animal! You want to shoot somebody, you bastard? Shoot me! Shoot me!"

McLarty grinned. "Okay," he said.

And he shot Bob.

twenty-five

Bob Carson seemed to fall in slow motion. He collapsed in sections, head dropping first, torso bending at the point of impact, arms coming up to protect what was already wounded, legs buckling, then giving way, the whole of him, falling. It seemed to take all day. Seemed something other than real. When, finally, Bob hit the floor, Malcolm stared at Amy, needing confirmation, he supposed, that this was actual, that it had just happened right in front of him. And of course, it had. He could tell with just a glance at her that she had seen what he had seen. Her eyes were pools of white in a face that hung slack on her skull like a bag on a hook.

"You shot him."

Pym's astonished whisper was unnaturally loud in the sudden, claustrophobic silence that filled the old warehouse.

McLarty shrugged. "Of course I did. Said I was going to, didn't I?"

Then, as if she had been too stunned to process it until this very second, Janeka suddenly cried out Bob's name and began crawling on her stomach—her ankles were still bound by duct tape—to where he had fallen, right near Malcolm's feet. McLarty stepped over and stood straddling her. "Look at this," he said idly. "Look at this, look at this. She had her fucking hands free and you didn't even notice. Piss-poor job of checking on the captives, Sergeant." He raised the gun.

"That's enough," said Pym.

"The fuck it is," said McLarty, the barrel of the pistol two inches off the back of Janeka's skull. "She goes next. Then that bitch over there who slugged me. We can keep this one if you want. He's not going anywhere with those cuffs on him. We can chain him to the front of the van just like we planned."

Janeka, still inching her way forward, seemed not to notice any of this, seemed oblivious to everything except the need to reach Bob, who lay there still as death, the blood on his shirt front glistening in the pallid light. "Bob," she whispered, "please, honey, please. Please don't...please don't..."

"'Please, honey, please...'" mimicked McLarty in a high, singsong voice. Then he laughed.

"I said, 'That's enough,'" Pym told McLarty. His voice had taken on a knife's edge of command.

McLarty noticed. His eyes came up. "How many times do I have to keep reminding you: I'm your commanding officer, not the other way around. What the fuck did you join this man's militia for, Sergeant, if you're going to turn pussy over every little thing?"

"I joined it to carry out a mission," said Pym. "I didn't join it to be a fucking animal. Now give me the gun, Captain. I'll watch the prisoners."

Janeka had reached Bob and was cradling his head, still oblivious to this argument about her very life. She rocked back and forth with Bob in her lap, moaning through her tears.

McLarty said, "What? The hell I will. Who the fuck is going to help me paint the armor and finish wiring the bomb if you're in here babysitting?"

"You can handle it. May take a little longer, but you can do it."

"Well, why should I trust you to watch the prisoners? You're so soft, how do I know you won't just turn 'em all loose soon as my back is turned?"

"You know I won't," said Pym.

"Oh yeah oh yeah oh yeah?" said McLarty. "Funny thing, now that I think about it, how you never noticed this bitch had got her hands loose. For all I know, you're the one helped her do it."

Pym raised one of those big hands. "You know better. Now come on, Dwayne, give me the gun. I'll keep an eye on them, you finish getting the van ready, and we can accomplish our mission like soldiers."

McLarty said, "You do know we got to kill them, don't you?"

Pym said, "Maybe. We don't have to do it now, though, do we?"

They stared at one another for a long time. Finally McLarty heaved a sigh. "Aw fuck," he said. "Aw fuck, aw fuck." There was something in his voice of the petulant child surrendering to his mother. He put the gun into Pym's hand. "Just keep an eye on them, okay? Can you do that at least?"

"Yeah," said Pym. "Let me know when you're ready."

He watched as McLarty took one of the lanterns and went out to the van. McLarty opened the front door and removed cans of spray paint. In the dim glow of the cabin light, Malcolm was able to make out an evil sight: two assault rifles were propped against the passenger seat side by side, twin promises of carnage.

"Jesus," he breathed.

Pym watched McLarty go with no apparent interest and then nudged Janeka with his foot. "How's he doing?" he asked.

"How do you think he's doing?" she spat. Her eyes were glistening. "He needs a doctor. He needs a hospital."

"That's not going to happen," said Pym.

He motioned to Amy with the pink pistol. "You get over here with these others, so I can see you," he said. "Behave yourself and I won't have to tie you up." Amy did as she was told, taking a seat on the floor to Malcolm's left, right at Bob's feet. She did not speak. Terror had made her mute.

"What kind of man are you?" demanded Janeka, tears in her voice.

Pym grunted as he sat down at the table. "Right now, I'm a man who could use a beer," he said.

"You know this is wrong," said Malcolm. "Your friend out there might be crazy, but you're not."

Pym ignored him. He turned his back and started tapping on the computer keyboard until he had brought up the live stream from the conservative cable news channel. The handcuff key, noted Malcolm, was still on the table at his elbow. "America's news," Pym intoned with rich satisfaction, "unbiased and unafraid." This was the news channel's much-parodied slogan. "Unhinged and untrustworthy" would have been more accurate, in Malcolm's view.

"Please," said Janeka, her voice rough. "He's going to die if he doesn't get help soon. Please, sir. I don't want him to die."

Pym picked up the roll of duct tape and tossed it back to Janeka without looking. "Tape that tight over the wound," he said. "Keep the pressure on. Might stop the bleeding." He rummaged on the table and found the gauze he had meant to use to dress the wound on his face earlier that day, and the antiseptic he had sprayed onto it. "Use these," he said, tossing it all over his shoulder as well. "Best I can do."

Janeka picked these things up from the floor. "This is not good enough," she said. "He didn't cut his finger. He was shot."

"It's all you got," said Pym. "Besides, Dwayne's probably right. Probably have to kill all of you anyway before it's done. I'm just too soft-hearted."

"Your mother must be so proud," said Malcolm.

Pym looked around. "You leave her out of this," he said.

"Actually, she's a nice lady." Amy's voice was soft. They looked toward her.

"She's right." Bob said this.

His voice was raspy and weak, but hearing it, Janeka laughed in happy surprise. "Bob?" she said. "Oh, thank God. Don't try to talk."

Bob shook his head. "She's right," he repeated. "You look at her, you look at this guy, and you wonder what happened. How did she give birth to this?"

"Bob, save your strength, honey." Janeka was peeling tape off the roll with fresh energy. Unable to tear it with her hands, she used her teeth.

"Janeka," he said, "there's so much I need to tell you."

She wouldn't hear it. "Shush," she said. "Tell me later. Tell me later." Bob fell silent as Janeka opened his jacket and tore at his shirt to reach the wound in his side.

Amy spoke on, spoke over them, still marveling at the mystery of Pym's mother. "You want her to be a monster," she said in a soft, wondering voice. "After you see her son on the video? You expect that. But she's not a monster. She's this nice lady in this nice house who's had a real hard time of it in her life, including marrying a couple of really shitty men and raising a son with special needs. But she persevered, you know? You have to admire that. She did everything she could for her boy. I felt sorry for her."

Pym had been looking down at the live stream on the computer. Now he looked at Amy. She said, "When this comes out, it's going to kill her. You realize that, don't you? It's just going to kill her."

"You shut up talking about her," said Pym. "I swear, you shut up about her or I'll make you sorry."

Amy fell quiet. There was silence then except for the tinny music from the laptop's speakers. It was a fanfare of drums and horns and then, on the screen, the august, snowy-haired anchor, who had covered every presidential election since 1960, gave the latest results. As he intoned the name of each state, a white image of that state turned the appropriate color, pinwheeled three times, and then flew, trailing red, white, and blue stardust, to deposit itself in either of two columns: one on the left headed by a stern image of Barack Obama, the other on the right headed by a smiling John McCain. A counter directly beneath each man's chin kept tally of his electoral total. Headlines of other news crept across the bottom of the screen just above a ticker that was at this moment announcing the Dow Jones industrial average had closed that day at 9,625.28. A station logo was in the bottom right corner.

It was a busy screen.

But when the states had finished their pinwheeling and flying to opposite corners trailing stardust the color of patriotism, it turned out that Connecticut, Delaware, Maine, Massachusetts, Maryland, New Jersey, and New Hampshire had all turned blue and placed themselves in the column headed by Obama. Oklahoma, Tennessee, West Virginia, and South Carolina had gone for McCain.

Out of nowhere, Pym rose from his chair, looming over Amy as redwoods loom over shrubs, his fists clenched, roaring at her. "*You don't know anything about it, do you hear?*" It took Malcolm a moment to process this, to realize Pym was returning to the subject he had ordered Amy to abandon several minutes before, as if unable or unwilling to leave it alone. "Just because you talked to her for a few minutes, you think you know something about her or me? You think you know *anything*? You got a lot of nerve, you know that? Fuck you, lady. Fuck you!"

Amy cowered beneath the onslaught.

"Hey, look," said Malcolm, feeling not unlike a man trying to lure a bad dog with a juicy steak, "there's M.J. There's Jordan."

The election coverage had gone to a commercial break and on the screen Michael Jordan, tongue wagging behind him, was climbing through the air toward the basket in slow motion, bringing the ball down like a hammer on some backpedaling defender who looked as if he just wanted to get out of the way. Flashbulbs twinkled behind them like stars in the sky. In the voiceover, Jordan was saying something wise about the virtues of hard work and persistence. The logo of an athletic shoemaker came on the screen.

"Best there ever was," said Malcolm, "best there ever will be."

Pym's glare was dull. "You're just trying to change the subject," he said. "You just want me to leave her alone."

"Of course I do," said Malcolm. "She doesn't deserve you yelling at her just because she thinks your mother is a nice lady. You ought to take that as a compliment. Most people would."

"I ain't most people."

"No, what you are is embarrassed," said Malcolm. "You don't like anyone to mention her because it reminds you that what you're doing is not something that nice lady would approve. I bet you it would horrify her, wouldn't it? I bet you you're not the man she hoped you would be, are you? She raised you to be better than this, didn't she? What would she think of you right now, Clarence?"

Pym shook his head. "You won't let it go, will you? Always trying to get inside my head. Always trying to get a rise."

"I just think you're not nearly as stupid as you pretend to be," said Malcolm. "Not stupid at all."

"Oh yeah? I got news for you, Clarence. Thinking you and that jumpy little meth head out there are superior human beings because your skin is white? That's stupid. Thinking you're going to get anywhere near that park? That's stupid. Thinking you're going to kill Obama? That's really stupid. Thinking that two lone idiots constitute a militia? Stupid. Thinking you're going to do anything except hurt a bunch of innocent people and then die for no reason? Supremely, incredibly stupid."

"Shut up."

"And the worst thing is, you know it. You know all of this without me even saying it. Because you're right. You're not really stupid at all. But you pretend to be. You let yourself be led by that loser out there even though you know it's wrong, even though it's useless, even though you know you're smarter than he is. You're better than he is."

"I told you to shut up."

"You smarter and you're better," repeated Malcolm.

"I said, 'Shut up.'" Pym raised the gun.

"Go ahead," said Malcolm. He lifted his chin. "Shoot me because you don't have the guts to face the truth. Go ahead and do it. I don't care. I'm sick of you. You're a coward and a hypocrite. Go on, Clarence. Pull the trigger. You'd be doing me a favor."

Pym pursed his lips. He looked confused.

Amy piped up in a trembling voice. "You know, your partner killed his family, probably with that gun. Bob climbed through the window. He saw their dead bodies."

"You're lying." Pym glanced over at Amy, kept the gun trained on Malcolm.

"She's...telling the...truth. I did climb in. I did...see." Bob tried to say more. His face contorted in a spasm of pain and he fell silent.

"She *is* telling the truth," said Janeka. "I know because I was there when he did it. It was when he was on the way here. He stopped by a house and he took me in there and he shot some guy. Then he went down a hallway and I heard a woman's voice and two more gunshots. The house was on Winnebago Street. Is that where his mother lives? How would I know that if I wasn't there?"

"You're all lying. Just shut up! You hear me? Just shut up."

He looked from one of them to the other. The gun had gone limp in his fist. "I don't want to hear anything else out of any of you," he said. "You're lying."

"No we're not," said Malcolm. He spoke with a cold resolve. "And you know that, too."

Pym stared at Malcolm for a long moment. In the sudden silence, Malcolm heard the sound effect for a state pinwheeling and looked up to the screen in time to see Pennsylvania deposit itself in the column beneath the unsmiling Barack Obama. The Illinois senator had 80 electoral votes. His opponent had 39.

Pym turned his back on them. He laid the gun on the table within easy reach, sat down, and focused his attention on the news live-streaming to his computer. Malcolm could no longer see the screen—Pym's bulk precluded this—but he could hear the states spinning and the white-haired anchor commiserating with conservative pundits who analyzed the developments in tones that could only be described as morose, if not downright funereal.

Bob's breathing was labored and Malcolm wondered how much longer he could last. From overhead, the buzz of traffic from the highway drifted in. From outside, there came the hiss of an aerosol can as McLarty sprayed paint on the armor plating. He was idly humming a happy song.

Malcolm seethed with frustration. Pym was just sitting there, no gun in hand, his broad back unprotected. It wasn't a good chance, but it was the best one they were ever likely to get. But Malcolm was chained, Janeka's feet were bound, Bob was shot. The only one who had the opportunity to make some crazy, desperate play for freedom was Amy. A glance told Malcolm that was not going to happen. She sat on the floor with her knees under her chin, eyes seeing nothing, drawn up inside herself and shivering as if naked in a blizzard. She would not try anything.

"You really met my mother? You're not just bullshitting?"

Pym spoke without moving. His voice surprised them. It seemed to issue from some desolate cave within him.

Amy glanced up, surprised to be addressed. "Yes," she said. "She has a very nice house with flowers out front. She lives over on Baxter Street. All your school pictures are lined up on the mantel. Up above on the wall is a big portrait of you and her together. You don't look too happy, but you can tell, Mrs. Funicelli really loves her son."

Pym grunted. "Yeah," he said. "Never did like taking pictures on account of my size."

A silence intervened. Then he asked, still without moving, "You got any kids?"

"I have two," said Amy. "Daughters. Cynthia and Ella."

"You're a good mother?"

"I try to be. Probably work too many hours."

"You got a husband?"

"Anthony. He's a corporate lawyer. Out of town on a business trip. Though I expect he's probably rushing home right about now."

Pym nodded. The silence fell again.

Janeka spoke. "What about you?" she asked. "Do you have any children?"

"I don't want to talk anymore," said Pym.

Janeka looked up at Malcolm. The whites of her eyes glistened in the shadows cast by the battery-operated lantern.

Time passed.

On the computer screen, the sound of states spinning and changing colors continued every so often, mixed with the drone of talking heads analyzing numbers. Janeka cooed softly to Bob, who drifted in and out of consciousness, occasionally grunting with pain. From the alleyway outside, McLarty continued to hum as he painted his armor and tinkered with his bomb.

Malcolm barely heard.

He closed his eyes. He hung his head.

He walked the streets of Memphis again, 20 years old again, angry again, crying "Black power!" again, a gun sitting heavy in his pocket again, just waiting for some cracker, some whitey, some honky, to give him an excuse to use it. He stared at them again, convinced again that they were fundamentally different from him and that whatever they had of humanity inside them was a flame too small, too flickering, too fleeting, to matter. He watched them watching him, seeing him but not seeing him at all, seeing him but really seeing whatever it was that came up in their minds when they plugged in the tape marked "nigger" and let it play. He watched them and knew that they were beyond redemption. And he was glad he had his gun.

This was the man he had been. But then life had happened, as life will.

And he had grown away from that rage, away from that unfocused fury toward a faceless them, had come to accept as true the old axiom that hatred corrodes the vessel that carries it, and this had made him a better man. He had seen 40 years pass and in those years, he had married and mourned a glorious woman, raised two children, and lived a celebrated life. Yet all of it had only brought him to last night, and to writing an angry column that said, "I am sick and tired of white folks' bullshit." He had announced that he had given up on the idea that white people might ever be redeemed. He had told America to go to hell. It was as if he had lived those 40 years thinking he was going forward, only to find he had simply traveled in a great wide gyre to become again that angry 20-year-old walking the streets, loaded and ready.

Malcolm's disappointment with his own life was matched only by his sense of estrangement from American dreams.

Not only had he traveled 40 years to become again who he once was, but had not America done the very same thing? Look at all the young black men in jail or shot to death just for being black. Look at the poverty rate. Look at the unemployment rate. Look at the achievement gap. And look at these two, this ridiculous, delusional pair who fancied themselves an army of redemption, this raggedy little meth addict and his giant companion whose hatred, whose burning sense of birthright stolen, whose conviction that they had been done wrong by all the forces of history and change, was so palpable and deep they might as well have stepped into this warehouse straight out of 1953, 1921, or 1878. Looking at them, how could you believe time had passed? How could you believe progress—*any* progress—had been made?

So what good was any of it? What good were Malcolm's years of writing columns, seeking by the force of his reason and the excellence of his words to cajole and convince white America? For that matter, what good were King's speeches, what good was Malcolm X's fire, what good were the NAACP's court filings, what good were Jesse's singsong rhymes or Stevie's brotherhood songs, if at the end of it all, 40 years later, you wound up chained to a chair pleading for your life with a giant misanthrope who called you nigger in one breath and in the next cited to you events from the legend of Michael Jordan?

What good? What good? What damn good?

The question covered him like ground fog on tarmac. The realization did, too: Malcolm had wasted his life. It had all been for nothing.

"Looks like this is it."

Pym's voice tried to tug Malcolm up out of himself. He did not want to come. What was the use of opening his eyes only to bear witness to some new obscenity or insanity? What was the point of being in the world if the world was only going to shit on you and disappoint you and make you feel like a goddamn fool for ever having dreamed or believed? Malcolm did not want to open his eyes.

He opened them anyway.

Pym was standing, his hand cupping his mouth, calling to McLarty. "Dwayne, you might want to see this."

A moment later, McLarty came in, wiping his greasy hands on a greasy rag. "What's going on?" he said.

"They're about to call the West Coast," said Pym. "I think this is it."

Malcolm looked at the screen. He blinked. He blinked again. Obama had 207 electoral votes, McCain, 135.

The white-haired anchor faced the camera. He looked drawn and sad, like a surgeon after a long night in the operating room about to tell a mother that her son has died on the table. "With results coming in from some key western states," he said, "we are now ready to make a projection. Polls are closed now in California, Washington and Oregon and it appears—"

The screen went black.

The screen went black!

Malcolm caught himself straining toward the dead computer. "Fix it!" he told Pym.

"Battery died," said Pym with a shrug.

The two of them stared at one another helplessly, silently.

Then Malcolm heard it. It was a sound so faint that at first he wasn't even sure it was a sound, wasn't sure it wasn't just his mind playing tricks on his ears. Then he saw Amy's eyes and Janeka's eyes, saw Pym looking meaningfully at McLarty, and he knew they all heard it, too. Distant and dim but real, carrying across the night and through the door of the old warehouse.

A roar of delirious joy lifted from Grant Park.

In that moment, something rose inside Malcolm that he had not expected and could not name. Something proud. Something with gnarled roots and feathered wings. He felt unexpected tears massing behind his eyes. He felt the painful warmth of dawn breaking behind his sternum. He saw Janeka, tears wetting her face, put her forehead to Bob's and whisper something Malcolm could not hear. From somewhere deep within the cavern of his own suffering, Bob smiled.

It had happened.

Holy hell, it had happened.

Barack Obama had won the election. Barack Obama was going to be president. Of the United States. A black man, president.

Holy hell.

"I guess that settles that," said McLarty. "No turning back now. Time to do this time to do this time to do this. Go get the suits, Sergeant. Let's get dressed. Let's do this with style."

Pym did as he was told, using his lantern to light his way to the other side of the cavernous room.

McLarty lifted his own lantern, casting harsh light upon his four captives. He grinned a malignant grin. "I guess you niggers and nigger-lovers are happy now. You got what you wanted. Your socialist nigger was elected. Old Hussein Obama goes up on the wall next to Ronald Reagan and all those other great men. Well, I wouldn't celebrate too much if I was you. Because tonight is the night white Christian America finally wakes up and starts to take its country back."

"Here's your suit." Pym had come up behind him. In one hand, he carried the two white suits in their clear plastic garment bags, in the other, the two top hats.

"Good job, Sergeant." McLarty accepted the smaller bag and hat. "Let's get dressed."

"Where are we going to change?" asked Pym.

McLarty gave him a surprised look. "Right here, of course. Right here right here right here."

"You mean, here...in front of...right where they can...?"

"Yeah. What do you expect? We're going to go over there in the corner and give one of these bitches the chance to go running for help? 'Course, we wouldn't even have that problem if I'd gone ahead and killed them like I wanted."

Pym was still hesitant. "What about if I go over in that corner behind those pallets and change first while you watch the prisoners, and then you can—"

"We don't have time for your bashfulness, Sergeant. We've got a time-table here. Ol' Barry Hussein Soetoro is probably already on his way to the park. Let's go let's go let's go."

Pym gazed around him with the glassy eyes of a man trapped inside his own nightmare. Malcolm had the sense he wanted to run. There was a moment when he thought the big man might do it. Instead, Pym dutifully unzipped his garment bag and pulled out the white suit. McLarty did the same.

The smaller man was quick and matter of fact about it, stripping out of his windbreaker and jeans down to his tighty whities, which were in fact not tight, but sagged on his bony, drug-withered frame. His movements brisk and businesslike, he stepped into the pants, pulled on the shirt—his filthy hands left black smudges on each—fastened the cummerbund, and fixed the clip-on bowtie.

Pym, by contrast, stood there for a long moment with his great head falling almost to his chest, his eyes downcast. He didn't begin tugging at his T-shirt until McLarty was mostly dressed. The little man stood there tapping his foot to show his impatience, but Pym would not be rushed. He peeled off the T-shirt as if he were peeling back his own skin. Malcolm wondered if Clarence Pym had ever undressed in front of another human being before.

Then the shirt came over his head and Malcolm saw. Pym's flesh dripped off him like wax from a burning candle. It tumbled down, hanging in great rolls, creasing itself in deep crevices. There was simply too much of him, a fact of which Pym, with his dazed face and slow movement, seemed freshly and painfully aware as he stripped in front of these strangers. Slowly, he pulled down his pants to reveal the red boxer shorts hanging like a flag from his massive behind.

"Come on come on come on!" snapped McLarty.

Still Pym ignored him. With the same dazed and deliberate movements, he pulled on his tuxedo shirt. His hands were so big he fumbled with the buttons, but eventually, he managed. He pulled on the pants next, got them zipped, sat down and stuffed his feet into patent leather shoes the color of snow. With slow, awkward hands, he clipped on the bowtie. Finally, he shrugged on the coat. Then he stood next to McLarty, his head still down. "About time," McLarty said. "About time about time."

McLarty donned his top hat. Pym followed suit. McLarty tipped his hat to the side. "Well, how do we look?" he asked Malcolm brightly.

They looked ridiculous. Pym, in particular. He looked like a sad polar bear in a top hat. But for some reason, Malcolm could not make himself say that. He settled for saying, "You look like you're going to the prom."

"Didn't go to no prom," said Pym in a baleful voice. "But you probably already guessed that."

"I wasn't trying to insult you," said Malcolm.

"What the fuck do I care what you were trying to do?" said Pym. "You think I give a shit what you think?" But his eyes carried wounds.

"Come on," said McLarty, speaking to Pym but looking at Malcolm, "let's get him hitched up to the front of the van. I'll get the ordnance. You bring the prisoner. When we get him hitched up, then I'll come back and take care of these others."

"I don't want to kill them," said Pym. "This guy, he's enough."

McLarty's eyes were windows of his disgust. "Goddamn it," he said. "I knew you were going to do that. I knew it I knew it I knew it."

Pym's head was still a weight, sitting heavily upon his chest. "Let's just leave them here, Dwayne," he said. "The white woman there, she's got kids. And the other guy, he's already been shot. He probably won't live anyway."

"You know, Clarence, I was afraid you were going to pull some shit like this. Here we have a chance to really make a mark, really do this with some style, and you're too fucking pansy to go through with it. What we do right here, this could ignite a movement."

"I don't want to hurt them is all," mumbled Pym. "I don't see the reason."

"The reason is because I say so, dummy!"

Pym's head came up. "Don't call me that, Dwayne." He was no longer mumbling.

"What else can I call you? What else what else what else? You're worried about killing three people? If this mission goes like we plan, we'll kill 300. Maybe even 3,000!"

"Yeah, but we won't see any of those people. It's different. These guys, it's more...personal."

"Personal? Personal? Personal? That's the stupidest thing I've ever heard. It's always personal when you kill somebody, Sergeant. You can damn well bet it's personal to them if nobody else!"

He paused, disgust blowing out of him in great angry gusts. Finally, he said, "Okay, you don't want to lay a hand on the other three, fine. Can we at least take care of this guy?" He thrust an index finger toward Malcolm. "That's what we got him for, isn't it? Can we at least do that? Or is that also too much for your poor tender conscience?"

Pym shrugged. "I guess we can do that," he said.

"Well, halle-fucking-lujah," said McLarty. "Bring the prisoner. I'll get the ordnance."

McLarty went to the van to retrieve the guns. Pym snatched the pink pistol from the table where he had laid it while pulling off his T-shirt. He also picked up the handcuff key. He handed that to Amy, waving her over to Malcolm with the pistol. "Let him loose," he said.

Amy rose to do as she was told. With a crisp click, the cuffs around Malcolm's ankle sprang open. Then the cuffs around his wrists did the same. Malcolm ached in too many places to count. His joints were solid like something forgotten in the back of the freezer. He could barely make himself move.

"You." Pym was pointing one thick finger at Amy. "You wait until we're gone, you hear? Then you can leave and call for help. But you don't move til we're gone. You understand that?"

Amy nodded briskly.

"Don't do this," Janeka pleaded. "Those people in that park, they've done nothing to you."

Pym wasn't listening. He looked down at Bob. "Hope he makes it," he said. "That's a hell of a thing he did, finding us here when even the cops couldn't. He must really like you."

Then Pym's attention turned to Malcolm. "Get up," he said.

"Hold on," said Malcolm. "I can barely move."

"Oh, and I guess I'm supposed to come over there and help you and you're going to jump out of that chair and stick a thumb in my eye. Is that how you've got it planned?"

"No, I..."

Pym swung the pistol around. "Get up," he said. "Don't make me tell you twice."

Malcolm put both hands on the chair and pushed. It was agony. He came off the chair slowly, joints and tendons screaming curses and protests. With an effort, he stood upright.

Pym motioned with the gun. "Walk," he said.

Malcolm complied as best he could, his gait shuffling and slow, favoring his right leg. Behind him, he could hear Amy crying. Ahead of him, he saw the little meth freak standing at the door, an assault rifle in each hand, grinning his maniac's grin.

Malcolm went back to Memphis. He went back to the balcony of the Lorraine Motel. Martin Luther King stood there in the gathering twilight, feeling pretty good for a change, bantering with his men, getting ready to go to dinner, sensing Malcolm coming up on his left, about to turn and smile in greeting. And across the street, the window opens. And Malcolm sees it, sees the snout of that rifle, that Remington Gamemaster 760, poking through.

And in the very instant of his seeing it, there is a bang and a 30.06 bullet, a bullet with enough stopping power to fell a buck dead in its tracks, strikes King on the right side of his face and he drops like a sack of flour and gore flies up and paints the overhang of the balcony and everybody ducks and Malcolm just stands there impotent, useless, and pathetic.

For 40 years, that failure had been with him. He had never told anyone, he had sought no psychiatric help, he had said nothing. He had simply lived with it, this secret shame that haunted his dreams, the knowledge that he had seen, yet done nothing.

Not again. Not this time.

He might die tonight—no, he almost certainly *would* die tonight—but he would not just allow the thing to happen in front of him while he failed to act. Not again. That much, he swore.

Malcolm knew that whatever it was he did, he had to do it now, while he was still free. Once they chained him to the hood of the van, he wouldn't have a chance.

But what?

He thought of all the hours of television he had watched as a boy and a young man, all the times he had seen the likes of Joe Mannix and Little Joe Cartwright move like lightning and disarm men who had the drop on them, knock the gun away in one quick motion, deliver a solid haymaker in the next. But that was television and besides, after having his car rear-ended this morning, after sitting in that chair for 16 hours, after blowing out candles on his sixtieth birthday cake, Malcolm knew one thing for sure: there was no lightning caged in his bones.

But he had to do something. He couldn't not do something. Not again.
Think. Think.

He was struck by the sheer ridiculousness of what he was demanding of himself. He was no action hero. Indeed, as a man who spent his days crafting arguments on a computer screen, he was about as far from an action hero as it was possible to get. All day, he had tried to use the skills he did have to move Pym, had tried to use logic and provocation to persuade this strange and somehow tragic man to see what he refused to see, but that had netted him nothing. Pym refused to see, refused to be moved. So Malcolm's options had come down, absurdly, to trying to think of what Joe Mannix might do in his place.

Malcolm went through the door, hands held high. Behind him, McLarty handed one of the assault rifles to Pym, who slung it over his shoulder.

Malcolm took inventory, tried to see everything, to view it the way an action hero would. There had to be something here that could help him. He felt the pistol poking him in the back and realized he had stopped just outside the door.

He walked around toward the back of the van. Except that it wasn't a van anymore. It was a tank, its every surface and window covered with armor plating. The plating had even reduced the windshield to a mere slit of glass. Neon hate slogans festooned its sides.

WHITE AND PROUD!

NOBAMA!

WHITE AMERICA, RISE!

One of the panels carried a crude rendering of the Confederate battle flag. "She's a beauty, ain't she?" McLarty had come up on his side.

Malcolm did not speak.

Think. Think.

Now he stood behind the van, the back door of which still hung open. The back seats were gone. The cargo area was filled with two rows of barrels, linked by a profusion of wires running across the floor. This, Malcolm supposed, was the bomb.

McLarty had pulled the van up into a narrow alley closed off at the front. In that tight space, the doors to the cab could not be opened wide enough to accommodate someone of Pym's size. And the sliding door could not be opened, covered as it was with armor plating. Pym would have to climb in through the back, between the drums that constituted their bomb. And they would have to pull the van out into the open space on the other side of the warehouse if they intended to chain Malcolm to the grill.

They seemed to realize this at the same time Malcolm did. They looked at each other. McLarty shrugged. "Didn't think about that," he said. "Go on and climb in. I'll watch this guy."

Pym nodded. He pocketed the little pistol and began to shrug the assault rifle higher on his shoulder as he braced to climb into the van.

Now.

The thought and the action were simultaneous. Malcolm jabbed his elbow into Pym's side. It didn't hurt him much, but it surprised him. His hands went automatically to his stomach. Malcolm yanked at the rifle. The gun slid free.

Somewhere, Malcolm had seen—maybe he read it, maybe he saw it on television—that Timothy McVeigh had had a failsafe for his terrible device. There were multiple fuses, but in the event they failed, there was also some sort of contraption—a blasting cap, Malcolm supposed it was called—that could go off with the impact of a bullet and set off the unholy bomb. These two had aped that Opie-faced killer in so many other ways; Malcolm prayed to God they had also aped him in this. He lifted the rifle toward the rear of the van and pulled the trigger.

Nothing happened.

He pulled the trigger harder.

Nothing happened again.

Then Malcolm was on the ground, his skull throbbing from the impact of a rifle butt. McLarty, who had hit him, didn't even look at Malcolm beyond the instant it took him to snatch the rifle back and thrust it at Pym.

"How fucking stupid are you, Sergeant? What kind of soldier are you, you can't even keep hands on your own fucking gun?"

He smacked Pym on the back of the head with his open palm.

"You fucking idiot! Do you realize what almost happened here because of your carelessness?"

"What the *hell*, Dwayne?" Pym stared incredulously at the smaller man.

McLarty reached up and smacked Pym again on the back of the head. "Fuck fuck fuck, Clarence!" he snarled. Dwayne McLarty had become something...feral.

"Ow! " cried Clarence. "Dwayne, I told you not to hit me any—

McLarty cut him off by hitting him. And this time, McLarty smacked Pym hard enough that the big man hunched his head and bent double. When he did, his eyes met Malcolm's. It was like looking into a cauldron.

Rage burned there. Hatred burned there. Shame burned there. And hurt—years and years of hurt—burned there, too.

McLarty screamed. "Goddamnit, Sergeant!"

Pym's burning eyes met Malcolm's. Malcolm said, "What will your mother think, Clarence?"

He might have said more, but all at once, Pym was roaring like some wounded beast and bringing the rifle up. Malcolm closed his eyes and cringed, wondering how bad it would hurt, wondering if he would hear the shots.

But all he heard was the voice of Clarence Pym. It said, very clearly, "I'd run if I was you."

Malcolm opened his eyes. He saw Pym flip the safety selector on the AK-47 to fire mode.

Oh, shit.

Malcolm was coming to his feet as Pym was straightening up. Malcolm was running as Pym faced the bomb inside the van. Behind him, McLarty screamed, "No no no!"

Malcolm ran.

The rifle chattered.

The van exploded.

twenty-six

That morning after getting off work, Malcolm rode his bike downtown.

He was aware of the eyes on him, white people watching, their faces hard with suspicion—and also, he realized with a jolt, fear. A police officer riding shotgun in a cruiser eyeballed him hard. Malcolm pretended not to notice and kept on riding.

He rode until he got to an office building on Front Street with a Western Union in the lobby. He chained his bike to a lamppost outside and walked in. Some stubby white man in a straw fedora was ahead of Malcolm in line. He turned, shifting a bitter-smelling cigar from one corner of his mouth to the other as he stared at Malcolm with frank interest and even franker malice. Malcolm stared back. Eventually, the man turned away.

When the white man had finished his business and Malcolm reached the counter, he asked for a telegraph blank and then wrote out a message and handed it to the white woman in the cat's-eye glasses on the other side.

Writing to apologize. STOP. Behavior was inexcusable. STOP. Understand that now. STOP. Would like to return to school. STOP. Please give me another chance. STOP. Promise you won't be sorry. STOP.

She glanced up at him and he could see the questions dancing in her eyes, but she didn't ask. "Who's this going to?" she said.

Malcolm gave her the name and address of the dean at the white college who had suspended him. He paid for the telegram, went outside, and retrieved his bicycle. He rode past the white man with the smelly cigar, who

357

was making his way very slowly, leaning heavily on a cane. Malcolm felt the burn of the man's gaze in the center of his back.

He rode south through the wasteland of yesterday's violence. National Guardsmen stood on street corners smoking cigarettes, chatting together. They glanced up, appraising him as he passed. A personnel carrier went in the opposite direction, its treads rumbling and squeaking. The soldiers all turned their heads.

A few people were out in the riot zone, curious onlookers come to see the destruction for themselves, insurance adjusters with clipboards in hand, men with hammers and plywood nailing up the gaping maws of looted stores, merchants and proprietors scraping push brooms against the sidewalk. Glass glittered in dustpans that were emptied into cardboard boxes because no trashcans were available. Mounds of garbage towered over alleys and side yards.

People watched him as he passed. Without knowing anything about him beyond the color of his skin, their eyes found him guilty of all this. And he was. He always would be, more than they could ever know.

Malcolm fixed his gaze on a point in the middle distance and rode toward it.

Finally, he reached home, hauled the bike up the familiar stairs, and up to the familiar door. He walked in. His father was in the kitchen making breakfast. Pop looked up, but did not speak. Malcolm stood in the doorway separating kitchen from front room and watched. He could not make himself cross the threshold.

Behind him on the television, a white man with a brush cut and black frame glasses was excoriating Martin Luther King for, he said, starting the violence and running away. He called him a hypocrite. He called him a coward. He called him "Martin Loser King."

Pop said, "You gon' eat, or you just gon' stand there?" He was dishing up two plates. Oxtails and eggs.

Malcolm sat down. "Look, Pop..."

"What happened with that old lady?"

"She died."

Pop had been scraping eggs onto a plate. He stopped and some emotion Malcolm couldn't quite read filmed his eyes. "Sorry to hear that," he said. He went back to fixing the plate, passed it over to Malcolm.

Malcolm lifted his fork. "Look, Pop, I want to talk to you about..."

"She wasn't a bad old lady. I know me and her ain't never got along, but still..."

Malcolm put his fork down. "Pop, would you listen to me?"

His father regarded him with sober eyes. Finally, he said, "Junior, some things, you got to leave them alone."

"Pop..."

"What's that y'all young ones say? 'Let it all hang out?' Can't always do that."

"But I just wanted to say that I didn't mean..."

"Don't," said his father. Malcolm stopped. The older man looked at him. Then he shook his head. "You think I don't know what you see when you look at me, June? Tired old man ain't never been nowhere, ain't never learned nothin', ain't never done nothin', ain't never gon' be nothin'. And you, look at you. You shiny and new like a penny. You the future. I guess the future always look down on the past. I guess that ain't no big surprise."

Malcolm felt the tears leaking onto his cheeks. His voice was ashen. "Pop, listen to me..."

Pop plowed right through the barrier of Malcolm's protests. "But see," he said, "you might be future and I might be past, but we tied together, you and me. We tied together 'cause we live in this house. We tied together 'cause we blood. I'm your father and you my son. Ain't nothin' gon' never change that fact. So what's the use, you sayin' somethin' to me right now? About yesterday, I mean. That's done. That's over. And here we are, still in this house, together, still father and son. That's why I say, Junior: some things, you can't do nothin' about. Some things, you just got to leave them alone. Look past them. Live with them. Do you understand what I'm saying?" His father was watching him closely.

Malcolm nodded. He didn't trust his voice.

"Good," said his father. "Now eat."

Malcolm did not know whether to be grateful or ashamed. He did not know whether he had escaped something or been set free. He picked up his fork and began to eat. His father did the same. They ate together in the darkened kitchen of the little house. They didn't speak about the awful thing Malcolm had said. They never would.

The letter came five days later.

Malcolm was dozing in his room when his father came in with the mail and shook him awake. "Thought you might want to see this," he said. And he dropped a large envelope on the bed next to Malcolm. The return address showed that it had come from the dean's office at the white college.

Malcolm sat up and broke the seal eagerly. He pulled out a course catalog for summer classes. Clipped to that was a neatly typed letter from the dean. It began: "I am in receipt of your telegram asking for readmission. I have given it serious consideration and I have come to this conclusion: if you are willing to buckle down and take your obligations seriously, I am willing to extend you another chance." It went on to advise him that he would need to take summer courses this year and next to make up for the work he had missed during his suspension. He would also need to agree to work to pay off the cost of cleaning his graffiti off the wall. He was to report back to school next month.

"They lettin' you back in?"

Malcolm was surprised to realize Pop was standing above him. "Yeah," Malcolm told him. "I go back next month."

Pop smiled. "That's good, Junie. That's real good. I ain't even knowed you applied to go back."

"I guess I didn't tell you," said Malcolm. "I met Martin Luther King last week. We talked. He's the one who told me I should take my ass back to school."

"No shit?"

"Yeah. It was at the hotel, the night after, well, you know... He was standing out back where I usually take my breaks."

Pop said, "What's he like?"

Malcolm considered this. He thought of the sad, exhausted eyes. He thought of the grim determination. "He gave me a lot to think about," he told his father. Pop looked at him, waiting for Malcolm to say more. Malcolm shrugged, unable to put words to what he was trying to convey. "That's it," he said, almost apologetically. "I've just been thinking about a lot of things since then, is all."

Pop regarded him for a long moment. He said, "King coming back to town tonight. He say he got to have another march in Memphis; he got to prove it can be nonviolent. I was goin' over to hear him. You want to go with me?"

Malcolm didn't even have to think about it. "Yes," he said.

They rode the bus over to Mason Temple that evening under a sky mottled with black and gray clouds. When Malcolm and his father got off on

E.H. Crump Boulevard, they stepped into the sort of wind that would rip an umbrella inside out, snatch it from you, and fling it down the street. So they didn't even bother with opening the one they had brought, simply turned up the collars on their coats, adjusted their hats, and staggered doggedly against the pushing and shoving of the air.

Lightning blasted the world white and then came thunder, crashing so hard and so close Malcolm could feel it like a solid thing against his chest. The rain had not come yet, but it would. It was only a matter of time.

A car rushed past. It was full of men his father knew, probably going where he and his father were going. He saw Pop glance over and knew he had seen the same thing. It made the guilt flare up like a toothache that just won't stop.

"You didn't have to do this, Pop," he said. "You could have rode with Sonny."

Sonny had not explicitly said that Malcolm was not welcome in his car. But his silences and his ice-water stares had spoken more clearly than words ever could. And that was when he came around, which was not so often now as it once had been.

"Yeah," said Pop. "I could have."

"He's your best friend, Pop."

A bolt of light stabbed the earth and the thunder detonated again, more ferocious than before, so loud that Malcolm almost missed what his father said in response. Almost.

"Yeah, but you my son."

It was a simple declaration, little more than a statement of fact, but it set emotions colliding in Malcolm's chest so hard he actually gasped. He felt ashamed of himself. And he felt a sudden, overpowering love. He draped an arm across his father's shoulder, surprising them both. There was a moment. Then his father did the same.

Staggering together against the wind, father and son walked toward Mason Temple. The rain had just begun—stinging darts that felt like tiny knives against the skin—when the building came in sight.

The room was not full. The weather had kept the crowd down. White men with microphones and TV cameras were arrayed before the pulpit—crews from national television networks. A union leader was addressing the crowd.

Malcolm and his father were still standing just inside the door, shaking the water off, when there came a sudden burst of applause. Malcolm craned

his neck to see what had caused it. He saw Ralph Abernathy entering the
auditorium by a side door. Malcolm looked for King. He saw his father looking for King, too. But King was not to be seen. Abernathy had come alone.
Disappointment and confusion rumbled up from the crowd in an audible
murmur.

"King not gon' be here?" his father asked.

Before Malcolm could even hunch his shoulders to indicate his own bafflement, Sonny was there, holding out a flier for Pop. "Mo? You seen this?"
He spared less attention for Malcolm than he would have a chair or a table.

Pop took the flier. Malcolm read it over his shoulder.

> **MARTIN LUTHER KING has proven himself to be a
> yellow Uncle Tom. YELLOW instead of BLACK. Now
> BLACK POWER will have to finish what the YELLOW
> KING could not.**

It went on like that. It promised violence. "Burn, Baby, Burn," it said.

"These all over town," said Sonny. "Young niggers and that black power
bullshit. They gon' fuck up everything, Mo. Everything we tryin' to do."

He eyes were on Malcolm as he spoke.

Pop, still staring at the flier, missed this. He shook his head slowly. "This
town is a mess," he said. "This whole thing is a mess. King shouldn't of never
come back. I wouldn't have."

"They callin' him coward," said Sonny. "They sayin' he run away. What
else he gon' do? Ain't had no choice. He had to come back."

"Yeah," said Pop in a reluctant voice, "I know."

Sonny said, "He had to prove he could have a march without young
fools tearin' it up." And again he stared pointedly at Malcolm.

Malcolm stared back. Then he looked away. He said, "Let's get our seats,
Pop."

From outside came the hiss of rain on stone and above that, the eerie rise
and fall of civil defense sirens. Pop looked to the ceiling as they edged their
way into an aisle. "Storm warnin'," he said. "Must be gettin' bad out there."

Pop and Malcolm sat together on the unforgiving wooden seats. Sonny sat behind them—close, but not too close. A local preacher was at the
podium. Malcolm looked into the pulpit and was surprised. Abernathy had
disappeared. He wondered where he'd gone.

"I heard King's not comin'," said Sonny.

At that, a man in the row ahead of them turned. "I heard he is," he said, through a broad smile. "They goin' to get him now."

So they waited to see. Storm shutters rattled. They waited. Yet another preacher who was not King spoke. A student from Northside High spoke, promising that he and his classmates would participate in the next march nonviolently. Someone sang. Ralph Abernathy reappeared in the pulpit. They waited.

And then the side door opened and Martin Luther King walked in. The small crowd rose to its feet, all as one in their adoration, palms banging together in an ovation that rose and rose in volume. King grinned and waved at them before mounting the pulpit to shake hands with the various ministers and dignitaries.

Everything was all right now, in spite of the storm.

Malcolm remembered the small man standing out back of the hotel just a few nights before and how, soul-weary as he was, he had not backed down from Malcolm's anger but engaged it. Malcolm remembered how the man had defined and claimed "black power" and made it something somehow higher than a clenched fist and a broken window, how he had defended, with heartfelt earnestness, the crazy idea that letting a man beat on you without resistance was some greater calling, how he had stubbornly refused to admit that white people were beyond redemption.

He gave me a lot to think about.

Malcolm leaned over to his father. "I'm going to try to talk to him afterward," he said, still applauding. "I told him I'd let him know what I decided to do."

Pop was beaming. It made him look like a different man. "That's a good idea, Malcolm," he said.

And it was a moment before Malcolm realized: his father had called him by his name, his *new* name, the one Pop had seen as a rejection just a few weeks ago. Malcolm was about to speak, about to say something to acknowledge this. But then the ovation crested, the audience began to be seated, and Malcolm took his seat as Abernathy came to the microphone. Abernathy's introduction was a speech in itself. He spent almost half an hour lionizing this great friend with whom he had fought shoulder to shoulder for 13 years in the trenches of human rights. His remarks took King from birth to school, to college, to Montgomery, and finally to Memphis. "He has not yet decided to be president of the United States," Abernathy joked, "but he is the man who tells the president what to do."

Finally, Abernathy sat and King came to the podium with a puzzled smile playing on his heavy features. He waited for the applause to pass, then started speaking in the slow preacher's baritone so familiar from TV news. The great voice was back on duty, no longer addressing one college dropout out back by the Dumpsters. No, now it was addressing history. "It's always good to have your closest friend and associate to say something good about you," said King. "And Ralph Abernathy is the best friend that I have in the world."

He spoke for 45 minutes. He used no notes. His voice strong and true, King took them on a "mental flight" through history, the audience laughing appreciatively as he rattled off the names of Greek philosophers—"Plato, Aristotle, Socrates, Euripides, and Aristophanes"—even as he assured them that no matter the magnificence of that age, no matter the majesty of Rome's empire, no matter the glory of the Renaissance or the courage of Franklin Roosevelt railing against fear itself, there was no era he would rather live in, if given the choice, than this one.

This, he acknowledged, was a strange thing to say, given the sickness and troubles roiling the land. "But I know somehow that only when it is dark enough can you see the stars. And I see God working in this period of the twentieth century"—he tapped the lectern for emphasis—"in a way that men in some strange way are responding. Something is happening in our world."

King noted how the violence that destroyed the previous march drew attention to itself and away from the plight of the sanitation men. So they had to march again, he said. He spoke of the need for Negroes to make use of their power, to "redistribute the pain" by withdrawing economic support— boycotting—companies that did not treat black people fairly. Boycott Coca-Cola, he said. Boycott Wonder Bread.

The preacher turned to the Bible then, recounting the parable of the Good Samaritan, the man who stopped on the Jericho Road to help a stricken man of another race. After others had passed by without stopping, the man from Samaria aided this stranger without thought to his own safety or inconvenience. And King located in that well-worn tale why the plight of Malcolm's father and 1,300 other sanitation men mattered, or should matter, even to people who had never toted a tub of garbage or picked maggots from their hair.

Perhaps, said King, the men who passed by that stricken man were afraid for their safety—after all, the Jericho Road was dangerous. Perhaps they wondered what would happen to them if they stopped there to help this stranger. But the man from Samaria, said King, reversed the question and asked himself: if I do not stop to help this stranger, what will happen to him? This, he said, was what people should be asking themselves about the sanitation men in Memphis.

Something seemed to seize him then and he began to talk about the old days. He told them about the time he was stabbed by a deranged black woman while he was signing books in New York and how he almost died. And, oh, what he would have missed if he had.

He would have missed students standing up for great American ideals by sitting down at lunch counters, he said. He would have missed students confronting segregation head on by riding for freedom in interracial groups on interstate buses. He would have missed Selma and Birmingham. He would have missed the chance to stand at the temple of Lincoln and tell America about his dream.

He would have missed Memphis.

Malcolm sat up straight. He looked at his father. Pop was clapping and cheering, yelling in response to the preacher's call. "Preach, Doctor! Tell 'em about it!" All around Malcolm it was the same, sanitation workers and women and young people, all roaring loudly enough to drown the storm. So maybe they didn't hear it. But Malcolm did. Some ghost of valediction haunted those words.

And then, even in the cacophony of the people's adoration and applause, the valediction turned somber. Memphis, said King, was where he had been warned not to return because there was too much danger, too much risk, too many threats.

"Well, I don't know what will happen now. We've got some difficult days ahead. But it really doesn't matter with me now, because I've been to the mountaintop"—his voice trembled on that word—"and I don't mind."

Don't mind what?

But Malcolm knew. Didn't want to know, but he did.

"Like anybody, I would like to live a long life," King was saying. "Longevity has its place. But I'm not concerned about that now. I just want to do God's will. And he's allowed me to go up to the mountain. And I've looked over. And I've seeeeen"—singing the word, making it almost musical—"the

Promised Land. I may not get there with you. But I want you to know to-night, that we as a people will *get* to the Promised Land!"

The audience was on its feet roaring love. Malcolm stood slowly. He stared at Martin Luther King and he could tell that King did not see them or hear them. His eyes ticked back and forth in their sockets, as if he were listening to some voice only he could hear, as if he viewed some vista visible only to him. And then all at once, he threw his head back and thundered one last time in defiance.

"And so I'm happy tonight! I'm not worried about anything! I'm not fearing *any* man. Mine *eyes* have seen the glory of the coming of the Lord!"

He turned abruptly from the pulpit, still speaking. The microphones did not catch the words and no one would ever know what they were. King all but slumped into the arms of Ralph Abernathy as he took his seat. All around Malcolm, people were cheering, people were calling, people were weeping with unrestrained joy.

Malcolm applauded, too. His hands seemed to have a mind of their own. He cheered. And this was something his throat had decided on its own to do. His body was moving without him. But his mind was stunned. He felt as if he had been struck between the eyes with a hammer.

"You still going down there?" Pop was at Malcolm's shoulder.

Down in front, people were swarming the podium, reaching for King, straining to touch him, to talk to him.

"I'll see him tomorrow," said Malcolm, finding his voice. "He's at the Lorraine, I think." He still wanted to tell King about the decision he had made, the decision King had pushed him to. But there was something else, too. That ghost of valediction that had walked through the great man's words, that had peered out through the great man's eyes, seemed to demand something of Malcolm simply because he had seen it and heard it. Yet Malcolm had no idea what that something was. Was he to question it? Challenge it? Console it?

Something.

"I'll see him tomorrow," repeated Malcolm in an absent voice and they began to file toward the exit.

But of course, tomorrow came too quickly. And what happened happened.

Bantering one moment, about to turn a smile toward Malcolm one mo-ment, and in the next lying on the balcony floor with one leg drawn up, the side of his face obliterated in a mass of wet, red pulp. And Andrew Young wailing. And Billy Kyles kneeling. And Ralph Abernathy cradling his best friend's head. And policemen running with guns drawn. And people pushing past Malcolm. And a camera flashing. And Malcolm staring.

And Malcolm staring.

And Malcolm staring.

And Malcolm backing slowly away. Sirens wailing. People screaming. Malcolm walking away now, the things he'd intended to say lost to him. Slowly, he went down the stairs. Slowly, he passed through the courtyard, buffeted by people running past, people screaming orders, people crying.

He heard it from a distance, saw it from some far place. He found the bicycle he had left downstairs and climbed slowly aboard. One last glance above. He saw the sole of King's left shoe. Malcolm put his head down and rode away.

He rode without seeing and without destination, the riding itself being the entire point. He rode past people glued to car radios listening to terse bulletins. He rode past police cars traveling at high speed. He rode past black men with clenched jaws, their eyes dancing with fire. He rode past a white man who exulted to another white man, "They finally got the son of a bitch!" He rode past mountains of trash.

He rode and then stopped. To his surprise, he found himself at the hotel. And right that instant, as if on cue, Melvin Cotter came boiling out the front door, ripping off his busboy's smock as if it were burning his skin.

"Malcolm! Did you hear? They done shot him! They done shot Dr. King!"

"I was there." Malcolm spoke in a voice he didn't recognize.

Melvin threw his smock to the ground. His eyes glittered with raw fury. "They done done it now," he declared. "Fuck them! Fuck all of 'em! You was right the whole time, man. Black power! Black *power!* Violence the only language fuckin' honkies understand!"

"No, I was wrong," said Malcolm in his new voice.

But Melvin didn't hear. "Done shot Dr. King! *Jesus!* They done gone too far now. You hear me? They done gone too fuckin' far! We gon' burn this motherfucker down tonight!"

He stormed away, cursing the uncaring night.

Malcolm walked inside. He met dazed eyes. The young white girl at the desk had her hand to her mouth. White people stared at him, waiting, he supposed, to see what he would do. Malcolm entered the Employees Only area. He opened Rupert Pruitt's office without knocking.

Pruitt looked up in alarm. He was behind his desk, holding his shotgun braced against his lap. He had been feeding shells into the breach.

"Toussaint? What do *you* want?" Fear had stretched his eyes wide.

"Wanted to give two weeks' notice," said Malcolm. "I'm quitting. I'm going back to school."

Pruitt was incredulous. "Give notice? Jesus Christ, boy! Ain't you heard what just happened?"

Malcolm spoke softly. "I heard," he said. He closed the door and walked away.

Back in the lobby, he paused a moment. The front door, the door through which he had entered, was to his left. Malcolm went right. He walked through the lounge where white people were hunched together, speaking in hushed, urgent whispers. He went out the back of the hotel to where far below, the Mississippi River carved its restless path to the sea.

And there he stood. Just stood. Just breathed.

The word was going out now, spreading by telephone, radio, teletype, television. Pretty soon, the whole world would know what Memphis knew, would know what Memphis had *done*. And when they heard, how many black people would feel like Melvin? How many would say, *This is enough! This is war!*

Most of them, he supposed. Maybe all of them. Even now, he could hear the distant scream of sirens.

Violence the only language fuckin' honkies understand! We gon' burn this motherfucker down tonight!

And Malcolm would have been right there with Melvin, last week. Indeed, would have stormed ahead of him. A very long time ago, last week.

But the memory of the tired man he had met in this place would not allow it.

He knew what many black people would think. What had happened here was a reason to give up on all of it, all those sweet, integrationist dreams, all those homilies about the mystical power of nonviolence, all those gentle hymns of perseverance and overcoming and, most of all, the idea that white people would ever be anything other than white people, the idea that they would ever think of you as a brother or a sister in the human family, and treat you accordingly.

King's murder, they would say, tears in their eyes, Molotov cocktails in their fists, was a reason to give up on all those things. But for Malcolm, it was the opposite. It was the reason he could not.

Because the question King had asked was profound: *what happens then?* And Malcolm still could not answer it.

All at once, he became aware of the weight in his front pocket. He reached in and fished out the pistol he had bought when he was broken and looking to be whole again. He studied it for a moment in the light of a streetlamp near the Dumpsters, then turned it over in his palm. It was a snub-nosed revolver, an evil, ugly thing.

Without even knowing he was going to do it, Malcolm suddenly screamed some cry without words, clenched the gun hard in his fist, and flung it with everything he could muster. The pistol traced a high arc against the paling moon. By the time it landed with a distant splash in the river, Malcolm had already turned to leave.

He wanted to get home before the fires started. He wanted to get home to his dad.

twenty-seven

Once they had established that he was not going to die on them immediately, the authorities had descended on Malcolm's hospital bed—the Secret Service, the Department of Homeland Security, the Federal Bureau of
Investigation, the Bureau of Alcohol, Tobacco and Firearms, the Chicago
Police Department. They wanted to know if McLarty and Pym had said
anything suggesting they might be part of a larger terrorist plot. They wanted to know if there was any hint of foreign involvement. They wanted to
know how the homeless man (whose name turned out to be William Lincoln Washington) wound up dead. They wanted to know what the whole
thing was all about.

By this time, Malcolm had not slept in well over 24 hours. His body
ached. His head thudded heavily. Between having his temperature taken,
his chest palpated, his wounds dressed, he told them all the same story. He
got rear-ended. He got kidnapped. He was held all day. And then one of
the kidnappers turned on the other and started shooting the bomb and the
resultant explosion—the roar, the wave of overpressure, and the feeling of
being lifted off his feet—was the last thing he remembered until a paramedic
stood above him, yelling to someone else, "We got another one over here."

At some point in their marathon interrogations, the various personnel
from the various agencies all asked him variations of the same question: why
him? Was it because of that inflammatory piece he ran in the paper yesterday? Each time it was asked, Malcolm tried to answer the question as if it

370

were not stupid and as if they didn't all know it was stupid, tried to answer patiently and reasonably, reminding his interrogator that it was next to impossible for Pym and McLarty to put together so elaborate a scheme mere hours after the piece came out.

Each time he said it they looked disappointed, as if they had expected him to make sense of this thing for them and he had failed.

"Then why you?" asked a Secret Service agent, a black man with light skin and more salt than pepper in his thinning hair. He was standing at Malcolm's bedside, scribbling notes into a pad.

Malcolm looked at him. "Why not?" he said. And even as he said it, it came to him that that answer was probably as close to the truth as they were ever likely to get. It was 5:00 in the morning. A nurse was reading the meter on a blood pressure cuff that tightened against his forearm. He was tired.

The other man seemed to sense this. "Well, I guess that's enough for now," he said. He closed the notepad and put it in his breast pocket. "We'll let you get some rest, but I'm sure we'll have more questions for you once the forensics come back."

"Thanks for the warning," said Malcolm.

The man left. The nurse, a stolid-looking black woman of late middle age, was making a notation on his chart. Her smile was wry. "They startin' to get to you?"

Malcolm said, "Was it that obvious?"

"Yeah," she said. "Can't blame you, though, what you been through. By the way"—and here, she leaned close, spoke in a confidential tone—"I *liked* what you wrote. You ain't spoke nothin' but the God's truth." She leaned back, all business once again. "Try to get you some rest. You need anything, you push that button there." With her pen, she indicated a large contraption shaped vaguely like the sole of a shoe. It had many buttons on it, a handful of which controlled the television that had been playing silently from a ceiling in the corner. As the nurse walked out, Malcolm, finally alone, brought up the volume and flipped to the news.

On the screen, the nation's newly minted First Family was walking out onto the stage in Grant Park, waving at the massive crowd. Flashbulbs sparkled like diamonds. Oprah Winfrey was leaning on some man, weeping. Jesse Jackson had an index finger to his lips, his eyes shining. And the president-elect addressed the nation. "If there is anyone out there who still doubts that America is a place where all things are possible, who still wonders if the dream of our founders is alive in our time, who still questions the power of our democracy, tonight is your answer."

Then the story cut to an image of Malcolm—an old sig photo, ten years out of date. "Meanwhile," said the anchorwoman on camera, "authorities are still piecing together details of that bizarre assassination plot yesterday in which *Chicago Post* opinion page editor Robert Carson and disgraced *Chicago Post* columnist Malcolm Toussaint were both held hostage."

Disgraced columnist.

In that moment, he knew: this would be part of his name from now on. It would be the first sentence of his obituary. It was how he would be introduced at parties.

With a grunt of disgust, Malcolm turned the channel. He found another morning news show, this one running a helicopter shot of McLarty and Pym's van, or the remains of it, sitting blown apart in a circle of light outside the old warehouse. A man identified by the caption beneath him as an "explosives expert" came on then, speculating about how McLarty and Pym had apparently bungled. It was possible they did not properly wire the bomb, he said, or failed to mix the chemicals in the right proportions. Whatever the cause, the expert went on, the bomb failed to explode with anywhere near the force they had apparently anticipated. And the armor plating on the van had acted to channel the greatest force of the blast to the path of least resistance—right out the open door where McLarty and Pym were standing.

McLarty had died instantly, shredded by his own shrapnel. Pym was critically injured and was said to be in surgery at that very moment, "In fact," said the anchor, "he is at the same hospital where doctors are treating the two *Chicago Post* journalists wounded in the attack: opinion editor Robert Carson and disgraced columnist Malcolm Toussaint."

Malcolm turned off the television. For a long moment, he just lay there on the bed, contemplating blessed silence.

Somewhere in that long night, at some point when doctors and cops had given him a momentary break from their interrogations and their palpating, he had taken a walk and found Amy Landingham standing at a nurse's station, apparently being signed out. She had a daughter in her arms, another clinging to her pants by a belt loop, and a man—her husband the corporate lawyer, Malcolm assumed—standing right behind her. He looked frightened. He needed a shave.

"Malcolm," said Amy when she saw him.

The little girl in her arms giggled at the slightly distorted voice that came through Amy's wired up jaw. "Mommy, you talk funny!"

Amy handed the child off to her father. "Give me a minute," she told him. She approached Malcolm. "How are you doing?" she asked. There was something guarded about her gaze.

"I'm fine," he said. "How about you?"

"They're letting me go home. Finally."

"Good for you."

"You've talked to the FBI?"

"I've talked to every cop in America."

"You know," she said, "they're going to have me write about this, a big first-person takeout for Sunday tying everything together. Of course, that's assuming I can get it together by then. But we're talking front page and everything."

"Great," he said, genuinely pleased for her. "Might be your first Pulitzer."

This made her smile. But then that look returned. "Are you willing to be interviewed? By me, I mean?"

"Sure."

"Can I have the exclusive? I know you don't owe the paper anything, but..."

Malcolm smiled. "I'll talk to you and nobody else until after Sunday. Or maybe never, I don't know."

"Thank you," she said. She turned away. Then she turned back. "You know, I did have one question for you now—do you mind?"

"Sure."

"When I asked you yesterday morning why you did what you did, you told me you just got tired. And I've been wondering about that ever since. What did you mean? Tired of what?"

Malcolm had sighed. "You want to know the truth? I'm just tired of having to explain the same things to white people, year in, year out, over and over and over again. I'm tired of saying the same things and them not listening."

She gazed up at him thoughtfully. "*I* was listening," she said.

They had regarded one another for a long moment. Then she had given his shoulder a quick squeeze and left to be with her family.

Now, a few hours later, sitting in his bed beneath the blank and silent television, Malcolm groped for the word to describe what he had felt in that moment.

Startled? No, it was more than that.

Ashamed? No, it was less than that.

Embarrassed?

He turned the word over in his thoughts a few times. Yes, he decided, that was what Amy's words had made him feel: embarrassed. In writing that angry, impulsive column, he had treated "white people"—whatever those words still meant—as an undistinguished lump of malfeasance and ignorance. He had forgotten the things he learned at the river's edge on the night he sat with Martin Luther King. He had forgotten about Amy and people like her, and become undiscriminating in his antagonism. He had become like the worst of them, those people he had railed against for so many years. And that was deeply embarrassing.

He'd been wrong to do that. And yet—he remembered the nurse leaning in close to whisper her confidential agreement—he knew he had not been wrong about everything.

Lord, he was tired. Body, soul, tired.

Still, there was something he had to do. Malcolm got out of bed. He slipped into the terrycloth slippers the hospital provided and tied tight the flimsy gown the nurses give you to make sure you don't accidentally maintain some shred of dignity while in their care. He grabbed hold of the wheeled IV stand feeding painkillers into his body by way of plastic tubing and walked out of the room.

The hallway was full of nurses and doctors. Some of the FBI agents, Secret Service agents, and police detectives who had been questioning him all morning were also loitering there. "Where are you going?" demanded the black agent with the more salt than pepper hair.

"Visiting," said Malcolm. "Is that okay?"

He didn't wait for an answer.

Malcolm's step was lively for a banged-up man of a certain age. The drugs were good. He took the elevator two floors up. This was a quieter floor, the lights lower, the walls done up in soothing earth tones. It was the surgical suite. He found his way to the waiting room. They were all sitting there on plush couches—Lassiter, Perry, Lydia, a few others from the newsroom, and some young man Malcolm recognized from desktop photos as Bob's son. At the sound of him, they all looked up. Lydia's eyes narrowed.

She came and stood before him. Seeing the flint in her gaze, it was only through an act of conscious will that he did not step back. Or indeed, run. "Are you okay?" she asked. Her voice was soft, but hard.

"Yeah," he said.

"I can't imagine what you've been through."

"Doctors say I'll be fine."

"Good." She leaned closer. "You do know you're fired, don't you?"

"Yeah," he said. "I know that."

"Good," she said. "I wouldn't want there to be any misunderstanding." A pause. She gave him those fiery eyes. "Here's what's going to happen," she said. "Amy Landingham is going to contact you, probably later today, to participate in a story about this whole sordid disaster. And you're going to cooperate; you're going to give her the exclusive. Otherwise, so help me, I am going to find some way to sue you til your eyeballs—"

"We've already talked," said Malcolm, not wanting to hear what gruesome fate Lydia had in store for his eyeballs. Or, indeed, any of his other balls. "I already told her yes."

Lydia did not bother to hide her surprise. "Oh," she said, eyebrows arching just slightly. "I'm glad to hear that." She regarded Malcolm for another long moment. "You know," she finally said, "if I had been able to get my hands on you 18 hours ago, I would gladly have ripped out your spleen with my bare hands. I have never been more furious with a human being in my life. I cannot believe you did that." Another pause. The fire in her eyes dampened almost imperceptibly. "How are you, Malcolm, really? Are you all right?"

He pondered this for a moment and decided that, yes, all things considered—his body sore, his head aching, his life, career, and reputation in tatters—he actually felt pretty good. Better than he had in years. Maybe it was just the drugs, but he didn't think so. "I'm fine," he answered. "I really am. How's Bob?"

"Resting comfortably, as they say. Thank God the wound was through and through and did not hit anything vital. Ms. Lattimore is in with him. They're trying to keep the visitors down; they don't want him to have too much excitement."

"I just want to apologize to him," said Malcolm. "I apologize to you, too, by the way. I don't blame you for being furious with me. You have every right."

"Why did you do it, Malcolm?"

"I just had enough," he said. "I just couldn't deal with it anymore."

She thought about this. She nodded. Malcolm was grateful she was black. It meant, at the very least, that he did not have to explain what "it" was.

He moved past her toward Bob's room. Just as he got there, a woman's cry stopped him. He looked back toward the waiting area. The woman was white, about 60. She was pretty. Gray hairs were just beginning to streak the brunette fall that framed her face. At that moment, she was speaking with a surgeon who had apparently just delivered bad news. The woman wept inconsolably and Malcolm studied her for a moment. There was something familiar about her, but he could not place it.

He went into Bob's room.

Pale dawn sunlight filtered in through the lace curtain. Janeka sat in a chair pulled up to Bob's bedside. She had his hand in hers, her head resting on his thigh. They both appeared to be asleep and Malcolm turned to leave, but she lifted her head at the sound. Her face was still bruised from where McLarty had slugged her.

"Malcolm?" she whispered.

"I'm sorry," he said. "I didn't mean to disturb you. How is he?"

Bob spoke then through closed eyes. "He's doped up pretty good from abdominal surgery, but he bets he's going to be in a heck of a lot of pain when that wears off." Bob's eyes fluttered open. "But considering the alternative, he doesn't mind."

"Bob," said Malcolm.

"Malcolm," said Bob.

The silence that filled the next moment was as awkward as a newborn colt. Janeka tried to lighten the tension. "Well," she said, "now that the two of you have been introduced..."

Malcolm cleared his throat. "Look," he said, "I just came to apologize."

"So apologize."

"I'm sorry," said Malcolm.

Bob regarded him for a long moment. Finally he said, "You know, if I could have gotten my hands on you this time yesterday—"

"You'd have pulled my spleen out through my nose. Yes, I know. You'd have had to wrestle Lydia for the privilege, though. I really am sorry. I knew I was torching my career when I did it. I accepted that and I really didn't care. But it didn't occur to me that I'd be taking you with me. If I'd known that was going to happen—"

Bob cut him off. "They offered me my job back," he said.

"Really?"

"Yeah," said Bob, wincing a little as he adjusted his body slightly in the bed. "Turns out I'm a hero, though all I did was blunder in there and get shot. Still, how are you going to fire the hero editor?"

Malcolm was relieved. "That's great," he said. "I'm really glad to hear it."

Bob hunched his shoulders. "Don't know yet if I'm going to take it."

"You don't?"

He looked at Janeka. "No," he said. "We've got to talk about it. Got a lot to figure out."

Malcolm arched an eyebrow. "We?"

Bob grinned. "Yeah," he said. "We."

A white man came into the room then. Close-cropped hair, an earpiece in his ear, nothing but business in his eyes, which surveyed the room like a general mapping a battlefield. He might as well have borne a neon sign that said, Secret Service. Malcolm sighed. Obviously, they had come to drag him back for more questioning.

But the man looked at Janeka instead. "You're Ms. Lattimore?" he said.

"Yes," she said.

"You have ID?"

Puzzled, Janeka released Bob's hand, went into her purse, and produced a California driver's license. The stranger studied it for a long time.

"And you are?" prompted Janeka.

"Secret Service, ma'am." He handed the ID back to her, pointed to Bob. "You're Carson, right?"

"Yes."

"And you?" The finger was pointing now at Malcolm.

"Malcolm Toussaint."

"The guy who was kidnapped. The columnist."

It occurred to Malcolm that he should probably be grateful the guy hadn't referred to him as "the *disgraced* columnist."

"Yeah," he said. "That's me."

He gave Malcolm a hard look. His eyes roamed the room once again. Then, without another word, he spun on his heel and disappeared.

Malcolm stared after him, then turned to find his own confusion mirrored in Bob's eyes.

"What the heck was that all about?" asked Bob.

"Your guess is as good as mine," said Malcolm. "Place is full of cops and Secret Service agents. I'll be glad when they're done with me so I can get out of here."

Janeka said, "So, what are you going to do, Malcolm? I mean, now that you're—"

"Unemployed?" Malcolm sat on a couch near the foot of the bed. "I have no idea. My kids are on the way, flying in from California to make sure the old man's okay. I'm sure I'll get the usual full-court press about how I need to give up snowy old Chicago and come live with them in the land of earthquakes and perpetual sunshine."

"Maybe you should," said Janeka. She spoke gently.

"Maybe I will," said Malcolm.

"I hear a 'but,'" she said.

"Oh, it's no big thing," he said. "I'm thinking that whatever else I do, the first thing I want is to go down to Memphis and spend a little time with my dad. He's 81, still living in the house I grew up in, still working for the city in the sanitation department."

Bob said, "He was in the 1968 strike, wasn't he? You wrote about him once."

"Yeah," said Malcolm. "I don't know how many times I've offered to help him. Move him to a better place or even bring him up here to live with me. He won't do it. Still hauling garbage. He's such a hard-headed old man. Too much pride for his own damn good." He smiled as he said it. "Haven't seen him in awhile. I think I'd like to."

"That's good," said Janeka. "I bet he'll be happy to see you. I bet if you ask your kids, they'd—"

And then she stopped. Her eyes widened. Malcolm followed her gaze. He felt his jaw drop open. The president-elect of the United States had just come through the door.

He was tall and lean, impeccable in dark suit and tie, smiling his toothy smile. "Hey, everybody," he said. He crossed the room to Janeka, hands outstretched. "Janeka, how are you? You okay?"

She rose and he took her hand in both of his. "Mr. President-elect," she said. "Congratulations, sir. Yes, we can."

"Yes, we did," he replied.

He took the two men in with a glance, then returned to Janeka. "I don't mean to interrupt," said Obama, "but when I heard that you were hurt in that incident yesterday, I wanted to come and check on you personally to make sure you're okay."

Janeka touched her bruised mouth self-consciously. "I'm fine, sir. Just got punched in the mouth is all. It's Bob here and Malcolm who got the worst of it."

Obama shook Bob's hand. "Mr. Carson? How are you doing? You going to be all right?"

Bob had a dazed look. "I'm fine, Mr. President. I mean, Mr. President-elect. They say I'm going to make a full recovery."

"That's great news, Bob. Glad to hear it."

Now Obama turned to nod at Malcolm. "Toussaint," he said. His gaze was cool.

Malcolm was not surprised. He had written a number of unflattering columns about Obama back when the president-elect was a senatorial candidate in a hurry. He had dubbed him "Flash," both for the speed of his ascent and for Malcolm's argument that the bright young lawmaker would ultimately prove himself a flash in the pan. They had not enjoyed a cordial relationship since then. Now Malcolm came to his feet, extended his hand. "Mr. President-elect," he said, "I suppose this is my day for being proven wrong. Congratulations, sir. And godspeed."

Obama accepted the handshake. "You know, brother," he said, his voice as cool as his gaze, "that was a heck of a column you wrote yesterday." He measured Malcolm with his stare, making sure Malcolm knew this wasn't a compliment. "And it was a heck of a day you chose to publish it," he continued. "Or to sneak it into the paper, I guess would be more accurate. Reporters have been trying to get me to comment on what you said for the last 24 hours. Thanks a lot."

"Yes, sir," said Malcolm. He almost said, "Glad to help" but choked the sarcasm back.

Obama gave him a look as if he'd heard the words anyway. He turned back to Janeka. "Well," he said, "I won't keep you any longer. I just wanted to say I hope you feel better soon and thank you for everything you did for the campaign. When you feel up to it, I hope you'll contact the transition office. I'm sure we'll have need of your talents in Washington. Tell them I said so."

"Yes, sir," said Janeka. "Thank you." She took Bob's hand again. "I'll certainly think about it, but to tell you the truth, we haven't figured out yet what we're going to do."

And there was that word again: *We.*

Malcolm liked the sound of it. Obama seemed to as well. "Well, let us know," he said. He smiled the toothy smile, lifted his hand—"Thanks everybody," he said—and disappeared from the room.

Malcolm stood, watching through the door as the next president shook hands with doctors and nurses in the hallway under the watchful gaze of Secret Service agents.

"You said he could never win." Bob spoke from behind him.

"Yep."

"Wrote it in that column."

"Yep."

"You were wrong."

Malcolm turned. "Yes, I was."

"The country's changing, Malcolm. That's what you haven't figured out yet. You're still living in the past. And yeah, the past was bad, but it's still the past. All that old racial stuff, we're moving beyond that. These next four years, you'll see. It'll be different from now on. We just elected a black president! You can't tell me that doesn't mean people are finally getting over all this stuff. It's changing for the better. I mean, don't you think?"

He looked at Malcolm, then at Janeka. There was hope in his eyes.

Malcolm looked at Janeka. Her eyes reflected back his own doubt.

Malcolm's gaze returned to the president-elect, surrounded by Secret Service agents, smiling and waving to well-wishers as he moved toward a waiting elevator. And then Malcolm was standing at the river's edge in the darkness many hours before the dawn and Martin Luther King was telling him again that there would be no armed revolution, no black separatist state, no mass emigration, and that the only option he had was to wrestle with white people in the faith that someday his humanity would touch something in theirs.

"Don't you think?" Bob repeated it.

Malcolm turned to look at him. He and Janeka were still holding hands. And there was still hope in Bob's eyes. Hope, asking for reassurance. Hope, needing to believe.

Malcolm shrugged. "Yeah," he said. "Maybe so." And he tried to believe it himself. Because King had been right.

He had no other choice.

ACKNOWLEDGMENTS

There is one question I expect to be asked a lot by people when they read this book: How much of this is real?

The answer: it depends on what you mean by real.

For instance, while Clarence Pym and Dwayne McLarty are complete works of fiction, their outlandish plot to kill Barack Obama is, in fact, based on a real plan hatched by two white supremacists.

According to their scheme, which was broken up by law enforcement, Daniel Cowart and Paul Schlesselman would first have murdered 88 African Americans in a killing spree at a black school and then beheaded another 14. The significance of the numbers? Well, "h" is the eighth letter of the alphabet, so in the world of white supremacy, 88 is understood as a coded salute: "Heil Hitler."

The other number, meanwhile, is a reference to the so-called "14 Words" of white supremacy: "We must secure the existence of our people and a future for white children."

With 102 black people thus butchered, Cowart and Schlesselman planned to somehow drive toward Obama, firing automatic weapons. And yes, they reportedly planned to wear white ties and top hats. Some things are simply too bizarre to be anything but true.

Barack Obama and Martin Luther King, Jr., are, of course, real historical figures. The quotes from King's two speeches in Memphis and Obama's election night speech in Grant Park are both accurate. Obama's election day quip while voting and the banter between King and his men in those final moments on the balcony of the Lorraine Motel is also true to the historical record. Everything else mouthed by both men in this book is made up by me, though King's arguments against the term "black power" are paraphrased from what he actually wrote. And yes, on the night of the riot, Dr. King did, indeed, stay at the Holiday Inn.

"Eddie" is not real. No history of the Memphis riot that I have ever read has definitively indicted any one person or group for what happened. The superheated atmosphere and the collision of interests that marked that day may have made the conflagration simply inevitable.

On the other hand, the email that sends Malcolm over the edge *is* real, if by "real" you mean typical of what passes for dissent in the Internet age. Every pundit gets this stuff regardless of his or her race, creed, or political affiliation. But the hatefulness, coarseness, and sheer intellectual incontinence of these communications, particularly when they are based in race, is truly startling. Indeed, "Joe MacPherson" is an amalgam of thousands of different folks who have cluttered my *Miami Herald* inbox every day, dozens of times a day, for 20 years. For what it's worth, "Your so stupid" and "Your such a racist nigger" are complete and verbatim quotes from two of the more memorable missives.

That said, I would be remiss if I left the impression that the only folks who write me are miserable maggots with a perilous grasp of English grammar. So allow me to lift my figurative glass to those many writers of thoughtful dissent and all-too-generous praise who have helped me maintain my sometimes-tenuous faith in human decency over the years.

Here's something else I expect someone to ask: Have I ever come close to doing as Malcolm does, writing a fiery, kiss-my-backside letter to white America? The answer is an emphatic "no." I am not Malcolm Toussaint, nor he me. This is a work of *fiction,* an attempt to grapple with the tantalizing question, What if...? Though there are obvious similarities between us, I try always to remember what Malcolm allowed himself to forget: there are Joe MacPhersons in the world, yes. But there are Amy Landinghams, too. The momentary satisfaction of lashing out at the former will never be worth betraying the trust of the latter.

And no, I have never been tempted—nor am I aware of anyone who has ever tried—to sneak something into the paper.

And on that note, let me proceed to some thank-yous.

As always, first and last, I thank God for this and every good thing in my life, and also for the not-so-good things, because it is in life's challenges that we find growth—and learn faith.

Thank you to Marilyn, my wife (34 years and counting!) and former elementary school crush, for always believing, always supporting, and always having my back.

Thank you to my agent, Janell Walden-Agyeman of Marie Brown and Associates, for her quiet toughness and unfailing good humor in a partnership that now has 20 years of mileage on it.

Thank you to Doug Seibold, my publisher, for believing in this odd duck of a book and for supporting me over the years as I follow the sometimes-fickle dictates of the muse.

Thank you to Judi Smith, my assistant, for her sharp proofreader's eye and for filtering out enough of the Joe MacPhersons of the world to protect my aforementioned faith in human decency, though perhaps at the cost of her own.

Thank you in advance to the citizens of Chicago and Memphis for overlooking the intentional (and, probably, a few unintentional) liberties I have taken with the geography of these two great American cities. I am aware, for instance, that the freeway interchange where the Funn Toys warehouse is located is arguably too far from Grant Park for the sounds of celebration to have carried there. What can I say? I worked hard to respect the geography of your cities (to the point of spending a morning hiking the route Malcolm takes along the banks of the Mississippi the night of the riot) but when the realities of geography conflict with the needs of the story, I chose the latter every time.

Thank you, also, to: Dr. Ziad E. Batrouni, DDS, who answered some questions for me regarding the treatment of Amy's injury; my cousins Richard Wesley Pitts, Jr., and the Reverend Tony Pitts, Sr., my go-to sources for questions about their hometown of Chicago; my friend and colleague Wendi C. Thomas, my guide to all things Memphis; Detective Victor Moore, retired L.A. County Sheriff's detective, who answered questions about police procedure—and attitude; retired Secret Service agent Orlando Lee, who helped me shape my characters' meeting with the president-elect; Earl Caldwell, who was the only reporter at the Lorraine Motel on the night of King's assassination, and who helped me get a better handle on the man; Rick Hirsch, managing editor of the *Miami Herald*, and Nancy Ancrum, editor of the

opinion pages, who helped me understand how a newspaper might respond
to a situation like the one Malcolm creates; Lem Jones, who works at the Mason Temple in Memphis, and who allowed me to wander through that sacred
space, communing with its ghosts; Officer Jose Estrada of the Chicago Police
Department, who confirmed that I was on firm ground in having Detective
Raintree threaten Bob with a "Class B misdemeanor;" Jan Smith of the *Memphis Commercial Appeal*, who gave me access to photos of Memphis "back in
the day," and also to some images of the King assassination and its aftermath
that I had never seen before (and I've seen a lot); and Billy Do, who stepped
in from the Twitterverse when I needed some last minute reassurance that my
Vietnamese dialogue was correct.

   I am also indebted to the Memphis Public Library for opening a trove
of vintage photos for me, and to the staff of the map room at the Library
of Congress for providing maps of Memphis as it was in 1968. Michael
K. Honey's book, *Going Down Jericho Road: The Memphis Strike, Martin
Luther King's Last Campaign* and Joan Turner Beifuss' book, *At the River
I Stand* were invaluable to me in trying to recreate not only what happened
during those troubled days, but also, how it *felt*.

   To whatever degree I have managed to achieve verisimilitude here and
to tell a story that compels, I am indebted to all of the above. To whatever
degree I have fallen short of those goals, I have only myself to blame.

ABOUT THE AUTHOR

Leonard Pitts, Jr. is a nationally syndicated columnist for the *Miami Herald* and winner of the 2004 Pulitzer Prize for commentary, in addition to many other awards. He is also the author of the novels *Freeman* (Agate Bolden, 2012) and *Before I Forget* (Agate Bolden, 2009); the collection *Forward From this Moment: Selected Columns, 1994–2009, Daily Triumphs, Tragedies, and Curiosities* (Agate Bolden, 2009); and *Becoming Dad: Black Men and the Journey to Fatherhood* (Agate Bolden, 2006). Born and raised in Southern California, Pitts now lives in suburban Washington, DC, with his family.

Q & A with Leonard Pitts, Jr.
AUTHOR OF *Grant Park*

What was the genesis of *Grant Park*? Where did the idea first come from?

My books usually start with themes, and then characters and plotlines flow out of them. So this particular book began with a frustration not unlike what motivates Malcolm when he reads the racist email from Joe MacPherson. I was less interested, though, in exploring the racial aspect of communiqués like that than the sheer illogic and incoherence of them. In my experience, as in Malcolm's, that sort of facts-optional absurdity has become pretty ubiquitous in discussions of race—and other contentious social issues—in the last half-century or so, whether on cable news, online, or in the local paper. If you're emotionally invested in resolving such issues, it's a deeply frustrating thing.

So I decided to write about one man's response to that frustration and, through him, to talk about how our approach to the things that divide us has changed in the last 40 years. That was the nugget of it. From there, of course, the book sprawled to include themes of fathers and sons, the splintering of the civil rights coalition, and the loss and reclamation of hope.

Your book explores themes that have everything to do with the civil unrest that has affected Baltimore, Ferguson, and other parts of the country. Does a fiction writer have any advantages over a journalist when it comes to shedding light on these issues?

Oh, yes. Reality is seldom neat, for as much as pundits like myself like to try to impose social and ideological order upon it.

In dealing with serious real-life issues in a fictional venue, however, you can order the world according to your own specifications to show whatever it is you're trying to show and to say whatever it is you're trying to say. The world is what you say it is, subject, obviously, to the constraints of internal logic. But within those constraints, you can manipulate the "facts" in hopes of finding the truth.

As a journalist, was it challenging to fictionalize well-known political figures such as Martin Luther King, Jr., and President Barack Obama?

Writing Obama was not challenging at all. In the first place, he doesn't have a whole lot to say in the book, and second, he is in our ears almost every day, so I'm very familiar with his speech patterns. For instance, the whole "Hi, everybody" with which he enters the room in the book is pretty well known to us after six-years-and-change of his presidency. My biggest challenge in writing him was to get the behavior of the Secret Service correct.

King was just the opposite. The only scene of him not taken directly from the historical record, of course, was the long dialogue with Malcolm out back of the hotel. I rewrote that scene several times. I think I was intimidated by the idea of putting words into the mouth of a man who is so revered and well remembered. I wanted to present an off-duty King, shorn of the marble in which he has so long been entombed, but on my first pass at that scene, I had him speaking essentially in bursts of rhetoric, all of which could be sourced to his speeches and books.

Problem is, even great speakers, when they are off duty, do not speak in rhetoric. They speak like people. So I really had to struggle with giving myself permission to write him just as a man. Much of what he says and does (the drinking and smoking) are still traceable to the historical record, but I also consciously pushed myself to go beyond that and speculate about what he would have said in this particular circumstance.

It was really kind of a scary, but exciting, thing.

Your rendering of King plays a very active role in the story. How do you think your King compares to other popular depictions, such as the King depicted in *Selma*?

Well, as already noted, I wanted to present him in a less formal and structured way than we are used to seeing, and I think that's what the depiction in *Selma* was about. At the end of the day, I think my novel and that movie are both doing the same thing—trying to free him from the amber of our reverence.

It's interesting. Over the years, we've seen warts-and-all cinematic portrayals of other revered figures—John F. Kennedy, Franklin Roosevelt, Thomas Jefferson—but only now are we beginning to see that view of Dr. King. He was a great and noble man. He was also a drinker, smoker, and philanderer who suffered from depression in his last days. Only now are we getting around to presenting this truer, fuller portrait of who and what he was.

This novel unfolds primarily through two distinct points of view: that of celebrated black journalist Malcolm Toussaint and that of his white editor Bob Carson. Which character's story was more difficult to tell?

Neither character was particularly difficult, though I did have to take a few passes at the chapters of young Malcolm to get the tone right. For some reason, the scenes of him in Memphis as a teenager interacting with his father were difficult to get a handle on.

Otherwise, the characters were pretty easy. I particularly enjoyed playing with each man's late-life disillusionment and how each reflected the other.

What are you working on next?

It's called *The Thing You Last Surrender*. It's about George Simon, a Marine during World War II. He experiences a kind of racial coming-of-age when his life is saved by a black Navy messman at Pearl Harbor. He forges an unlikely friendship with Thelma, the sister of the man who saved him.

As the war grinds on, George finds himself in a very real sense struggling to hold onto his humanity while fighting under brutal conditions in the South Pacific. Meanwhile, Thelma is in their shared hometown of Mobile, Alabama, facing a very different racial coming-of-age of her own.

35674053683091